Greyson Gray:

Camp Legend

B.C. Tweedt

DEDICATION

This novel is dedicated to all the grown-up boys and girls who dare to fight those who wish to harm innocent people, both home and abroad. Thank you for doing what is right, even when it's hard.

ACKNOWLEDGMENTS

This delicious book which you are about to devour was actually produced by hundreds of people. Many of the hundreds have no knowledge of this fact. I deliberately swiped their personalities, gestures, and impromptu dialogue, and used those ingredients to cook a story stew. Much of the meat of this story comes from my experiences at a camp very similar to Morris All-Sports Camp, and sweet memories of my time there are peppered throughout. Also, I could not go without thanking my mother who stirred this stew over and over in a long editing marinade that ultimately made this novel digestible. And finally, thank you to my wife, who feeds me when my hunger pervades my every thought.

Prologue

Wednesday Night

Brandon's weary body hit the sofa like a sack of concrete, and its springs groaned as a comfortable crater formed around his backside. Camp counselors filled the lobby of Bickford Hall, some rubbing red, swollen feet while others sprawled out on the floor, their arms shielding tired pupils from heavy fluorescent lights.

CJ sighed wearily, massaging his own neck. "I don't know *what* went wrong during these kids' childhoods, but someone must'a dropped them on their heads or somethin'."

The counselors grunted in agreement.

"Well, at least your group's not as bad as Brandon's," Tristan declared. "His group reminds me of a circus – they look like a freak show and act like animals!"

"Hey!" Brandon pulled himself up to the edge of his seat and glared at Tristan. The laughter melted to silence. "Don't talk about them that way, okay?"

Tristan looked up. "Yeah, okay. Sorry, dude, I was just joking. I actually do admire some of them, like that kid with the red hat. He's somethin'."

He sure was, Brandon thought to himself.

"You keep good track of him at night? That cop car pulled up outside and I immediately thought it was for him."

Everyone laughed – except for Brandon. He knew the kid was already gone.

"There's a trainer watching our hall," Brandon sighed, "he'll be fine."

"Unless he tries to go out the window," Tristan joked, "good thing it's three stories to asphalt."

CJ laughed. "From what I've seen, I wouldn't put it behind him."

Outside the window, a shadow approached and all eyes converged on the winding sidewalk where a heavyset figure lumbered through sheets of rain. His bulk rushed up to the front door, rain cascading off him like a waterfall. A sudden crack of lightning flashed his portly silhouette against the wall and filled the doorway just as thunder shook the glass doors. Squinting his eyes as they adjusted to the bright, blue lobby, the man shook the remaining water from his poncho.

"Woooee! We'll have some scared campers tonight, boys – especially the young'uns. If they come to ya crying 'cuz of the storm, just comfort 'em as much as ya can."

The head counselor hung his poncho on a peg and wiped the rain from his buzzed head.

"What if they want to sleep in our beds, Mac?"

Mac smiled and tucked his shirt into his shorts. "Well, we don't want anything like what happened to Dan in '89."

A few laughed as Mac took his seat in front of the twenty male counselors.

"Why? What happened?" a new counselor inquired.

Everyone hushed and turned toward Mac. He dropped his bulk into his favorite recliner and took his time adjusting his weight into the old cushion.

"Well, back then, counselors were allowed to go out at night, and Dan was a big night owl. One night he came back to the dorms at 3 AM, exhausted and not thinking too clearly – ya know what I mean?"

The older counselors chuckled as the newer counselors leaned in closer to catch every word. Brandon stood up and looked out the window toward the observatory.

"Well, Dan stumbled to his room and just fell into bed. Didn't take time to undress or nothin'. Just fell on his bed and drifted off asleep thinkin' all was just fine an' dandy."

Mac paused, creating more tension and suspense. "The problem was, he hadn't found his room — he'd stumbled into one of his camper's rooms!"

The counselors laughed lightly, waiting for the rest of the story.

"Yep. Dan slept all through the night with that camper right next to him! An' the next day when he told us what happened, we asked the kid why he hadn't done anything..."

Mac paused and reached down to remove his soggy shoes.

"Well, tell us what he said!" one of the new counselors demanded.

"He said…," Mac continued, accentuating each word, "…and I quote: 'For the first couple hours, I thought it was a joke!'"

Wild laughter echoed down the halls, where a sole figure slowly padded down the center of a dark stretch of carpet.

"The first couple *hours*! I can't imagine what was going through that kid's—"

A flash of lightning illuminated the hall as a young boy crept toward them like a drugged zombie, ignoring their presence. His blue, striped pajamas hung loosely around his youthful frame.

Rain hammered the roof, creating multiple rivulets down the glass doors as the boy's labored breathing competed against the pounding rain. He stopped in the center of the room – head low, mouth agape, eyes closed as he rocked back and forth.

"Are you okay?" Mac asked.

"10." The boy spoke plainly, eyes still closed.

A frown creased Mac's brow and his large head tilted to the side. "What? Ten what, son?"

"9."

"Whose kid is this?"

"He's mine," Brandon stated as he rushed over to the boy.

"8."

"Austin, are you awake?"

"He's counting down. What is he counting down to?"

"I don't know."

"7."

The room grew tense as the counselors sucked in their breath and slid to the edge of their seats.

"6." The boy's whisper grew louder – his eyes opened and stared blankly out the window.

"Austin. Look at me."

"5."

Brandon knelt and grabbed the boy's arms, looking straight into his eyes. "Austin. Wake up, Austin!"

"4."

"Austin, listen to me, what are you counting down to?"

"3!"

The counselors in the room stood up, muscles taut, eyes frantically darting from the boy to wherever his gaze led.

"Wake him up! Quick!"

"AUSTIN! Wake up! What happens at zero?"

"2!"

"What happens? WHAT HAPPENS AT ZERO!"

Austin snapped awake and turned toward Brandon with a desperation and fear he had never seen before. The boy's dry lips formed the last word...hesitated...then spoke.

"One."

Chapter 1

Four days ago. Sunday afternoon.

"I still remember the legends and pranks my counselor pulled on me ten years ago," CJ said as he stuck a loop of masking tape onto one of the incoming camper's room signs on the third floor of Bickford Hall, the future home of eighteen seventh-grade campers. "The Observatory Legend, the Legend of Paul Newton, squirt gun wars at night..." The veteran counselor closed his eyes as sweet memories played like a movie in his mind.

Brandon smiled and shook his head as he pressed the last room sign onto a door of one of his future campers.

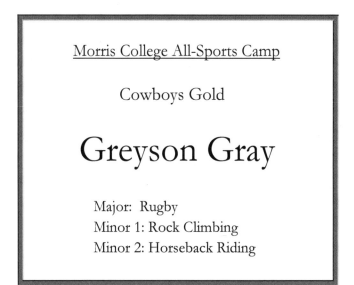

Morris College All-Sports Camp

Cowboys Gold

Greyson Gray

Major: Rugby
Minor 1: Rock Climbing
Minor 2: Horseback Riding

He smoothed the sign out and turned to CJ. "Legends, huh?"

CJ grinned mischievously, mounting one of his own 'Cowboys Purple' signs up across the hall. "I'd tell ya all about them, but the Legends are not something to be shared in such loose atmosphere," CJ whispered. "Tonight, prepare your kids — you know — build up the suspense, turn out the lights and all. I'll come by and let you see how it's done. Then, the fun is all yours. You can even make up your own legend if a kid asks some stupid question you don't feel deserves an honest answer."

Brandon's thoughts wandered to the week ahead. *Babysitting nine seventh-graders from morning to night…will it be as bad as some say it can be?*

"Well, it's almost that time," CJ warned, interrupting his thoughts. "The early ones are probably heading here from the Rec Center right now."

Brandon shook off the nerves tingling up his spine and was about to head to the room for one last moment of peace when he heard voices rising from the stairway.

"This is it, Sammy. Third Floor."

"I'm a Cowboys Gold! Does that mean I have to paint myself gold? Then I'd rather be a Cowboys Albino!"

A boy emerged from the staircase with a suitcase in his left hand, an over-sized backpack that hung down to his knees, and a huge box fan wobbling precariously under his right arm. His short, black hair was matted to the side and his thick eyelashes were dark enough that one might think he used eyeliner. A slightly lazy left eye offset a ridiculous smile that revealed a need for braces in the future. His grey-haired grandmother followed him closely, lugging another two suitcases.

Brandon sighed inwardly but rushed over to introduce himself. "Hi! I'm Brandon. I'll be your counselor for the week."

"Or *are* you…?" the boy furrowed his brow and puckered his mouth to one side as his lazy eye rolled inward toward his nose.

Brandon froze, his arm still extended for a handshake. His lips moved to speak, but he didn't know how to respond. "Uh…*yeah*. I am. And your name is?"

"I'm Sammy, but only people call me that."

Brandon laughed, thinking this might all be a joke. He glanced at the grandmother, hoping for an ally or some explanation of Sammy's strange behavior, but she was glaring at him like he had just farted in church.

"Aren't you going to take his things, boy?"

6

"Uh...yes – sorry. Let me take those for you, uh...Sammy," Brandon offered as he reached out for the suitcase and fan. "If you'll follow me, your room is just down this hall."

As Brandon led them past his own room, he could hear CJ laughing inside. *Does CJ know this kid?*

"There's a window, Grandma! I can see outside!"

Grandma's words were softened with love. "That's good, Sammy-dear."

"But that means the squirrels can look in, too. They'll be eyeing my nuts."

Brandon choked and quickly faked a cough to camouflage his shock before Sammy removed a large package of salted peanuts from his backpack and hugged them close to his chest.

"I'm nuts for nuts! Even my tears taste salty!"

Brandon nodded awkwardly and blurted his exit plan. "Well, feel free to unpack your things and make yourself at home. I'll be in my room just down the hall if you have any questions."

He left before he could hear a response and rushed into his room where CJ was on his bed, laughing uncontrollably, his radish-red face wet with tears.

Brandon flopped face-down onto his bed. "What...the... *heck*?"

CJ wiped his eyes and turned toward Brandon. "Good luck with that one! He comes every year and is always a handful. He's funny, though."

"Are they all gonna to be like him?"

CJ took a reassuring tone. "Nah. There's always one that makes it worth it. Well – usually."

———————————————————————————

Greyson Gray held his mother's hand, her wedding bands lightly pressing between his fingers. He felt his mother's attention and looked up at her as they approached the large, capitol-like building with shining, golden letters printed on the side – BICKFORD HALL.

Greyson's mother let go of his hand and ran her fingers through the brown hair sticking out the sides of his worn, red baseball cap with a white G stitched on the front. Smiling faintly, he tried to put on a happy face for his mother, but something restrained it. He hadn't been happy enough to truly smile in months. In fact, it had been ten months and thirteen days.

"Greyson."

"Yeah?" he replied in his quiet, still boyish voice.

"This is Bickford Hall."

"I know."

His mother smiled bleakly and knelt beside him. Their eyes held fast to one another for a moment, knowing each other's pain – but she was first to look away, not able to bear it much longer. With a new determination, she reached around him, pulling and shifting the straps of his heavy backpack to help it fit him more comfortably. "You sure you have all you need?"

"Yup."

"Do you know where you're going?"

"Third floor."

She nodded slowly, smoothing out his snug, white t-shirt and taking one last look into his calm green eyes and tanned face.

"Remember. Do to others what you would want them to do to you."

"I will."

"And try to have fun, Greys!"

She smiled and pinched the tip of his nose. He wiggled his nose in response, but his smile remained stagnant.

"Grey – I want to see your smiling face and hear you laugh again!" Tears welled up in his mother's eyes, but she brushed them away, laughing lightly. "And I'm sure all the cute girls here will, too."

Greyson blushed and looked at his feet. "Okay, Mom. I'll try."

"Dad was a little ladies man at your age, you know."

Greyson's face stiffened and he looked into his mother's eyes.

"Or at least he claimed he was." She smiled and lost herself in a daydream for a moment. Snapping back to reality, she spoke softly. "He would want you to be happy; you know that, right?"

"I know."

"Then do something about it. If you know something needs to change and you have the power to do it, you just do it."

"Dad thought he had the power—"

"Greyson," she snapped.

The boy stopped abruptly. He looked past her at the giant concrete building just paces ahead and watched the parents and children parading to their destinations – children with their moms and dads.

"Greyson. I'll be back on Friday to watch you in the Camp Olympics. Promise me you'll be smiling by then. I need you back."

His mother held out her hand with her pinky outstretched; Greyson sighed and noticed a group of boys gazing at the woman holding out her pinky.

"Oh, don't mind what they think of us. Do you promise?"

Greyson reached out his pinky and grabbed his mother's. They shook twice, and released; then, before he could resist, his mother pulled him to her and squeezed him so close the brim of his hat pressed against her and fell to the ground.

Feeling the unfamiliar breeze on his hair, Greyson gasped and squirmed free from the embrace. Like a whip, his hand shot to the hat and shoved it back onto his head. Crisis averted, he repositioned it just right and offered a faint smile to his mother.

She stood up and nodded with an understanding sigh. "Have a great week. Love you."

"Love you, too."

Greyson watched her walk down the winding sidewalk until she turned a corner past the Recreation Building. Once she was gone, he turned, looked up at the colossal Bickford Hall with glittering gold letters, and made his way to his room.

"Hi, I'm Brandon. I'll be your counselor for the week."

The twin boys with identical blonde hair hanging down to their eyebrows and over their ears smiled at him mischievously. The one with slightly pudgier cheeks jerked out his hand.

"Jarryd Aldeman," he said excitedly, pumping his chin upward. "Pleasure to meet you. This is my brother, Nick."

Nick extended his hand and shook Brandon's hand. "I was born second."

Brandon smiled and nodded. "Good to know."

The boys' father reached between the two and thrust his hand toward Brandon's.

"Thank you so much. You shouldn't have any trouble with these two. I've got to run, but it's good to know they're in capable hands."

"No problem." When Brandon removed his hand, he felt paper. He looked down and caught a glimpse of a green bill. "Uh, yeah. I'll take them from here. Let's go boys, follow me to your room."

As he walked past his room, rubbing the smooth paper in his hand, he smiled at CJ. *Things are finally looking up.*

"Wow. Nice pad. The chicks will dig this suite," Jarryd quipped.

Nick laughed quietly and blushed at Brandon.

"You wish. The 'chicks' are staying in Binz Hall," Brandon informed him.

"Hmm...who is this Ben and how can I get to know him?"

Nick shook his head and began unpacking his things. Jarryd's eyes twinkled and his eyebrows jumped in anticipation of Brandon's answer.

"Binz. B-I-N-Z. It's a hundred yards away."

Jarryd pumped his chin again with a sly smile. "Just a quick dash."

Brandon smiled and watched Nick start to put the sheets on his bed as Jarryd walked over to him and reached for his hand. "How much my dad give ya?"

Brandon withdrew his hands. "Ah, no. That's between your dad and me."

"He gave my last counselor a hundred."

"What?"

Brandon opened his hand and looked down at the green bill. His eyes frantically scanned the bill and landed on the number in the corner.

1,000,000. A fake.

Brandon's crestfallen gaze rolled upward to Jarryd who then burst into laughter and jumped on his bed, the veins in his neck pulsing out as his face grew red. Nick merely shook his head and giggled to himself. "He paid Dad a dollar to do that to you."

Brandon crumpled up the bill and threw it at Jarryd.

Freakin' kid.

"Brandon," CJ's voice came from the hall. "Got another couple kids here."

Great. More angels.

He turned to the twins. "Boys, please stay on this floor and...feel free to visit with the other campers—why are you still laughing?"

Brandon shook his head and sped to the hallway. CJ was down the hall visiting with a few of his campers. *They look normal enough. Why can't I get normal campers?*

"Brandon?"

"Yes?" Brandon spun around. A young, frail boy looked up at him with the biggest eyes he'd ever seen. They were deep eyes, sunken into his pale face, but they were glazed over with a deep concentration or focus, like they were looking right through him.

"You're my counselor. I'm Austin," the boy stated plainly.

"Uh...yeah, nice to meet you."

"I've already moved my things in and my parents have left. They've given you this note to help you with my condition. It basically says that my psychiatrist doesn't believe that I can tell the future...yet. Can I sit on my bed until I'm needed?"

Brandon took the small, folded note. "Yeah, sure, bud."

"Thank you."

The boy turned on his heels and slowly walked toward his room.

"Wow," Brandon muttered under his breath.

"Brandon?" Austin poked his head outside of the room.

"Yeah?"

"Your next camper is about to arrive. I think he needs some help."

"How do you know he needs help?"

"It would be easier if you just read the note."

"Um…okay."

"Too late to help now."

BANG! A series of loud thuds reverberated throughout the stairwell.

"Patrick!" A woman's voice echoed loudly. "Why did you do that? Think!"

"I hate my stupid suitcase. It's stupid."

"Your case isn't stupid, Patrick. Just because something isn't what you want it to be doesn't mean it's stupid."

"I *hate* it!"

Brandon stepped into the stairwell as Patrick passed him empty-handed. His mother stood several steps down, holding a broken suitcase with one hand, trying to stuff clothes back into it with the other.

"Here, let me help, ma'am."

"Thank you very much," the middle-aged woman responded with a tired sigh. The two filled the suitcase and Brandon carefully carried the broken case up to the hall and into Patrick's room, where Patrick sat in the center of the floor, legs crossed and arms folded.

"This room sucks."

Brandon hesitated for a moment in the doorway. "Well, it's the same as all the other rooms. It'll look better when you get your sheets on and a fan blowing…"

"No it won't."

"Patrick," his mother intervened, "you're going to have a blast. Your dad and I are paying a lot of money for you to go here and learn your sports and make friends."

"I hate sports. And friends."

"Oh, that's silly, Patrick. Of course you don't hate your friends."

"I hate 'em."

"Don't say that."

"Why not? I do."

"Because hate is a strong word."

"I don't want to be here. I want to go home."

Brandon stepped over to the mother and son. "Patrick, we'll have lots of fun this week, I guarantee it. It's the fourth golden rule here: Have fun!"

Patrick glared at him. "Following rules isn't fun. What a stupid rule!"

The kid has a point.

The woman sighed and touched Brandon's shoulder. They took one last look at the sulking child and walked together into the hall.

"You should know…," she began, whispering, "…Patrick has ADHD. But for this week we have upped his medication at breakfast and lunch. There's a danger of some light depression with the medication, but you can get him to snap out of it with some encouragement. Please be patient with him."

"I'll do my best, ma'am."

"Thank you. Good luck."

The woman gave him a look of sympathy before turning to leave. As soon as she was out of sight, Brandon rubbed his throbbing temples.

"ADHD with depression, huh?" CJ stood down the hall, shaking his head at Brandon. "I feel for ya."

Brandon looked down the hall to remind himself of the challenges he had in each of the rooms, and the situation began to overwhelm him. He let out a deep, frustrated sigh, put his arm against the wall, and slammed his forehead into it.

"Hey, Brandon."

Brandon heard the unfamiliar boy's voice and cringed. *What will be wrong with this one?* He reluctantly looked to his right through the open door. It was Greyson Gray and Liam Swank's room.

Each boy sat in his bed across from the other, watching him with expectant eyes. Already, he began to calm. There was something about this boy with the red baseball cap that made him feel at ease.

"Hi…Greyson?" Brandon walked into the boy's room.

"Yeah. And this is Liam. We just met."

13

"H-h-hi," Liam said shyly, avoiding eye contact and raising his hand for a timid wave.

Greyson arched one eyebrow. "He says he has a stuttering problem when he gets a little excited or nervous. And he says he's pretty much always nervous."

"Oh, yeah?" Brandon asked, looking at the freckled boy with buzzed blonde hair. "I have a little speech problem myself. Whenever I get around girls, I've been known to get kinda nervous and say things I don't even understand myself."

Liam smiled widely and giggled. "R-r-really?"

"Yeah. But most of them can see right through that and are flattered by the attention."

Liam looked at his shoes and lost himself in thought for a few seconds.

Greyson nodded with a faint smile directed at Brandon. "Cool. You kinda seem like a good counselor already."

Brandon's face lifted and he hesitated for an awkward pause. "Yeah? Well, thanks, Greyson. It's going to be a great week."

The boy needed, then shrugged. "We're not doing anything. You need help or something?" Greyson asked.

Liam jumped up, bright-eyed and eager to help.

"Well, alright. How about helping Patrick move in? Cheer him up a bit, huh?"

"Alright," Greyson agreed, shifting his hat. "We got to be unified to beat Purple, right?"

"That's right! Go Gold!"

"G-g-go g-gold!"

Not far from the glittering golden letters of Bickford Hall, but well hidden from any prying eyes, a man's thumb stroked the black barrel of his glistening shotgun, his fingers wrapped around the solid, mahogany pump. He sat in the dark, alone, but the arrays of flashing buttons on a control panel in front of him lit his pasty white, pockmarked skin in hues of green and red. He spoke in the empty room, as if to himself, but a small, wireless earphone that looped over his ear blinked methodically.

His calm, husky voice whispered. "You have the destination? Good. Then that is all we need. The storm should move in midweek. No more delay."

He paused, listening to the response in his ear.

"There hasn't been any suspicion."

He put his legs up onto the control panel next to the small security television. The tiny screen displayed the front entrance of Bickford Hall where boys and girls flooded in with uninhibited excitement. A moment later, the screen flickered and a silvery hallway appeared where two grizzly men armed with automatic rifles guarded a thick, metal door.

"Camp has begun. It should be no problem."

Chapter 2

Sunday Evening

"Down, set....hut!"

Bodies flew at each other from both sides and collided in a tangle of hands, arms, and torsos before angling off in different directions. Brandon took three strides backward, eyes focused on the field, hands clasped around the football.

"I'm open! I'm open!"

"I'm open!"

"I'm OPEN!"

"BRANDON!"

"Don't all go long! I can't throw it that far!"

The boys waved their arms frantically, their defenders within arm's reach.

"Four apple, FIVE APPLE!"

Two boys ran at Brandon, but the Aldeman twins were ready. As linesmen, they pushed back the rushers to give Brandon more time to throw.

Brandon scrambled to the side, the rushers close at his heel. No kids were open; they all stood in the end zone, wanting to catch the go-ahead touchdown. But Brandon coiled his arm and, in desperation, chucked the ball high into the air just before the rushers tagged him with two hands.

The ball spiraled through the warm air and peaked at the lowering sun. In the crowded end zone, legs tangled and boys collapsed in a small heap.

But one boy remained standing. Hands raised, Sammy stood in the ball's crosshairs. He opened his arms wide, his good eye focused intently on the rapidly approaching ball, his mouth agape in anticipation.

The brown spiral slammed into Sammy's face at high velocity. His arms clamped together after the fact and his legs gave way. His body crumpled to the turf and the ball bounced next to him, settling by his side.

A collective, "Oooooo," rose up from the boys.

Brandon sighed deeply as the twins broke into laughter in front of him.

I just broke a kid's face. Great.

CJ ran to Sammy's side and examined his face. "Wow. You took it pretty hard, but you look fine."

"I almost caught it!"

"Yeah, nice tr—wait, your eye is a little…uh…"

"The ball didn't do that. My mom dropped me out a sunroof."

"Oh."

Brandon ran up as CJ lifted Sammy to his feet. His entire forehead and nose were red, but his smile cleared him to keep playing.

"Well, we have two minutes before it's time to head in," CJ stated, glancing at his watch. "That was fourth down, so what do you say about giving Purple one play to win?"

The Purple boys erupted into "Yeah! One play!"

"Yeah, sure," Brandon agreed. "We'll stop ya cold. Let's go Gold!"

Purple began to huddle around CJ and Gold gathered around Brandon.

"We'll stop them," Austin said plainly.

"That's right we will. And we've been down one man all game! I'm proud of you guys."

Patrick sat on the sidelines, where he had been all game, digging at the grass.

"Patrick! We need you, bud! Come on!"

"I hate football!"

"The team needs you!"

"Stupid team."

Brandon shook his head and looked at the boys in his huddle. "Alright. We'll only rush one. Greyson?"

"Yeah?"

"Do whatever you can to get in there and get CJ. The rest of you, stay on your man. No touchdown! Gold on 3. One, two …"

"GOLD!"

The boys spread along the line of scrimmage just as Purple lined up. Two of Purple's more mature, muscular boys stood in front of CJ and glared at the lean Greyson. One scoffed. "You're not going to cry when we knock you down, are you?"

Greyson merely reached to his hat, spun it on his scalp, and fit it facing backwards.

"Oh, snap. Now he's serious, Tucker."

"Haha. He does look serious, Trevor."

Greyson took a deep breath. He was in good shape and always had been; he had never lifted weights or even been on an organized sporting team, but he couldn't remember the last day he hadn't broken a sweat running, riding his bike, creek hiking, mowing the yard, or trying one of his dad's creative dares.

One day his dad had dared him to run to the adjacent town and back in an hour – a distance about four miles. As he got older, the time got shorter and he would throw in some obstacles. Once, he ran with a backpack full of sweet corn and another time he had to do a pushup every time a car passed him on the road. Luckily he lived in small town Iowa, but he counted 132 during one round trip.

The challenges never amounted to much of a tangible reward – an ice cream cone, small binoculars, first dibs on the Friday movie choice – but Greyson would have done them without any reward, because his dad was always there to congratulate him in the end.

"Down! Seeeeet…hut!"

Greyson darted left and took Tucker's hands to his chest. The force pushed him farther left, and he spun with the momentum. In a moment he was past, but CJ had felt the pressure and rolled right. Both blockers stood between him and the quarterback once again.

Greyson didn't hesitate but flew straight at the blockers; he knew they would be cherishing this moment – a straight on collision would certainly send him to the ground, probably broken, possibly dead.

He feigned a leap directly between them and they both bit hard. Trevor extended both hands in a hard push, but found only air as Greyson stopped on a dime. Tucker missed as well and stumbled forward into Trevor's thick legs. As Tucker fell, Greyson jumped and kicked off of Tucker's back, giving him the momentum he needed.

The counselor struggled to find an open receiver, but it was too late. Greyson stretched out his arms.

But CJ had never been sacked.

With a stiff arm, CJ shoved his palm hard into the side of the boy's cheek, sending him reeling to the grass.

With his pursuer out of sight to the left, he looked out at the field and finally found an open receiver streaking toward the back right corner of the end zone. He cocked his arm and –

Two hands pushed into his side. The ball left his hand, but the play had ended.

"Sacked! Game over!" Brandon yelled, running to his victorious players.

Stunned, CJ stared at Greyson, who stood two feet lower. Greyson casually wiped the dirt from his shoulder and ignored the sore cheek that had turned as red as his hat.

"He cheated! He spiked me in the back!" Trevor yelled.

"I'm not wearing spikes."

CJ shook his head and slapped his thigh in anger. "Can't you two even block one kid? Geez!"

Brandon stopped in his tracks and watched the fuming CJ from the corner of his eyes. Morris All-Sports Camp emphasized good sportsmanship over athletic prowess and winning...or at least it was supposed to.

Careful to avoid eye contact with CJ, Brandon blew his whistle and addressed the group. "Good game, Purple and Gold! It's a solid tie. Let's line up, shake hands, and get to the Rec for our next activity."

The boys did as they were told, making two single-file lines across from each other and shaking the other team's hands as they filed past. Greyson held out his hand for Tucker and Trevor, but at the last moment, both withdrew their hands and smoothed the sides of their sweaty hair with joy.

Greyson seethed with anger, his cheek burning even hotter, but he restrained himself. His mother's familiar words rung in his ears: "Do to others what you would want them to do to you." *Punching them in the face would probably not be the best way to follow that command.*

Greyson took a deep breath, shook the last Purple's hand, and jogged to the sideline with his team. He reached for his water bottle, but Liam jumped to it before he could and handed it to him. "N-n-nice s-sack."

"Thanks, Liam. It was fun." Taking his water bottle, he caught a hateful glare from Tucker and Trevor, who walked stride in stride with CJ.

"Gold! On me!" Brandon shouted with his hand up. "We'll stick together everywhere we go, so don't wander off. Patrick, let's go!"

Patrick abandoned the grass pile he had made on the sideline and sauntered to the rest of the group as they followed Brandon off the football field and joined groups of kids flowing toward the Rec Center from all angles. Some had played cricket, others lacrosse, others water polo, and many others had tried a range of sports from the regulars like basketball and baseball to sports unique to Morris College like Powerball and Speedaway.

A group of twelve girls walked in front of the Cowboys Purple, chatting intensely. Jarryd's eyes lit up and a sly grin spread across his lips. With his grin plastered on, he stepped abruptly to the side of the group and back in again, right next to Greyson and Liam. Greyson recoiled, but Jarryd had already leaned toward his ear.

"Dare me to make a move on one of them?"

Greyson glanced at him from the corner of his eyes. "You need me to *dare* you?"

Jarryd cocked his head, the grin still as wide as ever. "Yah. Duh."

"Umm…okay." Greyson scanned the group of girls for the candidate most out of Jarryd's league.

So many options…blonde, brunette, red-head, athletic, tall, trim, bright smile…

And then he found her – a girl that could make any boy who hadn't yet started liking girls, start instantly.

Wow.

"Alright. Ask the one with the blue shirt and ponytail. I dare you."

Jarryd searched the twelve girls as they entered the Rec. His head swung to Greyson. "Nice, choice, my friend. Very nice. Watch the magic."

Jarryd scurried ahead of the group and past Brandon to the girls' group.

Catching them inside the huge triple-gym area, Jarryd jogged next to the girl in blue and pumped his chin at her. "Hey, baybay."

The girl in blue jolted in surprise and her arm reflexively curled in between her and the bold boy. "Do I know you?"

"Haha. Most people do. Some more intimately than others."

The girl's brow furrowed. "What does that mean?"

Jarryd smiled. "I don't know, but I know I would like to get to know you. Do you want to know me?"

The girl in blue looked over at her friends, who giggled some kind of response Jarryd didn't understand. One girl leaned over to her and whispered into her ear; the girl in blue gasped, but laughed softly afterward. Regaining her composure and hushing her friends, she looked back over at Jarryd.

"Sure. I've never known a boy who looks like a chipmunk."

Jarryd's grin disappeared, his larger than average two front teeth slipping behind his lips; his high, rounded cheeks blushed bright and his feet stopped moving. The girls broke into uncontrollable giggles and moved past him like a herd of laughing hyenas.

Jarryd scrunched his brow in thought. He was used to rejection, but that was just plain mean. *Oh well,* he thought, *there are many more fine ladies around, anyway.*

His brother, Nick, caught up to him first, worry spread on his face. "Jarryd, what happened?"

"Oh, nothing," he lied, waiting for Greyson and Liam to catch up. "She just didn't look *nearly* as good close up."

21

"Oh, yeah? They looked like they were laughing pretty hard," Greyson pointed out with a smirk.

"They did?" he asked nervously.

"Yeah, you tell a joke or something?"

"YEAH! Oh, yeah, I forgot. I did. I did."

The boys stared at him as Brandon continued to lead them through the giant gym area.

"And the joke was…"

"Oh….uh…" Jarryd dug deep for a joke, any joke, "it was about a chipmunk…a chipmunk and…"

"Did they say you look like a chipmunk, Jarryd?" Nick put his hand on Jarryd's shoulder.

"No, of course not. Why would they say that? I don't look anything like a chipmunk! *Do* I?"

Nick whispered into Liam's ears, "Girls call him 'Chip' at school."

Liam tried to hold in his laughter and snorted. Greyson patted him on the back and looked toward the blushing Jarryd. "If you look like a chipmunk, you're the thinnest chipmunk I've seen. And anyway, everyone looks like some animal in a way. Better a cute little chipmunk than a boar or a rat or…"

"Or a deer," Jarryd inserted.

"A deer?"

"Yeah, that's what she looks like."

Greyson and the others glanced left as the Cowgirls Gold gathered on the gym floor next to their counselor. They started giggling again, but the girl in blue suddenly flinched and froze. Her eyes seemed to be directed straight at Greyson, or perhaps right behind him, but either way he felt the uncomfortable attention and quickly examined his laces to make sure they were still tied.

Jarryd laughed. "Did you see her stop dead when she saw me? Yeah, a deer in the headlights for sure! Wow. Right, Greyson?"

Greyson looked from his shoes to Jarryd. "Oh, uh…yeah, definitely a deer."

The best-looking deer I've ever seen.

22

Brandon finally came to the end of the gym and found the small piece of paper labeled Cowboy's Gold taped to the wall.

"Alright, boys, have a seat here in a circle."

The nine boys sat on the hardwood floor as Brandon took a binder from his backpack and turned to the first page. "Great job on our first activity boys, really. That was tons of fun!"

The boys shook their heads, licking their emotional wounds from the tie. Brandon ignored their dejection and moved on. "We'll have a competition like that every evening and then three during the Olympics; each victory is worth *three* points to the victor. But even more important is what we call Fairplay points. Basically, each team is eligible to receive *five* points based on sportsmanship. If you're good at math, you'd already realize that it is possible to win a game, but lose overall."

A boy jammed his hand into the air, "Brandon! Brandon!"

"Yes, Ryan?"

"Uh, uh, so how many points did we get today?"

"Good question. Both Gold and Purple will get 3 points for the tie, and CJ and I will award Fairplay points later. But I can tell you now that we can easily do better. If the whole team plays to their best ability, and is respectful to the other team and the officials, then they will receive all five. I think we earned about 3 points today."

"No way! Then they should get zero! Did you see how CJ got angry at his own team?"

"And Trevor said we cheated, but he was only mad 'cuz Greyson schooled his –"

"Alright, alright, I know. But is that an excuse for us to be bad sports?"

The boys grew silent and settled down as Brandon turned back to the binder.

"Going on. You all have a schedule in your rooms, but just in case you are confused…you all have one Major and two Minor sports. You will spend 3 hours in your Major instruction in the morning, and an hour and a half in each of your Minors in the afternoon. When you are done with Majors we will have lunch together. Then, after Minors you

23

have free time, our competition versus the Purples, then supper. Finally, we have evening activity which is different each night. Who has been here before?"

Two boys raised their hands.

"What is on Wednesday evening?"

"The Dance!"

Brandon smiled, "That's right. There's a DJ and some sweet music."

"And women!" Jarryd blurted.

"Right," Brandon scoffed, "and the pool is open if you don't wish to dance."

Half the boys look relieved, half rolled their eyes. Greyson examined his shoes.

"Do you know what the Paddle is, Greyson?"

Greyson looked for the answer in his huddlemates' eyes, but found none. "Uh…"

"That's okay. You'll get very familiar with it. Just like we are rewarded for great athleticism, like you showed today, Greyson, we also award for great character. The Paddle is a 16-inch wooden paddle, and you can receive a total of six awards, two each year. When you receive one, it is branded onto your paddle. Each letter of PADDLE stands for an award: Perseverance, Attitude, Dedication, Discipline, Love, and Enthusiasm. As you train in your sports this week, I hope we also train ourselves to show these traits even more."

"What if you're like Patrick, and never compete?" Ryan asked before Brandon could go on.

"Please don't single anyone out like that. We're a team, and I bet Patrick will join us for the next competition."

Patrick sat, holding his knees close to his body, rocking back and forth.

"Would he get 'perseverance' for continually not playing?" Ryan spurted.

"No, it doesn't work that way…"

"Would he get 'love' for his love of hatred?" Sammy chimed.

"Or, uh, 'attitude' because he has a pretty awesome bad one?" Ryan spurted again.

"STOP! Wow, okay! I will call on you to talk. Otherwise, let's go on." He looked over his shoulder at the wall. "This place where we are now is called our shield. It is called our shield because we are going to make a paper shield and tape it to the wall. We will meet here after all of our events and meals."

Brandon reached into his bag and laid a large paper cutout of a shield on the gym floor. Next to it he rolled out five or six markers. "First, we need to write Cowboys Gold in big letters. Who has good handwriting?"

Liam jumped in and grabbed the gold marker. In a moment, the shield was labeled boldly with the team name.

"Okay, good. Now, let's put down some words or phrases that best define our team. What do we want people to think of when they hear, 'Cowboys Gold'?"

"Hot!"

"No, Jarryd. No."

Jarryd smiled. "They'll think it anyway." He stared from the corner of his eyes to the Cowgirls Gold huddle just 15 feet away.

"Sure, Chip," one of the boys muttered.

The boys laughed under their breath, all except Jarryd and Nick.

"Anyone else?" Brandon burst in.

"Go Red!" Sammy yelled.

Brandon turned to him, confused. "You mean, Gold?"

"No, I like red better. Or red *and* white!"

"What? Why?"

"I know!" Jarryd yelled as he raised his hand. "Because red and white make pink. And pink is hot."

"No," Sammy stated. "Because red and white are the colors of dead unicorns."

Brandon raised both hands in the air. "Whoa! What? Why? No one wants to be like a dead unicorn."

"I wish I was a dead unicorn." Patrick hadn't moved, his legs hugged tight and head hanging low.

"Ooookay, besides Patrick," he grimaced. "We don't want to be any color but Gold and no mascot but the Cowboys. Do I dare ask for any other suggestions?"

The group descended into thought. The other groups spread around the gym were all working on their own shields, discussing wildly, coloring liberally.

"How about daring?"

Greyson had nearly whispered; the boys leaned in expecting more. Brandon cocked his head. "What do you mean by daring?"

Greyson shifted, immediately regretting bringing the attention to himself. "Well, I, uh….I know Jarryd likes dares, too, and I also like them…um….it shows you're not afraid?"

"Hmm…I like it. It means we take risks, holding nothing back, not caring what others think about us or how we might get hurt or embarrassed."

"Yeah."

"Sweet, bro," Jarryd said with his grin.

"Shoot," Brandon breathed, looking at his watch, "we're running low on time. 'Daring' is great. We'll put that on and tape this up. Then boys, we are going to supper."

Austin smiled and muttered to himself. "Daring will fit perfectly."

Chapter 3

The Cowboys Gold merged into the long string of groups headed to the Cafeteria. Boys and girls chanted in enthusiastic unison for their own color: "P! U! P, U, R! P, U, R, P, L, E! Purple! Power!" or "G, O! G, O, L! G, O, L, D, E, N! Golden! Glory!" The shouting match lasted the entire long flight of stairs to the cafeteria where counselors once again counted their kids before ushering them inside to wash their hands.

"Hats! I need your hats! No hats in the caf!" Brandon yelled as he grabbed ball caps from several kids.

Greyson froze, Brandon's hand outstretched toward him.

"I'll take your hat for ya. Just 'til we get back out."

Greyson stepped back. "Why? I want to keep it."

"It's an old-school sign of respect and manners. Camp rule, bud."

The group gathered, antsy and ready to eat.

"Let's go eat! I'm going to starve to death!" Ryan complained, holding his stomach.

Brandon waved Ryan off. "Greyson. Take it off."

Greyson chewed on his lower lip, breathing through clenched teeth. *I can't take my hat off. Something could happen to it.*

"Greyson, you'll have to stay outside if you can't take it off. What's wrong? You need to see the nurse about your head or something?"

"I'm going to DIE of HUNGER!" Ryan bellowed as the last group passed them into the cafeteria.

Panic filled Greyson's lungs, his eyes searching the area for an absent solution. "I…I can't take it off. I always have it on."

Brandon cocked his head, bewildered, and leaned down to his level. "You take it off to go to bed."

"No, I don't."

"Oh." He looked to the side, thinking. "When you go to school or church?"

"No, my teachers and pastor let me."

"Oh…," Brandon stiffened, his strategy failing. "You wear it when you shower?"

Greyson shifted and looked deep into Brandon's eyes, wanting to say no, but he couldn't lie. He usually hung it on the shower handles.

Brandon's lips curled up. "Good. So you know you *can* take it off, and it's still okay. The hat might actually like a break every now and then, huh?"

The boy looked to his shoes. "I guess."

"My INSIDES are CRAMPING!"

"Shut it RYAN!" Brandon snapped. He turned one last time to Greyson.

"You can keep it in your hand the whole time, okay? Now let's go or Ryan will kill us all…then eat us."

Greyson whipped his hat off in frustration.

Brandon sighed and waved the boys in. "No running!"

The long wait through the line was torture for Ryan and everyone who had to listen to him, but it was even more torture for Greyson. Every few moments he fought off the panic, feeling the absence of his red hat. Only clutching the cloth harder in his grasp relieved the fear.

Eventually he took a tray and brought it around the various lines, choosing his favorite fruit, bread, vegetable, dessert, and a healthy helping of meat. If there was one thing he enjoyed about living in Iowa, it was the abundance of pork and beef.

"Can I have another hamburger, sir?" he asked a square-jawed, muscular man behind the sneeze guard. The man looked very out of place, especially with the transparent hair net crumpled over his shaved head.

The man looked up at him and sneered in disdain. "Nice hat hair, kid."

Greyson drew back. "Nice job, baldy."

He spun on his heels and left, a smile on his face. A moment later, his smile left him. *What did I just say? Where did that come from?* That was not something his parents would have been proud of. He had to apologize. He quickly spun back around and –

SMACK!

Greyson's tray flipped into the air with the impact; salad, brownie, and burger careened up as his back spanked the tiled floor. The tray and silverware clashed first in a spectacular noise and hundreds of heads turned. The food hit second, splattering cold mustard and dressing over his clothes and face. Then, like an exclamation mark at the end of an already cruel remark, his brownie fell with a dull thud onto his crotch.

A collective "ooooh" rose into a crescendo of hysterical laughter throughout the cafeteria, girls and boys both joining in the fun. Greyson lay on his back in the middle of the mess, still frozen in surprise as Tucker hovered above with a burger in hand.

"Ah, dude. I'm sorry. You really shouldn't just stop like that."

An evil grin gleaned through his false apology as he stepped over the tray and strutted toward his table, taking a sloppy bite out of his burger.

Greyson burned with anger, let out a deep growl, and scrambled to find traction in the mustard and dressing; but the mess only grew messier and the laughter even more hysterical. His cheeks squeezed close to his eyes and a lump rose in his throat.

"Here, grab my hand."

Greyson found the voice to his right, and looked up at its source through blurry tears. He gasped.

"Grab it."

It's her! Her shirt matched her eyes perfectly – ocean blue – and her voice matched her face – confident, yet sweet.

He hesitated only a moment before grabbing her wrist. She gave him a hard yank and his feet found traction; she pulled him to her with both hands, nodded once only inches from his face, and hurried away, her pony tail swinging with her bold walk.

"Thanks," he muttered pathetically at her disappearing figure.

All at once, counselors were around him, asking him how he was and cleaning his mess with urgency. Brandon was there, but Greyson ignored him. Something was missing. Something important. His hands grasped hard at air.

"My hat! Where's my hat?"

"What?" Brandon asked, looking into the boy's panicked face. "You lost it?"

"It was in my hand!"

He scanned the floor – tray, lettuce, bun, bowl, silverware – no hat! He scanned back into the line, then out in the seating area. Nothing.

"It's okay. We'll find it. Let's get you cleaned off."

"No!" Greyson swatted his counselor's arms away and burst into the seating area. He marched forward, his jaw set, fists and teeth clenched. Determined, he ignored the stares, the pointing, and the laughing.

He zoomed past Liam, Jarryd, and his table, the dressing dripping down his shorts onto the carpet. Finding his mark, he grabbed the back of a sitting boy's collar and pulled him backward. The chair teetered precariously on its back legs and the boy squirmed. Greyson looked hard into Tucker's face.

"Where is it? Give it to me!"

"What?"

"My hat! You took it!"

"Let go of me, you freak!"

Greyson snarled and drew back his hand. He had only hit two people before in self-defense, and both had drawn blood. This would be no different.

He aimed for the nose and…

"D-d-don't!" Liam grabbed his arm from behind. "It-it-it-its-it-its…" Liam pointed to the corner of the cafeteria where a conveyor belt carried dirty trays behind the wall to be cleaned. On one of the trays being carried away, his red hat lay on a plate of half-eaten mashed potatoes.

Greyson squirmed free of Liam and burst away from two counselors rushing toward him. By now every eye was on him, mouths agape in rapt attention.

He sprinted around a table, ducked a boy with a tray, and dodged a flailing female counselor; he watched her tumble on the carpet behind him and one thought flashed in his mind as a hundred gasps sucked the air from the tense room.

WHAT am I DOING?

But the hat drew closer to the hole in the wall.

"Greyson, stop!"

He ignored the plea and drew in a quick breath. Two counselors stood on each side of a long table filled with campers who sat with eyes fixated on him, some still with food sitting unchewed in their mouths. The conveyer belt was just beyond their table.

I've already gone this far…

Taking a step back for momentum, he dug into the carpet with his toes and dashed toward the table. The female counselor mouthed "No," but it was too late. Leaping with all of his strength, his left foot barely made the front edge of the table and propelled him up, shaking the silverware and cups in a cacophony of plastic and metal.

Keeping the momentum, he pounded across the top of the table, spraying Jello and milk from his shoes as the girls flung back their hands and screamed. The counselors reached at his legs from the sides, but Greyson broke through them like twigs. With one last stride he pushed off with his right leg and flew toward the conveyor belt as the hat entered the tunnel. He landed and reached.

His mind screamed. He had missed it by one second.

But there was no time to scream; the counselors converged on him from all sides. He looked desperately into the hole.

It's big enough.

He flew face-first into the hole as the counselors grasped at air.

Sounds of shock and awe filled the cafeteria as the boy disappeared into the hole. The counselors remained frozen in disbelief for only a moment before snapping into search mode.

Greyson squirmed in the cramped tunnel, shifting on top of trays, plates, and… a sharp fork! He recoiled and a bowl tipped over; liquid soaked through his boxers and he cringed. He could smell the tomato soup, and he figured he'd smell it until his next shower. Ignoring the discomfort, he peered past his legs to his prize: the red hat moving toward the light.

He couldn't sit up; he could barely lift his neck, but open space was approaching. The hat entered into the light and his body soon after. When the harsh light hit his pupils, he rolled off the belt to his feet and surveyed the surroundings.

Large carts full of trays filled the yellow-tiled room; sounds of high-pressure water and splashing came from behind a row of carts to his right.

He took two quick strides forward and snatched the hat as the tray turned the corner and followed the line of trays to another hole leading back to the cafeteria. With a relieved sigh, Greyson pulled the hat onto his naked head.

"Get in here!" A loud whisper erupted from behind the wall of carts.

Greyson's heart skipped and his body tensed. The anger behind the voice was frightening. But it wasn't directed at him.

The spraying water stopped and a door closed.

"Do *not* interact with them!"

"But I was just—"

A resounding slap echoed in the tiled room. An awkward, silent pause followed and Greyson became deathly aware of the sound of his breath. Mustering his courage, he breathed slowly, taking small, soft steps toward the nearest cart. He could just see enough of the figures through the trays and leftover food to justify the risk.

Stalking closer and closer, Greyson could make out two men: one he recognized as the tall and muscular cafeteria worker with a square jaw, the other was shorter and had bulging eyes that were freakishly near the sides of his head – like the eyes of an insect he had once found in his backyard. A praying mantis.

SquareJaw and Mantis.

"Do you need to be reminded of what is at stake?" Mantis asked, poking his finger at the larger man's chest.

"No, sir."

"Do it again–you're *done*."

"Yes…sir."

"We are too close for your stupidity to ruin everything. Stay here and shut up."

The door opened and Greyson reacted with a jerk, finding shelter just as it clicked shut. SquareJaw shuffled around the carts to the conveyor belt where he snatched a tray and threw it on a cart.

"Dumb boy…" he muttered under his breath. "I'm not *bald.* It's shaved. There's a *difference.*"

Greyson grinned and shifted in his tight hiding place. He shifted too much.

Squeak.

SquareJaw's eyes snapped to the carts.

"Who's there?" He released the tray in his thick hands and slowly stepped toward Greyson's hiding place, his eyes beady and focused.

Greyson gulped.

The angry man has the snotty boy who called him baldy…alone in a back room. He's going to kill me!

Greyson watched through a half-empty glass of milk and trembled as the monster of a man drew closer.

"Hello?" A girl's voice reverberated from the tunnel. "Are you in there?"

The man stopped just feet short of him, turned and ran to the tray hole. "Shut up! No yelling in the hole, you little brat!"

Seizing the moment, Greyson dashed toward the hole, only slipping in a glop of dressing before making the mad crawl over clacking trays, cups, and silverware. Fear and adrenaline rushing through his veins, he burst from the hole into the waiting arms of two angry counselors. They yelled something at him, but he could only exhale a long sigh of relief in response. The hole was behind him, hiding the angry man – at least for the moment.

CJ yanked him toward the exit and glared down at him, shaking his head as he escorted him past the Cowgirls Gold table where the girl in blue had just sat down. She tried to stay focused on her food, but in a brief moment her eyes slid upward and connected with Greyson's.

"What the heck did you think you were doing, kid?" CJ questioned. He smiled shyly at the girl in blue, and then spoke plainly.

"Getting my hat."

Chapter 4

Sunday Night

Brandon dropped his backpack to the ground with a long sigh, slapped his cheeks with both hands, and rubbed at his tired eyes. CJ watched him from his bed with earphones on.

"The Jensens have much to say?" CJ asked, knowing the camp directors would have been quite upset that a boy had almost attacked another boy, run from counselors, trespassed dangerously, and shown little remorse afterward.

"They had more to say to me than him. They let him off with a warning and an apology to Tucker and the food service." Brandon shed his staff shirt and reached for a fresh shirt in his suitcase. "As for me, apparently I need to keep him on a tighter leash, try to get to know him better so he'll listen to me more, and find that perfect balance between friend and authority."

"Is that all?" CJ laughed, taking off his earphones. "That's crap. What we need is a match and some gasoline to burn his baby-blankety hat. *And* a leash sounds good, too."

Brandon turned to hide his reaction. "He's the last kid I'd thought would do something like that."

"It's only the first day."

Brandon sighed wearily and put on the fresh shirt. "You still doing the ghost story tonight?"

CJ sat up, eyes on the open doorway where kids ran back and forth from the showers. "Don't say that so loud, but yeah. Ten o'clock. Maybe scaring the crap out of 'em will get them to behave, eh?"

Brandon raised his fist to knock, but hesitated in Greyson's doorway. Seemingly oblivious to Brandon's presence, Greyson stood next to the sink, watching himself brush his teeth in the mirror. He still wore his red baseball cap, pointed upward at a sharp angle, giving the front of his scalp some fresh air, but he had shed his shirt and donned loose, red pajama pants that flowed to the floor and gathered around his ankles. Night passed through the open window in thick, humid breezes, carrying the crickets' sharp, rhythmic chirps from the dark into the light.

Brandon smiled mischievously, waiting in vain for the boy to notice his presence, but Greyson continued brushing in a steady peace, massaging his gums in small, circular strokes with his eyes focused on some place beyond the mirror as he hummed with the crickets.

The calm brushing sounds and Greyson's humming mixed with the crickets' chirps in odd harmony. The melody gradually sank to the background of Brandon's mind; the seconds passed by and his attention strayed to daydream until the boy spat a mouthful of foam into the sink and sipped tiredly at the water cupped in his hands.

Finally, taking the towel from the rack beside, he wiped the foam from the corners of his mouth, lowered the towel, and sighed.

"Why do people do that?" he asked, turning toward Brandon in the doorway.

Startled, Brandon shook his head. "Uh…do what?"

"Watch other people brush their teeth." He smirked accusingly, walking toward Brandon.

Brandon tried to suppress his laugh. "You knew I was watching?"

"Yeah, the *whole* time."

The counselor laughed at himself. "Yeah, well, I don't know. You were taking your time."

The boy shrugged and pursed his lips, which Brandon noticed were redder than most. And with vivid, green eyes, he could certainly look serious if the time came. At present, though, the boy looked shy, but at ease. "I guess I like the feeling," he responded timidly, giving intermittent eye contact. "And I can think."

Walking in from the doorway, Brandon lowered himself to Liam's bed. "I usually just try to rush and get it over with."

"Yeah," Greyson nodded. "Liam says he doesn't even brush his."

Brandon laughed, shaking his head. "Gross. He use mouth wash, though?"

"No, but I offered him some of my new pop brand and he tried it. He swallowed some of it then spat it out when he realized it was Listerine."

Brandon lay back on the springy bed, laughing out loud. Greyson plopped down on his own bed across the room, his familiar faint smile pushing at his stiff cheeks.

After his laughter eased, Brandon lay still for a moment, his eyes fixed on the ceiling and his mind debating how to understand this kid.

"What do you think about?"

Greyson jerked from his own reverie. "What?"

"What do you think about? When you brush your teeth."

Greyson flinched and his mouth failed to speak the words he wanted. "Uh…I don't know. Stuff."

"Ah. Stuff." Brandon put his arms behind his head. "Like what hat you should wear tomorrow?"

Greyson shrugged, grabbing his knees nervously. "Nah. I got that covered."

Brandon felt the boy's reserve. *The kid is vulnerable. He's hiding something personal, or embarrassing – but it would be wrong to push his tender spot.*

"BRANDON!"

Jarryd's voice echoed through the halls and felt like cymbals in Brandon's ears. He groaned and sat up. "I'm in here!"

"BRANDON!"

Greyson gave him a half-smile and dropped to his pillow. "Aaah. It feels good to lie here with no obligations. Sooo nice."

"Jerk." Brandon threw Liam's pillow at him.

"Someone stole my towel!" Jarryd screamed. "I'm NAKED!"

Brandon's eyes squinted and his lips curled in disgust. "I'm *not* in here! I'm *not* in here!"

Greyson glimpsed Brandon's panicked face then suddenly stuffed his face into Liam's pillow to stifle his laughter. Brandon eyed the boy and kept a cautious look at the doorway, stuck between two unique situations; finally, Greyson had broken his stubborn reserve, but he had an odd, naked boy to clothe in the hall.

"W-w-w-w-w what…" he heard from the hall. Liam had happened upon Jarryd.

Jarryd laughed hysterically, "What are you looking at? This is my body. God gave it to me!"

Liam rushed into the room, soaking wet, a towel wrapped around his waist.

"Ja-Ja-Jarryd's naked!"

Brandon got up and cautiously approached the hall. "I'm coming out and you better have clothes on, or you're spending free time with me tomorrow."

"Oh, geez!" Jarryd expressed from out of view in the hall. "Nick, throw me my boxers! Quick!"

Brandon looked back toward Greyson and rolled his eyes. Greyson dropped his hat over his face, his stomach still bouncing with inner laughter.

"Are these my boxers? These are yours!"

"I'm coming out in three…"

"Can I wear them?" Jarryd asked his brother.

"NO!" Nick shouted.

"Two…"

"I'm putting them on!"

"One!"

Brandon stepped out with a hand over his eyes, peeking through his fingers. With relief, he dropped his hand and exhaled audibly. "Good. Jarryd, keep your clothes on!"

"Someone stole my towel!"

"No, they didn't. You lost it. Find it. Meeting in one minute in Greyson and Liam's room. Hurry up!"

Brandon walked back into the room, shaking his head. "You two ready for the meeting? Tonight we get a little history lesson."

"Nice," Greyson muttered from underneath his hat. "I like history."

Liam held out his hand and turned his thumb down. "Pppthhhh!"

Brandon pumped his eyebrows. "Not a fan, Liam? Well, you'll like this kind of history. After this lesson, you'll see the camp in a whole different way. It might just change your life."

"Get out," Greyson glibbed.

"Really. It will."

"No, get out. Liam needs to change."

"Oh."

"The year was 1818. Iowa was the next frontier."

A sole flashlight shone on CJ's face, and the shadows shifted as he spoke, hushed and dreary.

"Vast plains of prairie grass flowed in wind unimpeded by buildings, the Mississippi River had never known a motor or a bridge, and miles of wilderness offered no safety to the daring pioneers seeking new lands for the young nation, America."

"Daring, like us!" Ryan blurted.

"Like Greyson!"

Greyson retained strict focus and shook his head.

"Shhh!" CJ shifted, annoyed at the loss of atmosphere he had achieved with absolute darkness and silence. He went on.

"The plains were dangerous. The men, women, and children traveling from the East met with new disease, harsh weather, but worst of all…a brutal new enemy. The enemy – fierce, stubborn, and motivated by a rage and fury of a mother protecting her young. For this was *their* land. And the settlers —daring as they were—were unwelcome."

The boys leaned in, stiff and tense. They hung on every word.

"The natives were not ignorant or primitive like mothers told their children in order to make them less frightened; they were shrewd, calculating the risks. The trickle of pioneers could be repelled…*butchered*…but they knew…every trickle of blood…"

Brandon reached and turned the faucet to a steady drip…drip…drip.

"…could turn into a flood!"

The faucet burst into a full stream then dwindled slowly.

"So the tribal chieftain sought the will of the gods for the answer: attack or retreat? The great oracle, Eye of Eyes, a beast of a man, older than any man should live, required sacrifice to seek the favor of the gods…thirteen pure children."

"Oh, geez," Jarryd moaned, fear spread across his face.

"The chieftain despaired for days, not wanting to take children of his own tribe. He prayed to his gods, 'Oh, gods who provide. Please provide for me and your faithful followers the means to sacrifice what you require.' Then, like a gift from above, a scout returned with news of a caravan of covered wagons, making their way across the plains. Amongst the wagons—thirteen pioneer children."

"Oh, GEEZ!"

"The children were taken by night, the warriors silencing them with an herbal tea that squeezed their throats, making them unable to utter a sound." He focused the light on his throat and grasped it with his free hand. The light shifted, ever so slowly, back to his face.

"The warriors dragged them away, leaving no evidence of their presence. Sunrise came, and the mothers' cries woke every creature within five miles. And the children—innocent, young, pure—were forced to kneel in a small, circular clearing in the center of a dark forest. They thought of their mothers and fathers, but they could not cry out loud. Instead, their tears soaked the ground…making it so salty that no plants would ever grow there again."

CJ paused and stared directly at Greyson. Greyson swallowed the lump in his throat.

"And then, with a single knife…Eye of Eyes…his dark eyes rolling up into his head, his skin hanging from his bones, his scent stinging the children's nostrils… sacrificed them…one…by one…forcing them to watch."

Liam's mouth quivered, his shorts clenched in his fists.

"Until he came to the last boy…who had watched twelve of his companions bleed and die. Eye of Eyes cleaned the knife with his fingers…and looked into the boy's eyes. He recoiled back in surprise…because the boy had not shed a tear. Instead, he looked up at Eye of Eyes with furious defiance. Eye of Eyes saw the boy's courage and grew afraid…for he knew that this boy had a father…and his father would have bred such courage. So, in an instant, he released the boy and took his own life instead, adding his own blood to that wooded clearing."

CJ looked around at the wide-eyed boys, some with tears, some so tense that they were in pain, and he was satisfied. So he leaned in for the finale.

"Now, that boy ran back to the caravan without stopping. He gathered his father and men and weapons, and watched as the natives were driven from the land by the power of guns. The boy's name was Josiah Morris. He became a great man, cleared the forest, and used the wood to create a town – Morris, Iowa. And in the clearing where they recovered the bodies, where grass would not grow, where Eye of Eyes sought the vision of the gods, they built an observatory, where great vision could be sought *without* sacrifice. Some still say they can hear the cries of the mothers rising from the earth, shrill and blood-curdling. And some say they see lurking shadows of warriors still seeking that last, thirteenth child to sacrifice to the gods."

Silence sunk into the humid room, CJ's last words hanging in the air. Visions of the violence, the warriors' lean, muscular frames with angled, painted faces, and the knife-wielding Eye of Eyes haunted their minds.

Suddenly, CJ's flashlight went out and Liam jumped out of his seat with a yelp.

"Good night boys. And remember to obey your counselors or we just might take you to the observatory!"

CJ laughed maniacally and inched open the door. Then, with a sudden burst of energy, he darted out and slammed the door behind him. A few boys laughed and Brandon smiled knowingly at them, but others grew serious.

"Holy mackerel. Is it really true, Brandon?"

"It is, Jarryd. Sad, but true." He shrugged. "Well, I'm going to leave you guys alone for a bit. Lights out in your *own* rooms in five minutes, okay?"

"You're leaving us alone?"

"Yeah, five minutes, lights out."

Brandon opened the door and left. The door closed with a click.

"We have to go."

Jarryd's voice was unmistakably confident. The boys swung their heads toward the sound of his voice. He stood by the window with the faintest moonlight glowing on his back.

"Go? Go where?"

"To the observatory."

The room's silence broke as boys shifted on the bed and in chairs. "What? No way."

"Why would we do that?

"To find out the truth! If the counselors are lying, we can shove it in their FACES! But if they are telling the truth, we'll have evidence…and we'll be famous…and girls will dig us."

"Yeah!" Nick added, standing up next to his brother.

"No!" Sammy yelled as he stood, mocking Nick with a goofy smile.

"Shut up, Sammy. Who's in?"

"Will we be killed if we go?"

"Patrick, you're not going."

"I hate you."

"Anybody?" he asked again, ignoring Patrick. "Who's going with me and Nick to the observatory?"

The boys were silent. Sammy sat down.

"Greyson will go," Austin stated abruptly.

Greyson looked up, confused. "What? No, I won't. I've already gotten in enough troub—"

"I dare you."

"You what?"

Jarryd pumped his chin and crossed his arms. "I dare you."

42

Liam swung his gaze to his friend. Greyson wrinkled his forehead. He was tired and already on thin ice, but he had never turned down a dare. Ever.

I so shouldn't, he thought. *But then again, what was THAT wrong about taking a peek at a building at night? Especially if we don't get caught.*

"Just there and back?" he asked timidly.

Jarryd nodded.

Greyson grabbed the top of his hat with both hands and swung his head back. "My mom's gonna kill me!"

Jarryd pumped his fist. "Yes! Anyone else?"

Liam sprang to his feet, an answer in itself.

"Anyone else?" Jarryd looked around, but found no other volunteers. He swung to Greyson. "Alright. So how do we do it?"

Greyson was still shaking his head when he realized they were all looking at him. "What, me?"

"Yeah. What do we do?"

He scanned the room at his eight peers. *Why me?*

Greyson spoke while gathering his thoughts. "Uh…well…we'll need to make some preparations…"

Brandon opened the door and poked his head in. "Lights still off…hmm. Nothing *weird* goin' on in here is there?"

The boys were awkwardly silent. "Uh…no. We'll be in bed in a sec," Greyson answered finally.

Brandon furrowed his brow, hesitated, then closed the door. Outside, he shook his head and looked at CJ. "Are we done?"

CJ scoffed. "Yeah. Wednesday I'll bring a classic goodie out. But you see how it's done? Tomorrow it's your turn."

"Cool. I'll think of somethin'." Brandon put his ear to the door and barely heard voices. "I wonder what they're talking about."

CJ began to walk toward his kids' doors, but turned to Brandon.

"They're probably too scared to even *move*."

Chapter 5

Monday Morning

The sunrise stretched over the horizon and into Greyson's weary eyes. He lowered the brim of his hat to his brow and took in a deep breath of already humid air. It was going to be hot. Steamy hot.

"I hope they have omelets! And crepes! And bagels with *cream cheese*! And assorted fruit! And—"

"And shut up, Ryan," Chase interrupted. "Your hot air is making the humidity rise."

Chase was born in Dallas, Texas and was proud of it. He gave evidence to the claim that everything was bigger in Texas; he stood six inches taller than the second-tallest boy in Cowboys Gold and had caught two touchdown passes in yesterday's football competition. No one dared mess with Chase, because, as he liked to say: "Don't mess with Texas."

"It's hot like this in a Dallas December. But our Junes are so hot, if you don't drink a gallon of water, you'll pee dust."

Greyson squinted skeptically through the glaring sunlight at the Texan. Chase squinted back. His low, serious brow gave his eyes a slight amount of shade, but he never seemed to stop squinting, even when inside or wearing a hat.

"I would laugh, but it's too early to make the effort," Jarryd whined, trudging up the long flight of stairs to the cafeteria.

Brandon rubbed the bags under his eyes and slapped his cheeks to get his blood flowing. He hadn't slept well in the muggy night. He had set the fan on high setting and right next to his face, but the noise kept him up. When he turned the setting lower, sweat beaded all along his back and forehead. At least he hadn't had a homesick kid the first night. If anything, *he* was the one who was homesick.

"Hats everyone. Let's have 'em!"

Greyson flung his hat off and grasped it tightly in his left hand. Brandon gave him a look.

"A peaceful breakfast today? Please?"

Greyson winked and held the door for the group.

Greyson slid his tray along the metal counter to the square-jawed man's station. Today he was handing out tator tots in the shapes of smiley-faces. The man's face betrayed his product.

"Good morning." Greyson stated politely.

"Eh." The worker dropped a single face on Greyson's tray.

"Sorry 'bout yesterday."

The man eyed him, his beady eyes unwavering for seconds beyond an awkward silence.

"Hey, I want my tots!"

Greyson turned to the impatient boy in line. "He looks good bald, doesn't he?"

The boy scrunched his face and looked at the worker, who still stared at Greyson. "Uh...yes?"

Greyson turned again to the worker, attempted a smile, then cringed under his stifling gaze.

I tried, SquareJaw.

Shrugging, he escaped with his tot. When he stole one last glance back, he caught SquareJaw watching his feet walking away.

Besides that encounter, breakfast began peacefully; but with each morsel digested, another ounce of energy stirred in their veins. Greyson held his hat in his lap with his left hand, slurping at the last of his cereal with his right as conversation flowed all around him.

"What will we do today in archery?"

"Probably shoot some arrows."

"Think we'll beat Purple today in soccer?"

"I don't care. All I care about is Fairplay points. I looove *sportsmanship!*"

"Which girl are you going to ask to the dance?"

"Which girl? You mean, 'which *girls*'?"

"I heard that if it gets over 100 degrees, we all get to wear swimming shorts everywhere we go."

"Why? Just don't wear underwear and it's basically the same thing."

"I heard that they might just cancel camp and let us lounge around eating grapes in the pool."

"Grapes? How will we earn our brands eating grapes?"

"Yeah, I want a butt-load of brands."

Brandon almost choked on his toast. "Well, speaking of that, I got to run to the bathroom. Put your trays away if you're done. I'll be right back."

Brandon pushed in his chair and exited the large cafeteria. Like someone had flipped a switch, the group's attention snapped to the center of the table. Conversation ended, chews were abandoned, and Greyson froze mid-slurp. Sixteen eyes stuck to him.

"Greyson, man. You still up for it tonight?"

He slurped his cereal and set the spoon in the bowl. Glancing left and right nervously, he leaned over his tray.

"Well, let's see. Chase, you're getting the walkie-talkies, right?"

"Yeah, I saw them lying out in the nurses' office yesterday."

"Ryan, the mirrors?"

"Uh, uh, yeah. The bike helmets all have 'em."

"Good. Then tonight, Sammy's got the distraction, and Patrick will back him up."

Sammy nodded and patted Patrick's head. Patrick sneered.

"And I'll get the ropes. Should be enough."

The table hushed with nods of approval. Gradually, the boys returned to their unfinished breakfasts and whispered their anxieties to their neighbors. Liam leaned toward Greyson.

"W-w-what if we g-g-get caught? W-w-w-we could g-g-get sent home."

Greyson shrugged. "I don't know. I guess."

46

"Th-th-th-th-th-th…." He sighed and started over. "Th-then why are we d-d-doing it?"

"I was dared."

Liam's eyes flinched and his fingers pinched at his tray. Greyson took a long swig of orange juice, but felt Liam's continued stare. He turned to him and shrugged again. "What?"

Liam's eyes glazed in puppy-like worry, but after a pregnant pause, he shrugged and turned back to his breakfast.

Brandon strolled through the doorway and smiled at the table, but only for a moment. He stopped midway to his seat and scanned the entire table and the whole cafeteria. "Where's Jarryd?"

The Cowboys Gold craned their necks and searched the cafeteria.

"There he is! He's sitting at a girl's table at the end."

Jarryd sat with legs straddling the back of the chair, hands folded in front of him. All signs from a distance suggested he was listening intently to what the girls were saying. He nodded his head slowly, furrowed his brow in thought, and leaned in with interest. Then, he turned toward the Cowboys Gold table and pointed; the girls' heads turned like dogs toward a treat.

"What is he doing over there?" Brandon asked, once again feeling left out of the loop.

Nick swallowed some egg. "He's getting us dates."

"Sweet," Ryan glowed, his arms wrapped around his heaping tray of food.

"What?" Greyson glared at Nick. "What do you mean 'us'?"

"Me, you, Chase, Liam…"

Liam choked on a tator tot.

Brandon shrugged with a smile. "He's at the eighth-grade table."

"What?" Greyson glanced from the Cowgirls Gold table across the aisle to a few tables down where Jarryd was waving goodbye to a flock of smiling eighth-grade girls.

"Eighth-graders! AWEsome," Sammy drooled through closed teeth.

"No. I don't want a date," Greyson said defiantly.

Jarryd skipped over to the head of the table and pumped his eyebrows. "How awesome am I, huh? I just got Greyson a date to the dance."

Greyson gritted his teeth. "What if I didn't want one?"

Jarryd smiled wider. "Good. Cuz you have three."

"WHAT?"

Jarryd chuckled. "Yeah. Lisa, Melanie, and…and….uh…the other one."

The boys laughed and congratulated Greyson with pats on the back and thumbs up. Jarryd began reveling in the glow of approval, listing names and pointing toward other tables as he told happy boys who could potentially be waiting for them on Wednesday night.

"Nope!" Greyson stood up, his chair jolting backward into the back of the boy's chair behind him. "I don't want a date. I'm gonna go tell them so."

Brandon stood up. "Whoa. Greyson, wait a sec."

Greyson ignored him, sliding his chair back into its spot and mumbling an apology to the boy behind him.

"Greyson…"

Greyson stopped and shot Brandon a frustrated look. "Don't worry. I'm just gonna talk to them."

Brandon squinted and cocked his head. After a brief pause, he sighed like a father first handing his car keys off to a teenager. He was free to go.

Before he knew it, Greyson stood in front of the table of eighth-graders. Their eyes were twinkling, their long eyelashes batting like butterfly wings, and their glittered lips pursing in the kind of smiles girls get when staring at a puppy.

Greyson began. "Uh…"

The girls' counselor gave him a look. She looked familiar. A brief memory of her trying to tackle him flashed before his eyes.

"Uh…I…my friend Jarryd was over here…."

"I'm LISA!" Lisa stuck out her hand, pink painted fingernails and all.

"Uh…hi…"

48

He reached out his hand and she grabbed it with gusto. Her nails dug into his skin, and leftover hand lotion oozed between his fingers.

Lisa giggled, "Oooo….big hands for a little guy."

It took all of his strength not to show utter disgust on his face. After a long shake, his hand finally slipped free.

"I'm MELANIE!"

Melanie's hand jutted outward, but Greyson could still smell the raspberry and melon emanating from his now silky-smooth hand.

He said it quickly in monotone. "I just wanted to say that I don't want a date for the dance."

The girls' smiles wavered. "Uh…what?" Lisa asked. Her attitude was thick.

Greyson shifted and gulped. "I just wanted to say that I don't want a date to the dance. Sorry."

"Oh, I get it!"

Melanie whispered in Lisa's ear and Lisa's smile returned. "You are so CUTE! Playing hard-to-get…"

Greyson nervously wiped the lotion from his hand onto the back of his mesh shorts. "Uh…"

"Well, hard-to-get or not, we got you! And Jarryd told us how badly *you* wanted us."

Mental note. Kill Jarryd.

"No. I don't want you. I don't want to dance at all. I'm going to swim or something else."

She giggled. "You're good! I almost believe you!"

Lisa's perfectly straight teeth were unnaturally white. *Her parents must be dentists. Mentally slow dentists…*

"I'm just going to leave now. No date."

"See you there, GreyHUN!"

Greyson squeezed his hat's brim and clenched his teeth as he escaped their giggles. *Why are girls so dull? They were okay to look at, but not much more than that. And it looks like they just get worse as they get older!*

He hid his face from his friends as he approached their table. He could sense their gaze already. They would be waiting to pounce on everything he said, every look he made, and every…

"Greyson?"

A girl's voice. Straight ahead of him. It was her.

He looked up. The girl in blue was now the girl in red. And Jarryd was wrong. She looked just as good close up as far away. In fact, quite better.

"Uh…hi…"

"Sydney. My name."

"Hi."

She smiled shyly and looked at her shoes. Curious onlookers were staring. "Do you…uh…," she began.

"I don't want a date to the dance."

It took a moment for the words to register. When they did, the air seemed to suck out of the room. *What did I say?* He had spoken quickly without thinking.

Sydney's face turned a mixture of surprise, despair, and then anger.

"That's not what I was asking," she punctuated. "Why are boys so full of themselves?"

Before Greyson could respond, she stormed off toward the bathrooms without looking back.

What did I DO?

"What did you do?" Jarryd asked excitedly, feeding off the drama.

"I told her I don't want a date to the dance."

Jarryd playfully punched him in the stomach. "Nice! Playing hard-to-get! You sly dog."

The whole camp was burning. Heat lingered like a thick, wooly blanket over the oven-like fields. Everything sweated – especially boys who hadn't discovered antiperspirant yet. Even the water jug sweated.

Greyson was tempted to step out of line, kneel low, and lick its gloriously cold perspiration from bottom to top.

On the fields, his shirt seemed to melt like molten lava and clung to his body as it solidified into igneous rock. He wanted so badly to take it off – if he could pry it off – but rugby was a coed sport and the girls could be offended.

He ran to the verge of collapse and then ran more, using all of his pent up anger and sweating it out on the field. He sweat out his rejection of Sydney, his anger at the freaky eighth-grade girls, Tucker and Trevor's bullying, the stupid hat rule, and the fact that every other boy out there probably had a father.

By lunch time he looked like he had woken up and rolled right out of bed and into a swimming pool. His hair was dripping, his red hat looked more maroon than anything, and his underpants felt like a wet diaper. Walking past the eighth-grade girls to his table felt good.

Still want me, now, girls? Want to dance with this?

"Lookin' hot, GreyHUN!"

Greyson rolled his eyes and tried to avoid looking toward Sydney's table as he went to his seat. He had gotten in the habit of avoiding people: Sydney, Tucker, Trevor, SquareJaw. And this was only the second day of camp. Maybe the list would grow.

He saw his huddle-mates for the first time since they had left for their majors after breakfast.

"Greyson! We missed you!"

Greyson smiled and set down his tray. "I missed you, too, Jarryd."

Suddenly he felt arms wrapped around him and a head on his shoulder. Liam smiled up at him and giggled. He was being hugged.

Greyson laughed and pulled Liam's arms off his wet body. "Sick! I'm a ball of sweat!"

"S-so am I!"

"Greyson." Chase peered at him from down the table. He was holding something underneath the table. Slowly, a black pencil-like pole slid up from below. An antenna. Chase nodded. "I got 'em."

51

"Good work," Greyson approved. He had gotten the walkie-talkies. *Now, where is Ryan with the mirrors?*

"Is Ryan here?"

"He's in trouble," Nick noted grimly.

The table hushed. Brandon's absence made sense now.

"What happened?"

Nick picked up a banana and banged it on the table. "Our instructor caught him trying to knock the mirror off of his helmet." He banged the mangled mess again and a chunk flew into the air and down on his tray. "He might get charged with vandalism or something." He pulled the peel away from the messy goo and shoved it in his mouth.

"Do you know if he gave our plan up?"

"I don't know. Brandon and the Jensens are talking to him now."

Greyson cringed. He remembered his talk with the same crew. Luckily, the Jensens had been lenient on him. They seemed to understand why he had done what he had done. The same couldn't be said about Ryan. *Why would someone smash an expensive bike helmet repeatedly on the ground?*

"So...are we still on for tonight?" Jarryd asked.

"Until we hear back from Ryan, we're on."

"And another thing. What if the myth is true? What if there really are warriors still looking for the thirteenth child? What if Eye of Eyes still has his knife?"

"It's not true."

"But if it IS?"

"It's not."

"But if it IS, we need *weapons*. I'm taking skeet shooting. Nick is taking archery."

"And Liam is taking Gymnastics. We'll be fine," Greyson interjected.

"But..."

"Can you imagine if we get caught carrying shotguns and crossbows around campus?"

"That would suck. But so would Eye of Eyes cutting out my Adam's apple."

"SHHH!"

Brandon walked through the entrance with a gloomy Ryan in tow. They took their seats in silence, but Brandon broke it without hesitation. "What is with you guys?" He waited for their response.

"I'm having fun," Jarryd spoke with the perfect innocent smile. "It would be better if it wasn't as hot as Chewbacca's crotch outside."

Brandon's serious demeanor took a hit, but stayed on its feet. "Why are the Cowboy Golds the only ones to have to see the Jensens so far – and twice in the first 24 hours?"

The boys put down their silverware and nervously looked around to see if the other kids had noticed their scolding.

"Is there something I need to know that I don't already?"

Sammy unscrewed his bottle of nuts and took a quick gulp of their salty goodness. He hated confrontation.

Greyson gripped his hat tighter. *Does he know? Had Ryan told?* He examined Ryan's face. *He looks gloomy. Almost guilty.*

"Seriously, boys. Are you hiding something?"

The tension was thick. No boy wanted to break, but if they had already been turned in, breaking would be the best thing to do.

"Okay, okay." Jarryd sighed and looked Brandon straight in the eyes. "I am hiding something. I will confess."

Brandon blinked thankfully. He leaned in for the confession that he thought must take courage for a twelve-year old.

"I…have a third nipple."

Chapter 6

It was his turn.

The rock wall towered above him. A climbing rope tied securely to the harness was uncomfortably wrapped around his waist and between his legs. The wiry-thin instructor yanked at the strap around his waist and all the straps tightened. He yelped, but the instructor gave him the thumbs up. Greyson returned a dumb smile and watched the instructor take his place behind with the rope in hand. It was the instructor's duty to give him enough slack to climb freely, but not too much slack in case he fell and needed the rope taut to break his fall.

But he knew he wouldn't need the rope, because he wouldn't fall. He had done riskier challenges than this for his father. One of the riskiest was to scale their two-story house using only the clothes on his back and a garden hose. It had taken several failed attempts, but he could still feel his feet hitting shingles.

"Climb on!" the instructor shouted.

"Climbing!" he replied.

The climb was quick. There was a challenging part where the wall jutted out at a 45 degree angle, but lingering there would have sapped his strength. Speed was the key. Secure a foothold, find a fingerhold, push with the legs and make the grab with your hands, then repeat. Before he knew it, he was ringing the bell at the top. It was simple and fun.

The climb tonight will be tougher.

Ryan hadn't told. They'd asked him on the way back from lunch. Also, he'd somehow managed to snag one of the mirrors he had broken off without anyone checking his pockets. So, even with the minor snag, they'd gotten the walkie-talkies and the mirror.

Now they needed a rope.

"You need help putting the stuff away?" he asked the instructor when it was time to go.

The instructor jumped at the chance to let a kid do his work and piled the long, strong ropes in his arms and pointed him to the equipment shed just outside the huge gym area.

The old, wooden shed door was slightly open, so Greyson kicked it with a purposively manly grunt. The door swung with a creaking groan like an opening coffin, releasing a rush of thick, musty air as he pushed through the narrow doorway with the cumbersome pile of rope in his arms. He tottered to the corner and dropped the rope to the dusty floor with a thud, causing a plume of dust to rise in a huge cloud where the shape of the light slicing through the doorway revealed itself in floating particles. Greyson coughed and closed his eyes.

Suddenly, his nerves twitched and a shadow flashed over him. *I'm not alone.*

The door slammed like a shot and utter darkness squeezed out the light.

Greyson gasped in fear and adrenaline shot through his veins like ice. His heart thumped in his throat.

"Who did that? I'm in here!"

He squinted through the dark and dust – a hulking shape loomed near the door. The shape seemed twice his size, and it was looking right at him.

"Who's th—?"

It rushed at him with a ferocious growl. Greyson sucked in a deep breath to scream for help when something clasped around his throat. His body hit the flimsy wooden wall and tennis racquets clanged to the ground.

A massive hand pressed his throat hard against the wall; not even a yelp escaped his mouth. He could barely see the shape of the man in the dark, but he knew who it was.

"Listen, boy," the man growled. "I know it was you in the back yesterday, so don't deny it."

Greyson squirmed hard and tried to punch the man, but he couldn't get any leverage with the wall right behind. The man squeezed his throat harder and pressed his other hand deep into the boy's stomach. Greyson squealed in pain.

"You will not tell a soul about whatever you heard. You will not tell a soul about what is happening now. None of it is your business and does not concern little boys. You understand?"

Tears welled in his eyes. It hurt to breathe.

"I will know if you tell. If you rat me out, I have friends. Mean friends. Big friends with knives. You understand?"

He nodded, the tears flowing to the man's rough and calloused hands.

Suddenly the hand was gone and Greyson collapsed to the dusty floor. The sliver of light returned, and then with a creaking groan, he was alone in the darkness. He collapsed to his knees and elbows, gasping for deep, dusty breaths through staggered sobs, still feeling the man's fingers wrapped around his throat. His tears beaded on the dust layer below as he tried to catch a full, painless breath.

Thoughts raced through his scattered mind, but suddenly the pain in his throat unclenched and gave him his first few deep breaths. He sucked at the air and whimpered in exhale. Finally, oxygen flowed in his lungs and seemed to wash out his panic and return his mental clarity.

He pushed off his elbows and knelt, looking at the ceiling to stretch his red, aching throat. He felt at the lump forming on the back of his head, but he was alive. He was okay. The man was gone.

I'm okay. Get a grip and figure out what to do.

The dust finally seemed to be settling, and he hacked and gagged the last of it. He rose to his feet with a shuddering sigh, rubbing at the raw marks on his neck and grimacing in anger.

What did I do to deserve that? The man's insane!

Greyson stepped on a racquet, then kicked it away.

Why would he do that? So I wouldn't tell about what I'd heard? What did I even hear? Something about them getting too close to mess things up. Then he got slapped.

Greyson sniffed and wiped the tears from his eyes.

That's it. He's scared. That little fight in the tray collection place was more than I thought. SquareJaw must be protecting something bad enough to risk life in prison – he almost strangled a kid!

He leaned down and picked up a tennis racquet, then searched for its place on the wall.

SquareJaw had to be stopped from doing whatever it is he was doing. But how to prove it? And why would anyone believe him?

He had to have evidence.

He straightened his clothes, picked up the remaining racquets, and left the shed with a rope tucked under his arm. Looking around for any curious kids, he walked to the back of the shed, buried the rope deep inside a bush, and walked back to his instructor who would lock the shed later that afternoon...with one less rope inside.

Sammy waddled onto the yellow school bus, his large backpack waving left and right with each step. He smiled at the bus driver.

"Does this bus go to the horses?"

The driver laughed and stroked his thick mustache. "I believe so."

"Yaaaay!"

Sammy squeezed down the aisle, searching each seat for enough room for both himself and his backpack. Kids filled the crowded bus with raucous conversation and laughter. Sammy whined. "There's no room left!"

A few kids turned to him from their seats.

"There's plenty of space. Right over there."

"No...there's only one space," he said slowly, holding up one stubby finger. "I need twooo..." he added, holding up two fingers now.

"No, you don't. You're not that fat," a freckled redhead joked.

"I do, too!" he shouted. Then, crossing his arms in a mock pout, he sat in the middle of the aisle.

The laughter caught Greyson's attention. Leaning out from his seat where he sat alone, he got up and scurried to Sammy's location.

"Hey, Sammy. Come sit back with me."

Sammy craned his neck straight back a little too far; the weight of his backpack shifted, and he rolled backward. Greyson snagged his collar and pulled him back to a sitting position. "Come on."

"No. I need two spots."

"Oh."

He looked at the smiling kids to the left and the right. They all had a comment:

"Leave him there."

"Let him be."

"He has to learn somehow."

"Don't force him. I heard he bites."

Greyson shook his head. "There are two spaces where I was sitting in the back."

"Thanks! My nutbag is thankful."

Sammy got up with some effort, squeezed through the narrow aisle and sat in Greyson's spot with his backpack full of nuts at his side.

Greyson smiled and lifted himself up on the seatbacks to get a view of available seats. He found a spot two rows up, made his way there and slid in next to a girl looking out the window. The girl heard him slide in and turned.

He froze for an instant in awkward eye contact. It was her again. Recognition flickered in her eyes and he immediately turned and left, mumbling his apology. She scoffed and turned back to the window with an angry huff.

Sydney is taking horseback riding. It figured. His mom had made him choose it because she claimed, 'it would be fun like old western movies', but really, he bet it was because she knew only girls would be there with him. *She was like that.*

He found another spot next to a fourth grade girl who offered him half her gum which she had found under the seat, but he politely refused. The short eight minute drive felt like an hour. Finally, they exited the bus at a ranch just outside of Morris.

The sticky heat hadn't let up all day, and outside on a ranch listening to professional horse handlers droning on about taking care of horses, different kinds of saddles, and riding safety only made the heat more annoying. How could he pay attention to them when he felt the urge to sprint away and hide, or to yell, "I need the police! He's going to do something wrong! I want to go home!"

His face contorted with the nagging thoughts as he brushed the backside of a particularly large horse, sweat dripping from his hat line like a steady bleed. Wiping it away with his hand didn't seem to help when his hands were just as sweaty. Sydney seemed to glance at him every few minutes, but each time was more awkward than the next. *Why does she keep looking at me? Can she still see the red finger marks on my neck? Is she disgusted with my sweat? What?* Not knowing the answer annoyed him even more. He wanted to walk right up to her and rub the brush through her own pony tail. *Now you have a real reason not to like me!*

But instead, he shook his head and brushed the horse's butt.

An hour of sticky, frightened boredom later, he boarded the bus to go back to camp without getting on one horse. That was for tomorrow. Competition was next. Was it legal to force kids to play soccer under a blazing hot sun for an hour? Where were all the overly protective parents when he wanted them?

"Want some peanuts?" Sammy asked from the seat behind him.

Greyson turned and grimaced at Sammy's stuffed mouth, full of dry, salted peanuts.

"It's a hundred degrees outside. How can you eat those things?"

Sammy shook his head so that his wandering eye floated toward Greyson. "It's only 98.6 degrees in my mouth. If you were a nut, you would rather be in my mouth than outside."

Greyson paused. Strands of sticky, salty saliva slimed from his upper to lower teeth as he chewed like a dog eating peanut butter.

The kid has a point.

"Punt-kick it! Punt-kick it!"

Greyson held the soccer ball in his hand, squinting through the hot sweat dripping from his brow. He had made the easy save, and now he had to get it out to his offense. Chase was their star and needed the ball.

He dropped the ball out in front of him and swung his foot toward it with all his strength. The ball cut through the thick humidity and arched to Chase at midfield. Chase let the ball bounce once before knocking it down from his chest to his feet. In a flash, he was at a dead sprint toward the Cowboys' Purple goal.

"Nice kick. But they'll be back," Austin, one of his defenders, stated plainly.

"Yeah. I know. You just don't let them get a shot off and we'll be fine. We keep the tie for another couple minutes and we'll go to a shootout."

Austin shook his head. "Here they come."

Tucker had violently swiped the ball from Chase who was now on the ground by the Purple goal.

Now, the Purples had numbers. Tucker passed it to Trevor, who dodged Jarryd and Sammy with one quick side step. The ball stayed close to his feet as he crossed the midline. Nick tried to cut him off, darting toward the ball, but Trevor tapped it forward, where Tucker came to intercept.

Austin and Liam stepped forward and bent their knees. They were the last line of defense.

Tucker slowed with the ball, waiting for Trevor to make a move; but when Trevor flew around the left side, Liam stayed close on his heels and Austin stepped between Tucker and the goal, determined to keep the lead. Tucker eyed Trevor, and lined up for the pass.

He swung his foot back for the pass, and Austin stepped right in the line of fire, ready to take the impact of the ball.

Austin grimaced, waiting for the impact, but it never came. Tucker had stopped mid-swing and juked to the right, flying to the now-empty space between him and the goal.

Greyson stepped forward, arms and legs at the ready. Tucker dribbled once more, twice more, approaching the goal without shooting. Greyson balanced on his tiptoes, waiting for the last moment, watching for any telltale signs of a shot.

There it was. Tucker's eyes caught Trevor coming from the left at breakneck speed. He had beaten Liam and was wide-open for the pass. Trevor would want the header.

Greyson stepped left and Tucker felt the newly open goal. With a slight, upward kick, the ball spun toward the back left of the goal where Trevor jumped, his head ready for impact.

But Greyson had seen it coming. Diving with the full length of his body, his right fist intercepted the ball a foot before hitting Trevor's forehead. The ball flew out into the goalie's box as Greyson hit the ground hard.

The Gold team erupted in cheers at the amazing save worthy of the highlight reel. But Greyson's eyes never swerved from the ball, which bounced freely toward a purple player.

"The ball! Clear it out!"

All eyes shifted to the ball.

He scrambled to his feet as the purple player set up for the shot. He had gotten to his knees when something pounded his back from behind. He flailed forward, face-first into the dirt and sharp turf.

He heard the impact of foot to ball, rolled to the side and reached up for it, but it was no use. The ball slammed the back of the net.

Purple players burst into jubilation, bumping chests, high-fiving, running with arms outstretched like airplanes, or pulling their shirt-fronts over their heads. Brandon came running in, blowing his whistle. "Knock it off Purple! Sportsmanship! You're going to lose Fairplay points!"

CJ strutted out to his team. "Ahh, come on Brandon. They scored! Let them celebrate."

Greyson ran up to Brandon, the right side of his face smeared with dirt. "Did you see that, Brandon? He pushed me! That's a red card!"

Brandon wiped at his face and could sense the boy was on the verge of tears. "Really? I'm sorry, bud, but I didn't see it. Things like that happen and you can't always catch 'em."

"What? Look at my face!"

"Yeah…" He shrugged and glanced at CJ. "I don't know what to say. We'll get 'em the next competition."

"But…ugh!" Greyson punched the air in frustration and scratched at his burning cheek.

How do people keep ATTACKING me and get away with it! Aaagh!

A water bottle stood in front of him and a moment later he felt himself kicking it with all his strength. It twisted through the air, squirting its now warm water in a spiraling spectacle.

"Hey! That's my water, freak!"

Trevor came running over and stood face to face with him. His sweaty face stank of body odor.

"So what? HIT ME! No one cares!"

He clenched his fists but Brandon was there, pulling them apart with help from Jarryd and Liam. "Knock it off! Both of you! No Fairplay points for my players, that's for sure."

The teams split apart, throwing threatening gestures toward each other as they left.

Brandon's mind raced with desperation. "Seriously, Gold. You were doing so well and playing so hard. Who cares if you give up a goal near the end?" The boys gathered around him silently, sucking on water bottles with breathy huffs.

"Now get back out there. We have a minute left to tie it up!"

The boys sprinted out, but Greyson shook his head, his lower lip quivering with anger. "I'm not going."

Brandon sighed. "Come on. You can't give up! Get out there!"

"No."

They exchanged stares and Greyson's red, wet eyes won. Brandon shrugged. "Fine. Go join Patrick – and watch your teammates persevere without you."

He marched away.

Patrick moaned. "See? Sports are stupid. They make everyone stupid, too."

Greyson flipped his hat back around and plopped down next to Patrick with streaks of sweat and tears in a mixed line down his cheeks. "You're right," he sniffed. "Maybe if we all just sat next to you the whole time, we'd all be friends. And... maybe Tucker never would have taken my hat...and...yeah...things would be different now."

Patrick nodded. "Well...you'd be different. But what else would be? The world would still suck."

Greyson sighed and let that be the end of it.

The two boys watched Purple score one last time before Brandon blew the whistle. The teams lined up and shook hands. Brandon whispered in Greyson's ear on the way back, "We need to talk tonight. This can't go on."

Greyson's eyes drooped and he pulled at the grass with Patrick.

"Let's go! Air conditioning, fresh fruit, Gatorade. It all waits for you. Stay together!"

Patrick and Greyson gave each other a quick glance and stood up despite the heavy load of gravity and sweat.

Something tripped in Greyson's brain. Some kind of switch turned off the part of his brain that said he should care what others thought of him. The same switch seemed to affect even what he thought of himself.

He took his tray right past the bald, square-jawed cafeteria worker. The man gave him a knowing glare, and Greyson returned it with indifference. No words were said, but a conversation was had. Greyson wouldn't say a thing, because he didn't care.

He passed by the eighth-graders table, his face still smeared with dirt. The girls pointed and giggled, but he didn't even roll his eyes.

He sat by Liam and Jarryd who tried their best to cheer him up, but the switch was firmly in place.

Even food tasted bad. He had a few grapes and four glasses of Gatorade, but he wasn't hungry. He gave Liam his taco and Chase his brownie.

"Dude. What's wrong? Who cares if we lost? It's not your fault, man."

He shrugged.

"We'll get 'em for ya. Next time. When Brandon's not looking."

Brandon perked up. "I'm *right here*."

Jarryd blushed. "Oh. Oops. I meant we'll get em'…something nice. Like a scented candle or somethin'."

Brandon smiled. "Right. They'd like that."

"And then shove them right up their—" Jarryd whispered loudly.

"Whoa! I'm eating."

Greyson remained stoic, his eyes glazed and daydreaming. *Why don't people just shut up and leave me alone?*

"You catch the Patrick disease or somethin' man?"

"Yeah, it's like you're a wounded puppy. You need some lovin'? Or maybe you just need to be put down?" Chase asked sarcastically. "I had to put down an ol' mare once. But it had mad cow disease or somethin'. You just lost a game."

"Heat rash, maybe? Mine's like a volcano, but Gold Bond's an ocean of relief."

"Girl trouble?"

"Homesick?"

Liam thrust forward with a mouth full of taco. "L-l-leave him alone!"

The table hushed.

Brandon sighed. "Yeah, guys. I think it would be best. Just let him be."

And they did for the rest of the evening. After supper the entire camp took pictures – first as a large group, then as huddles. The photographer tried to take Greyson's hat away, but Brandon spoke with the photographer alone for a minute and nothing more was said.

After pictures, the entire camp met at the football field for teambuilding games where each huddle was to try to use teamwork and cooperation to overcome obstacles. Huddles raced to secure the most fun-looking activities using objects of all kinds – long jump ropes, parachutes, tubes and marbles, wooden blocks, plastic towers, strings and orange cones, and more.

They even turned the stadium lights on, which to most kids made the experience feel like a Monday Night Football game, but to Greyson and Patrick it was like the dentist shining his light on you right before he began to drill.

Brandon took the Cowboys Gold to the high jump mat near the north end zone of the football field and had them sit on the hard, rubber track. "Listen up. Our team needs work. Everyone should see that. That is not so bad. All teams need work. Where it goes bad is when the team doesn't even *try* to improve – they give up, getting down on themselves and each other."

Greyson kept his eyes on his shoes, hoping to avoid eye contact.

"So, today, we're going to try to work together to achieve some goals. To do this, we first need to trust each other."

"Are we supposed to tell you all our deepest, darkest secrets now and then hug and make up?" Jarryd interrupted.

Brandon laughed. "Nah. That's later. For now, we're going to do the *Trust Fall.*"

The boys perked up, hearing the excitement in Brandon's voice.

"One at a time, we are going to stand on that mat, four feet up, turn our backs, close our eyes, and fall backward toward the ground."

"Ah, snap!"

"Yeah. That's the fall part. The trust part comes in when the rest of us are lined up with our arms ready to catch our huddlemate before he hits the ground. To fall backward blindly, we have to trust our team to catch us."

"What if we don't want someone to catch us?" Patrick asked predictably.

"Well, then find a different huddle. 'Cuz the Cowboys Gold don't let each other fall."

The boys nodded their approval. "Nice, Brandon. Corny, but nice."

Brandon smiled. "Thanks, Jarryd. I think you just volunteered to go first."

"Yeah!"

Jarryd sprang up and climbed on top of the mat.

"Okay. Four people each in a line. Line up across from a partner and spread your arms."

The boys followed the instructions.

"Now, bend your knees in your best bracing-for-impact stance. Jarryd will yell, 'Falling', we will respond, 'Fall away!', and then he will turn and fall light as a feather and stiff as a board. Do not let him hit the ground, boys."

Jarryd smiled, pumped his eyebrows, and took his best swan-dive stance. "Falling!"

The boys bent their knees and smiled with anticipation. "Fall away!"

Jarryd turned and hugged himself. He breathed in deeply, and just when he was about to fall, he turned on a dime. "Wait. I'm not ready."

The group lowered their arms in frustration. Jarryd looked down at Sammy who smiled as far as his arms were still open.

"I'm supposed to trust *him*?" Jarryd arched his eyebrows at Sammy's face. "Why should I trust him if he can't even look me in the eye? I can't tell if he's looking at me or the bleachers!"

"Hey don't make fun of –"

"Both!" Sammy replied.

Jarryd laughed. "See?"

Brandon's tired face turned angry, "Is there anyone who trusts this group and who would like to show it?"

Jarryd piped up first. "Ah, come on. I was just joking. I'm doing it."

At that, he turned, went stiff as a board, and fell backward.

"Wait!"

He fell away.

Chapter 7

Monday Night

Jarryd lay stomach down on his bed. A thick ice pack rested on the back of his head, leaking condensation down his neck. Brandon stood over him shaking his head, running the event back through his mind over and over.

"Light as a feather, stiff as a board, dead as a doornail," Jarryd moaned through his pillow.

Brandon laughed softly. "Well, why don't you go 'out like a light bulb' now and get as much sleep as possible like the nurse said."

"Nick has to give me a sponge-bath first."

Brandon bent over with tired laughter. "Now that would be brotherly love, if I've ever seen it."

Nick came through the doorway, a wet rag in his left hand, a red bucket in his right. A bath towel was thrown over his right shoulder.

Brandon's mouth dropped open. "Wait. You were serious?"

Jarryd gave him the thumbs up without moving his sore head.

Nick laid the bucket down with a soapy slosh. "Can he have some privacy please?"

Brandon laughed under his breath and closed the door behind him. *Weird, freaking kids.*

Boys ran past him on both sides, relishing the new energy that the showers gave them. Brandon longed for a shower of his own. He had thoroughly enjoyed his shower and short nap during Majors, but he had gained several new layers of sweat after that.

CJ sat out in the hall, selling candy bars to the kids who had brought money.

"New special! Six for three bucks! Six for three!"

Brandon slid down the wall and sat next to him. "Weren't you just selling them for fifty cents a piece?"

CJ smiled. "They're kids. They can't do math."

One of the Purples fresh out of the shower and in a towel came up to them and dropped a five-dollar bill. "I want six!"

CJ looked up at him. "Six? I'll give you a better deal. Ten for five dollars! Just for you, Sam."

"Really?"

"Yeah, no doubt. You're my favorite camper."

"Awesome! Deal!"

CJ dished out ten candy bars into the boy's arms. He dashed down the hall and into his room. CJ waited until he disappeared to wink at his younger counselor friend. "You have a lot to learn about these kids. But don't worry. You do have a tough group. That Greyson kid needs a good whipping. Spoiled kid thinks the camp should revolve around him."

Brandon didn't know how to respond. "Eh...maybe. Maybe he just wants things to be fair and right." He felt stupid as the words came out.

CJ furrowed his brow. "Yeah, whatever *he* thinks is fair and right, like him winning everything and getting to disobey any rules he wants."

Another kid came up and dropped a five-dollar bill. "You gave Sam ten for five! I want ten for five, too!"

Brandon took the opportunity to get up, but CJ stopped him halfway. "I don't know. What do you think, Brandon? Should I give him ten for five?"

Brandon scoffed. "Yeah. But only if you go into room 339 and ask Nick if you can help him with what he's doing."

"What is he doing?"

"Ah...you'll find out. Just do it."

The kid looked to CJ and CJ shrugged. "Okay. Ten for five."

Brandon turned and smiled smugly to himself. He walked past his own room and eyed his pillow with jealousy. *Soon, my soft friend. Soon.*

He sauntered down the hall of his kids' rooms and gravitated to Greyson and Liam's room. The door was open and drew him in. Taking a deep breath, he stood in the doorway and spotted Greyson lying shirtless on his bed with his fan directed on his face. His eyes were closed, mouth agape, and hands crossed peacefully over his chest.

Brandon tiptoed into the room and sat on Liam's bed. The bed moaned under his weight. Greyson didn't stir. *He must be asleep.*

"How long you going to watch me this time?"

Brandon smiled and leaned back, using Liam's pillow as his own.

"You here for our talk?" Greyson asked melancholically, glancing at him through the corner of his sad eyes.

"Nah. I've had enough talking. I think I'll just listen and think for a while. Maybe I'll use your toothbrush if I need to."

Brandon breathed in and let it out as slow as possible, taking in the beautiful silence as he closed his eyes. He could sense the boy across from him, still and somber. It wasn't like he was depressed like Patrick, but something was weighing on him. The boy just wasn't himself. *Why?*

"I think about my Dad, mostly."

Brandon opened his eyes and blinked once, making sure he had heard correctly. He sat up, the springs moaning as he shifted his weight. "What?"

Greyson shifted on his bed, unsure of whether to sit or lie down. "When I brush my teeth. I caught him watching me every now and then."

Brandon chuckled. "What do you remember when you think about him?"

The boy lifted his hat and scratched the top of his head. He rubbed his chest and scratched where it didn't itch. "He...I don't know. I guess I just like to remember when we did stuff together," Greyson looked at the ceiling and spoke nervously, the words catching in his throat and bringing moisture to the bottom of his eyes. "He left. Maybe he'll come back. They say he won't...but I don't know."

Brandon had leaned in, his elbows on his knees. "Where did he go?"

The question caught hold of a reluctant memory and forced it to the forefront of Greyson's mind. It played back in front of his eyes, a dark mood covering his emotions. He put the memory into words as best he could for Brandon.

He was in their kitchen, a stream of orange and yellow sunset light coming in through the window. His hands were working steadily, pressing the dry towel against the wet dishes, wiping them until they shined without streaks. His mother worked in the soapy sink to his left, her brow furrowed in worry, the wrinkles at the corners of her eyes more evident than before.

"He's going to Africa, dear. A country called Sudan."

"Why does he have to go?"

"It's what he's always done best and it's what he wants, Greys. He took the job at the Register because we had you. He wanted to be with you as you grew up."

"But he was happy with us here."

His mother let a dish slip into the deep, soapy water, and she wiped her hands on Greyson's towel. "Of course he was! And he'll still be here for most of the year. This is just one assignment. And he hasn't had an opportunity like this since, well, about 13 years ago."

"Before I was born."

His mother leaned down to his level like she often did, her hand stroking his face or resting on his shoulder.

"Yes, but, dear, don't think—don't think it was your fault—don't think you were something he didn't want. Ask him, Greys. We had you to put some good in the world and now he is going away because he thinks he can do some more good for the world. A few pictures can affect a lot of people, and your father takes the best pictures."

Brandon sighed in sympathy. "Did you get to ask him?"

"Yeah. He gave the same answer. He thought I could do fine by myself for two months. He thought it would be good for both of us...and 'the world'."

He returned to the story.

"Greyson. You might be angry with me, I know. But please, son, don't be angry. Your mother needs you to be the man now. What have I told you to do for 12 years? What is our duty here?"

"To take out the trash?"

His dad smiled and ruffled his boy's hair. Greyson smiled and laughed, pushing at his father's powerful hands.

"Nah, come on, son."

"Do the good that should be done."

His dad's eyes sparkled. "Right. Now I'm trying to stay true to my own advice."

Greyson's mouth quivered. His eyes hurt from holding the tears back. He sniffed and wiped his face with his hand and wrist. The words seemed to echo in his ears. *Do the good that should be done.*

Brandon sat across from him, nodding his head sympathetically. "What happened next?"

Greyson sat up slowly, his fingers kneading his mesh shorts, his eyes searching the space beyond.

"I have to go, and you have to let me, son." His father paused and a coy smirk formed on his lips. "I dare you."

Greyson looked up, tears in his eyes, his lips quivering.

"I dare you to let me go. If you do, you get the prize."

His legs felt weak. He wanted to scream, 'No!' and clutch at his dad's legs like he used to when he was young. But he couldn't anymore. He was older now. And old boys could never pass up a dare. This would be his hardest dare; it would hurt and challenge his mind and strength. And just like the challenges before, he could do this…and his dad would be there in two months to congratulate him.

"Fine. Go."

His dad grabbed his shoulders and pulled him close in a long, tearful embrace. Then, ten times faster than he wanted, his father grabbed his camera bag and his suitcase and left through the front door. The taxi waited outside as his father and mother embraced one last time.

Then, after a brief kiss, his father reached up and removed his lucky red baseball cap with a white G stitched on the front. With a glance toward his son in the window, he handed the hat to his wife and stepped into the taxi.

The taxi drove away, kicking up gravel and dust into the front yard and down the road for a mile. His mother turned reluctantly, the hat gripped in her tense fingers. Tears pouring down his face along the same familiar path on his cheeks, Greyson opened the door for his mother and hugged her without shame. Overwhelmed with grief, he barely felt the hat being fitted to his head.

"Your prize, Greys."

Greyson sat still on his bed; his red hat now in the grasp of his shaking hands. His cheeks tensed to hold the tears back, but one escaped and dripped from his chin to his lap below. He swiped it away and smiled sheepishly at Brandon.

"Sorry," he sniffed.

Brandon watched helplessly from the bed across. *How could they train me for this?*

He rose to his feet and approached the anguished boy, his mind racing for the proper way to comfort a camper. *How much counseling could a counselor really do? Was he even allowed to hug him?* He glanced toward the open door, hoping no one had been listening for Greyson's sake.

He sat next to Greyson on the bed and cautiously put his arm around him.

"That's why you went after your hat like you did."

Greyson sniffed and nodded with a smile. "Yeah."

"And is that why you were so sad today? Were you thinking about him?"

Greyson gazed at a space past Liam's bed, pondering the question. There wasn't one answer to it. *I was attacked by a man, threatened with death, bullied by Trevor, ignored by Brandon, and hated by girls. Was it because I was thinking about Dad?*

No. I haven't been thinking about him at all. Suddenly, the switch that had flipped earlier, flipped back. *The good that should be done.* He hadn't done much good at all. A memory flashed of when he'd sat by Patrick. "You'd be different. But what else would be?" Patrick had said. *He'd been right. If I just sat out, the world wouldn't be different. Tucker and Trevor would still be evil, and SquareJaw...SquareJaw would still get away with whatever it was that he was doing. What good have I done at all?*

"I'm sorry. I—I've just been dumb."

Brandon awkwardly grabbed the boy's shoulder. "I agree." He smiled at him. "But I think you'll turn it around. You might even get that Perseverance brand."

Greyson feigned a smile. "Thanks. I'll try."

Liam stood in the doorway, cocking his head inquisitively. "W-w-what are you doing?"

Brandon yanked his arm away from the boy and stood. "Hey, Liam. Just chatting. Have a good shower?"

Liam nodded, but didn't move.

"Meeting in five minutes guys. See ya then."

Greyson smiled and waved. Liam stepped out in the hall to let him pass, but came back in with a coy smile.

"Don't look at me like that."

Liam shrugged. "A-are we s-still on?"

Greyson took in a deep breath and held it, rubbing his eyes. He put his hat on his mess of wet hair and let out the breath. He felt new.

"I don't think so. Jarryd's hurt and I just told Brandon I wouldn't be dumb. We can just have fun here telling stories or something."

Liam's mouth hung open and he almost dropped his towel.

The meeting dragged on. The dark night had brought relief from the heat, but the humidity remained. Boys sat shirtless in Nick and Jarryd's room, snacking on candy and drinking from juice boxes their parents had packed for them.

They called the nightly meetings "paddle talks" where counselors shared their wisdom and discussed the brands for the day. Tonight, Brandon spoke of the first and second brands, perseverance and attitude. Boys groaned at the moral platitudes – in the back of their minds they awaited the night to come. *Would the distraction and escape work as planned?*

"Attitude is contagious. It's like a wildfire. One spark and the whole forest can light up. One negative comment, one act of bad sportsmanship can affect the whole team in a bad way. Would you all agree to that?"

Jarryd mumbled from his bed. He still lay face-down, the icepack now a soppy mess mingling with his drool. "Uh ugree. Fiah sucks."

Ryan's hand shot upward. "I, uh, agree, too!"

"Thanks for sharing. So, would anyone like to share how we should try to change our attitudes for the rest of the week?"

He looked to Greyson. Greyson sat on Nick's bed, back to the wall. "My mom always tells me—"

"Your mum's *HOT.*" Jarryd laughed and sucked in his drool.

The room erupted in laughter. Greyson smiled. "That's what my dad used to tell me."

The laughter died down as Brandon shushed them.

"Used to?" Chase asked. "Does he not think so anymore?"

More laughter, but Greyson gritted his teeth and smiled meekly. He ignored Chase's question and went on, speaking through the soft laughter. "My mom always tells me to do to others what you would want them to do to you."

Thoughtful nods and "hmms" joined the hums of the fans. Jarryd rolled over, drool all over his face, and sat up straight. "So...should I go up to Deergirl and just start making out with her?"

The laughter took another minute of their free time before bedtime. Brandon looked at his watch and gave up, calling it a night. "Alright, boys. Jokes aside, I think Greyson's hot mom has a good idea. Let's try to think of others tomorrow." He stood to leave. "Lights out in three minutes!"

"Three minutes? Ah, come on!" Ryan complained. "It's only 10:27!"

Brandon laughed. "Yeah. Do the math. Lights out every night at 10:30. That's the way it is."

"But WHY?"

He smiled and remembered CJ's advice. Sitting down, he began thinking out loud. "Because, Ryan, we have twins in our huddle."

Nick and Jarryd turned to him with keen interest. "Huh?"

Brandon nodded and tried to look serious. "Groups with twins need to be especially cautious about not being up past 10:30."

"Why?"

"Because of Paul Newton."

A hush fell across the room and the boys shared confusion. "Who's he?"

"Well, long story short, he was a counselor here six years ago, something happened, now we have to lock kids' windows at night and watch any twins' rooms very carefully after 10:30."

Jarryd and Nick stared at each other as Brandon walked to them.

"But what – happened?" Nick's voice trailed off.

"Oh, I wouldn't want to scare you..."

Greyson tried to cover up his smile with his hand.

"Tell us! We have the right to know!"

Brandon sat on Jarryd's bed, but kept his distance from Jarryd's face. He sighed and started, "Paul Newton was a lucky counselor of five sets of identical twins and he loved it for awhile – he only had to meet with five sets of parents, they were easy to split into pairs, and they had an uncanny ability to communicate in competition."

Nick smiled at Jarryd.

"But...things quickly turned for the worse. They confused him, switching identities, sports, and clothes regularly. They harassed him at night, each one asking to go to the bathroom twice and claiming it was the other one. Eventually, there was one straw that broke the camel's back. At 10:30, all five sets of twins refused to go to bed. They said that if he couldn't remember their names, he couldn't tell them what to do. He tried to tell each one to go to bed and turn the lights out by name, but they'd just say, 'I'm not Jarryd, I'm Nick,' then run around to confuse him."

Jarryd smirked.

"Then, suddenly, something snapped…and the next morning, there were ten bloody beds and no sign of any bodies – or of Paul Newton."

Jarryd tensed and Nick grabbed his hand.

"Then…a year later…another set of twins. Bloody beds. Gone. Two years ago…another set of twins. I'm surprised your parents sent you."

"You're just making that up! Aren't you?"

Brandon sat up and slapped Jarryd on the thigh. "I don't know, boys. This is my first year. I'm just telling you what I heard." He walked to the door and turned, looking at his watch. "But it's 10:29. I'd go to bed."

Brandon gave one last look at Jarryd's wet face before closing the door behind him.

"Still want to go tonight, Jarryd?" Greyson asked.

Jarryd shrugged and sat up woozily. "An army of Paul Newtons couldn't stop me."

Nick gave him a slight push; Jarryd lost his balance and fell back into bed.

Greyson stood up in the center of the room. "Jarryd, you're hurt. Look at you. You're drooling all over yourself."

Jarryd wiped his face and looked at his hand. "Eww. But still…"

"We shouldn't go tonight. At least I'm not going."

"No way!" Jarryd sat up again. "I dared you!"

Greyson grimaced. *Ouch.*

"Jarryd. It's not just because of the twin-killer, but think of Brandon. We've given him enough trouble already. We don't want *him* to snap."

Austin walked past Greyson toward the door. "You'll go tomorrow night."

"Tomorrow night?" Greyson asked.

He looked to Ryan and Chase, who nodded their approval.

Jarryd held his forehead and fell back onto his bed. "Ugh. Fine. Tomorrow night."

Liam pounded the bed with his fist out of frustration.

Greyson patted his head. "We'll see. Good night."

As he left the room of disappointed boys, he still felt troubled. He believed what he had said. It would be good to obey and respect Brandon and the rules – especially if the only reason for disobeying the rules was to discover the truth about an ancient Indian curse in the middle of an Iowan college campus. But there was a greater good – to find out what SquareJaw was doing and to stop it. No more sitting on sidelines. He had to trade one good for another. *Sorry, Brandon.* So, for that reason, he would escape tonight. Alone.

Chapter 8

"Liam. I need your help."

Footsteps padded down the dark hall outside. Counselors were leaving for their meeting downstairs.

Liam turned over. The moonlight cast an eerie shadow across the room and reflected in Liam's white eyes.

"Don't tell anyone I'm gone," Greyson whispered. "If someone comes in here looking for me, tell them I'm meeting with the Jensens because they might send me home."

"Wh-what?"

"Can you do that?"

"Wh-where are you g-going?"

"To the cafeteria. Don't panic. I'll tell you more later."

"B-but…"

Greyson flung his covers off, threw on a t-shirt, and snapped a worn, red fanny pack around his waist. Next, he rummaged in his duffle bag and came out with a walkie-talkie, held it to the night-light and flipped the on switch to 'On'. He searched inside the fanny pack and emerged with the small mirror with a thin plastic connector that once held it to a bike helmet.

Zippy his fanny pack closed, Greyson tiptoed to the door, which was required to be cracked open at all times. His fingers ever so slowly pushed the mirror through the crack. Snuggling close to the door, Greyson kept his eyes peeled to the mirror, tilting it up and down until a small part of the hallway appeared. In the middle of the hall, about three doors down, a physical trainer sat reading a sports magazine, supervising for the counselors as they had their nightly meeting.

Greyson held the walkie-talkie up to his mouth, still watching the small view in the mirror. He had hid the other walkie-talkie under Jarryd's bed in the 'on' position. He held the 'talk' button and the walkie clicked.

"Hello, twins! I'm Paul Newton!"

The voice and light screams echoed from down the hall, coming from Jarryd and Nick's room.

Greyson smiled, watching the mirror as the physical trainer dropped his magazine and turned toward Nick and Jarryd's room to his right.

He put the walkie to his mouth. "If you find this, hide it!"

The physical trainer stood up and sped straight to the twins' room.

Satisfied with the results, Greyson pulled the mirror back in and slid it into his fanny pack. He took one last look at Liam and winked at him. "See ya."

He shoved the walkie next to the mirror, pulled the door open without a sound, and slipped out.

His heart raced, the open hall's air thick with tension as desperate whispers came from the twins' room.

"Why are you screaming? Kids are trying to sleep!"

"Who ARE YOU?"

"I'm supervising! Shut up!"

"Are you Paul?"

"Paul? What? Shut up and go to sleep or I'll go get Brandon!"

"We weren't talking! I swear!"

"I heard you!"

"It wasn't us!"

Greyson glided through the hall with long strides and turned into the stairway. He craned his neck up, heard nothing; he looked down, nothing. Putting his back to the wall, he took off his shoes. Then, with quiet, padded steps, he moved swiftly down the three flights of stairs.

Another flight descended to the basement where a glass door exited to the back parking lot, and a hallway led to the front lobby where he could hear the raucous laughter of the counselors in their meeting.

Getting out of the building would be no trouble; getting back in was the hard part. All doors were locked, including the fire door ahead of him that had an alarm that could be turned on at any time, though it wasn't now. Also, all the windows were locked except the kids' rooms, which always had screens that could not be pried off. His fingers were still raw from trying.

That's where the rope would come in.

He put his shoes back on and opened the door to the back parking lot. Rich yellow lights gave the empty lot an eerie glow. Bugs flew in herds around the buzzing bulbs, seemingly attracted to sound and light – the two things Greyson sought to avoid. He sprinted to the dark, grassy ditch behind the lit parking lot and slid to his stomach.

His eyes scanned the back of Bickford Hall to the rest of campus. Winding sidewalks and buildings were well lit, but no one wandered them this late. Far across campus, beyond the football field, he saw the cafeteria on the hill. To the right near the far end zone of the field, the small domed observatory seemed a huge metal pimple on the concrete and grass campus.

To the left, the giant Recreation Building stretched over the corner of campus. He couldn't see the shed, but he knew where it was. He looked at his watch. *The physical trainer should have finished giving the twins their scolding by now.* He pulled out the walkie and flipped it back on.

"Jarryd," he whispered. "Jarryd. Did you find it?"

He released the talk button; his eyes peeled over the lot and through the glass door to the stairway.

The walkie crackled. "H-hello? Greyson? You frickin' scared us!"

It was Jarryd's voice.

"Shh! Keep the walkie under your covers."

"It is. Where are you?"

"I'm outside. I'm going to need your help in a minute or two."

"Sweet. I knew you couldn't pass up a dare. I wanna come."

"No. Stay there. I'll call back in three minutes or so. Radio silence until then," Greyson demanded with a smile. He was living a spy movie.

He clicked off the walkie and dashed to his feet. The humid air rushed at his face, and when his hat almost blew off he turned it backward for the sprint. He sped around the back of the lot to the dark side of the Rec Building and paused for a short breather at the corner. He used the mirror just long enough to see the empty path to the equipment shed.

Zipping the fanny pack again, he raced to the shed, pulled the rope from the bush, and wrapped it around his shoulder. The run back was awkward, but he made good time. Three minutes after he had left, he slid to the same ditch, sweat beading on his forehead.

He clicked on the walkie. "Jarryd."

"Yeah?"

"I need you or Nick to go to the bathroom."

"Now? *Here?*"

"No. No. Listen. The bathroom down the hall. Leave the walkie in your room; open the bathroom window."

"Pee out the window?"

"What? No! Please don't. I'll be below. Just look out. I hope you can tie a knot."

"Can do. Over."

Greyson smiled. "Oh, and don't let the trainer say no."

"See you soon. Over and out."

The walkie clicked.

Jarryd hid the walkie under his bed and stood quickly. Before he took his first step, his head swooned and vision blurred. He sat down and blinked away the fuzz in his eyes.

Nick stood over him. "I can do it."

"Do what? Go back to sleep?" he whispered, dripping with sarcasm.

Nick blinked. "No. I've acted in school plays; I know how to act."

"And musicals," Jarryd mocked.

"Yeah…" Nick shook his head. "So?"

"You're a regular thespian."

"Shut up. I'm going."

Jarryd nodded. "Fine. Whatever."

Nick's face flashed a smile, but he covered it with his hands. He breathed deeply, rubbed his eyes, and ruffled his hair. When he lowered his hands from his face, his eyes were open halfway and his lips smacked slowly. He looked at Jarryd like he'd just gotten up.

Jarryd rolled his eyes.

Pushing the heavy door open, Nick lowered his head woozily and walked out. The physical trainer put down his magazine in a jolt and gave him the death stare. Nick didn't acknowledge him, only shuffled past him.

"Where d'ya think you're going?"

Nick turned around, visibly holding himself. "I need to pee."

The trainer closed his eyes in disgust and motioned him on without looking.

Nick smiled to himself and padded to the bathroom. Once out of view, he skidded across the tile in his socks and unlocked and slid open the window. Leaning out in the fresh air, he saw nothing but an empty parking lot. But then, a moment later, a figure burst from the dark ditch and through the lot, a large rope in his hands; the red hat on the figure's head gave him away.

"Greyson! Up here!"

Greyson waved and ran to the side of the building. He whispered as loud as he could, making motions with his hands, "Catch the rope. Tie it to the radiator."

Nick looked down at the radiator next to the window. It looked solid enough.

He gave the thumbs up and reached his entire torso outside.

Greyson held several loops in his right hand, the rest in his left. He bent his knees like a coiled spring and shot upward, the loops of rope spinning in the air toward the boy in the window. Nick snatched the top end of the rope and pulled it to his chest on the first try. Greyson pumped his fist in excitement as Nick took the rope inside and began to tie his end to the radiator.

The night was still dank and quiet, and Greyson breathed a short sigh of relief. *The plan has been flawless.*

Nick waved outside and gave the thumbs up. Greyson returned the wave and gave the long rope a hard tug. It snapped taut and secure.

With one last thumbs up to Nick, he threw the rope up against the building and glanced in the glass door.

CJ stood right there.

Greyson's heart nearly burst out of his chest; he hugged the wall as tight as he could as CJ's shadow loomed into the lot like a monster about to devour a hapless victim.

Each second seemed an eternity, but the door handle glinting in the yellow light remained unturned. A key jangled in the door and a faint red light started to flick on and off. Then the shadow shifted, footsteps plopped up the stairs, and CJ was gone. He hadn't been seen.

Greyson exhaled. *That was close.* And now he knew when and how the alarm turned on.

Using the mirror, he checked the doorway just to make sure. When he was convinced, he sprinted to the ditch and took out the walkie.

"Jarryd, come in."

A pause.

"Yeah, the thespian just got back. Mission accomplished."

Greyson laughed silently. "Thanks. The counselors are back now, so be especially quiet. I'm headed to the cafeteria now. I'll fill you in tomorrow."

"The *cafeteria*? Wait, why?"

"I'll tell you later. Over and out."

"Bring me back a brownie…"

He clicked the walkie off and stored it in his pack.

Soon, his legs were churning and his arms pumping. The free run felt good. No ball, no defenders, no pressure. He ran around the dark end of the Rec Building to the equipment shed for the second time, and slowed at the bush where he had stored the rope.

Kneeling, he quickly surveyed the campus. *Quiet. Too quiet.*

He shook his head. *Why do I think in clichés?*

He took off again, along the chain link fence blocking off the football field and track, up the long flight of stairs to the cafeteria, and finally to the front entrance. His lungs sucked in the air; his legs bounced with energy until a sudden realization hit him like a brick to the face.

This is where his plan ended.

Stupid! Now what? Knock on the door? Look through the windows? Or break the windows?

He had to do *something*, try everything before he even thought of giving up. Mentally slapping himself, he began touring the perimeter of the building. He began to check every window and try every door; he searched for ways to get to the roof, but there were no trees anywhere close enough for a jump or even a daring swing.

Making his way through flowers and around an air conditioner, he came to the back corner of the building. He stopped suddenly, his toes tottering in the air above an eight foot drop. He grasped the building's corner and pulled himself back. Below, a ramp cut into the ground from the alley to a loading dock beneath ground level.

This must be where trucks load and unload all the cafeteria's goodies.

He leapt down and knelt, examining the dock. To the right, a dumpster, to the left, a single door – the last door to check. *It had to be open!*

He jumped to his feet and tugged at the door.

"Uh!"

Locked. He noticed an electronic keypad to the right glowing red. *Really locked.* Suddenly, he jerked and looked into the lens of a security camera.

He hopped to the side and hugged the wall. Clutching its bricks, he shuffled to the side and out of the camera's angle. He pushed away and stood near the dumpster.

Stupid. All for freaking nothing! He stomped the ground in frustration.

On cue, a light blasted through the door's window. *Geez! Hide!* Greyson snapped his gaze left, then right. He found a hiding spot, leapt, banged inside the dumpster, and rolled into something wet and pungent.

An electronic buzz sounded briefly and the door opened. Male voices spoke quietly.

"...the most casualties. It makes perfect sense."

"Ah, I don't care." The voice was obvious. *SquareJaw*. "As long as I get my cut and get to Maui before they figure out what hit 'em, I'm good. Chicago, Kansas City, Minneapolis…I could care less."

The door closed and the voices started to fade. Greyson didn't move a muscle, though his leg was awkwardly bent under him and the smell made him want to vomit.

"Shoot! Wait. Can you buzz me back in? I forgot my card."

"You forgot your card?" The angry voice was also familiar. This one was Mantis. "What, do you think it's just a set of car keys?"

"Ah, I know," SquareJaw replied. "Just buzz me in."

"Just take my card. Meet me at the observatory. I am not waiting for you."

Greyson tensed. *This is my chance.*

Beep. Click!

The door unlocked; SquareJaw opened it as his friend's footsteps clomped away. Waiting and hoping the door closed just slowly enough, he paused for one last moment.

Wait…wait…

Every instinct urged him to stay quiet and safe, but he fought them back.

His mental alarm beeped. *Go.*

He untangled his legs and scratched at the sides of the wet metal. He scrambled for a grip, found the edge and pushed himself over with a soft metallic clang; he rolled over the top and landed on both feet, but too hard to keep his balance. He fell to his hands, tearing them on the hard asphalt, but he ignored the pain; out of the corner of his eye – the door was closing its last foot.

He pushed off the cement and shot like a missile to the doorway. His right hand slipped through the narrow gap and the door slammed against it.

"Uhh…"

He grimaced in pain, stomach on asphalt and hand stuck in the door. Behind him, he could hear Mantis rapidly approaching.

"What the *heck?*"

Greyson grunted to his feet and pulled open the heavy door. He slipped his thin body through, the angry man coming at him like a raging bull. The door clicked closed and buzzed locked as the man slammed against it and pounded the window.

Greyson whipped around; SquareJaw was out of sight – an open doorway to the right. He darted through it just as SquareJaw popped out from around the corner, peering at Mantis banging on the window.

"What?" SquareJaw shrugged his shoulders, smiling.

Mantis frantically pointed down at the door; he didn't have his card.

SquareJaw muttered under his breath and strutted to the door to let Mantis in. Greyson hid behind a stack of boxes as the lumbering figure flashed past the doorway.

"What do you want? Forget your card? They're not just a set of car keys!"

Greyson dashed from behind the boxes and flew around the corner. SquareJaw turned at the door and caught sight of the boy. His eyes went as wide as Mantis' in the window. "What the heck?"

The banging on the door continued. SquareJaw scrambled for his keycard, swiped the door open, and took off after the boy.

"I'm going to kill the little freak."

"No guns! This has to be quiet."

Greyson fled down another hallway, opened a large freezer, but decided against it.

I have to get out!

He flew around another corner and found the kitchen. Huge machines spread across the entire floor – boy-sized bowls with mixers like the motors on motorboats, wall-sized ovens, racks of pots and pans, and columns of knives. He felt he would get cut just looking at the room.

Footsteps pounded behind him. He shot through the machines, weaving left and right, avoiding every type of blade. The men rushed to the entrance behind.

"There! Get him!"

He dashed to the far door which exited to the cafeteria. SquareJaw snagged a knife from a cutting board and leveled his shoulders. His target darted left, then right toward the doorway. He drew the knife back and hurled it at the door.

Greyson turned, the knife glinting as it cut through the air.

CHING!

The knife passed his shoulder and hit the door handle-first, leaving a deep dent, and clattered to the tile. Greyson slid to a stop at the doorway and glanced behind. Mantis had gone another way. *He's going to try to flank me — cut me off from the exit.*

He had to double back; but one thing stood in his way.

"You!" SquareJaw recognized the boy.

Greyson froze.

"I *warned* you."

Greyson's lip quivered. The man was going to kill him.

SquareJaw took a step toward him. "Now look, kid. Just come here and I'll make it painless. Maybe your mother will even be able to recognize your face at your funeral."

He searched the area. *Can I get past him? Should I try the door?*

SquareJaw took another knife from the large counter in the middle. "You're not getting out of here."

Greyson felt his fanny pack. Quickly, he zipped it open, grabbed the walkie and turned it on.

"Jarryd, come in!"

SquareJaw paused in disbelief.

Please, please, be there!

"Yeah?" Jarryd responded.

Greyson put his mouth to talk, but did not push the button. "If you touch me, I scream that I am going to be killed in the cafeteria! People will know!" His voiced cracked with fear.

SquareJaw's knuckles cracked as he squeezed the knife handle; his massive biceps twitched. "Don't say anything or you die."

"Can't you see I already have a death wish? Try anything, I scream to my friend."

88

SquareJaw laughed, then shrugged in surrender. He put the knife down slowly and backed away. Greyson turned to the door and twisted the lock in case Mantis decided to try it.

"Let me leave. Get away."

SquareJaw shifted toward the giant mixer, backing away. But he suddenly stopped. "Your friend, Jarryd. He have a death wish, too?"

No! How could I have said his name? Stupid!

"Escape and we'll come for you. Get me arrested, we'll come for you *and* your friends."

"You think I would use his real name, stupid? Come on!" Greyson bluffed.

SquareJaw scoffed while Greyson began to walk along the outer edge of the kitchen, his finger near the talk button. On the outside, his face was stern and confident, betrayed by the tears forming in the corners of his eyes. On the inside, his heart pounded and his lungs shook from adrenaline.

"What are you going to do?" he asked the man. "What are you planning for Chicago, Minneapolis, or Kansas City? Why do you go to the observatory?"

SquareJaw gritted his teeth. The boy knew too much. Suddenly, like a snapping cobra, he shot forward and snatched the knife from the counter. Greyson pushed the talk button.

"I'm in the cafeteria, they're going to –"

The knife slipped between his chest and arm, tearing his shirt and slicing his ribs; he yelped and dropped the walkie; it slammed to the ground, the batteries flinging to the tile and skidding under counters.

Greyson felt his ribs, feeling something sticky. A shock of pain and fear jolted down his spine. But he had no time for a band-aid. SquareJaw growled like a lion and shot toward him.

Run!

He dashed left toward the door to the cafeteria; SquareJaw slammed into a cart of empty trays, and they exploded across the room. The cacophony of falling trays echoed throughout the enclosed kitchen, piercing Greyson's ears. He reached the door and fumbled with the

89

lock, hearing SquareJaw's deep breathing and clomping feet right behind him.

The lock clicked undone and he swung open the door with SquareJaw almost within arm's reach; he took one long stride toward the deli counter just as Mantis stepped out from behind it with an evil grin spread across his wide-eyed face.

Down!

Greyson hit the ground like sliding into home base. The man's hands grabbed at him, but only snagged a hat. Snarling, Mantis looked up and his face flashed into horror just as SquareJaw slammed into him, SquareJaw's large knee smashing into his friend's cheek. The collision's momentum carried them over the boy on the ground and into the deli counter with a loud metallic BANG! They crumpled in a tangled heap.

Greyson watched the mess of groaning men from his sliding position, the sudden release of danger yet to sink in. But it didn't take long. He rose to his feet, breaths coming in short gasps, and snatched his red hat from underneath SquareJaw's leg.

He started to turn away for his escape, but something caught his eye as he turned – the keycard. He took it from the ground and sprinted through the kitchen.

Like a blur, he was through the tiled hallway, arms pumping and legs churning out in the dark. Lights flashed past his eyes like fuzzy comets. His lungs burned and his side ached, but he ran almost soundless; there was no sound but that of his breath and his feet hitting the grass to block out the ringing in his ears from the clanging trays. Time passed slowly until he finally reached the back of Bickford Hall.

He almost collapsed; his lungs and legs were burning and sweat streamed down his face. Looking down at his white shirt, he saw a red triangle seeping down from around his armpit. He felt his ribs, and could feel the thin gash in his side. Not stitches worthy, but deep enough to bleed a lot.

Shaking off the pain, he jogged to the rope and looked up to the window three stories above him. He sniffed and wiped his face with his sleeve. It was a long way up.

He knew if he hesitated much longer, he would talk himself out of it. He had to do it – there was no question about it. Mustering all of his strength, he held the rope tight, jumped for a higher grab and raised his legs to the wall. Grimacing through the pain, he waited for his side to numb.

He began walking up the wall, pulling at the rope with his arms and pushing off the brick with his legs. He took three steps, four more steps, then paused for a breather. He looked to his left and right – the men hadn't followed.

He took another three steps and his arms began to shake. Another step, this one much harder. *I'm not going to make it. I can't.*

His feet slipped from the wall and he swung shoulder-first into the brick. "Ughhhh!"

He suppressed his scream and searched the brick for a foothold. His feet pushed and slipped, his knuckles cracking with his full weight; just as he felt his grip loosening on the rope, he found a crevice and stuck his foot into it.

Finally, his arms could release some of the weight and he paused there, one and a half stories up, breathing in long, deep breaths. He could feel fresh blood dribbling from his wound, but the sharp pain had numbed to a deep ache.

He fought the urge to scream out for help, hoping someone could hear him through the open third story bathroom window. Instead, he dared himself to make it. *I dare you to make it to the window with a gash in your side. I dare you. If you make it, I'll give you a nice shower and a soft bed.*

And so he did. He started his walk again, one step at a time. He felt woozy and light-headed with each step, tiredness coming on fast, but he made it to the end of the rope. He lowered his feet again, taking the shoulder-hit to the brick, and reached for the windowsill. The pull-up into the window felt like it was ripping his gash open across his chest and back, but all that mattered was getting inside. He fell hands-first onto the bathroom tile, his feet hitting the radiator on the way down.

He lay there for some time, relishing the safety of the room. But the time came to get things done. He pushed himself up and pulled the rope inside the room.

Now, to my bed. Just down the hall. He tottered through the bathroom and passed by the mirrors on the left; he caught his reflection and stopped. *Oh, geez.* Then he smelled himself – he stunk like rotten eggs or worse. He shed the shirt and hid it with the rope behind the radiator.

He stripped and stood under a dripping shower for a few minutes, wiping away the dried blood and smell of dumpster. He dried off with paper towels and donned his hat and boxers again. Looking in the mirror briefly, he turned to the doorway and walked out into the hall.

Brandon stood outside his room, leaning in. "Where's Greyson?" he asked Liam.

He could hear Liam whimpering. "H-h-h-he …."

"I'm right here, Brandon."

Brandon turned, his panicked eyes dimming. "Oh, whew. Where were you?"

"Just doing my business. Should I wake you up next time?" he asked with soft sarcasm, walking toward him with his arms consciously hiding the gash in his side.

Brandon smiled tiredly. "Please don't. Good night, Greys."

Greyson came to Brandon and wrapped his arms around his waist. Brandon paused, surprised and awkward. He patted the boy on his back.

"Who do they let in Bickford at night?" he asked, his face buried into Brandon's stomach.

"Uh…no one. Only counselors, head-counselors, and the physical trainers."

"No cooks?"

Brandon arched his eyebrows. "You hungry?"

Greyson let go, relieved, making sure to hide his gash with his arm. "A little. But I can wait."

"Heh. No cooks allowed. Get some sleep. We got another big day tomorrow."

Greyson smiled and almost passed out. "Good night."

He walked to his bed and fell on his pillow headfirst. Liam stared at him from his bed as Brandon closed the door slowly and whispered. "Night."

"G-g-good night," Liam whispered with concern in his voice.

But Greyson was already asleep.

The control panel blinked in greens and reds like a perfect Christmas display. The man paced beside, the wireless receiver attached to his ear adding another twinkling light to the otherwise dark room.

"I see four options. Maybe more," he spoke, anger still evident though he tried to contain it. "One, we kill him. Two, we kill him *and* his friends. Though those two options are tempting, they are unreasonable so close to zero hour. We can't rely on Sheriff Roberts if police come anywhere near here."

He walked to his shotgun propped against the wall; his finger played around the edge of the shiny black barrel. "Three, we kidnap him. This is possible, but again, the police presence is a negative. We want to keep this to the least amount of people as possible." He held up four fingers. "Four. We trick him. He's just a kid."

On the other side of the line, SquareJaw held his cell phone to his ear, looking over the mess of a kitchen.

"You've told me everything?" The man asked. "The boy in the red hat and his friend Jarryd?"

SquareJaw gulped. "Yes. That's all." His hand searched his pocket one more time. *No card.*

The man held the shotgun and pumped it so that SquareJaw could hear.

"Watch him closely, both of you. Let him know you're still there. For now, clean up. It was a raccoon scrounging for food. Got it?"

SquareJaw scanned the floor – but his card was gone. "Got it."

Chapter 9

Tuesday Morning

Greyson woke up with the sun. He rolled over, taking with him a string of drool trailing from his lip to a small puddle on his pillow. *Must not have moved much last night.* He'd had a wild dream. SquareJaw had found him, tied him up, and thrown him into a giant mixer. When the blade first hit his side, he'd woken up.

His fingers wandered to his side and touched the wound. He recoiled. *Ouch.*

"D-d-does it hurt?"

Greyson's heart jumped. Liam stood over him, holding his bed sheets over himself like a cape.

"You scared me." Greyson sat up and tried to see his gash. "Not bad – just a little."

Liam continued to stare. Greyson looked at his friend and sighed. "I'm okay...seriously!"

Liam burst toward him and hugged him tight. Greyson grimaced as the dried blood cracked over his wound.

"W-w-was it Eye of E-e-yes?" Liam released him, wide-eyed.

Greyson rolled out of bed and wandered to the mirror. "No. Worse."

Liam gasped. Greyson turned and smiled. "Just kidding! If you go and get the twins, I'll tell you all what happened."

Liam dropped his sheet and ran out into the hall. Glancing at his watch, Greyson saw that they had twenty minutes until they had to leave for breakfast. *Would twenty minutes be enough to tell it? It didn't matter. They have to know. And we have to start planning.*

Jarryd and Nick came sprinting into the room, followed closely by Liam.

"Oh, geez!" Jarryd eyed his wound. "What'd you do to your armpit? Try to shave your pit hair and miss?"

Greyson lifted his arm. No pit hair. Jarryd laughed, "Nope. You got it all."

"Close the door," Greyson commanded as he sat on his bed. Liam shut it with a slam and took a seat on his own bed beside the twins.

Greyson took a deep breath and exhaled. "You're not going to believe this…"

The trek to breakfast seemed especially long. It felt like only minutes ago he had been sprinting up the same flight of stairs. Rewinding the night and replaying it over and over in his mind occupied his thoughts. He thought about the glinting knife, the men racing at him with wild eyes, dripping fangs, and claws. He didn't know how the men seemed to now be vampires in his memory, but they were.

When his mind wasn't thinking about last night, it was searching for the future.

I should call the police. Tell them what had happened. But be anonymous.

No. SquareJaw's buddies would know it was me who turned him in.

Maybe I should call home, ask Mom what to do.

No. She'd have a heart attack, panic, and call the police all at the same time.

Maybe I should tell Brandon. He might understand.

No. He'd do the same thing as he did when I told him Trevor pushed me in the back in soccer – nothing.

Maybe I should just run.

No. There's something good to do that has to be done. SquareJaw had to go down.

He sighed, the decision already made. *It's up to me. To us. We'll stick to public places all day, so that if they try something, there'll be witnesses. Then we'll go tonight. But this time we'll bring back evidence.*

"Greyson!"

Greyson snapped from his thoughts. "Huh?"

Jarryd looked at him and pumped his eyebrows. "Whatcha thinkin' about?"

He glanced up toward the front of his group where Brandon led them on. "Tonight."

Jarryd slugged him on the shoulder. "Nah you're not. You got a *girl* on *your* mind. I can *tell.*"

Greyson blushed. "You got me. I was thinking about your mom."

Jarryd burst into laughter, breaking the morning quiet. "Good one, GreyHUN. Good one."

Brandon yelled from the front. "Alright boys, hats off. We're going to start the day thinking about others like we talked about last night. We're going to hold the doors open for the other huddles."

"What?" Ryan screamed. "We're letting them go first?"

Brandon nodded, walking backward toward the front entrance. "Why? I'm hungry!"

Brandon smiled. "Think of *others*, Ryan. Others."

"EEHHHHH! I don't want to!"

The rest of the boys put distance between them and the temper tantrum.

"Ryan. You'll survive, you'll get your food, and others will thank you for your service. It's all good."

"But it's not *fair*! Why don't they serve *us*?"

Brandon shook his head. Greyson took two large steps up to Ryan and put his arm around him. "Ryan, what do you say you open the door for others today, and then I'll open the door for you tomorrow so you can go first?"

Ryan's brows shot up. "First-first?"

Greyson nodded. "That okay, Brandon? First-first?"

"Yeah." Brandon smiled wide. "Sounds like a plan."

"Okay!" Ryan burst ahead, sprinting to hold the front door.

The other boys followed and grabbed one of the many doors to hold open wide as the other groups meandered from their dorms to breakfast. They received some muttered 'thank you's' and a few nods of appreciation – nothing to earn a gold-star sticker, but it felt good to

Greyson nonetheless. At least it did until Sydney and her friends walked through Chase and Austin's doors, not even looking toward him. Greyson tried to ignore the twinge of anger and pity poking at his heart. *I can make this right, too, if I can only get the guts to talk to her.*

Once inside, rumors spread quickly that the large dent in the front of the deli counter was due to a rabid raccoon that snuck in during the night. Kids excitedly reenacted the crazy event in their minds, as if it were as real as anything they'd ever heard. Only four kids and two disgruntled cafeteria workers knew the grisly truth.

Greyson made a point to take his empty tray straight to SquareJaw's counter. He had to show the man he was still alive, strong, and not intimidated – though he really was only *one* of the three.

SquareJaw's eyes squinted at him from above large, dark bags, and the corner of his mouth sneered viciously. Greyson noticed for the first time he wore a nametag reading, "Hi, I'm Carl."

"Hi...*Carl*...can I have three pieces of bacon instead of two?"

SquareJaw glared at him.

"No? I'll just take two, then."

The muscular man picked out two shriveled, extra crunchy pieces and threw them on his tray. The kids in line behind Greyson jolted in surprise and watched in awe.

"Thanks. Just like I like 'em."

SquareJaw grunted. The next kid in line looked up from the tray that was almost as big as he was. "I want what *red hat* got!"

Greyson smiled at SquareJaw, but reluctantly turned his back to him. He could almost feel the knife sliding into his back, handle-deep. But it didn't come. Yet.

The morning clouds parted, and the sun punched the ground with its heat. Its rays burned through Greyson's shirt, melting away the sweat that had leaked through. Still, this day was not as bad as the day before.

He ran the rugby drills, gave an effort in the scrimmages, but he was not sweating out anger today. His sweat was pain, and a little fear.

Up on the bleachers, sitting alone with elbows on his knees, leaning forward, a lone man watched the children practicing below. Greyson squinted through the sun and held his hand over his eyes like a salute. The man didn't move. His eyes were wide apart.

I'm being watched.

Greyson paused for a breather during the game, turned his back to the man, and bent over with his legs straight, stretching toward his toes. It was a good stretch to keep his hamstrings loose, but it was also a good way to stick his butt straight at the man's face.

He leaned his neck around and smiled at the man. If only he could lower his pants and give him a full moon – but he would probably get sued by some extra-caring parents.

He was suddenly reminded of two winters ago. It was the first snow of the year, sometime in November. With his mother's help, he had set the perfect ambush for his father when he got back from work. His father didn't have a chance and took several snowballs to the face and chest before wrestling him to the ground. His father had simply said, "You're asking for it, son," and let him go.

Then, six months later, long after the snow had melted, his father ambushed him at three in the morning with a bucket of snow he'd saved in the freezer. His father laughed his head off and helped him clean up. "You asked for it," he'd said.

Knees straight and butt skyward, he was asking for it again. But this time, it wouldn't be a bucket of snow at three in the morning. It could be much worse.

After majors, the Cowboys Gold sped ahead of other groups and rushed to hold the doors open for them. This time, kids were much more awake and noticed the selfless act of service.

"Thank you!"

"How nice!"

"How sweet!"

"Who are you trying to impress?"

"What? I can't even open my own door?"

"Thanks!"

"What gentlemen!"

"Oooh. GreyHUN treats the ladies right!"

"Well, done, men. Keep it up!"

And the comments went on. The last group, the Cowgirls Gold, 'ooh'ed and 'ahh'ed more so than other groups. Sydney approached the doors smiling until she found herself in a group of girls heading through Greyson's door. She tried to pull up and switch directions, but awkwardly continued with the group.

She found herself passing right by him. She smiled slightly, and spoke softly. "Thanks, Greyson."

Greyson mouthed, "You're welcome," but nothing came out. Instead, he muttered, "Yeah."

He swallowed and shook his head.

I suck.

Finally, after the last girl had passed through, they left their posts and went to lunch. Greyson avoided SquareJaw's line and sped to his table without deli meat. He sat down, set his hat on his lap, and dug into the food.

"How was Rugby?" Nick asked.

Greyson looked up with his mouth full. He gave him thumbs up and returned to his food.

"Tennis was fun today."

Greyson looked back up at Nick, confused. He was usually pretty quiet. He gave another thumbs up.

"We got to videotape ourselves serving so we can see our form."

Greyson put down his fork and chewed until he could swallow. "Yeah? That's cool."

Nick glanced down the table at Brandon then back at Greyson. "The video cameras were pretty cool."

It clicked. "You…got to use one yourself?"

Nick nodded 'yes' and looked down toward his lap where there was a camera-sized lump in his shirt. "I saw that I had a problem with my form, though. I don't know where to put my…*left elbow*." He glanced down twice to the lump.

Greyson smiled. Brandon looked up from his food, showing little interest in their conversation.

"Hmm…," Greyson began. "I was talking to a friend down by the *equipment shed*. He said you should keep your 'elbow' *down* and make sure to *plant* your right foot, then you'll be good."

Nick smiled and nodded approval. "Thanks."

"No problem."

"You play tennis, Greyson?" Brandon asked.

Greyson bobbed his head. "Off and on."

"Nice."

Nick and Greyson laughed, prompting Brandon to drop his fork to his tray and survey the table. "What? What did I miss this time? Gosh!"

The table laughed at his feigned anger. He was the best counselor they could imagine. He let them be kids.

Brandon smiled, shaking his head to himself. "Freakin' kids."

"Did you see how he opened the door for you?" Melinda asked Sydney, who sat next to her on the bus. "He's a gentleman!"

Sydney peered out the window at the kids sprinting to their second Minors. She was unimpressed with Greyson's act of chivalry. "Their counselor was making them."

Melinda scoffed. "He was looking straight at you when he did it, though."

Sydney turned and looked her friend in the eyes. "Mel, give it a rest. He said no."

"Uh, uh! You said you didn't even ask him!"

"That's right. He said no even *before* I asked! That means he really, really doesn't want to go with me."

Melinda shook her head and pushed her small glasses to her nose. "Or maybe he's just playing hard-to-get!"

Sydney rolled her eyes just as Melinda spotted a red hat coming toward the bus. "He's coming." She rushed toward the aisle when Sydney grabbed her arm and tugged her down.

"No!" Sydney shouted. "Don't do it again!"

Melinda smiled and tugged back. "Let me go! He's coming!"

Melinda pulled free and flung herself into the empty seat across the aisle. She adjusted her clothes and smiled coyly until she spotted a young boy coming down the aisle. With a sudden jerk, she pulled him into the seat next to her, leaving the seat next to Sydney as the first open seat.

Greyson came up the stairs and said 'hello' to the bus driver. When his eyes scanned the bus, Sydney and Melinda looked at their shoes.

He strode down the aisle, his mind elsewhere. He had stayed near his instructor as long as possible, checked the bush to make sure Nick had stored the camera safely, and then sprinted to the line for the bus. He hadn't seen Mantis following him, but he also hadn't gone to the bathroom out of fear that he might be caught in there alone.

Melinda bit her lip as Greyson found the open seat.

Sydney stared out the window trying her best to ignore him, but she could see him looking at her in the window's reflection.

"Can I…sit here?" he asked timidly.

She acted shocked. "Oh. Yeah, sure." She could hear Melinda squealing to herself as Greyson sat down; the young boy next to Melinda gave her an odd look.

VRRRRooooooooom.

The bus driver turned the ignition as the instructor stood to take roll. "Yesterday another instructor of a sport I won't mention left a camper behind at the golf course. So today we're going to take roll before and after we leave. If you're here, raise your hand and say 'here'. Madeline Adams?"

"Here!"

"Rachel Abraham."

"Here!"

Greyson tuned out the shouts and fingered his fanny pack's zipper as he played the conversation out in his mind. *"Sydney. When I said that I didn't want a date to the dance, I didn't know what I was saying. I had just turned down three eighth-graders...."* No. *Too stuck up.* *"Sydney. When I said that I didn't want a date to the dance, I meant I didn't know how to dance. I would rather swim. Would you like to swim with me and my friends?"* Yeah, he liked that one.

"Greyson Gray?"

"Sydney!" he shouted, hand raised.

Time froze. Heads turned, eyes glued to him. Greyson's cheeks flushed bright red and burned with heat. The giggles started slowly as kids rose in their seats to look at the weird boy.

"Uh...I mean...here."

Sydney's jaw dropped open and she eyed him, stunned. Melinda's lips curled into a wide smile.

Greyson could hear murmurs throughout the bus: "Who's Sydney? Why'd he say that?"

And then it came, like cruel fate. The instructor looked to the next name. "Sydney Hansen?"

Sydney's face shot up, her eyes wide and mouth still ajar. Giggles and laughter renewed, young boys and girls searching for the girl named Sydney.

Greyson pulled his hat down over his face, trying in vain to hide as Sydney faced Melinda in disbelief and fear.

"Sydney Hansen? Are you here?"

She had no choice. Her hand shaking, it timidly peaked out from behind her seat. The murmurs continued: "There!"

"That's her!"

"She's sitting right next to him."

"Here," she muttered.

She closed her eyes and turned toward the window, pretending that the last minute had not happened. Greyson continued to hide his face until finally the giggles and pointing faded away. Roll continued, though, and the few boys there would shout out a girl's name, mocking him.

"Bethany!"

"Mildred!"

"Sydney! Chicka chicka bow wow!"

And the laughter didn't stop. Even the instructor was amused. When he had finished, he put the attendance list down. "Alright. We're all here. Let's Sydney – I mean go."

Finally, four minutes into the eight-minute ride, the laughter had passed and natural conversation began.

Greyson spoke through his hat, muffled, "Sorry. I didn't mean to."

Sydney opened her eyes and turned to him. "It's okay," she sighed. "I guess if it wasn't me I'd be laughing."

Greyson tried to look at her from beneath his hat, but all he could see was dark red. "I say things I don't mean sometimes."

Something in Sydney's heart leapt. *Like when you said you didn't want a date to the dance?* "Like shouting random names?"

"Uh...yeah. Or whatever I'm thinking about."

Aack! Greyson grimaced and flushed red again. *Did I just say that? I wish I would stutter like Liam so I would have more time to think! Would she catch it, though?*

Sydney turned to the window to hide her smile. *He had been thinking about me!* Her heart fluttered. She could feel Melinda peering at her from across the aisle. In fact, Melinda held the young boy's ear, forcing him to listen to the conversation across the aisle and report everything her friend and her friend's soon-to-be boyfriend said to each other.

"Yeah," Sydney shrugged. "It happens."

From the outside, Greyson slouched and appeared cool and at ease. Inside the hat, he was mentally slapping himself silly.

Sydney fought her instincts to lift his hat and peer into his eyes. Instead, she sought to talk about him – something her mom had advised

104

her to do whenever forced into a conversation with a male. She looked at his fanny pack out of the corner of her eye. *What could he have in there? Didn't he care about the reputation fanny packs had?*

"I like your fanny pack."

Greyson removed his hat from his face and looked down at his pack to make sure it was still there. He glanced at her, his eyes still adjusting to the new light. "Thanks. It helps me keep track of all my things."

She grinned. "Like a purse?"

Greyson recoiled, but caught her smile. "Yeah, I guess. But stuff more important than lipstick, lip glaze, lip balm and other girl stuff."

Sydney laughed. "Oh, yeah? Like what?"

Greyson pushed himself up from his slouch and looked to his pack again. He had a mirror and a very important access card inside. That was it.

"Uh...man stuff. I can't tell you about it. It's secret."

Sydney reached toward it and he instinctively slapped her hand away. Her mouth dropped open in feigned surprise. Greyson laughed.

The boy leaned over to Melinda. "He hit her and laughed."

"I can see that!" Melinda whispered angrily.

Greyson turned his pack away from her and felt the need to fill the awkward silence he had created by hitting a girl. "You like horseback-riding so far?"

She rolled her eyes. "You mean horse-butt combing?"

He smiled. *She has a good sense of humor.*

"No. I want to ride!" she continued. "You know, full-gallop with nothing but a free, grassy meadow in front of me."

"Riding into the sunset?"

She looked at him and hit his shoulder with her knuckles. "Yeah! Like the end of—"

"—Indiana Jones?"

"Yeah!"

Greyson nodded. *She has a good taste in movies.*

Sydney eyed the red hat in his hand. "Do you wear that hat every day?"

Greyson suddenly realized that he might have hat hair. His right hand shot up and ran through his sweat-mess of brown hair, making sure the sides were swept back and the front was spiked just a little.

"Uh...pretty much. It fits just right."

Sydney nodded. "It looks good on you."

Oh, geez. He hid his face behind his hat again as his cheeks flushed deep red. If he blushed again, it might be permanent. "Thanks."

Sydney nervously smiled and leaned back. *Was that too forward? It was. He'll think I'm desperate.*

Greyson put his hat on and stared at the back of the seat in front of him. It was time for his planned conversation. The bus was approaching the ranch; it had to be quick.

"Sydney."

"Yeah?" She looked him in the eyes. Or at least the sides of his eyes. He was looking straight ahead.

"When I said that I didn't want a date to the dance, I really meant that I didn't know *how* to dance. I would rather go swimming. Would you like to go swimming with me and my friends?"

Perfect! I said it! The perseverance brand is mine!

Sydney paused. Her heart dropped and her world seemed to dim.

"I *can't.* My parents won't let me."

Greyson gulped down the lump in his throat. "Won't let you swim?"

"Not with boys."

"Ahh..." *She had those kinds of parents.*

He looked down at his pack again and fidgeted with the zipper.

"But I could teach you how to dance."

Greyson's eyes widened. "Uh...no thanks."

"Come on. It's not hard."

"Neither is playing with dolls. That doesn't mean I should do it."

"You find it easy to play with dolls?"

Greyson tried to hide his smile. "Well...if I wanted to...but I don't and haven't."

"Yes you have. GI Joes are dolls."

"Are not!"

"Are, too! And you can't diss dancing 'til you've tried it."

"Nope. Not gonna happen."

Sydney laughed. "Is that boy-language for yes?"

"Uh…no." *I will never, ever dance. Ever. Someone would have to kill me, tie my limbs to string and dance me like a puppet.*

"So, it's a yes?"

Greyson turned to her. "I *don't* dance."

She cocked her head. "Yet."

"No, never. Like, I'll never dance. Ever."

"You will?"

"No! I won't."

"You will?"

"No! I do sports. Manly things."

"Dancing is manly."

"No, it's not."

"Yes it is."

"Are you really this dull?"

"Your *face* is dull!"

"Your *mom's* face is dull!"

"Your *butt* is dull!"

"No it's not!"

The young boy tapped Greyson on the shoulder. He turned.

"Sir, can you please slow down? I can't keep up."

Melinda pulled the boy back to her by his ear and smiled at them sheepishly.

The bus's airbrakes hissed to a stop inside the ranch and the instructor stood up with a clap. "Alright! Let's Sydney!"

Chapter 10

Sydney rode toward Greyson, her horse at a soft gallop. Her blonde hair bounced with the horse's tail, smooth and shining. She looked a natural, her hands gently holding the reins, her legs pressed to the horse's sides, moving flawlessly with its gait. She even had the dainty black helmet and gloves. Greyson nearly drooled, but realized it was just sweat rolling down his cheeks.

"Hey, Greyson!"

"Hey!"

"I named my horse after you!"

He smiled. *I'm so in.* "What is it?"

"Dancer. She's a pretty horse."

Greyson's mouth dropped. Sydney flashed him a quick smile and rode off with a press of the stirrups.

He yelled after her, pumping at the reins, but his horse didn't move. "Well! My horse speaks your name!"

Sydney turned her horse back to him with a sharp pull and sauntered to his side. "Oh, yeah? What? Sydnaaaaaaay? Clever."

Greyson shook his head no. "No. Your name comes out his *other* end."

"Eww!"

He laughed and shook the reins vigorously. "Let's go, GreyOne!"

But GreyOne didn't move. Greyson's arms pumped harder. "Go!"

Sydney scoffed as she rode in front of his unflinching horse. "You know your horse isn't grey, right?"

Greyson looked around at all the other campers riding around the large fenced-in area. They all seemed to have the hang of it.

"Yeah he is. Really *dark* grey."

"He's black."

"Whatever."

Sydney dismounted and walked her horse parallel to GreyOne. "Should Dancer and I teach you how to ride a horse?"

Greyson pumped the reins one more time. "No way! How about I teach *you* how to ride?"

Sydney smiled. "You *are* stubborn. Or arrogant."

Greyson pulled off his helmet, turned his hat around backwards, and resnapped the helmet over it. "Nah – just…confident."

Sydney mounted again and adjusted her helmet. "Alright. Teach me."

"Race ya. To the far fence."

She squinted. Over a hundred yards. She glanced left and right. The instructors were occupied with the younger campers.

"You're on."

Greyson pressed the stirrups into the horses' side and GreyOne thrust forward with a jerk. Its hooves flung dirt back, its sinewy haunches tense and strong. Greyson held the reins loosely and bent low, GreyOne's mane patting his face as he galloped.

Sydney hesitated in disbelief, but only for a fraction of a second. She kicked, "Yah! Get 'em Dancer!"

And Dancer sped after, toward the fence.

The wind flowed over his head, blowing the sweat from his brow. The smell of fertilizer swept by, the feel of freedom zooming by in blurs of green and blue. His legs grasped the horse's sides, his feet pressing the stirrups toward the dirt.

It had all been an act; he'd done this before. They had owned a horse for several years with a small stable for her in their large backyard. She hadn't been a beast of burden – she carried no load, pulled no cart – she was like a pet. She ran no races, but she ran like the wind. Greyson had ridden her for several years until her joints were just too old. He cried the day she was put down and they never owned another horse. She was the one and the only. Her name – Graycie.

The fence grew larger, its wooden beams rising from the earth. Greyson knew the fence could be jumped. This horse was strong, fast, and young. It could be done.

109

"Greyson! Stop!" Sydney shouted after him.

The fence approached, but GreyOne didn't slow. He wanted to jump it; he was born to be free. A long meadow curved into the horizon beyond the wooden beams.

Greyson rose on the saddle as the wind pressed his shirt against his skin and caused his eyes to tear. But through his tears, he caught sight of a figure beyond the fence and to the right. A man stood facing him, leaning against a four-wheeler. He had eyes that were almost to his ears.

"Whoa!" Greyson tugged on the reins and the horse whinnied loud. GreyOne dug into the loose dirt, skidding toward the fence. Greyson felt himself about to topple over the front of the horse, but his feet pushed down against the stirrups, pressing him back into the saddle as the horse jerked to a sudden stop, feet from the fence.

Dust plumed from the horse's hooves through the fence toward the man watching from the large, four-wheeled vehicle called a 'gator'.

The man clapped his dirty hands and gave a crooked smile. Then, he raised his hand and pointed behind Greyson to Sydney approaching on horseback. Greyson followed his gaze then turned back to him. The man slowly pulled his pointing hand back to his throat, thumb extended. Then, in one gruesome motion, he pulled his thumb across his neck.

Greyson sneered in disdain. He took a deep breath and patted GreyOne's neck. "Good boy. Ignore the ugly man. Good boy."

Sydney and Dancer trotted up to him, her eyes glued to the lone man out in the middle of the field.

"Who's that? You know him?"

Greyson shook his head. "I don't know. He probably owns the place. Let's head back."

Sydney shrugged and waved to the man. He waved back.

"And what's tonight?" Dr. Jensen asked the crowd of kids in the cafeteria.

"STRENGTH NIGHT!"

"Who's gonna win? Gold or Purple?"

The shouts mingled in a bizarre, "GOURPDLE!"

Greyson smiled and watched, rather a spectator than a rabid fan of a color assigned to him two days ago.

"Gold! Gold! Gold!" Ryan slammed his fists to the table, his eyes glazed in passion.

"White! Red! Black!" Sammy shouted, his eyes glazed and crossed. Jarryd rolled his eyes.

"Tur! Qoise! Green! Blue! Yell! Ow!" Sammy rubbed his shoulder. Jarryd smiled contentedly and rubbed his knuckles.

"That's right. Gold or Purple." Dr. Jensen stood at the microphone surveying the tables full of energetic kids. "One team will emerge victorious tonight. We have Cage Ball, Captain's Coming, and your favorite…"

"TUG OF WAR!"

Greyson put fingers in his ears. *Little boys screamed like girls.*

"Greyson!"

He turned to Brandon.

"Why aren't you cheering? Cheer!"

Greyson shrugged. "I'm saving my voice for tonight!"

Brandon nodded. "Good. I wanna hear you loud tonight then!"

He smiled and gave him thumbs up. With the loud cheering continuing, Jarryd tugged at his shirt. "We still on? To the observatory?" he whispered.

Greyson winked at him. "If we survive strength night."

And they did. Cage Ball – an intense game of soccer in the gym played on small scooters with a giant inflatable ball – was a close match, but Chase's speed gave them the victory over the Cowboys Purple with cheers of 'Golden Glory' filling the entire Recreation Building.

Captain's Coming was a game of intellectual strength. Similar to Simon Says, it required close listening and fast reactions. Sammy was usually the first to get out; Patrick never played, but the others did well. During the last round, Brandon stood eye to eye with Greyson with his shrill whistle hanging from his mouth, prepared to blow it in his face and shove him out of the group if he made one wrong move.

Once, Brandon tried to provoke Greyson's movement by pulling at the red hat's brim, but Greyson only growled until Brandon backed away. Greyson finished third that round, losing to two purples after they pushed him away when the game called for a group of only two.

The Cowboys Purple won Captain's Coming to tie Strength Night at 1-1, but Greyson and the others had an excuse. Their minds were somewhere else.

Tug of War was a different story. This was brute strength. No excuses. You were either stronger, tougher, and manlier than the other team, or you were pathetic little boys trying to play with the men.

Tucker and Trevor began their taunting before it began. "Hey GreySUCK! Look at these guns! Beat these!"

They both pulled up their sleeves and flexed. Greyson cocked his head, watching their gun show. "Uh…go ahead. Flex."

"We are flexing, dumb face."

"Oh. My bad."

Oops. Maybe I should be nice to them. 'Do to others what you would want them to do to you' and all.

He walked up to them, the rest of Cowboys Gold watching him with anticipation. He raised his hand to their flexing muscles. "May I?"

Their brows furrowed, arms still flexed. Then, with his thumb and pointer finger in the shape of a C, Greyson calmly gripped Tucker's bicep. He pinched it once…twice. "Hmm…impressive."

He felt Trevor's next. "Oh. That's nice, too. You guys must work out."

A nervous smile spread across their lips. "Uh…yeah, we do."

112

Greyson nodded. "Well, I admire that. Your work's paid off. I bet you'll do really well in Tug of War."

The Cowboys Gold stared in wonder. Where was the put down, the snide comeback?

"Pssst. Greyson," Jarryd whispered. "You don't get Fairplay points when you're not playing…"

Tucker sneered and rolled his sleeves back down. "That's right. You're going down! Aren't they Trevor?"

"Yeah, totally down, Tucker."

Greyson rolled down his sleeve and flexed his right arm. It was tight, but obviously not as large as Tucker's or Trevor's.

"It's not as big as yours but…wanna feel it?" he asked, biting his lip and pumping his eyebrows.

Tucker and Trevor eyed each other awkwardly; Trevor began to reach out but Tucker slapped it down. "No. We don't."

Then, stepping from behind the Cowboys Gold, a beautiful girl walked around Greyson and glanced at Tucker and Trevor, mischief glinting in her coy smile. The two boys' eyes grew as large as their biceps.

Sydney then turned to Greyson, who still flexed, and pinched his biceps. Greyson's legs shook.

"Hmm…I think he's got you boys beat," she said placidly. "Plus, he's a lot cuter."

Greyson blushed again and cleared his throat. "Ehem. You mean, handsome."

Sydney paused. "Oh, yeah. That, too."

Tucker scoffed. "What does she know? Let's go, Trevor."

Trevor scoffed, too. "You don't know anything. We're going!"

And they left amidst Gold's soft laughter.

Greyson muttered to her, "I was *trying* to be nice to them."

She shrugged. "What's the fun in that?"

Jarryd and the boys rushed to Greyson and Sydney. "That was hilarious! What's your name?" Jarryd asked.

Sydney blinked. "I remember *you*, Jarryd."

113

Something clicked in Jarryd's mind. "Oh, yeah. Deergirl."

Sydney recoiled. "What?"

Jarryd shook his head quickly. "Never mind." Then he looked to Greyson. "Is Deergirl coming with us tonight?"

Greyson shook his head with urgency and tried to slip away with the flock of huddles heading to the Tug of War station. Sydney ignored Greyson's escape and looked to Jarryd. "Where is he going tonight?"

Greyson turned backward as he walked away and put his finger to his lips. "Shh! Let's go!"

Shrugging, Jarryd jumped to follow him, but Sydney grabbed him by his shirt collar and pulled him in. "Hey, *Chipmunk* boy."

Jarryd's lip quivered, his arms curled to his body.

"Where...is...he...going?" she asked, her eyes piercing into his.

Jarryd broke quickly, his voice as shrill as a chipmunk's squeak. "To the observatory. See you at 11?"

Sydney released him and smoothed out his collar. "Yeah. I'll come. See you boys then."

Liam rubbed his aching biceps, moaning to himself as Greyson lay face up on his bed with his own thoughts. He felt bad. He hadn't tugged his hardest. If he had, his wound would have opened up again and bled through his shirt. Who knows how the adults would have acted if he hadn't been able to think of what to say about the knife wound on his side? *Uh...it was...rugby. Some freakin' kid's fingernails. He should really keep those trimmed down.*

"Sydney."

Greyson opened his eyes and turned to Liam. He was smiling wide. He held up three crooked fingers and clawed at the air. "Rarr!"

"Liam!" Greyson laughed, though he was right. *She is feisty. And I never thought a girl could be as cool as a boy.*

"S-s-she's hot."

"Yeah. I know,' he said happily, putting his arms behind his head. He felt like he should be smoking a cigar about now. It just seemed like what a man would do – talking about his babe, smoking a fat cigar and drinking a root beer on the rocks. *That's what I would do with Dad if he was here. Except the cigar part.*

Brandon popped his head in. "Hey guys. Meeting in two minutes."

"Hey, Brandon?"

"What's up?"

"Can we have a slumber party tonight? All of us sleep in one room? We could make a fort."

Brandon's eyes searched his memory. As far as he knew there was no rule against it. "Hmm…I suppose so. As long as you go to bed right after lights out."

"Awesome! Thanks, Brandon!"

"Are you going to give each other makeovers, play truth and dare and talk about your crushes?"

Greyson arched his eyebrows. "I don't know what you do on your sleepovers, but we don't do that."

Brandon shrugged. "Well. Whatever you do, keep it tame. No dares that get out of hand, okay?"

"Sure. See ya." Greyson turned to Liam. "Truth or dare? That's a good idea."

Liam nodded enthusiastically.

"I dare you to give Brandon a wedgie!"

Brandon laughed from the doorway. "I'm still here you know."

Greyson looked at him with a smirk. "We know. But no one knows why."

Brandon left, shaking his head and muttering, "Freakin' kids."

"Sammy, seriously. You're getting nuts all over the blankets."

"Soooooo."

"So, stop it."

"Oooookaaaaay. I won't."

"I will slap you so hard…"

"Jarryd!" Greyson interrupted the little feud. "Don't slap Sammy. He needs to be conscious for the plan to work."

Jarryd glared at Sammy who glared back with one eye and stuck his tongue out at him.

The fort was complete. Blankets hung from the ceiling and trailed to chairs and uprighted bed frames. Mattresses laid the foundation and pillows filled the interior. The most important part was the fact that the entire inside of the fort was hidden from the view of anyone in the hall. When spectators walked past, they had no way of knowing if there were nine boys inside – or none.

"This fort sucks."

"Patrick. If you say that one more time…"

"Jarryd. Pay attention," Greyson chastised. "I have the card and the mirror. The rope's still hidden. Jarryd, you got a walkie. Austin's got another."

"Yup."

"Got it."

"I hid the camera," Nick chimed proudly.

"Yeah. Good." Greyson checked the time. Almost 10:30. "Bedtime soon. Play quiet. At 10:50, the counselors should start heading down like they did last night. Then it's time."

Chase crawled over closer. "If y'all don't mind me askin', what do ya plan on doin' when ya get there?"

The boys eyed Greyson. He scratched under his hat. "Uh…we use the card to get inside, we hide. We take video and we leave."

"Ah. And what happens if this SquareJaw finds ya again?"

Greyson smiled outwardly, but his mind shirked. "Run?"

Chase nodded, his gaze somewhere beyond. "Well, good luck, y'all. Nice knowing ya."

The door creaked open and all at once the goodies were hidden. A hand reached under the front blankets and pulled them up; Brandon peeked under. "Oh, good, you're all still fully dressed. Kept the dares tame, huh?"

The boys laughed and Jarryd smiled. "Whoa. It's not that kind of party."

Brandon chuckled. "Yeah, sure. I once was a junior high boy. I know."

"Huh?" Jarryd crumpled his brow. "You used to be a boy? What kind of operation did that take?"

The blanket fort erupted in laughter.

"Jarryd, I see another concussion in your near future – that is, if you have a future after Paul Newton finds you."

"DUHDuhduh!"

Brandon laughed and held up his fist. "I'll put your lights out if *you* don't, freaks. Have pleasant dreams."

"Good night!"

"We love you Brandon!"

"Shut up. Go to sleep!"

The door creaked nearly closed, and the lights flicked off. Only a sliver of light slipped through from the hall.

The sudden quiet was numbing and brought an ominous tension that seeped through the blankets and closed in on them from all sides. Greyson heard soft shuffling in the fort and searched for a pillow himself. Twenty minutes. Twenty minutes until he did it all over again.

Chapter 11

Tuesday Night

There he was. The same physical trainer with the same sports magazine. *Must be a slow reader. Very slow.*

"Sammy? Ready?" Greyson whispered and reached back for the boy. Sammy crawled through the blanket door and to the room's doorway.

"Everyone else? Ready?"

"Ready." Jarryd nodded.

"Good to go." Nick nodded.

Liam nodded nervously.

Greyson turned to each one, maintaining eye contact with each for that perfect amount of time between indifference and annoyance. He felt their eyes with his own and found trust, fear, and pure adrenaline. They were ready.

"Austin?"

He flipped his walkie on and nodded. "Ready."

"You're our eyes and ears back here."

"I know."

"And our only hope if we're in trouble."

"Don't worry. You'll be fine."

Greyson looked at the floor. "I hope so." His mind searched for any last words. His watch read 10:51.

Sammy eyed Greyson and Greyson nodded back. "Go."

"EEEEEEEEEEEEE!!"

Sammy shrieked a shriek only a prepubescent boy could shriek. It rang throughout the hall and most definitely into the ears of the young trainer outside. Greyson smiled, the mirror shaking with his laughter. The trainer flung the magazine at the ground and rushed toward their room.

"Go, Sammy!" he whispered with a push.

Sammy shot from the doorway and into the hall; he streaked past the trainer and flew down the hallway, his arms flailing high above his head.

The trainer lunged after him and took off down the hall, the crazy kid flailing and screeching.

Greyson slipped the mirror in his pack. "Let's roll."

Four figures in black slipped from the door like cat burglars or ninjas – they hadn't decided which was cooler.

They padded quietly around the corner and into the stairway, Sammy's shrieks and the Cowboys Purple's angry and tired moans filtering in from the hall.

Greyson led them down the stairway three flights, checked the hall to the counselors' meeting with the mirror, and exited the building to the eerie, yellow parking lot. This all felt very familiar to Greyson, but to the others it was new and exhilarating.

"Cool. Now to get Deergirl," Jarryd noted, walking toward the girls' dorm which he knew to be Binz Hall.

Greyson shook his head and grabbed his shoulder to turn him back. "We're not getting Sydney."

His three friends cocked their heads and arched their brows.

"Uh…what?"

"We can't. How are we supposed to get in there to meet her?"

Jarryd rolled his eyes. "Are you kidding? You're going to stand her up on your first date?"

Greyson scoffed and sprinted to the ditch, leaving his three friends standing alone in the middle of the parking lot. A moment of realization passed until Liam suddenly burst toward the ditch after him; Jarryd and Nick followed close behind and slid down to their stomachs next to Greyson.

"She is going to kick your…"

"…I know. But it's just not possible. We've got to go and go fast. It can't be too long until Brandon figures out he's missing half his campers."

Jarryd shrugged. Greyson paused. "Well, yeah. So he might not notice. But still. We can't get in there. The girl's dorm is like a fortress. One girl sees us and their screams will shatter our teeth."

"That would suck."

"Yeah. So, let's go. Follow me."

Greyson pushed to his feet and set a hard pace around the long, dark back of the Rec Building until they came upon the bush behind the rickety equipment shed. While Nick dug for the camera in the deep bush, Greyson's eyes surrendered to memories springing from the wooden shed. SquareJaw's hands around his neck.

"Got it. It works."

The red light on the front of the camera flashed on and Nick swung the lens around to his friends. "Any last words?"

He panned toward Liam; Liam turned his face and ducked shyly. Nick smiled and panned to Jarryd who held out his tongue and made a rocker's sign. "Peace. To all the women of the world, I'll miss you. And you're missing out….if I'm dead. If I'm not, then why are you watching this? Anyway…Deergirl. I'm sorry I call you Deergirl. Peace."

The boys laughed softly, their eyes swinging out around the shed to the winding sidewalks and lit buildings. Still no one.

Nick panned away from Jarryd, and Greyson came into focus. He shyly scratched at his nose and sniffed, looking downward. Then, like some force below him rose through his lungs, his gaze rose straight into the camera.

"If anyone finds this tape and we're gone, you'll know what happened to us and who needs to be stopped. We tried our best. Please tell my mom that I love her. And…," he paused with a catch in his throat, "…and if you find my dad…tell him I missed him. Every day."

He fingered the bill of his red hat and tipped it to the lens.

The boys watched him with solemn reverence. The camera beeped once and the red light on its front went dark. Nick lowered it. "Well said."

Jarryd's wild eyes were suddenly dimmed. "Hmm…didn't know you didn't have a dad."

Greyson eyed him. "I have a dad. He's just gone."

Jarryd shrugged. "Ahh…makes sense. I think you've just seen too many movies."

"Whatever. Can we go?"

"Yeah! Definitely."

"Alright. Next stop – observatory."

The observatory gleamed, the moonlight washing over its silvery surface like ghostly, white ribbon. The boy's feet padded the grass one by one, slowly, left then right, crossing each other with deliberate aim. From their place the building seemed the head of a giant, metallic Cyclops. Its bald head rose from the earth and its single eye stared at their approach, waiting.

Greyson couldn't help but think the observatory was an eye in itself – an Eye of Eyes, gazing to the heavens with a power beyond all other eyes, searching for truth among the stars. But the eye in its side – the door – where a single red pupil pierced the night's dark, had them in its sight. Perhaps the spirit of the gruesome Eye of Eyes remained in the metal building built over the bloody clearing. Perhaps it was drawing them in, looking for that last child – the thirteenth sacrifice to the gods.

The boys approached with caution, four sets of eyes – one for every direction – open extra wide to suck in the slightest light. The breeze was light and cool, a welcome awakening but an ominous sign. The wind was blowing them toward the Cyclops, like gravity itself was pulling them in, sucking them into the metal beast.

They reached the side of the building and pressed their backs to the cold, rounded steel. Sliding their backs along its base like a thin path along a jagged mountain peak, they came closer to the door where a security camera scanned the lit sidewalk.

Greyson's fingers didn't need light to find the zipper, reach into the pack and remove the keycard. He held it at his side until he crossed underneath the protruding camera's width. *Would it even work here? Or was there a different card for every building?* His heart jumped.

The door was open.

Just slightly, a fraction of an inch, but it was open. Bright blue light played around the edges, and he felt drier air flowing from it. He glanced at the keypad again, just to make sure – it was red. *What's going on? Did someone forget to shut it?* He slipped the card back into his pack and zipped it shut.

Shrugging it off, Greyson gritted his teeth and pulled the door open with his left arm, still pressed against the steel to avoid the camera's view.

He grunted with the weight of the thick, metal door, but it opened just far enough for him to slip his foot in. Gaining the leverage he needed, he turned his foot, stuck his arm through, and pushed it open enough for his slender body to fit through.

Jarryd was next in line, and when his body pushed through the opening, Greyson turned his attention to the hallway ahead of him. Construction lights strained with an electronic buzz, blasting the hall with bright, blue fluorescent light. Greyson's eyes squinted from the bombardment of rays, his pupils shrinking painfully fast. Blinking hard and deep, the hall began to fade into clear focus.

The gray hall was cold with decades-old tile floor; nothing decorated the walls but spider-webbed cracks, and the ceiling tiles were sagging with age and dust. A small room opened up ten yards down the hall, its bare interior marked only by a collapsed couch and a mini-fridge. The floor was caked with dirt and the entire place smelled like old garage.

Empty. That's a good thing. Maybe they hadn't come here yet.

Liam and Nick slipped through the doorway; the door clamped shut behind them and buzzed locked as their gazes surveyed the old, abandoned hall with keen curiosity.

"Cool. It used to be like all high-tech."

Jarryd reached into the hall and pulled out a disabled key pad, its wires dangling like the cobwebs that hung in all the corners of the ceiling. Liam jumped to look into the half-open ceiling where venting shafts, pipes, and wires ran the length of the hall like miniature highways. At one time, this place had been alive and well, with power, running water, and air-conditioning. But now, if it weren't for the lights, it would be the perfect haunted house.

"I wonder what happened here. Why don't they use it anymore?"

Nick's question went unanswered as Greyson dared to take the first steps deeper into the hall. The dried mud crunched under his sneakers. Greyson watched his next step and found dried mud molded to a familiar shape. A footprint.

Someone had been here when tracking in mud was no longer a problem – after it had been abandoned.

"Quiet. They could be in here," Greyson warned.

"Why would they be in here of all places?"

"I don't know," he said. "But let's find out."

Not looking back at his three friends, he took another step.

BANG BANG BANG!

"AAGGH!" Liam screamed and swung to the metal door they had come from. Someone – or some thing – had knocked.

Greyson's heart raced after the start, frantically searching the hall for a hiding spot. *In the ceiling? Under the couch? Or should they fight?*

Jarryd flew to the door and grabbed the handle.

Greyson swung his view to him, panic covering his face. *Don't OPEN it!*

But he did. He turned the handle and pushed the door out just enough to see what was on the other side. His face turned to horror, his arms curling to his body to protect himself.

"Oh, no."

Sydney pulled the door open further and stepped in, her hands shielding her face from the light. "Geez! Lower the light, boys!"

Nick rolled his eyes up into the back of his head. "Whew. I thought you were Paul Newton!"

Sydney stared and her eyes flinched.

Greyson stepped in front of the path of the light, drawing his shadow over her. She looked away from Nick and smiled. "Thanks. For nothing!"

Greyson shoved his finger into his lips. "Shh! Quiet!"

Sydney surveyed the dirty, abandoned hallway. "Why?"

He gulped. *What am I supposed to tell her?*

"Uh...this place is uh...haunted...with the spirits of...ancient Indians."

Her face was a mix of confusion and annoyance. "Really? You stood me up for a haunted house?" When she had originally heard 'observatory' she had hoped for a long night gazing into the stars, looking for constellations and dreaming of the future with her new friend that happened to be a cute boy. Of course, that turned out to be another stupid fantasy. *What boy would want to do that? He wanted to mess with stupid, ancient evil Indians.*

Greyson mouthed something, but it didn't come out. Nick turned on the camera with a beep, turning their attention to him. "We're going to catch the spirits on camera."

Sydney nodded her head in feigned interest. "Okay."

"Any last words?" Nick asked with a smile.

"Uh..." she glanced around. "Are you recording?"

Nick nodded, looking at the flipped out LCD screen.

"I want to say..."

"...Nick, we have to go," Greyson interrupted, flipping the screen back into the camera.

Sydney recoiled. "What? But what if I get eaten by ghosts?"

Greyson rolled his eyes. "They're not going to eat you."

Sydney set her hips and gave him her best mother-stare. "Oh, yeah? Why not?"

Greyson sighed, every fiber of his being wanting to get further into the building to find a hiding spot for four boys and one very annoying, yet very good-looking girl.

"Because. They're looking for a boy to sacrifice. Not a girl."

Sydney nodded. "Hmm…I like how they think. Fine. Let's do it."

Liam and Nick smiled. Jarryd kept his distance.

Greyson shook his head, annoyed, but pleased with her cooperation. *Now, let's just hope her big mouth doesn't get us caught.*

"Contact Austin. We're going in."

Jarryd took out his walkie and flipped it on. "Home, this is Away, come in."

The walkie crackled and they paused a moment. Austin came through, "Home here."

"We're in. Heading deeper."

"Nice. All's good here. Nutty's back and asleep. Magazine boy hasn't a clue."

"Good. Over and out."

He flipped it off and put it back in his pocket.

Greyson nodded and led them forward, softly marching through the hall to the open room. To the right, a front desk still retained some of its chrome shine, but boxes and trash were thrown behind it carelessly. To the left, a collapsed brown couch laid on the ground next to a mini fridge. The fridge's electrical cord curved over the dirt ground like a snake but sat unplugged in the center of the hallway.

"A lobby?"

"Yeah," Jarryd muttered. A calm reserve had pressed into them as they passed further from the light.

Without exploring the dilapidated lobby, the group moved stealthily along the hall toward the dark.

"What's that say?"

Along the wall, a dusty sign hung from a lone screw. Greyson stopped in front of it and wiped his sleeve along its smooth surface. Letters, then words, appeared through the grime. They gathered around him, Nick zooming the camera to take in the message. He mouthed the words.

"Take...care. Careless mistakes...have great stakes."

Greyson sneezed and dust poured onto the ground at their shoes. Startled, the boys were speechless. Sydney voiced what they were thinking. "Who makes *that* sign?"

"Sounds like my math teacher," Jarryd opined.

Greyson shrugged and laid the sign on the ground. With a quick head motion, he led them toward the end of the hall. Their shadows grew longer and longer, the single large light becoming more distant. Their eyes played tricks on them, making them take double and triple-takes just to make sure that shift of light out of the corner of their eye was not some knife-wielding cafeteria worker, twin-killing counselor, or Indian warrior.

Just when they felt they had reached their destination, an obstacle blocked the hall with intimidating power; a thick steel door that looked like a bank vault. The worst part – the electronic key pad was missing and only a hole remained where it once was. Greyson tugged on the metal bar to open it, but it moved as much as the barbell did when he had tried to benchpress 200 pounds.

"Crap."

Nick panned the area with the camera, the dark almost too much for the digital camera to register much of an image.

Greyson took a step back and his foot hit something hollow. He half-tripped out of surprise and fell against the wall.

"It's a trap door!" Jarryd shouted.

"Shhh!" Sydney got in his face and he shied away.

Greyson pushed away from the wall, knelt and wiped the crusted dirt from the floor, slowly revealing the wooden panel made of several boards hastily nailed together. A slight cool breeze came from underneath; it was covering something.

"Here, help me."

Sydney and Liam grabbed hold of the boards and the three of them pulled the panel down the hall. The lid removed, a gaping, black hole seemed to draw them in. Only the edge of the dirt hole caught the light from the hall, and the darkness seemed to stretch forever toward the thick metal door.

"It's a tunnel underneath."

"Maybe the door was meant to keep something out...but that something found another way in," Jarryd whispered, as though talking to himself.

Liam shivered and grasped his shorts with white knuckles.

Sydney smiled and dipped her face down into the hole. "Maybe this place isn't that bad! Who's got the flashlight?"

Greyson looked at Nick. Nick looked at Jarryd. Jarryd looked at Liam.

"You didn't bring a flashlight? Boys. Hand me the camera."

Nick slipped his hand from the strap and handed it to Sydney. She searched the camera for its features on its sides and front. Finding the button she was searching for, she pressed it and looked into the screen. The screen flashed from color to greens and blacks. She pointed it at Greyson; his eyes glowed green, his face like a zombie's.

"Yikes. What is that?"

"Night-vision. Infrared."

"Really? Cool!"

Greyson leaned toward Sydney and watched the screen. "Good idea. It'll work as a flash light."

Nick nodded. "A digital torch."

The boys smiled, watching Sydney tighten the strap to her hand and sit on the edge of the hole with the lens pointed at her dangling feet. She turned back to the boys. "Follow me."

"Sydney...," Greyson halted mid-sentence as Sydney looked toward him, about to jump in the hole. "...can I go first?"

Sydney flinched. "Huh? No way."

He looked away. "You shouldn't be first."

The image of Mantis dragging his thumb across his throat flashed in his mind.

She played angry. "What? Cuz I'm a girl? Remember, the ghosts don't want to eat me."

Greyson exhaled slowly. *I tried.*

Sydney slid from the edge and found the ground with her feet. Kneeling low with the camera, she crouched and skidded further into the hole. Within a couple seconds she had disappeared.

Jarryd pinched Greyson's side. "Worried about her, huh?"

Greyson pushed him away and dropped into the hole after her. Jarryd winked at his brother and followed Greyson. Nick was next, holding onto Jarryd's shirt as they shimmied into the dark.

Liam turned back to the long hall where they had come from, alone now with his shadow. What seemed a mile away, the door was still shut as they had left it.

Whimpering in cold fear, he dropped into the hole.

The tunnel was wet and slippery with mud, caking their hands and knees as they churned their way in the pitch dark. Only the greens of the LCD screen were visible as it bobbed and weaved with the movement of Sydney's hand.

Greyson held the bottom of her jeans, trying to keep up with her fast crawl, and behind him, Jarryd held one of his shoelaces. Every once and a while he would feel a glob of mud hit his butt and Jarryd would giggle to himself. *Note to self, kill Jarryd twice.*

If he were claustrophobic, he would have been paralyzed. The walls of the tunnel were only three feet wide, the height about the same. The dark made it seem smaller, like there was no air to breathe, no way out, and there was no one with him. The earth could be collapsing in on him and he would have no idea until the mud started to hug him and squeeze the air from his lungs.

The wet was annoying. If he could guess what a turd felt like on its way out, this would be it. It even smelled like it.

"Sorry. That was me," Jarryd laughed.

Greyson gagged. Sydney stopped. She turned the camera back toward him. "You okay?"

"Yeah," he said breathily. He turned to where Jarryd would be if he could see past his own face. "You guys, okay?"

"Yeah."

"Fine."

"Y-y-yeah."

Sydney reached out and placed a muddy finger on Greyson's nose. "We're almost there."

Greyson grimaced and wiped the mud from his nose with his muddy hands. He heard Sydney slosh ahead and snagged her jeans.

It took only a few more seconds until he could start to make out a faint light source in the distance. It wasn't bright at all, but compared to the tunnel, it was like a sun on the horizon.

"Almost there."

"G-g-good."

"Shh!"

Sydney had hushed them from the front, the light now just above her head. Her face shone dully in the faint light filtering in from the tunnel's lid.

"I hear something." Her voice was hushed and serious.

Greyson held his breath so he could hear better, but all he could make out was the ringing in his ears and the light panting of three boys behind him.

"I can't hear any..."

"Shh!"

And then he heard it. He could hear it and *feel* it.

Footsteps.

And there was more than one set; one would start close and then fade away as another would come closer.

They weren't alone anymore.

Sydney looked to Greyson from her spot in the faint light. He didn't know if she could see him, but her eyes were searching for an answer. *I should have gone first.*

"The camera," he whispered.

She handed it to him and he cradled it with two muddy hands. She turned with two free hands and found handholds in the boards. Then, with a soft, womanly grunt, she reached up and pushed the lid a couple inches to the side with a gritty shake.

She flinched and gritted her teeth, ashamed of the noise. Greyson held his breath again, but there was no sound. Just the same footsteps. *They hadn't heard.*

Sydney gulped the lump in her throat and pushed the lid another couple inches. Light poured into the hole from above, and their eyes snapped closed. The cool, air-conditioned breeze blew in some flakes of crusted dirt, which fell like snowflakes into her hair.

Greyson exhaled and held the camera out toward her. When her eyes had adjusted, she snagged it from him and strapped it to her hand. Then, switching the camera from infrared and tilting the screen downward, she raised the camera up to the edge of the lid.

Sydney watched the screen, her neck awkwardly craning to keep it in view. She pushed the camera up through the hole, shaking with fear. When the lens passed the lid, the room came into focus. Something flashed across the screen.

She dropped the camera and gasped in fear. Greyson snapped into action; he grabbed her ankle and pulled her through the mud closer to him. Her face was frozen in horror.

He scanned the hole for any movement. No one was there; no one had come after them yet.

"What?" he asked in a panicked whisper. "What did you see?"

She could barely speak the words.

"An Indian."

Chapter 12

Greyson crawled over her. The awkwardness didn't matter – he had to put distance between them and her.

"Go. Get back to the lobby. Hand the camera to Liam. Go."

She didn't move. Her face suddenly softened and a sly smile curled at her lips. Greyson stared at her. *Has she gone mad with fear?*

"Are you serious?" she asked, suddenly feeling guilty for frightening him. "An *Indian?*"

He wanted to kick her. And then he did. Right in the shin.

"Stupid girl. You stinkin' scared me."

She rubbed her shin in surprise. After a stunned pause, the boys behind her began to groan.

"Uh…can we move?" Jarryd complained in a whisper. "I can't feel my knees."

She turned and kicked him.

"Feel that? Shut up."

She turned back to Greyson. Greyson shook his head at her then turned toward the hole above. Something *was* moving above them. A shadow passed over the sliver of light and he ducked.

"What did you see?" he asked her again, hushed.

She sighed. "A doctor or a scientist. Long white coat. Probably just an astronomer. Imagine that, an astronomer in an observatory."

Greyson hoped she was right. He hoped the whole thing was a misunderstanding. *Maybe SquareJaw is just a mentally insane astronomer. Maybe he tried to kill me because he was just really stressed about his work – what with his building falling apart and all.*

Duh. Who am I kidding? SquareJaw is not a frickin' astronomer. And this place is not used for stargazing. He didn't have a clue what it *was* being used for, but he planned on finding out. He grabbed the lid and pushed it another couple inches, making sure not to grunt like a girl when he did so. More dust sprinkled on his face and more light filled the dirt tunnel.

The gap was just wide enough. Mustering his courage and waiting for his instincts to click, he waited. When the footsteps felt a safe distance away, he peeked his head through the hole.

A large room. Scientists in white coats. Five of them. Walking around. Control panels. Buttons. Flickering lights. A huge, black window. *We're in the corner.*

He looked up. The rounded, metal roof was open just a crack and the starry night peeked in from above. *It looks like a freaking observatory.*

He lowered his head back into the hole. Sydney cocked her head at him expectantly. "Yeah?"

Greyson breathed heavily, his heart pounding. *No. This couldn't be right. Mantis had said for SquareJaw to meet him here. But what could they possibly be doing wrong by looking at the stars?*

Sydney reached out her muddy hand and placed it on his shin. "Let's go back."

Greyson shook his head. "Not yet."

He peeked back over the hole. He had to memorize every aspect of the room. Another hallway; *there's another way in.* A glass box on the wall with a lever inside – *an alarm.* Two large keys stuck into keyholes at opposite ends of the control panel. Vents along the walls, just below the ceiling. The place was clean – almost like new. A scientist with brown hair – two of them. One with blonde, one jet-black, and another –bald.

Yes. It was him. Near the far control panel, his back to him. *SquareJaw.*

What is he looking at? Light flickered on his white coat.

Suddenly, SquareJaw turned; his eyes snapped straight at the hole. *CRAP!*

Greyson dropped back under, adrenaline straining through his tense muscles. He couldn't breathe. *Crap, crap, crap. Crap!*

He saw me. He saw me.

A shadow blocked the light and the lid flew away. SquareJaw stood over him, ready to pounce. *Run!*

There was nowhere to run. They were finished.

"RUN! GO! RUN!"

But they could hardly turn in the tunnel. It was no use.

"It's okay, boy! Don't run. Come up out of there."

Another man walked up alongside SquareJaw's hulking figure. He had small, thin glasses, surfer-blonde hair streaking across his balding head, and a pock-marked face. His smile was friendly and confident.

Greyson's chin quivered, but he closed his mouth to hide it. Sydney froze behind him, kneeling in the hole, silent.

"Come on up, boy. That's not a healthy place to be. How many of you are there?"

Sydney pushed at his feet, but he didn't move.

"We have a walkie talkie," Greyson warned. "If you try to do anything to us, we'll scream and have the whole camp know what you did."

The man nodded with a condescending smile. "Sounds like a deal. Now come on up." He reached his hand out.

Greyson gulped, exhaled, and grabbed the man's hand. The man clutched him firmly, his large hand engulfing his entire hand and part of his wrist. He was yanked out of the hole and as soon as his feet hit tile, he pulled away from the man and pressed himself against wall.

Sydney came out next, SquareJaw himself helping her out with a kind smile. Out of the corner of his eye, he winked at Greyson.

Don't you touch her! Greyson nearly leapt at him there, but Sydney stood in the way.

"Thank you," she said to him, shaking his hand. The words bit deep into Greyson's heart.

Jarryd followed, his hand on the walkie, and Nick followed with Liam close behind. The camera was nowhere to be seen. *Good move guys. It's the only card we haven't dealt.*

And there they stood. Five muddy, tired children standing against the wall – five scientists staring at their pathetic figures.

The blonde one, clearly the leader, took the initiative. "Wow. You got dirty, didn't you?" He laughed to himself. "And you all look pretty nervous. Well…heh heh…I guess you should be."

133

Greyson clenched his fists.

"Running out of the dorms at night and trespassing on campus grounds could get you kicked out of camp." The man tried to look serious and grave, but failed. He had a good nature about him. "But…I once was a camper here, believe it or not."

Not.

"And we had some fun adventures – some legal, some not as much."

Jarryd and Nick laughed nervously.

"And this one you're on now has *got* to be cool, huh? Quite a *daring* escapade."

Liam nodded with enthusiasm, a smile breaching his fearful frown.

The man paced up and down the line of children, hands in his jacket pockets. He stopped in front of Greyson, bent his knees and looked him straight in his eyes. "Are you their fearless leader?"

Greyson glared at him, examining each pockmark like a crater on the moon.

The man reached his hand out to shake, the large gold band around his ring finger shiny and thick. "Dr. Jacob Emory."

Greyson broke eye contact and kept his hands at his sides, still clenched in fists. Dr. Emory lowered his hand and shrugged. "A little shy? I understand."

"I am *not* shy! You're a fraud!" He swung his hand to SquareJaw, his finger stiff and accusing. "He tried to kill me!"

Dr. Emory recoiled and glanced at SquareJaw. Then he laughed – a choking, raspy laugh – and turned to Greyson. "Carl? Carl, who is working the kitchen during the day and the observatory during the night to help his wife and kids get by, tried to kill you?"

Greyson nodded, his chin set. Dr. Emory motioned SquareJaw over to them and the hulking figure pounded next to him, standing a foot higher than the doctor.

"Carl? Did you try to kill the boy?"

SquareJaw shook his head. "Of course not," he said in his bass voice, "but I tried to kill a raccoon last night. I nearly got him before he ruined the kitchen."

134

Greyson scoffed angrily, "No! You threw a knife at me and it cut me! Look!"

He pulled his t-shirt up to his armpit and showed the wound to the whole crowd. Sydney grimaced in surprise.

"Whoa. That's quite a gash."

"Yeah, duh!"

SquareJaw shifted on his feet. "I did throw a knife at the raccoon. If you were in the kitchen, hiding or something, maybe it hit you somehow? Or the coon hit a rack full of knives. Maybe they could have…"

"No! There was no raccoon!"

His pleading eyes landed on Sydney and she scrunched her forehead in thought.

"Hmm…" Dr. Emory smiled. "You were in the cafeteria last night, fearless leader?"

Greyson nodded.

Dr. Emory rubbed his hairless chin. "And…why were you there?"

Greyson shrugged. "I knew he was up to something. And so are you."

Dr. Emory's condescending smile was getting on his nerves. *He's looking at me like I'm a little puppy and he's the master with all the treats.*

"This…!" Greyson suddenly moved, his sneakers popping from the tiled floor with the muddy glue. He ran to the control panel as the scientists watched him. "…this is not an observatory! What are you doing here?"

Dr. Emory strolled to the control panel and turned to the defiant boy with the red hat. He looked down at him and put his hand on his shoulder tenderly. "Son, we're not 'up to' anything. We're just studying the skies."

Greyson nearly lost it. "I'm not your *son*!" he screamed, the veins in his neck bulging out.

The astronomer glanced past him for a moment, lost in thought and ignoring his anger. When his gaze returned, he lifted his hand from the boy's shoulder and pointed up. "The stars. See them?"

All necks tilted back, all eyes gazing into the sliver of dark peeking through the metal roof.

"Right now, our telescope is surveying a very tiny fraction of a degree of space every day. Or night I suppose."

He pointed to a side counter, where monitors were slowly scrolling through numerical data. "Data logs and progress monitors." He grabbed a clipboard from one of the other astronomers and showed it to Greyson. "Prospects for further research."

Greyson wiped the dried dirt from his nose.

Dr. Emory's speech slowed and turned to a near whisper. "We…are here, young boy…to monitor its progress, log its results, and get our paychecks. That's it. Sorry we're not more interesting."

Greyson gulped and swung his defiant eyes to his friends. Their eyes betrayed his. They were all so still, so convinced, and so sad. The man – Dr. Emory – had defeated them with his words.

"But…," Sydney stepped out of line and glanced quickly at Greyson, "…but where is the telescope? I don't see one."

Dr. Emory coolly pointed to the large black window past the control panel. "In the main chamber through the window."

"Show us," Greyson demanded.

The doctor's eyes flinched momentarily. "The window is tinted heavily, as you see. This is to prevent any unnatural light that is not from the skies from reaching the chamber or the telescope's lenses. If we were to look at it now, we would ruin a large amount of accurate data."

Greyson turned to Sydney. She shifted on her feet and wiped a stray hair behind her ear. Liam shrugged, his puppy eyes pleading with him to stop. He searched the room, scrambling for a reason to disbelieve, looking for evidence of their treachery. But there was none. The only evidence was his wound.

"I know," Greyson said calmly. "I know he tried to kill me. You don't fool me here."

Dr. Emory sighed and clapped his hands on his thighs. "Well, then, I don't know what to say. I suppose we don't have to say anything."

136

SquareJaw smiled.

"The fact is that you are all trespassing, and you will have to leave."

SquareJaw's eyes locked onto Greyson and he stepped toward him. "I'll take them back to where they should be."

Dr. Emory gave the children one more look, sympathetically nodding like a bobbing head doll. "Carl, let's show them the door, but they know their way back." He smiled mischievously. "I trust they know their adventure ends here. The counselors and directors don't need to know about this deed done just out of good 'ol innocent fun. You agree, kids?"

Liam nodded with enthusiasm; the others just merely nodded.

SquareJaw walked in front of Greyson, his eyes never straying from the boy's face. "Let's go, *son*."

He grabbed Greyson's bicep and tugged him toward the hallway out of the control room. Greyson resisted for a moment, but decided against it. His anger seethed out of his very pores, but there was nothing he could do. He was no hero today. Sydney would watch him be dragged away like a naughty child to be spanked. It was his pride that was being spanked, whimpering and sniveling without a way out.

SquareJaw led them down a short corridor, lit and clean like new. It was night and day compared to the other side of the building and the kids were deathly silent. Only their shoes clapping mud to the clean tile made any real sounds. They passed several doors to their left and right, all shut and locked with a working keypad. Soon, they came to the end of the hall where another giant door blocked them. SquareJaw took out a card, swiped it through the pad and it buzzed green.

"Kids," Dr. Emory spoke loudly from down the hall. "You're welcome back any time on Thursday during the day and I'll show you around. I'll give you a complete tour. Sound good?"

They listened, but the night was growing longer and their brains were shutting down. Eventually, one of them muttered a "yeah" and they filed out the doorway into the muggy air with the air conditioning blowing on their backs. SquareJaw stood, silhouetted in the light, his huge frame almost filling the entire doorway. Greyson turned to him and watched a smile run across his face. Then, hanging his head, Greyson began the walk home.

"Wait a sec." Sydney whispered and cut back toward the closing doorway. SquareJaw saw her approach and held the door. Sydney stopped in front of him and looked up into his eyes. "Uh...I thought you looked familiar. I might know your wife. What's her name?"

SquareJaw froze, his eyes flared wider. "Uh..."

The boys watched from the sidewalk as the man searched his small brain. "Uh...she uh...uh..." His eyes wandered to the door in his hand. "Door....een. Doreen." He laughed nervously. "Heh. I...uh...never call her by her real name, though...heh...I just call her hun...and sweetie."

Sydney tried to hide her smile; she blinked rapidly and swallowed hard. "Ookay. I guess I don't know her. Thanks."

And she ran back to the boys, her ponytail bobbing left and right. SquareJaw snarled momentarily, then smiled and waved, then snarled again and slammed the door. The keypad turned red and a moment later, the security camera swung in their direction and stayed. Their welcome had run out.

Sighing deeply, Greyson took his hat off and held it in both hands. Sydney watched him with a patient smile, rocking on her heels. "Umm..."

Greyson turned to her, his tired eyes watery and sad.

"...you're right," she said plainly, looking back over her shoulder at the looming observatory.

Greyson's brow furrowed and he paused in silence.

"He's lying – they're lying," she continued. "Would you like to tell me what they're lying about?"

Jarryd cleared his throat. "Uh...what? It didn't look like they were lying at all."

"It was a trick," Greyson stated sternly. "Let's get back to the dorms."

He turned and walked toward Bickford Hall.

Sydney caught up to him, the boys close behind. "You're not going to tell me? Why did Carl try to kill you? What do you think they're doing there? And don't tell me Indians."

"No. Why should I? You shouldn't have even been here."

"But I *was* there!"

Her anger gnawed at his aching brain. *Why can't she just shut up?*

"Please. I don't want to talk about it."

She stopped and stomped her foot. Jarryd ran into her back and fell to the sidewalk; Sydney glared at him and then yelled for Greyson. "Greyson, stop!"

Greyson turned to her, his face contorted in anger. He spoke through his teeth, saliva sizzling with the words. "Please...be...quiet."

Suddenly, pain shot through his side and he jumped back. "Aaaghh!" *What the...?*

Sydney had pinched him hard, right on his healing gash. He grasped his side with both hands, glaring at Sydney. *Why had she done that? Some friend!*

Now, her eyes were no longer defiant, nor confident. Her shoulders had drooped and her muscles relaxed. She spoke softly. "Someone...tried...to kill you, Greyson. That much I know." She took a small step toward him. "Now...do you expect me, knowing that, to just let it go – to just go on with my life? Or...do you expect me to do something about it?"

Greyson breathed heavily as his anger quickly sank away. The pain in his side reverberated throughout his entire body, but his mind was clear.

A humid breeze blew through the trees to their right, the leaves shaking and convulsing. The wind blew them where it wanted them to go, and they did, peacefully and easily. Everything moved a little easier going with the wind.

Do the good that you know you should do.

The saying was so simple. It was not, 'do as much of the good as you can without getting yourself or others hurt or killed', though that made more sense to him. The saying was 'do the good that should be done'.

Period. No matter how daring they had to be to do it. Sometimes fighting against the wind was the right thing to do.

Sydney stood silently and expectantly, awaiting his answer.

"Okay," Greyson sighed. "I'll fill you all in on the way back so we're on the same page. What I do know – we're going to have to go back there. And before Thursday. Whatever they're doing is going down tomorrow."

Chapter 13

Boys' deep breaths rhythmically pulled and pushed the dank air in melody with the soft flaps of the fort's blanket walls. Austin peered through half-open eyelids to the clock – 12:14. It was past midnight. *Had something happened to them? They should have called in by now.*

The walkie crackled and Austin startled. He pulled it close to him and hovered over it.

"This is Away, come in." It was Jarryd.

Austin smiled, wide-awake now. "This is Home."

"We're coming in. We need the rope fast!"

Austin pushed on Ryan's leg. His breathing caught in his throat and he smacked his lips, but he remained asleep. Austin scooted over and pulled Ryan's pillow out from under his head; Ryan's head hit the carpet with a thud and he snapped awake. "Oww….whatcha do that for?"

Austin held the talk button. "Ryan's on his way. Be there shortly."

"My head hurts really bad!" he complained loudly.

Austin rolled his eyes. "Shh! Ryan. Go. Remember? The rope?"

Ryan sleepily rubbed his eyes. "Oh. It's time?"

"Yes!"

Ryan sat up with a long groan and waddled to the blanket wall entrance. He slid underneath and opened the door with a creak. He looked to the left – nobody. Even the chair was empty where the trainer usually sat. He looked right – the bathroom light was on, but the hall was empty.

Sniffing and rubbing his eyes again, he walked to the bathroom and glanced inside – no one at the three urinals, the three stall doors were closed, and the three shower drapes were open.

Catching his reflection in the mirror, he rubbed his bed head with both hands and tried to mat it down with a splash of water. He sniffed the air. *It stinks in here.* He rubbed his nose violently and crinkled his forehead. *Gross.*

Suddenly remembering what he had come there for, he walked to the last stall, holding his nose with both hands. He pushed the door open with his head and found the rope. *It's so big! Why did I volunteer for this again?*

Sighing despairingly, he lugged the rope over to the window and dropped it to the floor. Panting slightly, he rubbed his hands and brushed his pajama pants off.

He needed a break. And he needed to pee.

He waddled to the first urinal.

They came to the back of Bickford Hall and its glowing yellow parking lights. Something about the emptiness and the buzzing lights mixed with swarms of insects and his own tiredness made Greyson feel sick to his stomach. Or maybe it was the fact that he was losing and he couldn't stand it.

Sydney stopped in front of them and turned to Greyson. "Thanks for telling us everything. We'll get 'em back, okay?"

Greyson nodded with a tired smile. Sydney leaned in and gave him a shoulder hug. The contact felt comforting. There was something about a hug from someone other than his mother that made it special.

She released and backed away.

"How are you going to get in to Binz?" Greyson asked, just thinking of it.

She smiled. "Same way I got out. Let's just say my counselor loves me."

And with that, she pumped her eyebrows and took off running along the pavement. The boys watched her leave.

"She's amazing," Jarryd swooned.

Greyson nodded. They stood there another moment and then turned to the building.

"Radio in. There's still no rope."

"Home, this is Away. Where's the rope?"

Austin sighed. He had seen this coming. "Away, I'm going to see what's wrong."

He lunged up and hurried under the blanket-door and into the hall. The walkie crackled with a start, "What's wrong? Come in."

It was loud. The voice seemed like an explosion in the silence of the dark hall. Austin quickly turned the walkie off and glanced both ways down the hall. He heard someone stirring in a bed. He had to hurry.

He jogged to the bathroom and almost ran into Ryan at the urinal. "What are you doing?"

Ryan glared at him. "I'm peeing! Don't peek!"

Austin rolled his eyes and ran to the window. He twisted the lock and pulled the window up. Leaning out, he saw the four boys; they waved.

Working urgently, he tied the rope to the radiator and threw its long coils outside. It snaked outside and snapped taut. *Good to go.*

A toilet flushed behind him and he turned quickly. Ryan still stood by the urinal. He hadn't finished. Austin turned further. A different toilet had flushed. One of the stalls.

Austin froze. Someone else was in there. One of them? A purple? A counselor? He swung around and grabbed at the rope; hand over hand, he pulled it back up through the window. He glanced over his shoulder. Bare feet in the stall, pulling up shorts. He had no time.

The last of the rope flew through the window and into the bathroom. He knelt to the radiator and scratched at the knot with his fingers. It was too tight! He couldn't get it!

The stall door opened behind him.

No!

Suddenly, the door slammed back shut. Ryan stood against it, his shoulder pressed firmly and his bare feet trying to find traction on the tile; he nodded frantically at Austin.

Austin snapped back around and started at the knot.

143

"Hey! What are you doing? Let me out!"

It was Tucker. That explained the stink. And if he saw what they were up to, he was sure to turn them in.

Austin pulled a loose end through, and the knot quickly loosened. Tucker hit against the door and Ryan was sent sliding across the tile. He quickly regained balance and slammed back into the door, sending Tucker flailing back into the stall.

Austin's fingers worked like a frenzied pianist and the rope fell from the radiator. He grabbed it from the ground and threw it into the third stall. A moment later, he snagged the door and swung it shut.

Ryan saw the success and opened Tucker's stall door just in time. Tucker came barreling out, his panicked face searching for the door he expected to ram. His body flung across the bathroom like a missile and slid along the tile to the wall underneath the sinks.

Austin and Ryan shared a long panicked look as Tucker groaned on the grimy floor. Then, in unison, they burst from the bathroom together, leaving the larger boy behind.

They scurried into the hall but skidded to a stop on the carpet in an instant. *You've got to be kidding!* Poised outside the blanket fort's room like SWAT team members ready to infiltrate the enemy's fortress, Brandon and CJ hoisted massive water guns in their hands. They smiled at each other, knees bent, fingers on triggers.

Ryan and Austin froze. The counselors hadn't noticed them or the noise. They must have been too taken up with their own mischief to notice any other.

As the noise from Tucker scrambling to his feet grew louder, the counselors slipped into the boys' room, guns at the ready. Once their faces had passed the threshold, Ryan and Austin sprinted down the hall and turned at the stairway.

Austin flipped the walkie on and spoke into it. "Plan B. We're coming down the stairs."

They pounded down the first two flights of stairs at dangerous speeds.

"What?" the walkie crackled. It was Greyson. "No! Don't open the door. They turn on the fire alarm at 11."

Austin stopped, but Ryan kept churning down the stairs. "Ryan, stop!"

Ryan ignored him, panting down the stairs. "We have to hurry!"

"It's a fire-door!"

Ryan burst onto the first floor landing and ran to the door. Greyson stood just outside the glass door with hands waving and mouthing, 'no'.

Ryan read the large red warning letters across the glass:

> # Fire Escape Door Only
> Alarm will sound if opened
> when red light is flashing

He looked to door handle – a small, pulsing red light.

Austin slapped his hand on Ryan's shoulder and let out a relieved sigh. Together they peered through the glass to the boys outside.

Austin spoke into the walkie. "Now what?"

Greyson held his head back in a desperate moan. "I don't know. We need the rope!"

"Tucker was there. Brandon and CJ are awake, spraying our room with water guns as we speak."

As the realization of failure set in, Greyson lowered his walkie and laughed to himself out of frustration. Jarryd threw up his arms and laid his head on Nick's shoulder; Liam sat on the pavement and wrapped his arms around himself.

A faint echo reverberated through the stairway. It was a mixture of laughter and panicked screams. Amongst the voices, Sammy's shriek stuck out above the rest. *Poor kid*, Austin thought.

And then – Tucker's voice. It spoke quickly and loudly, with purpose. He was giving them up. This was how it would end.

Austin raised the walkie as Greyson walked closer to the glass, just feet from him. "I hear Tucker talking to Brandon and CJ. You should run."

Greyson shook his head 'no' quickly. "We have nowhere to run."

CJ's angry voice. Patrick complaining. More of Sammy's shrieks.

Ryan grabbed the walkie and pulled it down to his level. "Uh, uh, you could go to the pool and get clean. Then, then, they wouldn't know where you've been."

Greyson shrugged, indifferent. "I don't think so. We're done. Go tell Brandon to let us in."

"You can't give up!"

But he had already. Sitting next to his friends in the yellow light, they waited for their captors. It was only a minute or so before Brandon came rushing down the stairs, mouth agape in panic. Another minute passed before he had disabled the alarm with his key. Greyson thought of Sydney and how she had won her counselor over to her side. *How would things have been different if Brandon was on our side?*

Brandon held the door open and surveyed the dejected and dirty figures outside. His mind raced through possibilities, but he knew it was too much to handle at one time. Liam was already crying, and Greyson sat next to him, rubbing his back and speaking quietly in his ear. Nick shook his head methodically, avoiding eye contact and watching his brother, Jarryd, who was the only one looking at him.

"Sorry, Brandon," Jarryd whispered sincerely.

Brandon nodded. "Is anyone hurt?"

The boys looked up at him and Greyson stood, helping Liam up. "No. We're okay."

"Then come on in. We'll get you cleaned up."

CJ stood behind him with Tucker at his side. He glared at the boys as they trodded inside. "What were you doing? You want to get kicked out of here? Well you got it. The Jensens will…"

"CJ. Let 'em be," Brandon interrupted sternly.

CJ frowned and scoffed. Tucker took over. "One of those two locked me in the stall!"

Brandon followed his six boys up the stairs, keeping himself between the Purples and the Golds. "Okay, Tucker. We'll get to the bottom of it and there will be consequences. But it's late and we all need rest."

Tucker scoffed and frowned as CJ had, receiving a sympathetic look from his counselor.

The boys marched to their rooms, brought out their towels and bedclothes, and tiredly meandered to the showers under Brandon's watchful eye. Sammy, Patrick, and Chase dried off and changed to dry clothes, still bitter from their nighttime soaking.

Greyson stood under the shower a long while, longer than the others, the dried mud trailing to the drain like blood in water while Brandon stood in the bathroom doorway, painfully aware of the time and of the hard day he would have tomorrow. He might lose half of his campers – and his job.

"Greyson," Brandon whispered when they were alone, separated by the shower stall.

Greyson spit out some water to speak. "Yeah?"

"I'm disappointed."

Greyson let the shower speak for him, filling in the silence. *I am too.*

"You're a natural leader. It's a gift. The rest – especially Liam – they look up to you, you know?"

He lowered his head, the spray splashing his matted hair and making a waterfall over his closed eyes.

"And what you did with that gift...could have destroyed this team."

His chin began to harden and his cheeks pushed up into his eyes.

"It's not only your team, Greyson. It's mine, too. I think I deserved some say in what you were doing tonight."

A sob caught in his throat and he let it out. He knew Brandon heard it.

"I'm sorry, bud. I didn't want to make you cry....I...I just wanted to let you know that you can talk to me. Whenever. I'm on your side here."

Greyson sobbed once more into the water, took in a deep breath and let it out in a soft, shuddering sigh. His head pounded, the veins at his temples throbbing blue.

"You hear me, Greyson? There could still be a way out. A way to stay in camp."

The water had grown cold. His arms wrapped around his chest, his right hand covering the gash. When it grew too cold to bear, he turned the faucet off and the pipes clenched shut.

Brandon exhaled softly outside. "You tell me where you were, what you were doing, and maybe we could keep this between us and CJ. The Jensens don't *have* to know about it."

Greyson pulled the towel from the rack and buried his face into it. "Are you serious?" he asked, muffled into the towel.

"There will be conditions."

Greyson dried his hair and patted down his body. *He said he was on my side. But how could he be? How will he ever believe this story — I barely know what to believe! But if he did believe it, he would want tell the Jensens first off. Then, the Jensens would know what happened last night and I would get kicked out of camp.*

He tenderly ran the towel across the gash and dabbed it dry.

All I know is that something is going to happen tomorrow and I need to be free to do something about it. I can't get kicked out. I'll have to take my chances with Brandon and hope he will understand.

Wrapping the towel around his waist, he pulled the shower curtain open and slowly walked out of the shower stall. Brandon stood in the doorway, watching him.

Greyson lowered his head in submission and walked closer. "Okay. I have something to show you."

Turning his side and lifting his arm, he gave Brandon a better view.

Dr. Emory rested his heels on the edge of the control panel, his white scientist garb hanging from his chair's comfy arm rests. He slouched back into the chair, staring at the black window. Its tint was deep, and the image reflecting from it seemed to be admiring him. Behind him, two of his men had switched their fake coats for their favorite automatic weapons, which slung from their broad shoulders like deadly guitars.

His earphone beeped. An incoming call. He pressed his finger to the familiar button.

"Yes?"

From the other end came a gruff voice with anxious purpose. "Is everything on schedule?"

He smiled to himself and his reflection. "Of course."

Sitting up slowly, he reached to a small lever and pushed it higher with his pointer finger. The window brightened in front of him, like it had awakened from a deep, restful sleep. Little by little, the dark tint and his reflection left the glass, and a full picture of the observatory's belly revealed itself.

Dr. Emory's smile grew wider. Six men, some with soldering irons, others with handheld computers, worked tirelessly inside; the 'telescope' was almost complete.

"Good," the gruff voice approved. "The day we've been waiting for…"

"It's here."

"Yes, brother. This is how it begins."

"Call me when the time is near."

"I will. I will."

The receiver beeped again and the small red light faded away.

"Sir?" came a voice from behind.

Emory swiveled around in his chair. "Ah. Did they find their way home?"

Mantis nodded, dressed entirely in black. He stood completely still and rigid, his feet shoulder width apart and hands clasped behind him. "They were caught, sir, outside their dorm. They were locked out. I presume they will bring their story to the camp directors or the police in the morning."

Emory huffed and patted his knee. "Don't worry about that. The Jensens received a large donation for the camp a month ago, the college president another, in part so I could continue my 'research' here. They know my number and my importance to this college. They ask too many questions, I'll force their hand with my deep pockets. As for the police, Sheriff Roberts and I have an understanding as well."

"And the kids, sir. I couldn't hear what they were saying, but I didn't like the looks of it. They still seem suspicious."

Emory sighed, his elbows falling to his knees. He followed the trail of muddy footsteps from the control panel to the covered hole in the corner.

Mantis followed his eyes and felt the need to speak. "We made it too easy, literally leaving the door open for them. Too spotless. Kids saw right through it."

Emory eyed him and smiled condescendingly. "Noooo – some fool threw a knife at the kid. Not much to 'see through' there. The problem is our trick didn't overpower his friends' trust in him."

"But what will they do? They know nothing, can prove nothing."

Emory lost himself deep in thought, pondering all available options, both for the children and himself, and weighed the response. No matter what the kids threw at them, they would be ready.

"Find out as much about their fearless leader as you can."

"Greyson Gray, sir."

Emory glanced up at him. "Ah. That's his name, is it? Fitting."

Mantis sneered. He could still see the kid within his grasp – right before Carl came flying at him like a massive bowling ball.

"Well. I want to know everything there is to know about this Greyson. Parents, siblings, hometown, likes, dislikes, greatest fears, et cetera."

"Yes, sir. Won't be hard. Parents submit that kind of thing to the camp before it starts. The Jensens have it all on file."

"Good. As for now, close the tunnel, keep the place on lockdown. If they come back, they don't get in. And watch them. Gray could still be a pest."

Mantis nodded his approval, turned on his heels, and left.

Emory spun back around on his chair and stopped his momentum with his heel. He reached under the control panel, his fingers searching the dark underside. When his fingers felt the metal release, he pulled it and the heavy weapon fell into his hands.

Leaning back, he set the shotgun across the armrests, lightly stroking the wooden stock. His lips drew in and then forward, his tongue silently speaking a name.

Greyson Gray. Greyson. Gray. The name sounded familiar.

Chapter 14

Wednesday Morning

A deep blue curtain of clouds rolled over Bickford Hall, dropping a dark shadow over the early sun's rays that peeked through Greyson's window.

Greyson awoke with the sound of the wind beating at the edge of the windows. He walked drearily toward the blurred windows, the pressure of the front pulling at his eardrums. The front dragged with it a warm, wet wind that tumbled beads of moisture in its wake. For a moment he watched the beads of moisture pat the glass and drip down in smooth little waterfalls; a moment later, he had to see outside.

Taking the window by the base, he pulled it up just a few inches. The warm, heavy wind flooded the room, blowing the drapes like a king's long, flowing robe. He lowered to his knees and peered out the few inches of viewing space, his hands on the windowsill. From this height, he felt young again, a toddler watching the storm come in for the first time.

The moisture wetted his cheeks and tired eyes like a misty shower. Night seemed only minutes ago, his conversation with Brandon just a moment, but those recent memories faded quickly when he peered through the dripping water and dark shadows of coming storm. Across the sidewalks and over the football field, the real Eye of Eyes – the observatory – still stood, as solid and steel as ever. Nothing they had done last night had removed one ounce of its mystery or torn the veil that hid its true purpose. *But tonight,* he pondered, *tonight we'll tear it down, from silver ceiling to mudded tunnel.*

Sydney stood at the window, her hands on her hips, taking in the beautiful sunrise being eclipsed by a fantastic wall of dark storm clouds.

The wind picked up quickly, rushing over the campus and sweeping up dust and candy wrappers. Behind her, her roommate Melinda stirred in bed, sleeping peacefully the way she had left her last night.

Sydney turned toward her as the rain began to wet the windows. Suddenly she felt very old. Not old and gray like her grandma, but mature. She knew so much more than her friend who awoke to a world of camp, boys, candy, and a camp dance. It wasn't the same for Sydney; she felt the weight of a terrible secret – Greyson had been threatened and stabbed.

"Good morning, sunshine," Melinda said cheerily. She was a morning person. And an afternoon person. And an evening person.

"Not much sunshine today," Sydney said bleakly.

"Hmm…I see that," she rolled out of bed and joined Sydney by the windows. Beyond a long stretch of campus, Bickford Hall peeked over the top of the Recreation Building.

"Did you have pleasant dreams?" Melinda asked with a smile.

Sydney looked into space, her mind wandering.

"Syd?"

She snapped from her daydream. "Oh…uh…I'm not sure. I didn't sleep much."

"Hmm…something on your mind?" She hugged her shoulders. "Or some*one*?"

The wind blew in a sheet of rain that slapped the window. Sydney jolted and shook Melinda's hands from her shoulders. She played her fright off. "Uh…yeah. Yeah he was. Still is."

Melinda recoiled in surprise at her usually tightly-coiled friend's honesty. "Really? Nice. I hope he brought something special to wear to the dance so he can live up to your dreams."

Sydney sighed and turned from the windows. She could see him now. Neatly gelled hair, sides swept back, the front slightly wavy and spiked, and his old red hat lightly set on top. He would wear a matching red polo shirt with a sharp white collar and a green stripe across his chest to complement his eyes. His tan khaki cargo shorts would match his tan, and he would lose the fanny pack. His smell would remain, with only a smidgeon of cologne on the side.

A flash and a knife streaks into his throat, just above the collar. Blood splashes his face and he falls backward onto the dance floor. His red hat falls, too, and lands to his side. His green eyes are frozen in fright, lifeless.

Sydney shook her head violently and had to sit down.

"You okay? I'm sure he'll lose the fanny pack. I'll make him."

Brandon threw his cell phone on his pillow in disgust. The sheriff had apparently checked out the observatory during the night and found nothing of interest. As for the fact that a boy had nearly been killed by some maniac with a knife, Sheriff Roberts said he had heard more fantastic stories than that from campers through his career 'serving' Morris. He merely suggested that he 'keep a closer eye on the boys' and not let them 'wander off unsupervised'. *What a joke! To serve and protect, my butt!*

Sure, Greyson had asked him to be totally secretive with the story, but there were some things that had to be told. In training, he was told if he ever suspected, witnessed, or heard of some kind of child abuse, he was required to report it no matter what. He was what they called a 'mandatory reporter'. *But what good is reporting if nothing is done about it?*

Well, the next logical step would be to tell the Jensens. But goodness. What could they do that the cops couldn't do? Well, for one, they could kick half my kids out of camp and fire me and CJ for losing track of most of our kids – while shooting the others with water guns.

He lay back on the bed and glanced at his watch; he had to wake them soon. Maybe he'd let them have five more minutes this morning. They'd had a rough night.

"I hate rain. It's stupid." A long pause. "What can we do in this stupid camp when it's raining? Nothing! Nothing fun, just stupid talking." Another long pause. "Oh, not even talking. That's better. I hate you all any…"

Patrick tripped. A rock maybe…Jarryd's foot…probably. He landed hands-first on the sidewalk outside the cafeteria and rolled on his side with a squeal.

The laughter started softly, but soon the whole, tired group let it out. It was a release. The tension in the air had been as thick and heavy as the humidity the entire walk from Bickford as last night's events and possible consequences hung over them like the dark clouds above. Plus, they were late to breakfast – another downer on an entirely depressing day. But to see Patrick face plant after what they had listened to for five minutes – that was a release indeed.

Greyson bent down and offered to help the boy up, but he refused and nearly hit him. Greyson laughed and shrugged it off.

"Hats, boys. Get inside and eat healthy."

"Uh, Brandon, are we gonna have to talk to the Jensens during breakfast?" Ryan asked, his shoulders drooping. He remembered his last meeting with them.

Greyson held the door for the group. "No, we won't," Greyson answered for Brandon, glancing at Brandon timidly. "And, Ryan, come on in first. You're first-first today, remember?"

"YEAH!"

Brandon stood outside as the boys filed in. When he and Greyson were alone outside, he locked eyes with him. Both stared at each other gravely. *Will he make us? Did he even want us here anymore? Has he already told?*

Brandon grabbed the door for Greyson. "You have a plan yet, Greys?"

A sudden weight lifted from Greyson's chest and he smiled. As Brandon followed him in and put a hand on his neck, something new filled the spot where the weight had been. It was hope.

155

Breakfast tasted different that morning. The fruit was crisp and bright compared to the dreary grayness of the weather. The muffin was hot and moist, the blueberry perfectly melty. Even the water was pure and smooth. Greyson guessed at why it tasted so good, but could only imagine that the little things sometimes demanded attention when they needed it the most.

The boys sat together, talking softly, but when the food had begun to settle in and hunger diminished, there was another need lurking in their gut.

"We need a plan."

The table hushed and silverware rattled when it was set down in mass. Greyson surveyed his huddle and his counselor and began to ask questions: How do we stop them? When do we go? How do we get in? What if we're being followed? Do we need a distraction? What if the tunnel was filled? How do we escape? The questions were without answers at the moment he spoke them, but brought them forth rapidly, sometimes with such perfection that it felt like fate had led them to make that very plan at that breakfast table during that gloomy Wednesday morning.

It fell into place quickly. The dance that night – the place to lose their follower. The eighth-grade girls – the distraction. The keycard the bad guys must not know he has because they left the door open for him – the way in. The ceiling vents they spotted when reviewing the camera footage – the way around the tunnel. A gator provided by Brandon – the escape. And the way to stop them – teamwork, trust, and two large keys that stuck from the control panel.

But what was it they were stopping? This remained unanswered, but it didn't matter. They knew it was evil and they had the power to stop it.

Much of the morning announcements, chanting for gold, and the talk of the paddle brands slipped in and out of their ears. The rain began softly during majors, and the entire camp was forced inside. Some coaches had their campers run drills inside, others watched videos, and some merely talked strategy, teamwork, and sportsmanship. In the end, most coaches could not occupy two and half hours inside and merely let their children find their counselors by their shields.

Greyson sat under their large, paper shield, which had been hanging from the wall since Sunday afternoon. Under their group's name one word was scrawled in marker. Greyson eyed it with amusement, then yawning and rubbing under his eyes, he took off his shoes and placed them side-by-side beneath his head as he lay down on the hard gym floor. His eyes fixed on the gym rafters above, but soon his eyelids grew heavy and closed.

Liam woke him as he rested his head on Greyson's soft stomach. Greyson smiled at him and went back to sleep. Jarryd and Nick came from tennis next and as soon as they saw the situation, they matched the pattern – Jarryd's head on Liam's belly, Nick's on Jarryd's. Soon after, Chase, Ryan, Austin, and even Patrick joined in.

They lay there for half an hour, their heads bobbing with their friend's breathing. They filled in the gaps of the plan in quiet whispers, each new detail seeming as necessary as the next. They needed more walkie-talkies, a route to a police station, a climbing harness, a carabineer, and peanut butter. Also, Jarryd supplied advice on how to deal with women to Greyson – advice he would need when talking to the girls at lunch. Finally, they planned their wardrobe for the dance and for the actual 'dance' later that night.

"Should I tell my dates that I won't be able to dance with them tonight?" Jarryd asked, staring into the rafters.

"Dates?" Chase asked, confused.

Jarryd smiled. "Uh, yeah, duh. Who wants to dance with the same girl over and over?"

Greyson smiled but didn't answer.

"One's like a fourth-grader," Nick mumbled quickly from Jarryd's belly.

"Hey!" Jarryd sat up fast, scrunching Nick's head between his belly and chest. "Yeah! You like it, bro? Yeah!"

Austin's head popped up and down on Nick's stomach as he writhed in anguish.

The antics set the whole group off in laughter that spread without fail, heads and bellies bouncing all over.

Greyson laughed cleanly, eyes closed, enjoying Liam's giggles as his head jarred with the impacts of his belly laugh. But when he opened his eyes, three eighth-grade girls hovered over him like vultures over a carcass.

He sat up with a jolt and Liam squeezed away. "Uh…hi," he said meekly.

The girls' arms were crossed, hips jutting outward and lips pursed in glossy frowns. The one he remembered as Lisa looked to Melanie. "Hi, Melanie. Look at the time!"

Melanie held up her watch, pointed to it, and feigned surprise. "Oh, *my*. It's almost dance time! I wish I had a date!"

"Yeah!" Lisa said, some anger sneaking through the act. "But I bet there is a long list of guys just waiting for the last minute to ask us!"

"Oh, of course, Lisa. Very long list. But *whooo* will be the first to ask?"

They snapped back to him, arms crossed, lips pursed.

He sat there a moment, dumbfounded and mouth agape. Then it came to him. Jarryd's advice. A coy smile curled at his lips. He gave a quick glance toward the Cowgirls Gold huddle. *Forgive me, Sydney.*

When Jarryd winked at him, Greyson jumped up and stood in the three girl's huddle. They all stood a foot above him. He craned his neck up and peered into their eyes, one by one. He could see their anger melt like chocolate in a microwave.

"Ladies. I don't want to go to the dance, but don't get me wrong…I want to be with you."

Their neatly trimmed eyebrows furrowed. "Huh?"

Greyson glanced left then right, and then placed his hands on the girls' shoulders, pulling them down to him in an actual huddle. He almost gagged on their perfume, but held it back. "I want to be with you somewhere *else*. Somewhere more…secluded… and…romantic…than this gym with a dumb DJ and a hundred lame boys."

158

The girls' mouths simultaneously dropped. Jarryd bit his lower lip and nodded in anticipation.

"I know a place," he continued softly, trying his deepest, sexiest man voice, "where the rain falls on you but you don't get wet...where you search for heaven and it is brought down to you...where we can dance without supervision...and the only music we need is the beautiful symphony our dancing bodies will make together."

He almost lost it on that last line, but somehow he held it together. The girls almost fainted, their hands fanning their red faces frantically as small gasps and weird squeals leaked from their mouths.

"Ahh...uh...eee. That sounds so...so romantic. Where is it?"

Greyson nodded. "The observatory, by the football field. Go through the north entrance at 8 pm sharp. If there are men there saying it is off limits, do not use my name." He looked left then right again. "Instead, tell them you have come to see Carl again. He invited you."

The girls' faces were blank, dumbfounded and entirely ignorant. "How did you..."

"Shh!" He put his finger to his lips to hush them; then with a sparkle in his eyes, he lightly kissed his finger and let it fall from his lips. "No questions. I can't."

The girls' knees almost gave out; their hearts were beating too fast. "Okay. We'll be there."

Greyson winked at them and swung on his heels. He sat where he had been and lay down on his shoes. Closing his eyes, he hoped they would leave before he broke out in a fit of laughter.

Soon, Jarryd jumped on top of him, his mouth open in pleasant surprise. "Ah, ha! My young apprentice!"

"Would you like to eat my pancake?" Ryan asked Greyson.

"Uh...sure."

"Would you like my banana? I peeled it for you."

"Um...yeah. Thanks."

"My milk? It's two percent."

"Want to just give me your tray?"

Ryan shrugged and slid it over to Greyson. "You need it more than I do."

"I was just kidding!" Greyson smiled. "Take it back; I'll get fat."

Ryan immediately took his tray back. "You're right. Fat people can't run very well."

Run? He thinks I'll be running tonight. I hope it doesn't come to that.

Jarryd pushed his stomach out and patted his pregnant-like belly from across the table. "He speaks the truth. I can't run worth a crap."

Greyson nodded knowingly. "We know. We've seen you."

Jarryd shrugged. "Some girls like a little Buddha belly. A little girth, you know."

Chase choked on his sandwich and a piece of bologna flew to his tray. "Girth? Ya think ya have girth? Ya haven't seen nuthin'. Everything's bigger in Texas, includin' people."

The table laughed and chewed at the same time.

Jarryd pointed at Chase. "Who's the fattest person you've ever seen?"

Chase glanced at Brandon. "You mean, besides Brandon?"

Brandon dropped his fork. "I'm right here! Again."

The laughter mixed into the cafeteria's vibrant atmosphere. If the storm's goal was to dampen the kids' mood, it had failed. The camp was alive as ever – the dance was tonight and hormones were in the air. The counselors could smell it; hormones were like tiny microbes that infected all who breathed them in. Symptoms included shortness of breath, irrational thinking, excess perspiration, moodiness, and general stupidity.

"The fattest person ever, huh? Hmm…."

Nick held up his hand in a stopping gesture. "Please. I'm eating. Let's talk about something else."

Jarryd pumped his chin at Greyson. "Yeah, let's talk about Deergirl."

Greyson shook his head. "Duh. No."

"Why not? She's way over there." He pointed to the table three down and across the aisle.

"Because. It's not polite to talk about people behind their back."

"What if you talk *about* her back?" Jarryd winked at him.

Greyson's mouth hung open and paused, the table quiet in hushed laughter. "Did you just say that?"

Jarryd laughed. "Yeah. I went there."

Before he ended his sentence, a pancake hit him square in the face. The pancake stuck for a moment until Jarryd pulled it from his face, the sticky syrup stringing from his nose.

"Yeah. Don't go there again," Greyson replied, wiping syrup from the tips of his fingers.

Jarryd held the pancake in his hand and dropped it to his tray. "I respect that."

"Are clouds really water?" The table went quiet. Jarryd licked his syrupy lips and turned with the rest of the group to Sammy. "Cuz they look like cotton balls. Big, evil, fluffy ones."

Greyson shook his head, watching the crazy-eyed boy looking innocently out the far window at the dark clouds. *Where is he? Because he's not all here, that's for sure.* "Sammy?"

"Yeeeeeesss?"

"Do you remember what you are going to do tonight?"

Sammy nodded enthusiastically and picked at his ear. "I'm swimming!"

"That's right. At the rendezvous point. And what else?"

He smiled wide. "Keeping my nuts close by."

"Good boy."

Chase nodded at Greyson. "Shouldn't be too hard, should it?"

Greyson shrugged and watched the clueless boy take out his jar of roasted peanuts and hug them close. *I have no idea. I'm just as clueless as he is.*

After rock climbing, Greyson slipped two carabineers into his fanny pack and wore a climbing harness into the bathroom, only to take it off and store it into locker #22 before he left. No one noticed. Or at least he didn't think so. He walked from the gym into the light sprinkling outside. Kids walked and ran on both sides of him, sheltering their faces from the rain, umbrellas flashing in multicolor, exuberant young voices carrying over the splashing rain. But something stuck out of place.

Someone's watching me.

An internal alarm slapped his face. He snapped his gaze left, through the blurry darkness. Behind the equipment shed and streaks of rain, a shadowy figure stood in a wet, navy-blue raincoat. The hood covered his face in black, but somehow Greyson knew – maybe it was the way his feet spread straight and shoulder-width apart, maybe it was his thick knuckles clenched at his sides – it was Mantis.

Greyson gulped a lump in his throat and turned away quickly. Standing outside without any cover, the rain soon soaked his hat, but his feet didn't want to move. Kids swerved left and right around him, screaming joyfully in the rain, running to their buses or into the gym, but he stood alone.

His legs were heavy as cement and his bus was between him and the sinister figure that still stood, staring in his direction. No one else seemed to notice him; counselors and coaches were clueless. *How could they not see this creepy man stalking a child in their own camp?* He wanted to shout at the top of his lungs, "Look! A freaking creepy guy wants to kill me! Help!", but what would that accomplish? Only questions that he did not want to answer.

Taking a deep breath, Greyson lifted his legs and took the first step toward the bus, through the throngs of kids. One kid hit his left shoulder, another his right. The man watched him, the black hole of his face turning with his angle. Another small boy hit his waist, but he ignored him. All noise seemed to blend together into silence. Only the raincoat dripping with shiny rain demanded his attention.

Finally, an opening in the crowd of kids, and he jogged to the bus. When he reached the door, he turned to take one last look at Mantis – but he was gone.

162

"Come on up, Greyson. Out of the rain."

The bus driver smiled at him from his high-perched seat.

Greyson scanned the area outside the shed, but there was no sign of him.

"Go!"

A line of kids waited behind him.

He apologized, leapt up the few stairs and scurried down the aisle to a seat by Sydney. He avoided eye contact as he sat with a wet squishing sound next to her and said nothing, staring straight ahead at the seat.

"You okay?" Sydney leaned toward him, concern in her voice.

Greyson managed a smile and nodded. "Yeah. But don't look out the window."

Sydney recoiled in curiosity. "What? Why?"

And she turned – "What? I don't see anything. It's just wet and...and...."

She gasped and pushed away from the window into Greyson's side. Outside, by the chain-link fence, Mantis peered directly at them; his torso seemed to float above the throng of kids moving past him, oblivious to his presence. If only they knew that at any moment he may reach out, take their young body into the air, and smash it to the ground – all without a quiver in his conscience. Or at least Greyson imagined he could. *Maybe my imagination is getting the best of me.*

Maybe.

"He's watching me. Probably has been all day."

Sydney trembled at his side, shaking his arm and shoulder. "He...he is! What kind of creep..."

"It doesn't matter. We'll lose him tonight."

Sydney suddenly realized her close proximity to him and withdrew to her side of the seat. Melinda watched from across the aisle, perplexed.

"We have a plan?"

Greyson nodded and briefly looked at her. "Uh huh."

"What do I do?"

Uh, oh. Didn't plan that part.

"Uh....you will be in the dance. Ready to have your counselor dial 911."

She squinted at him angrily. "Yeah?"

He cowered further into his seat. *She's going to hit me.* "Yeah. It's important."

She leaned closer to him, still squinting skeptically. "Yeah? Really?" Her sarcasm was heated.

"Um...yes?"

"Um...no. I'm going with you. Whatever you're doing, I'm doing."

He swung his body around to face her. "You can't!"

"Why not? Cuz it's too dangerous? Cuz it's too hard for a girl?"

Greyson froze. *Yes? No! Don't say yes!*

"Yes."

Crap.

Sydney's face dropped and for a moment she looked like a hungry zombie ready to take a chunk of his brains. But soon she scoffed with a knowing smirk. "Right. You going back in? Back inside?"

Greyson nodded with his best fake confidence.

"Who you got going with you?"

He searched his memory. "Jarryd and Liam."

She laughed. "Nice. Liam will wet his pants if someone farts too loud next to him. Jarryd can run as fast as a dead cat. I guess that could be good if you're being chased by an angry bear...but seriously."

Greyson rolled his eyes.

"If you want the most able people with you, you'd take me and Chase."

"Chase has a job."

"Yeah? Well. You got two options. One, you let me come with you tonight."

Greyson shook his head.

"Or, two, I scratch your knife-wound open with my fingernails and use the blood to write out your plan for tonight on the bus windows."

He eyed her hands. She had fingernails. Not very long, but enough to do damage.

"You're bluffing. You wouldn't touch me."

She smiled. "I know how to handle boys. I have three brothers – no, wait, two now. Nathan stepped on my toe."

"Oh, yeah?"

"Yeah. You have five seconds. Which option: one or two?"

"Five seconds? Oh no! I haven't even written my will yet!"

"Five."

"Oh, geez. Can I call home?"

"Four."

"Should I be cremated?"

"Three."

"I have a blood disease you know."

"Two."

"It's very contagious."

"One."

Greyson pulled up his shirt and pushed his bare wound closer to her bared claws, tempting her.

"Greyson Gray?"

Greyson dropped his shirt and looked up at the instructor. He had a sly smile on his face, glancing between Greyson and Sydney suspiciously.

"Here," Greyson said, blushing. "So is Sydney."

The laughter felt better this time. Greyson looked over at Sydney and pumped his eyebrows like Jarryd would have. Sydney shook her head slowly, and then realizing it was futile, took a deep breath.

"Okay. You got me," she admitted. "I won't kill you."

*Hmmm….*she thought. *The stick didn't work. How about the carrot?*

She leaned her head back against the seat and folded her hands on her lap. "Then how about this? You let me come with you, I'll give you a kiss."

Aaagghh! Greyson was frozen stiff. His eyes snapped to his fanny pack and he quickly began fumbling with the zipper. "Uh…"

Sydney pumped her eyebrows back at him. "No? The offer only lasts five seconds."

Greyson smiled and buried his face in his hands, trying to cool his deep blush. She crossed her arms and began to count.

"Five...four...three...two..."

What would Jarryd do?

"Two kisses," he demanded.

The counting stopped. Sydney cocked her head and looked out the window at the passing trees. She turned back to him. "Fine. But only after you do good on your promise."

Greyson felt himself trembling and he felt cold. He usually shivered like this a few times a year: Christmas morning, right before blowing the candles out on his birthday cake, and when he was doing something wrong – like taking a peek into Victoria's Secret when he was supposed to cover his eyes. But this was like a combination of the three.

"Okay. You're in," he said, his chin trembling. "Listen carefully. First..."

"Are you cold?"

He shook his head, but realized his arms were wrapped in front of him. He jerked them to his side. "A little. It's the rain. Anyway..."

She listened closely, the plan flowing through him like a good story.

The day passed rapidly. It didn't feel like it was to the boys at the time, but it was the kind of day where looking back on it, they found it hard to imagine that it had been 10 hours ago when the sunrise had been engulfed by hordes of clouds.

Horseback riding had been spent in the stables, learning how to feed a horse and do other things Greyson found as boring as daytime television. Also, they learned not to ever startle a horse if at all possible. Apparently their kick could kill someone if hoof met head at the right angle. *Great*, he'd thought, *another way to die at this camp*.

Competition passed with little excitement. All huddles had been forced inside for their events, and thus, had to find some kind of inside sport and some kind of large enough space to compete. Brandon and

CJ had managed to snag a volleyball court before the girls could get to it. The boys had been extremely grateful for their effort, because every boy loves volleyball. *Not.*

The Purples won, 3 games to none. Sammy took two spikes to the head; one actually scored for Gold when the ball bounced back to the opposing side, but the score didn't matter. All felt Patrick's disinterest – and all without the aid of medication.

Dinner even passed by quickly. Ryan offered Greyson his best food again, casually mentioning that it may be his last supper.

"We should break bread and have communion!" Nick had suggested.

"And drink wine!" Jarryd exclaimed as Mac, the large head counselor walked past. He slowed and glanced in their direction. "Grape juice! Lots of grape juice!" Jarryd corrected.

And they had. Each took a piece of sliced white bread, dipped it into a cup of grape juice, and ate it together. Their last supper was complete.

Finally, then, the hour grew near. Kids shouted with excitement all the way from the cafeteria back to their dorms. For many, the dance was approaching. They looked forward to half an hour of hurried showers, fashionable dressing, accessorizing, and deodorant-spraying. Soon, the halls were saturated with the strong stench of wet body-odor and fresh body spray. The mixture tested every counselor's gag reflex but seemed to pass by the boys' nostrils without effect.

Brandon took off his wet shirt and threw it in his full hamper. CJ did the same, throwing his umbrella in the corner. "Hehe. Your kids were pretty tame today. You must have laid into them pretty thick."

"Oh, yeah. They know they owe me good behavior. Good call on not going to the Jensens."

CJ nodded and donned a fresh shirt. "What they don't know can't hurt them. The kids will be safe from now on and that's all they care about."

Brandon laughed nervously.

Down the hall, in Greyson's and Liam's room, Greyson slipped a pair of cargo shorts over his boxers and pulled on a red polo shirt with a sharp white collar and a green stripe. Putting some gel into his hair quick, he made it look presentable – like he really planned on staying at the dance.

Liam sat on his bed, already dressed for the dance – in his wet t-shirt and mesh shorts. "We c-c-could just c-c-call the police."

Greyson placed his hat on top of his hair and turned to his friend. "They won't believe us. We don't have any evidence. We have to *make them* believe, Liam."

Liam stared blankly ahead as Jarryd walked in carrying a short pile of dark clothes. "I'm ready."

He wore a polo and khaki shorts – and plenty of cologne.

"You smell like a funeral," Greyson scoffed, choking.

"Yeah? Like lots of flowers? Chicks dig flowers."

"And open graves?"

"Whatever. Are you ready?"

Greyson reached to his bed and pulled his fanny pack around his waist. Snapping it on, he looked inside. It was almost full.

"I have a golf-ball sized space left. Anything else I should bring?"

Jarryd shrugged. "A golf ball?"

Liam smiled and raised his hand. "I've got one!"

Liam ran to the closet and dug around in his suitcase. After several seconds, he withdrew with a shiny white golf ball in his hand. "It's l-l-lucky!"

He threw it to Greyson's waiting hands. Holding it up close, he could read the words on it. "Sea World?"

Liam nodded happily. "Ye-ye-eah!"

"Awesome, Liam!" He slipped the ball into the fanny pack and snapped it shut. "Thanks."

The rest of the boys filed into the room one by one, snapping photographs and making last second reminders of the plan. Nick whipped out the video camera again and swung around to each one of them, asking for their last words for the second time.

Patrick looked straight into the lens. "Life is pointless."

Nick gave him a thoughtful nod. "Depressing as usual. Thanks. Next."

Chase laughed. "Pa. If I'm dead, I'm sorry I disappointed you. I knew you wanted a football star. I tried." He laughed again and shrugged.

Nick gave a courteous laugh and turned the lens to Ryan.

"Uh…hi."

"Say something besides hi."

"Uh…I love you Mom! Love you Dad! Uh…and Mittens! And Snuggles! Uh, uh, and Aunt Mary…and Uncle Glen! And Grandma! Uh…Grandpa's dead…"

"Thanks! Moving on…Sammy?"

Sammy looked into the camera – and up at the ceiling – and giggled. "The squirrels must have got me. Avenge my death! Aaaavveeeeeennnge meeeeeeeee!"

The boys laughed and Nick swiveled to his brother. "Jarryd. Last words again?"

"Hmm…last time Greyson blew me outta the water. Let him go first."

"Okay. Liam."

Liam hid.

"Yeah, Greyson, then."

Greyson shook his head. "None of us are going to die tonight. I'll save mine for later. Years later."

Someone cleared his throat. Austin walked in from the doorway. "Are you sure, Greyson?"

"What?"

"Are you sure? No one will die tonight?"

Greyson nodded, looking oddly at Austin. "Yeah. We're going to do this right."

Austin paused, staring a long time at Greyson's face. Then, when the room felt awkward, Austin smiled. "Good. I hope you're right."

Nick panned over from Austin to Greyson, who put his hand over the lens. "I think that's enough, Nick."

"No, I haven't done mine yet!" Jarryd argued, jumping in front of Greyson. "I just want to say…Mom, Dad…I hope your lives go on

169

after I'm gone. You can adopt if you want. I'm cool with that. Or get a dog. Whatever floats your boat. But not a really handsome boy that's better looking than I am – if that's possible – because then you'd forget about me. And no really awesome dog that does everything you tell it to. Cuz then you'd think it was better than me, too..."

Liam smiled and gave him bunny ears behind his back.

"...and if you have time, please find Greyson's dad for him. I'm sure his mom will miss him if Greyson is goners as well. Peace!"

Jarryd turned to Greyson as Liam lowered his bunny ears. Greyson slowly let the words sink in. *Mom could be alone...*

The camera beeped and Nick closed the screen just as Brandon walked in, looking at his watch. "You boys ready for 'the dance'?"

When Greyson didn't answer, Nick answered yes for him. Jarryd and Liam carried their changes of clothes to Brandon and had him pack them into his backpack. Greyson snapped from his short daydream and added his pile of clothes to Brandon's backpack. While zipping it closed, Brandon looked over his shoulder at him and winked. He was on their side this time.

And at his side, they left in a pack, umbrellas covering them like smoothed rocks in a babbling brook. The rain had not let up since the afternoon and the ground was beyond soppy. Streams poured over the lower dips in the sidewalk and gushed from the gutters above. There was a flash flood warning for their area, and Morris River, which ran on the western border of Morris, was rapidly approaching flood levels.

Despite the wet, kids came flooding into the Rec Building from all angles like it was raining children and the lowest part of camp was inside. The DJ's music was already thumping, and flashing, multicolored lights drew the kids in.

Glancing in all directions, Greyson caught sight of the raincoat's tail for just a fraction of a second before it disappeared around the bend. He was following. The plan had begun.

Chapter 15

Wednesday Night

The dance was hopping. Boys, girls, and counselors joined in the mass of humanity in front of the DJ's giant table of CDs. The pop songs blared through four giant-sized speakers and red, green, blue, and yellow lights flashed to the beat, lighting the swarm of flailing arms and smiling faces. Every boy seemed to wear the same thing – but some popped their collars while others decided to play it low-key. Some girls wore dresses their mothers' and fathers' had approved – and others obviously did not.

"Snap! You see her?"

"Jarryd!" Greyson chastised. "We're looking for Chris, remember?"

"Oh, yeah. He looks kind of like you, right?"

Greyson stood on his tiptoes and looked into the crowd that seemed to convulse like an ocean writhing with each splash of bass. "That *is* the point. He's the closest camper to my size and hair color."

Jarryd tiptoed next to him. "There! Right in the middle."

"You see him? Go remind him to meet us in…," he peeked at his watch, "…four minutes."

"Got it."

Jarryd popped his own pink collar and piled headfirst into the thick of things.

Greyson watched him make his way through the dancers, but swung his head upward to the balcony. The balcony usually overlooked the entire three-gym area, but for tonight the middle gym was closed off from the rest with giant curtains – *apparently to make the noise louder and the stink stinkier.*

On the balcony, an elderly couple in Morris College t-shirts and mesh shorts leaned against the railing, watching their campers. The Jensens were kind, but in absolute control. No one – counselors or campers – dared to cross them.

Greyson scanned the rest of the balcony – a few parental-looking types, a head counselor, the camp photographer – no one wearing a navy blue raincoat. *Where is he?*

Jarryd reached the boy, Chris, and spoke with him before beginning his long journey out of the mass. Chris nodded, met eyes with Greyson, and looked at his watch.

"Greyson."

He turned to her. She wore an all-white dress, modest and elegant. Around her neck, a thin gold chain with a shining heart hung close to her body. Her hair was up and wound into some sort of layered cinnamon roll at the back of her head, with some curly blonde locks dangling down like curly fries. He realized two things…she was beautiful, and he was hungry.

Can I have an advance on those kisses?

"Hey. You're all dressed up," he said.

I'm an idiot.

Melinda stepped out from behind her. "He's wearing the fanny pack. Want me to take it off of 'em?"

Sydney held Melinda back and shook her head.

"Where'd you get that shirt?" Sydney asked.

He looked down at the polo he'd gotten from his mother last Christmas. "Uh…I don't know. Macy's? Is that a store?"

Sydney had seen that shirt in her daydream – and the dream hadn't ended well. Suddenly she felt paranoid. She glanced left, then right, then up at the balcony, searching for Mantis. "Have you seen the shadow?"

"Yeah. He was outside a minute ago."

Together they surveyed the dance one last time. Out of the corner of his eye, Greyson saw a man approaching the Jensens. Greyson turned away and whispered. "Don't look now. He's up by the Jensens. He's wearing a janitor's suit or something."

Sydney matched his gaze and exhaled quickly. "Let's dance, then."

172

"Huh?"

"Come on!'

She grabbed his hand and pulled him into the mix as Jarryd passed them.

"Hey, baybay!"

"Hey, Alvin."

"Alvin? Who's...oh."

She dragged him with her some ways into the crowd and found a breathable gap. Greyson shook his head and tried to resist, but she was strong and everybody seemed to be watching. When they arrived she spun around and grabbed his other hand, facing him.

"Ready?"

"No. Never."

"Come on. Just try it. Step left then right."

She stepped left, then right, still holding his hands in front of her. He arched his eyebrows. "That's it?"

"Yeah. Join in."

Greyson shrugged and mirrored her stepping with the beat.

I don't mind the handholding, looking into her eyes part...

"This looks stupid."

Sydney scoffed. "That's cuz you're not feeling the music. Swing your hips more. Like this."

She swung her hips with each step and Greyson threw her hands down. "Uh, uh. No way I'm swinging my hips."

"What?" Sydney sneered at him and huffed. "You know, looks only get you so far with women. You got to have some charm or something, too."

"Charm? Isn't that a toilet paper brand?"

Sydney stared at him. "So you talk about toilet paper?"

"You brought it up. What time is it?" Greyson glanced at his watch. *Perfect escape.* "Got to go. It's time."

"Already?"

"Yeah. Get changed. Meet ya in the boy's locker room. See ya."

Sydney shook her head in disbelief. *Worst date ever.*

Greyson edged into the crowd and imagined what he looked like to Mantis above. He would see just his red hat and polo shirt from above, and maybe some of his brown hair sticking out the sides. He would be seeing that all night.

He headed underneath the balcony toward the bathroom. Looking back when he went out of Mantis' view, he saw Chris making his way through the crowd. Jarryd was over to the side, waiting a minute after Greyson left as he was told.

He swung open the bathroom door and made a beeline for the lockers. Some boys were scattered around the locker room, changing into swimming suits or searching their lockers for extra body spray.

As fast as he could while walking to his locker, he stripped on the way – hat, polo shirt, fanny pack, cargo shorts. By the time he reached locker 22, he held his clothes in his arms and little kids were staring.

"What?"

The boys snapped back to what they were doing. A moment later, Chris walked in and ran up to him. Greyson waited for him and handed him his clothes, but took the fanny pack for himself.

"Alright. Get dressed. And remember…always face away from the Jensens."

Chris nodded and held out his hand. Greyson unzipped his fanny pack and fished out a rolled bill. He put it in his look-alike's hand.

"Ten now, ten tomorrow morning."

"Nice. Thanks."

Greyson nodded. "And please. Take care of the hat."

"Yeah, sure," he said flippantly.

Greyson stood in front of him, staring. "No. I'm serious. Lose it and you'll lose the ability to speak. Okay?"

Chris' eyes lit up and he gulped. "Okay. Sure."

"Thanks. We appreciate it."

"What are you doing to…?"

"Just get dressed."

"Okay."

Chris quickly dressed as Jarryd, Nick, Austin, Liam, and Brandon entered within the minute. When Chris was ready, Greyson set his hat on the look-alike's head just like he would wear it and sent him out. "Have fun."

Chris looked back at the group suspiciously as Brandon escorted him out. As soon as he was gone, Brandon locked the door.

"Okay, make this fast."

He threw his backpack to them and they tore into it. Dark clothes abounded, walkie-talkies crackled on and off as they tested them, and Brandon speed-walked to the fire door in the back of the locker room. Sticking his key into it, he waited for Greyson, Nick, and Liam to get dressed.

Austin and Jarryd helped the other three, pulling their shirts over them and tying their dark sneakers. Jarryd pulled Greyson's fanny pack around him and snapped it tight. When the last knot was tied, Greyson, Nick, and Liam stood side by side like three burglars or ninjas – they still hadn't decided which was cooler.

Brandon turned his key and the flashing red light blinked off. "You boys ready?"

Greyson looked to each one of them and nodded. "Jarryd, thanks for letting her go."

Jarryd shrugged and held up his walkie. "Keep me informed."

"Austin, don't let the shadow or the Jensens move without us knowing."

"Will do," Austin said plainly.

TapTap.

A thin knock on the door. Jarryd ran to it and unlocked it. Looking through it a crack, he pulled it open. Sydney came sprinting in with dark sweat pants and a black t-shirt. Her hair was still up.

"Nice hair."

"Shut up. We ready?"

Without explanation, Liam suddenly spread his arms wide and lifted his chin in the air. After a brief awkward pause, Greyson hugged him. The others followed, wrapping their arms around each other in a solid group hug. Brandon watched from the door with a patient smile, his key still turned. Slowly, he pushed the door open, letting in a gust of wet air.

"Go, kids. I have to get back out there and supervise."

The hug dissolved and Liam wiped his teary eyes.

"Good luck all. Stay low and they'll never know what hit 'em."

Mantis leaned over the rail and tried to look underneath the balcony. The boy had been in the bathroom for five minutes. *Had the little freak escaped?*

"What are you looking for, Ray?" Mrs. Jensen asked him.

"Ah, just checking the traffic flow to the bathroom. Jim was thinking of adding another entrance the other day."

"Hmm...that would be nice."

Mantis nodded and gave her his best fake smile. *Dumb broad.*

He had to check the bathroom. Maybe the kid was just dumping a load.

"Ray..."

Mantis stopped in his tracks and turned reluctantly to Mrs. Jensen. She pulled him in and pointed out to the crowd. "We've been doing this for 26 years."

"Yeah. It's amazing," he lied through his teeth.

"And each year the kids dance closer and closer together!"

"Uh, huh. Kids these days." He could strangle each and every one of them.

"Why *is* that, you think?"

The kid still hadn't come out. Did I lose the mark? Should I radio in?

"I don't know. Maybe it's television."

"You're right! I watched a show the other day, and there was this lady with the skimpiest outfit. It was like she was trying to show as much skin as possible without freezing to death!"

Should I push her off the balcony? It would be the most fun I'd had since Lebanon.

"And that boy. What is it, Bob? Greyson?"

Bob looked at his wife. "Yeah. Greyson Gray. Got to keep our eyes on that one."

The boy walked out from underneath the balcony, his red hat sticking out like a rose among weeds. He went immediately into the middle of the crowd and joined in the dancing.

Mrs. Jensen nodded and pointed him out to Mantis. "See him, Ray? In the red hat. Poor boy lost his father just months ago. Isn't that sad? Can you imagine the hurt he must feel inside?"

Mantis shook his head, finally breathing easy again. *Yes. He'll be feeling it.*

The door shut behind them with a click. There was no doorknob on the outside of the door, so there was no going back. Greyson knelt in the wet grass and took out his walkie. Sydney, Nick, then Liam knelt beside him.

"JearBear, come in."

"That's a 10-4," Jarryd responded.

"Aussie, you there?"

"I can hear you well," Austin replied.

"Nickel, how about you?" he looked to his left.

Nick raised his walkie and spoke into it with an echo. "Good to go."

Liam watched the rain fall on his face, squinting at the drops and opening his mouth to let them in.

Greyson looked at Sydney with a perk of excitement; then he swung his gaze to their surroundings and cringed. The observatory shone with a dull glow across the rain-streaked football field. On the far side of the field, he could see a group of three figures walking toward it in a cluster of pink umbrellas. He glanced at his watch – 7:56. They would be right on time.

"Let's roll."

Greyson bolted along the side of the building and curled toward the darkness on the edge of campus. Liam slipped on the grass and fell to his hands but scrambled to his feet, rain and mud spraying from his heels as he slapped across the grassy campus, avoiding the lights and windows.

"Is our – shadow still there?" Greyson whispered into the walkie in breathy gasps as he ran.

"Yeah. Balcony. Taking the fake."

"Good. Out."

He lowered the walkie and picked up the pace. Sydney and Nick matched his strides; Liam struggled in their watery wakes. They ran for over a minute on the outer edges of a tree line, circling around the way they had taken to the observatory the first day, but trying to keep well out of sight of that entrance.

When they reached the end of the Science Building, Greyson finally slowed and slid to the corner, peeking around it. The observatory was another 100 yards away. From this angle, they could see both sides – the back entrance and the front, where the cluster of girls approached the door. Two large men stood outside smoking cigarettes. He nodded to Nick. This is where he would stay.

Muffled beats of music from the dance still sounded through the pitter-patter of the rain as they stared at the coming scene. Squinting through the streaks of water that soaked their hair and dripped from their brows, they watched as the cluster of girls approached the two men.

This could be interesting.

Lisa lowered her mirror as they came to the front entrance; in place of where her mirror had been, a grim-looking man with a short beard looked her up and down. She returned his glare with her two girlfriends by her side, all wearing shades of pink with matching make-up.

"What are you girls doing here?"

"What is it to you?" Lisa replied with attitude.

The bearded man turned to his friend with an odd smile. The other man held a lit cigarette and tapped out some ash, uninterested.

"Uh...you aren't supposed to be here, are you now?"

Lisa looked to her friends and jutted out her hips. "What would you know? Can we get past?"

The bearded man laughed and hit his friend with his elbow. "Ha, feisty one. This place is closed at nights. University use only."

The man's friend held out his lit cigarette to her. "Wanna smoke, little girl?"

The men broke into a fit of laughter and the girls grew angrier. Melanie took a step forward.

"Our friend Carl invited us. He wants to see us again."

Both men's mouths popped open; the man on the right dropped his cigarette. After a long pause, they turned toward each other, eyes wide open in awe. Then, a chuckle rose up in their chests and threatened to break out in loud laughter.

The bearded man took out a cell phone and punched a number. "Jack! Jack, you got to come hear this."

The response mumbled in. "What? What is it?"

"He-he-haha! You just gotta come here, man."

"Alright, hold on."

Greyson clenched a bunch of his pants and released. *Yes, yes!*

"He's moving. We go now. Fast."

Brandon slid outside the dark office and quietly locked the door behind him. He looked down the hall both ways – empty. Glancing at

179

the small key in his fist, he had second thoughts. *What am I doing? I'm stealing from the camp? Am I trying to get fired? Not only fired – arrested!*

Before his conscience got the best of him, he clenched his fist over the key and bounded to the stairs. The pounding music shook the ground underneath his feet like small explosions and he even felt himself walking to its infectious beat. Somehow he felt like he was in a movie – one of those caper films where the good guys were misunderstood thieves. But those guys were usually geniuses, acrobats, or suave spies. He just wasn't.

He walked into the gym area and took a deep breath. Looking innocent was hard. *How did Greyson always do it so well?*

Chase found him by the drinking fountain and shook his hand. He felt the keys slip from his palm and almost panicked, but the deed was done.

They stalked to the edge of the observatory, out of view of the camera and the guard who walked slowly around the rounded corner to the front entrance, leaving the back exposed.

Greyson put his back to the steel wall and began to shimmy along its side toward the door while Sydney and Liam followed, mimicking his every move.

"You guys are good," Nick whispered from the walkie inside Greyson's fanny pack. "He's taking the bait."

They came to the keypad that shone with a sharp red glow. In this case, red was a good thing. It meant the bad guys didn't want anybody inside.

Greyson slipped his fingers inside his pack and pulled out the white keycard. He swiped it down through the slot and the keypad lit green.

Beep. Click!

Craning his neck to see the camera's angle, he reached to the door's handle and pulled it open just far enough to sneak his foot in. Then, with enough leverage, he pushed with his foot and arm to swing the heavy door open just enough for his thin body to slip in. Sydney followed like his shadow and Liam behind.

Immediately, they were engulfed in darkness. This time, there was no construction light. Another good thing. Darkness was their friend tonight.

Greyson held the door open as Sydney and Liam walked inside. Then reaching in the fanny pack, he felt the zip-lock bag and pulled it out. Using the light from outside, he opened it and removed the folded piece of paper covered in peanut butter.

He peeked outside, and finding it still empty, he reached around with the peanut-butter-paper in hand. He found the keypad's slot with his pinky, guided the paper in and forced it down in a slow swipe. He ran it through one more time, making sure to get the peanut butter deep inside the scanner without spreading it all over. No one would be using their keycard to get through that door any time soon.

He pulled his foot from the door and it clicked closed in a flood of darkness.

"F-flashlight?"

Greyson dug in his ever-useful fanny pack and took out a mini-flashlight. "I feel like Batman," he whispered as he turned it on his face.

Sydney smiled. "That makes me Catwoman. And Liam would be Robin."

Greyson shone the light to Liam. "R-robin sucks."

They stifled their laughter and turned toward the open hall. The small ring of light lit only a fragment of the dank, dilapidated hall. Every corner seemed a perfect place for a murderer or Indian warrior to hide. Only the flashlight meant safety, and only for a moment until it bounced away, leaving the darkness to flood back in.

The ground was a perilous mixture of broken tile and crusted dirt; they tripped several times, often running into each other. But soon they made it past the old lobby with the front desk and past the odd sign now on the ground. He lit it with the flashlight: 'Take care. Careless mistakes have great stakes.'

You got that right.

The walkie crackled. "It seems to be getting heated outside."

"Just let us in! It's getting cold outside!"

"No way. Carl will have to wait for another night, ladies!"

"UGHHH!"

Lisa looked at Melanie and Whatsherface looked at both of them. Hadn't Greyson told them to say that Carl had invited them? Had they said it right?

"Ca-rull! You know him, right?"

The bearded man nodded condescendingly. "Yeeeeaaaah. Ca-rull is a friend of ours."

"He's dreamy isn't he?" Melanie blurted.

The men snickered. "Are you girls for real?"

Even Melanie knew she sounded stupid. "Well, whatever! He said he would dance with us under the stars…and heaven would be brought down to us!"

The men burst into laughter, but stifled it, trying not to attract attention from the entire campus.

"What? Are you making fun of us?"

They were snorting and heaving with contained laughter. "No, no – we're definitely making fun of him!"

"Oh." Melanie looked to Lisa again and shrugged.

"Is he even *in* there?"

The bearded man sighed deeply, catching his breath from the laughter. "Whew! Yeah. Yeah he is. Should we go get him, guys? Show him what we found?"

Greyson shook precariously, his foot planted in Liam and Sydney's cupped hands. The flashlight lit their maneuver from the floor, pointing up from its perch on a box. They knelt at first, then pushed him up toward the ceiling where Greyson snatched the edge of the broken vent shaft and guided his upper body inside. Sydney and Liam pushed at his feet with all their might until Greyson disappeared inside, only the rope tied to his climbing harness trailing from his backside like a tail.

The bent shaft shook and crinkled, dust falling from the ceiling like snow. It looked like any minute the whole thing would collapse into the hall, but for now it held the boy and his hundred pounds and change.

"You okay?" Sydney whispered.

"Yeah," he whispered from the vent.

Down the long, dark shaft there was a small box of light that he hoped was the control room – where the muddy tunnel had led before the bad guys had drilled a steel panel over it.

Ever so faintly in the distance, he could hear a soft voice.

Dr. Emory watched the final preparations like a child waiting for Santa to come down the chimney. *Finally*, he thought. *Finally*.

SquareJaw stood behind him, stoic and tired. His cell phone suddenly shook to life. "Carl, come to the front. No questions."

SquareJaw walked from the room without a glance from Emory. *What could they want so close to zero-hour? It had better be pizza delivery.*

Mantis watched the red hat bob up and down with the rhythm. The kid was boring to watch. All he did was watch the DJ and dance with no one in particular. It seemed like his friends had even abandoned him. And he sucked at dancing. No wonder they had left him.

Wait a second.

He leaned closer, over the rail.

Where was the – where was it?

The boy jumped up and down, his waist popping in and out of view. *Oh, no. No, he couldn't have...*

Greyson crawled, closer and closer through the cramped tunnel that shook like an elevator with a large, gyrating crowd packed inside. Though it could collapse any second, the light grew brighter and he could make out the opposite wall now. *This could actually work.*

Brandon walked toward the Jensens, where he would take supervision duty. A gruff man dressed in a janitor suit brushed past him, muttering to himself in tunnel vision. He took a double take at him but shrugged it off, coming up to the directors.

"Hi, Brandon!" Mrs. Jensen greeted him. "How's it going? Better?"
I just stole one of your gators.

"Yeah. The kids are loads of fun." Brandon feigned a smile.

Mrs. Jensen nodded with a grandmotherly glimmer in her eye.

"Who was that guy?" Brandon pointed back toward the stairwell. "I haven't seen him around before."

"Oh, Ray? He's our maintenance director. He came on two years ago and did a fantastic job remodeling the observatory."

Brandon's heart jumped. *He was their shadow. Where had he been going so fast?*

"Oh, I forgot something. Sorry, I got to go."

Mrs. Jensen reached out to him. "Oh, you sure? If you ever need anything..."

"Yeah, thanks...," he said backing up. He turned and sprinted to the stairs.

SquareJaw opened the door and peaked out. The guards Jack, Mike, and Vince stood outside waiting for him. "What? What is it?"

"You have visitors," Vince said with a smile.

He stepped through the door and gazed around the men. Three young girls stood with pink umbrellas and pink dresses. They stared at him and gasped. "That's not Carl!"

Greyson shimmied closer and closer to the edge of the shaft where the control room lay below. He eyed the two tall, golden keys, still sticking up from the control panel, about ten feet apart. He would somehow have to grab both of them and climb back into the vent – preferably before getting caught. Only one man stood inside - Dr. Emory - his face fixed on the window to where the telescope was.

Crap. I can't do anything if he keeps staring like that. I can be fast, but not that fast.

Sydney fed Greyson more slack as he slid further in. *He had to be getting close.*

"Away, come in, this is Aussie."

Sydney reached down to the walkie he had left by the flashlight. She held the talk button. "Yes?"

"We could have trouble. You better get out of there."

She turned and met eyes with Liam. "Why?"

"He's gone. I think he's coming down – oh, there he is. He's coming toward…oh no."

SquareJaw arched his eyebrows and wiped the rain from his bald head. "Yes, I am! Who are you and what do you want?"

Lisa almost threw her umbrella at him. "Is this a joke? Where's Greyson?"

Melanie gasped and threw her hands over Lisa's mouth. Lisa's eyes went wide.

SquareJaw looked to Vince and Vince at Mike. "What did you say? Greyson?"

Lisa shook her head and pulled Melanie's hands down. "No. I didn't say his name."

Melanie sighed and rolled her eyes. Even she wasn't *that* stupid.

SquareJaw shoved Jack. "Get back to your post! Now!"

Jack took off.

SquareJaw snatched his cell phone from his pocket and dialed his first speed-dial. "Stay here, girls. I'll call Greyson for you quick."

The phone rang and someone on the other line picked up.

"Yes, Carl?"

"We have a situation."

Mantis marched through the gym, his fist clenched and teeth gritted. The boy in the red hat still bounced with the beat, children all around him.

He pushed a boy to his left and shoved through a group of girls. "Hey!"

He ignored them and plowed his way into the middle of the crowd. Kids shouted and jumped out of the way in fright; the boy in the red hat was still oblivious, facing the DJ and flailing his arms up and down. The crowd cleared from around him and it became clear – the kid was not wearing his fanny pack.

He reached out and grabbed the boy by his shoulder, spinning him around violently; the boy stared up at him like a deer in the headlights.

It wasn't him. He was gone.

Mantis pulled the boy's hat from his head and threw it to the ground. He snapped his gaze around the dance, searching for his mark. Children and counselors gaped at him alike, but no one dared advance on him.

And then he saw him behind a set of bleachers. One of Greyson's friends. The one with chubby cheeks and long hair; he held a black device to his mouth and he was speaking into it. The boy suddenly caught the look and froze. He jammed the walkie into his pants, but it was too late. They caught eyes again and he knew.

Mantis looked around. "Sorry about that." He wiped the look-alike's shoulder off. "I'm not feeling the best."

And he left – in Jarryd's direction.

Greyson watched from above as Dr. Emory tapped the device on his ear and cursed under his breath. And then – like a miracle – he left. The room was empty.

Greyson waited just a few seconds longer for Emory to get out of ear shot, and then pulled twice on the rope behind him – the signal that he was going down.

He gripped the edge of the steel shaft and readied himself for the face-first fall to the floor below. He had to trust Sydney and Liam. They would give him enough pull to gently lower him to the floor. At least – that was the plan.

The rope tugged at his harness, but too hard. *What the heck?* He slid back away from the opening and had to pull at the edge to keep from being dragged back into the vent. The rope continued to pull at him, almost pulling his pants off, and his fingers dug painfully into the sharp metal lip to the vent. *What were they doing?*

Sydney and Liam tugged at the rope.

"Tug! Tug! Tug!"

It was Tug of War all over again, and Liam didn't want to lose again.

Their walkie continued to crackle at them. "The guard is coming back! He's almost to the door!" Nickel warned

Then JerBear's panicked voice came on. "The shadow knows – and he's after me – run!"

Sweat started beading at Sydney's forehead, but she only pulled harder. He had to get out of there!

"Tug! Tug!"

The rope would not give.

"W-w-wait! It's stuck!"

Liam let go and pulled at Sydney's hands. When she let go, the rope flung into the shaft like a rubber band.

"Aaggh!"

They jumped at it and snagged it from the air in a sharp jerk; the force almost pulled their arms from their bodies – but it was secure.

Greyson hung outside the shaft, limply hanging against the wall only by the harness around his groin. He moaned and tried to get his bearings. One moment he'd been pulling himself out the shaft inch by inch, the next he was flying through the air before being jerked back against the wall, butt-first.

Regaining his composure, he fumbled with the straps, swinging and bouncing against the wall. Echoing down the hall, he heard a heavy door close. Was someone coming back in, or leaving? *Can't tell. Go fast. Faster!*

Emory closed the door behind him and scanned the girls' faces. SquareJaw watched his reaction.

"Uh...these girls say they were looking for Greyson here."

Emory flinched at the name, but his face curled into a smile. "Girls. Greyson made a mistake. He thought he could invite you here, but he could not. You must go back to where you should be, and tell no one of this – for his sake."

He turned on his heels and left no room for discussion. SquareJaw swiped the door for him and followed him in. As soon as the door clicked behind him, his earphone beeped.

"I lost him," Mantis warned. "It was a trick."

Emory shouted down the hall. "We know!"

He tapped the receiver and turned to SquareJaw, who pulled a pistol from the shoulder holster under his jacket.

"He's in here. Find him. Kill him."

His fingers flew over the straps, but they were too tight and he couldn't get a grip. And then he realized. He *could* just unhinge the carabineer. But it would hurt.

Lining his feet up with the ground, he grasped the metal oval.

Snap.

The rope and its carabineer flew into the shaft above him with a loud clang.

He fell like a rock, and the floor met him hard.

Oomph!

His feet and chest took most of the brunt, but he was free. Catching his breath and rolling to his feet, he looked up. A door closed again. Footsteps – getting closer.

He scrambled to his feet and hobbled to the control panel; he grabbed the first key with both hands and it popped free easily. He looked at it for a moment, gleaming in front of the window.

But then...the window came into focus.

His muscles tightened and he couldn't breathe. His eyes glazed in wonder, his gaze following the massive object from its base up its thick shaft to the rounded tip just below the retractable observatory ceiling. He stood frozen with key in hand, and all of the blood in his body fell to his feet, sending a long shiver down his spine.

"Oh, *geez.*"

Pointed toward the sky - a colossal missile.

Chapter 16

Jarryd skirted around the bleachers, looking back over his shoulder at the large-eyed man who walked with long strides toward him, his eyes dark and evil.

His heart beat like a drum in his chest and his legs felt heavy as he made the fastest line toward the far gym's exit. He raced around a group of boys with swimming towels and turned a corner into a hall of offices; frantic, his hand shot to a doorknob and twisted it left and right, but it wouldn't turn. He snapped across the hall and checked the opposite door. Locked!

Please, no. Please, no. He bounded to another door…locked! And another…locked!

His heart pounded in his throat as he glanced down the hall. Empty still. He glanced the other direction. At the end of the hall was one last door – a dead end.

He turned to run and flew toward the far door and slammed into it, grasping the doorknob. It opened. *Thank God!*

Gasping for breath, he pushed it open and rushed into the darkness. He quickly turned and caught a glimpse of the man bearing down on him; he slammed it shut.

The room had no windows and no light. In a frenzy, his fingers brushed over the doorknob, searching for the lock. Nothing to push, nothing to pull. *WHERE IS IT!?*

He feverishly searched with both hands; his right hand finally landing on the lock above the knob –

BANG!

A skull-jarring bang sent his body hurtling into the room and tumbling over the carpet. He rolled to a stop, but the world spun around him and a dull ache behind his eyes blurred his vision. Another concussion. The second in two days. But this one was worse. A man stood over him, silhouetted in the doorway from the light in the hall.

He felt something wet dribbling down his nose as the door slowly closed out the light.

"We know!"

The shout pierced Greyson's ears and shook him from his reverie.

Keys.

He dashed to the second key, pulled it from its hole, and pushed both into his fanny pack, zipping it secure. He dug into the tile and burst toward the shaft, but stopped on a dime. The shaft was eight feet up. The rope was inside the shaft.

Footsteps slapped outside.

With no other options, he shot to the swivel chair and rolled it underneath the vent; balancing his left foot on the seat, he jumped up and snatched the edge of the shaft, sending the chair spinning to the center of the room.

He pulled himself up and into the narrow hole, not looking behind him.

His feet wriggled inside just as Emory and SquareJaw came marching around the corner. The realization came fast – spinning chair, missing keys, shifting light in the vent.

"He's in the vent!"

Greyson crawled like a maniac, the vent shifting and shaking screws from their place. The rope lay limp a few feet in front of him.

"PULL!" he shouted, echoing down the thin metal passage.

He snagged the end of the rope and they pulled from the other side. He shot like a bullet through the barrel, his stomach and harness sliding along the steel like a painfully dry waterslide.

BANG!

Like lightning then thunder, a flash followed by a reverberating blast ricocheted like clanging cymbals all around him as he rocketed toward the end of the tunnel.

BANGBANGBANG!

The bullets sent sparks flying around him as he burst from the tunnel, head-first toward Liam and Sydney.

Falling!

They held out their arms and bent their knees in their best brace-for-impact stance, and he hit their arms in a speeding belly flop. The speed was too much and pulled them to the dusty floor in an awkward pile of flailing limbs. The flashlight bumped from its perch and fell to the floor.

The impact shook their brains, and it took a moment to regain coherent thought.

"Ugghhh…nice catch…you alright?"

He pushed himself away from Liam's chest and found the ground. Sydney squirmed free, rubbing her forehead.

BANGBANGBANG!

"AAGH!" Liam scrambled to his feet and raced down the dark hall, holding his hands over his ears and whimpering.

"Liam! LIAM!"

He cut into the pitch-black lobby, ignoring them.

Greyson winced as he pushed himself up and snagged the flashlight and walkie.

"They're *shooting* at us!" Sydney exclaimed in disbelief.

"I know!"

Greyson reached out and pulled Sydney to her feet, racing away from the fireworks behind them.

The walkie buzzed with activity. "Come in! The guard is going around to the other entrance! The peanut butter worked and I see Chase on the way. You're open!"

"We're coming!"

They raced through the dark hall hand in hand, the light bouncing ahead of them. They stopped at the lobby and pointed the light at the front desk.

"Liam! We've got to go! Where are you?"

Greyson scrambled over fallen chairs and boxes, and swung around the desk. Liam was curled into a ball beneath a small pile of cardboard boxes.

"Liam!"

He dashed to him and pulled at his arm; Liam resisted, squealing and shaking his head.

"Liam, please!" Greyson dragged him by the legs, but he reached and grabbed the desk, pulling away from Greyson's grasp.

The walkie shouted. "Chase is waiting! Where are you?"

"Liam!"

Liam curled closer to himself, ignoring his pleas.

"Greyson!" Sydney shouted. "We can come back for him!"

Greyson swung the flashlight to her.

"We can't leave him behind!"

She stood, eyes pleading with him, hands pressed together like in prayer. He swung back to his roommate, in shock; Liam whined and shivered, oblivious.

Then, Greyson shivered, too, and the picture of his friend, curled into a ball burned itself into his mind, forever to be a dark twinge of guilt in his conscience. "Liam…hide here. We'll come back for you. I promise!"

He turned, cursed to himself, and left.

Jarryd felt Mantis' hand brushing over his cheek, as tenderly as could be with rough, calloused knuckles. The room was bathed in dark, and sounds slipped in and out of his consciousness. The rough finger wiped under his nose and took the blood with it. Then, warm liquid splattered on his face. The man had flicked it all over him.

"What's your name, boy?"

Jarryd moaned and tried to sit up. Mantis helped him and pushed him back into a desk to keep him up. "Jarryd," he muttered.

"Ah…that's right. Jarryd Aldeman. How's your brother, Nicholas?"

Jarryd tried to move his swimming eyes to the man, but there was barely enough light to make out his figure. "Uh-uh-are...are you...are you Paul Newton?"

SMACK!

His neck cracked with the blow and his jaw seemed to pop out of place.

Jarryd began to cry, the pain and fear swelling over him.

"I ask the questions. Tell me...what are you doing with that walkie-talkie? Where is it?"

The man reached down and searched the boy for it. He slid it from his pocket, faked like he turned it on, and held it to his mouth. He spoke, his deep voice faking innocence.

"Hello? Greyson? Are you *there*?" He waited for the fake reply, watching the boy's reaction. While waiting, he wiped the tears from Jarryd's cheeks. "What are you crying for, boy?"

The door burst open and Brandon stood over them both, a baseball bat in his hands. Mantis stood up, the sudden light flashing in his pupils. The moment of confusion played in Brandon's favor; he raised the bat and swung once, connecting with the man's head in a sickly thud.

Beep. Click!

Greyson and Sydney pushed the door open and the night's cool light shone on the waiting green gator where Chase sat in the driver's seat, looking over his back and motioning them on.

"Hustle, y'all! He's coming back!"

Sydney jumped on the front seat and Greyson swung himself into the back cargo bed. The gator spun in the wet grass, churning mud beneath it until it caught traction and jerked forward. Chase put the pedal to the metal and squealed onto the sidewalk.

"Watch behind you!" warned the walkie.

A guard ran around to the back entrance and immediately saw the fleeing vehicle. He took aim with a large rifle.

Greyson pressed himself into the bouncing bed, but there was no shot. The guard lowered the rifle and spoke into his walkie.

The gator curled around the football field and zoomed toward the Rec Building. The rain hit their faces like icy needles and bounced off with the wind. The brief respite of the drive gave Greyson the first spare time to reflect, but much of what had just happened seemed to be beyond reach. *What am I doing? Is this really happening? Can I turn the movie off now and go to bed? Will Liam be okay?*

Chase expertly chose the smoothest path and took corners at crazy speeds. After turning the final corner, he skidded to a stop at the swimming pool entrance – their rendezvous point, where they would all return after one key had been delivered to the police. Until then, it was the safe-haven for one key just in case the other key should fall into the hands of the Emory or his henchmen. They had rightly predicted that he needed both, and they planned to never let that happen.

Chase pushed the gear into park and jumped out the open side with his hand outstretched. Greyson pulled one of the keys from his fanny pack and slapped it in his hand. "Guard it with your life. It's a missile."

Chase took a step away, but turned back. "What?"

Sydney turned to him as well as he leapt into the vacant driver's seat. "The telescope. It's not. It's a missile."

Chase smirked in surprise. "Nah way. Don't mess with me."

"I'm not."

Greyson pushed the gator into gear and held the brake. Squinting his eyes even in the dark, Chase shook his head once before running to the swimming pool's entrance where Sammy watched and waited.

Sydney hung on to the front dash with both hands, still trying to wrap her mind around what he had said. "A *missile?*"

"You know? A rocket with a boom? They're using the observatory as a missile silo!"

He released the brake and pressed the gas. The gator blasted forward, snapping their necks back with acceleration. *Oops. Too fast.*

"You want me to drive?"

He scoffed. "Yeah, the fate of the world resting on a female driver..."

"WHAT?"

He held back a smile and whipped around the dark side of the Rec Building. The hum of the gator's engine bounced off the brick wall – the only thing between them and the dancing hordes of kids being kids.

The walkie crackled, "This is Nickel. Where are you guys?"

Sydney took the walkie from her driver and held it close in the wind and rain. "We're almost to the road. Tex is at the rendezvous."

"Um...please go fast. They have a car."

Sydney squinted through the wet wind at Greyson in desperation. She shouted into the walkie. "A car?"

"More like an SUV. They just went out of view. I can't see which way they went."

Greyson sighed and wiped a hand across his eyes as he pulled off the grass onto a cement ramp and bumped to the road's asphalt. "Tell him to get back to the rendezvous. Everyone meet there until the cops come."

Sydney relayed the message. "Get to the rendezvous! Get everyone there and stay put! We'll be back soon with reinforcements!"

Greyson eyed her.

"And if we're not...they can't have your key."

The walkie crackled off, and a car passed them the opposite way, its headlights nearly blinding them.

"Roger that. See you soon."

The gator sped along the wet roads, splashing through thin rivers and puddles that reflected the streetlights in streaks of yellows and whites. The dance's music gradually faded behind them and they passed the sign for Morris College as the campus grew smaller. Their gator sped on, alone on empty and silent roads.

Brandon ran to Jarryd and held his face in his hands. Blood streaked across his face and his right cheek was already swollen. His eyes swam listlessly in his tears despite heavy blinking.

"Jarryd? Are you okay? Can you hear me?"

Jarryd sniffed and the blood drained down his throat. He jerked forward, coughing and gagging. Brandon reached over him to the desk and pulled down a box of Kleenex; Jarryd snagged one and coughed into it.

He looked up at him, his eyes finally finding a fixed spot. "Did you get 'em?"

Brandon glanced over his shoulder at the man's crumpled body. "Yeah. I got him."

Jarryd blew some chunky stuff from his nose and made a face at it. "Nasty."

He wiped the tears from his eyes and began to put the Kleenexes in a pile.

"Stay seated. Don't try to move, okay?"

He stood up and walked over to the man. Blood oozed from his ear and open mouth. *Did I kill him? No. I couldn't have. I didn't hit him that hard, did I?*

He knelt over him and checked his pulse. Still alive. He was relieved and panicked at the same time. Quickly, he searched through his janitor suit. A wallet. A cell phone.

He ran his hands down the sides of the man's legs. When he reached his ankle, a hard bump stuck out where it shouldn't. Gulping and pulling up the leg of his pants, Brandon saw the black metal strapped in a holster around his ankle.

This was incredible – and not in a good way. *Who is he? A murderer?* And a different man than the square-jawed one Greyson had pointed out to him. *The boys' story was real.* Whatever was going on in the observatory was more serious than he could imagine or handle himself.

He unstrapped the man's gun and cautiously carried it to the desk with both hands. He'd never handled one before and hated the thought of doing so now.

"Is that a gun?"

Brandon looked down at the boy and nodded before reaching back and retrieving the wallet and phone.

"He could have shot me!"

Brandon nodded again, shuffling through the wallet. "Yeah. He might have."

A credit card, a couple hundred in bills, and a driver's license. The name read 'Ray Yavil'. *Was it fake? Probably. But it would have to do.*

"You saved my life!"

Brandon scanned the office and found what he was looking for. He raced to the copy machine, put the license and credit cards under the lid, and pressed COPY.

"Um...sure, bud. Thank me later."

Jarryd blew his nose again and tried to crane his neck to see what Brandon was doing. The printer churned out a black and white paper with the images of both cards on it; Brandon snagged it and ran to the fax machine in the corner.

"What are you doing?"

He put the paper in the feeder and stopped. "Um...phonebook," he thought out loud.

"You're doing phonebook?"

Brandon shook his head, preoccupied. "No. I need one."

Jarryd could not see behind him and his head still swooned, but he still thought like a kid. "Use the computer. Online phone book."

Brandon smiled. "Yeah!"

He moved the mouse and the monitor faded on with static fuzz. The desktop picture was a picture of two men standing side by side in the desert somewhere. He ignored it and quickly maneuvered to the Internet browser.

"What are you looking up?"

Brandon typed in the online phone book and found the search box. He typed as he spoke. "Federal Bureau of Investigation, Morris, Iowa."

"The FBI?"

"Yes."

"Can't you just dial 911?"

He found the number for the closest FBI office. 140 miles away. *Awesome. I love Iowa.*

"No, Jarryd. I already tried that."

Jarryd furrowed his brow. "You called the cops already? When?"

Brandon typed the number into the fax machine. "This morning. They didn't believe anything and wouldn't even try to help out."

Brandon pressed send and walked to the desk as the paper fed into the fax. He picked up Ray's cell phone and scrolled through his contacts.

"Why wouldn't the cops help us?" Jarryd asked.

"I don't know. Maybe...maybe..."

He scanned down the list of names. And then he saw it. *Sheriff Roberts. In his contacts.* He looked again. *Sheriff Roberts. Oh, no.*

Jarryd watched Brandon as he looked worriedly into the cell phone's screen.

"What? *Why* wouldn't they help out?"

"Because they're on the bad guy's side."

Jarryd paused, letting the impact of the statement settle into his mind in a wave of despair. He looked up at the ceiling. "Do you know where Greyson is going now?"

"The observatory, I know."

Jarryd gave him a grave look. "No. After that, when he's stolen the keys."

Brandon nodded and it suddenly clicked. *What have I done?* He'd kept his little secret from the boy and it could kill him.

"Where's your walkie?"

Greyson turned on Birch Street, recognizing it as the street that their horseback riding bus would take to the horse ranch if they had turned the opposite way. They passed a curious jogger on the sidewalk across from them; they waved and she waved back. She was the first person they'd seen – the rain seemed to have kept most people inside in the small college town that lost over half its population over the summer schoolless months.

"We're almost there."

The next turn a block ahead would take them to the police station. There had been no sign of an SUV and Greyson hoped Nick had just made a mistake.

The walkie crackled, "Greyson! Are you there! This is Brandon!"

Sydney's eyes lit up and she frantically pressed the talk button. "Don't say our names!"

"Sydney? Is that you?"

Sydney rolled her eyes in anger. "No! What do you want?"

"Do not go to the police station! They have been paid off or something. They will not help you!"

The gator buzzed around the corner and Greyson braked the gator in a skidding stop. Sydney shouted into the walkie, "What? How do you know?"

Greyson pointed straight ahead, down the street to the police station. A black SUV was parked outside and two men talked with a portly uniformed police officer.

"Trust me! They're on the bad guys' side!"

"We know *now*."

Greyson pushed the gator into reverse and swung his arm over the seat as he pressed the accelerator to the floor. It peeled out in the slick road and spun backward into the curb. He popped it into drive and burst ahead, back where they had come from.

Sydney watched behind as the two men and an officer caught the movement out of the corner of their eyes. The men raced to their SUV and the officer watched with his hands on his belt. They disappeared out of view behind a row of houses.

"Go right! They think we'll be heading back!"

Greyson took her advice and cranked a hard right, holding on to the steering wheel as Sydney slipped into him with the momentum. The gator slid over the waterlogged street and snapped back straight with a lurch.

He glanced down at the speedometer as the rain hit his squinting eyelids. 25…30…35…36…37…37.

The engine buzzed loosely. They had reached their top speed, bumping crazily through the residential street, swerving to avoid the potholes.

Sydney spun around and faced the back, her wet hair coming undone from the bun, blowing past her cheeks and flapping in the wind. A black SUV flew past the intersection, not turning on Birch. *Yes!*

But then faintly, she heard the long screeching of tires; the slight reddish hue of reverse lights reflected off the white panels of the houses. They'd seen them.

"They saw us! We have to lose them!"

Greyson took another hard right into a rough alley and pressed the brakes just as they hit a deep bump. Sydney flew into the air and landed back in her seat with a harsh whip of her neck. She grabbed onto the front dash and swung her hair back around, glaring at Greyson. "Geez!"

Greyson flashed her an apologetic smile then turned back just in time to swerve around a garbage can, but not in time to avoid the cat.

"Meeeoooww – RAAYR!"

Bump, bump!

The gator heaved with the bumps, but sped along in the middle of the alley.

Sydney turned to him, mouth open and head cocked. "You swerved to miss the *garbage cans?*"

Greyson hadn't meant to hit the thing, but he shrugged it off. "I don't like cats!"

They watched as the SUV zoomed past the alleyway entrance behind them just as they turned left onto the road the police station was on.

"Go, go!"

The gator churned to top speed again as they flew toward the next intersection.

"Are they still following? Did they see us?"

They both looked back, waiting for the SUV to come barreling out of the alleyway.

When they turned back around, Sydney screamed; the SUV came at them from the left like a flashing, black meteor.

Greyson cranked the wheel right and held on for dear life as the SUV tried to turn into them. The gator spun out and its back side hit the side of the SUV with a metallic, glass-shattering crunch; the hard impact spun it the opposite direction in a fantastic lurch that sent Sydney banging into the steering wheel and Greyson's chest. In the middle of the spin pressing them to their seats, he managed to pound the brakes to the floor, and the gator screeched to a spinning, sliding stop in the middle of the intersection.

Both children gasped for breath as the intersection and houses seemed to spin around them in a blur like they were on an out of control merry-go-round.

The SUV put on its reverse lights and backed up into the intersection.

Greyson shook his head and blinked, trying to clear his head.

"Give us the keys, boy."

The SUV's door opened and a bearded man walked out with his hands in the air. "I'm not gonna hurt ya. Just hand 'em over."

Greyson's vision was swimming, but the man was definitely coming closer. Amidst the spinning image, Greyson noticed the pistol grip sticking out from underneath his jacket.

Greyson hit the gas and flew around what he guessed was the back end of the SUV just as the man cursed and drew his pistol. He put the SUV between them and the shooter, driving down the middle of the still-spinning street. The gator's crushed back bumper scraped at the asphalt in a shower of sparks until it fell, toppled over itself and skidded to a stop.

Sydney sat back up and moaned, holding her left shoulder. "Ouch. Where's the airbag when you need it?"

Greyson shook off the last of his cobwebs and turned down the next street just as he heard the SUV peel out once again. "Just hold on tighter next time."

Sydney sneered as Greyson swerved to avoid a pothole, forcing Sydney to lurch and grab the dash again.

"Away, come in. This is Nickel."

Sydney heard the voice and found the walkie somehow still working at her feet. She barely reached it with her sore left shoulder. "This is Away, the cops are on their side and we're being chased!"

"Jarryd told us. He's with Brandon in some office. They faxed the FBI and they should be on their way here."

Greyson watched his back and yelled to Sydney. "Tell him we're on our way. We've got to lose our tail first."

"We're on our way," Sydney relayed. "Get to the rendezvous and find Brandon."

"Roger that. Good luck."

The SUV's engine howled around the corner, bearing down on them with its brights blasting them with light. Its engine grew louder and its front grill grew nearer.

"It's gonna ram us!"

Greyson took a sharp left into a driveway and pulled it back to the right, tearing through a house's soggy front yard. The SUV pulled up alongside them on the street, watching as they bounced from yard, to driveway, to yard, recklessly snapping down young trees and churning through gardens.

"Mailbox!"

SNAP!

The wooden beam flew over their heads, the metal box still attached.

"NOW WHAT?!" she yelled over the sound of clanking metal and revving engines. Behind her, SquareJaw lowered the window and swung his hand out.

"DUCK!"

BANG!

The bullet whizzed over their heads and dug into a brick house with red splinters. Greyson turned right hard and pressed the brakes as SquareJaw fired twice more from the window.

Their gator hopped the curb and bounced hard on the street behind the SUV. Greyson fought to hold the steering wheel as the gator suddenly became reluctant to turn.

"Turn! Turn!"

He pulled at the wheel, but the gator held straight and slammed another curb. The shocks took the brunt of it, but both of them flew out of their seats and back down with another hard neck whip. The gator moaned in complaint and something hissed below them.

It was going to die soon. And if it did, they'd die with it.

"We're on our way."

Jarryd clicked off the walkie and Brandon helped him to his feet. He had to balance himself against the desk as the blood rushed from his head.

"Whoa. Almost passed out."

Brandon steadied him and looked around the office. Quickly, he snatched the paper from the fax, the license and credit card from the copier, and stared at the pistol.

"We have to warn the camp, tell the Jensens everything. If we have guys with guns running around..."

He picked the pistol and holster up with both hands and held it in front of him. "What do I do with this? He could still wake up."

"Strap it on yourself. And let's tie him up," Jarryd suggested.

Brandon thought to himself. "I'm wearing shorts and we have nothing to tie him up."

"Then shoot him."

"Shoot him?"

"Yeah, he was going to kill *me*."

"I'm not going to kill someone in…," he looked for the name of office's owner and found it on the door, "…Dr. Jacob Emory's office."

Jarryd burned a hole into the door's name panel with his eyes. *Dr. Emory.* "We have to get out of here."

"I know."

"No, seriously." Jarryd grabbed the gun and holster from him and hiked up his mesh shorts to his boxers.

"Hey, no, don't," Brandon objected, but watched as he managed to fit the strap around his pasty white thigh. "Dude, you have skinny legs."

Jarryd muttered, "Thanks," and swung his arm around Brandon's waist for support.

As they left the doorway, three men came around the corner. The man in front wore a doctor's robe and a condescending smile. They never broke pace.

"Hi, there. What are you doing in my office?"

Chapter 17

"Keep going!"

Greyson plugged the accelerator and the gator flew between two houses, rapidly approaching the tree line on the edge of town.

"Watch out for the forest!"

"How about the trees?"

He zipped into the tree line.

CRUNCH! The left side-mirror ripped away and rolled in the ground behind them. He looked to the right. *At least both sides matched now.*

Using what was left of the headlights to find the best path, he slowed and swung the dying gator left then right, weaving through the wet dirt and branches.

A burning smell rose from the engine and thin black smoke curled from under the hood.

"Uh, oh. Come on. Just a little farther."

"I can't see the SUV. Is there a road where we're going?"

"Uh…" He turned a hard right and headed to a far field where the trees ended. "Yeah. Gravel road to our left. It runs out to the ranch."

"The ranch…" Sydney leaned forward and scanned the horizon beyond the trees. Sure enough, the low-lying ranch was on the other side of the field. *He'd known where to go ever since they'd left the police station.* "Can we make it?"

"I don't know. If it dies, we get out and run."

A scary thought suddenly struck him and he reached down and felt his fanny pack. The form of the key was still there. He sighed in relief.

"They see us, Greyson."

Greyson matched her gaze; the SUV rolled off the gravel road and bounced in the water-logged ditch, sending a wave of water into the field. It barreled alongside the tree line then stopped suddenly.

Glancing at the SUV between flashing trees, Greyson gasped; a large rifle jutted out from its side window.

"Get down!"

A pregnant pause hung in the air, and the gator's engine idled as it bumped over rough ground. Bright muzzle flashes signaled a torrent of bullets had left the barrel.

RATATATATATATATA!

The bullets hit, blasting chunks from the trees all around them. Bark rained on the hood and their heads; sharp splinters stung their faces, forcing Greyson to stomp on the brakes and throw himself into the back cart, dragging Sydney with him.

Bullets slammed the metal frame as the gator continued to roll.

POW! POW!

The tires blew out with loud, airy explosions and the gator shook violently. They covered their ears and heads and the ominous sound of liquid pouring somehow leaked through the cacophony all around them.

RATATATATATATAT!

The final volley of bullets ricocheted off the green cart, leaving large, deep dents in its once shiny exterior as it came to a harsh stop against a tree.

Greyson listened for more bullets; his heavy breathing blew like heavy winds behind his eyes, and a shrill, maddening ring pressed at his eardrums. A last few pieces of bark shrapnel fell on them and the smell of gasoline seeped in his nostrils. It was over.

"Let's go!" he shouted, sounding like he was underwater.

Sydney rose with him and her shaking hand took his. They jumped from the side together and scrambled away from the dead vehicle, deeper into the trees. Both of them hobbled and stumbled, their legs bent and bruised from the worst thrill ride of their lives. The damp ground blurred underneath them as they ran as fast as their racing hearts could manage, curling around the field and following a barbed-wire fence.

The rain suddenly picked up again, and gusts of wind pelted their bodies with waves of thick drops. Lightning flashed across the sky, and the thunder cracked and rumbled through the air. Greyson squeezed Sydney's hand extra tight and watched the SUV back into the ditch, even its 4-wheel drive struggling to make it up the saturated mud and through the small river that rushed over the top of the road. They would try to cut them off before they reached the ranch. He tugged her arm and she kept pace.

The ranch felt out of reach; mud caked the bottoms of their shoes, the rain continued to weigh down their clothes and they slipped and slid along the rough terrain.

As they finally drew near, another lightning flash lit the side of the stable and revealed the door latched shut with a simple bolt.

Breathing heavily, Greyson gulped in the moist air as water dripped down his bent frame. Sydney bent over beside him and rested at his side. Over his back, she saw the SUV sloshing down the gravel road and slowing for the turn into the ranch.

"They're here."

Greyson turned and snapped to attention. Pulling the bolt back, he tugged open the wooden door and slipped inside with Sydney close behind. They instantly felt relief from the rain.

Loose hay layered the ground beneath them, formed a deep wall of bales along the left, and towered behind them. To the right were six wooden cubicles with high walls and metal gates, where the horses whinnied in fright each time the thunder shook their wooden home. The lone light bulb that lit the whole place from high above flickered with each lightning strike as rain pattered the roof with stronger and stronger intensity. Behind and to the right, a hastily nailed-together ladder towered up into an attic that spread out somewhere above.

"Go, behind the hay wall on the left. Wait for my signal to push."

Sydney nodded and raced down the aisle. She jumped to the first bale and found a thin, dark space behind the wall of precariously high hay bales.

Greyson swung to his right and bounded up the ladder to the attic above as bright lights from the SUV shone between the wooden walls. He frantically climbed the last few rungs and threw himself into the dark attic just as the large front doors swung open. Scurrying in the loose hay, he lay close to the ground and held his breath.

SquareJaw and the bearded man walked in together with pistols held at their sides. They peered left and right then directly at him. Greyson gasped, but the man looked back away. *It's too dark up here. He can't see me.*

"Come on, kids. You know how this ends. You can't run forever."

A lightning flash interrupted the silence and the stark shadows disappeared as the light bulb flickered and the thunder rattled the metal gates. From his high vantage point, Greyson could see every horse grow antsy – some pacing back and forth in their stalls, some bucking and whinnying angrily.

"Easy there, feller." The man laughed to himself and pointed the gun at Dancer. "Or I'll give ya somethin' to whinny about."

Greyson reached under himself and into his fanny pack. He pulled out the one item he'd thought he'd never need.

The bearded man approached the third stall and peered inside with his gun drawn. "Any boy in there with you horsey? No? Then what good are you?"

Sydney held her breath to thin, silent draws as the hay itched her cheek and ear. The man's shadow passed over her.

Greyson glanced at her hiding position and watched as the man approached the fourth stall. SquareJaw still stood by the doors. *Go forward you big idiot!* He inched forward, peeking over the stall. *That's right. Keep going.*

Waving his pistol in the air, the bearded man looked up into the dark attic. "If you're up there, little ones, don't be afraid. I'll be up there soon. HA!" He swung around to his left and pointed the gun in the fifth stall – GreyOne's stall.

Then, SquareJaw took another two steps forward, sneaking a quick look over his shoulder at the open door.

Perfect.

The bearded man opened the stall door and looked at GreyOne's butt. "Are you mooning me? You know where the kids are, horsey?"

A flash of lightning filled the darkness and the thunder struck soon after, blasting the stables with sound. The bearded man looked up into the attic as the flashing continued; he looked right at Greyson's face as the boy drew his arm back, fist clenched around the golf ball.

"There you are!"

GreyOne whinnied, frightened already – and everyone knew not to frighten a horse. Greyson hurled the ball with all his might. The bearded man flinched, and the ball clearly missed him; but with a sharp smack, it hit GreyOne's back end. The man turned and saw the flashing hooves too late.

His head snapped back unnaturally far and his body crumpled to the hay, leaving a bloody mist where he once stood.

"Now!"

SquareJaw raised his pistol as Sydney pushed with her arms and legs, her back pressed against the wall. The hay tower leaned as SquareJaw found the boy in his sights.

OOMMPF!

The tower collapsed over him, burying him in an avalanche of hay. Bales toppled over each other like giant ice cubes until they settled in the aisle below, and when the chaos was over – no part of SquareJaw could be seen.

Sydney stood on top of the first layer of bales, hay dust floating around her like yellow mist under a waterfall. Her hair was completely down by now, and falling over her smiling face in wisps of frizzy curls.

Greyson pushed off his stomach and scurried to the ladder. He dropped two rungs at a time and jumped into the aisle. Leaping over the bearded man, he ran to the hay avalanche. "Let's get out of here."

"Get the keys!"

He doubled back to the bearded man and cringed when he saw his distorted face. He had been right. *There were a lot of ways to die at this camp.*

Sydney ran up next to him as he searched the man's pockets.

"They're empty. SquareJaw was driving."

They both turned. A low moan escaped from underneath the hay. And then, the same thought crossed both their minds at the same time.

"GreyOne!" "Dancer!"

211

They eyed each other.

"We're not taking Dancer! She probably doesn't even want to get her hooves wet!"

"GreyOne just killed a man and you still trust him?"

"More than ever!"

She scoffed. "You're such a boy."

He shrugged both hands in the air. "And you…?"

"…a girl." She took a few strides toward the front entrance. "And girls go first."

"Wait, no!"

She jumped onto the toppled bales and scaled them quickly. Dropping to the aisle, she flew to Dancer's gate and swung it open. She looked back at Greyson. "Coming? Or are you going to let your girl ride out into the big, bad storm all awone?"

'Your girl'? I like the sound of that. He smiled and raced toward her.

Jarryd reached for the gun, but Brandon pushed his arm away. The men bore down on them and forced them to the ground.

"Close the door."

One of Emory's goons flipped the light on and shut the door to the empty hall.

"What did you do to him?" Emory asked, standing over Mantis. "Hit him with the bat?"

Emory put two and two together real fast. He was a doctor.

"He tried to kill us first!" Jarryd shouted through the pain in his head. Brandon watched Emory laugh and flashed Jarryd a confused look. Jarryd shook his head. "He's the bad guy we met last night."

Emory overheard and laughed again, finding his seat behind the computer desk. Brandon's heart skipped a beat, but he thanked God he remembered to close out the windows opened to the FBI's phone number. It's amazing how one careless mistake could have had such great stakes.

"Bad guy, huh? Heh. I suppose I would be that traditional role," he looked to his two henchmen. "But really, I'm just like every other American."

He swiveled in his chair, back and forth like a kid. "I want freedom. I *love* freedom. The revolutionaries – George Washington for instance, Abraham Lincoln another example – were both willing to kill to give every man the freedom they desired!"

Jarryd and Brandon listened intently. The man was obviously into himself. "And I'm no different. I want freedom. A lot of it." He sat up, pacing around the desk. "And you know what gives a man freedom nowadays? Not the freedom you or your parents think they have, not the freedom your government promises but fails to deliver - but real freedom? Freedom to do whatever you want, whenever you want?"

Brandon nodded with a knowing sigh. "Money."

"*Money*! You're right!" He came to them and leaned over, his pockmarked face burning with passion. "And I, too, am willing to kill for freedom." He paused for effect, staring into their eyes. "But no matter what you think of me, what I do tonight will be the start of something bigger than you can imagine. A catalyst for change for this country and the beginning of a new era of freedom in the world. This will just be the start."

Jarryd raised his hands to a golf clap. "Bravo. Nice speech. Are we dismissed?"

Emory wiped the shot of blonde hair across his perspiring forehead. "You are annoying, aren't you?"

Jarryd smiled bleakly. "Your *mom's* annoying."

Brandon elbowed him as Emory's lips flinched with an ounce of hatred. He stood up straight and turned on his heels, speaking away from them. "I see Brandon has had a handful taking care of you," he reached down and picked up the thick baseball bat, "and I'm guessing that he might even care about your well-being, as hard as that may be."

Jarryd scooted his back to the wall, away from the man with the bat. Brandon rose to his feet, his arms out in front of him in peacemaking fashion as Emory's henchmen drew their weapons.

213

"Brandon," Emory said gently with the bat hanging at his side. "I'm not a violent man, though I may hire them," he said as he glanced at Mantis's body. "But as you've heard, I'll do what it takes to get things done."

"Fine. Please. Just stop. We'll do whatever, okay?"

Emory took another step forward and Brandon backed to the wall. "I need two keys, and I take it one or both of you know where they are."

Jarryd glanced at the walkie-talkie lying on the floor by Emory's feet, then inched his fingers toward the bottom of his mesh shorts.

Brandon sighed and stepped between Emory and the boy. "Yes. I know where one is. The other..."

Emory's brow furrowed. "Your fearless leader, Greyson has them both, does he not?"

Brandon shook his head. "He has *one*."

Emory smirked. "Clever."

Jarryd peeked again at the walkie. They had to warn Greyson. Their key here was about to be compromised. And Greyson was heading back to the dragon's lair.

"And the other key? Where is it?"

"It's here. In the building."

Suddenly, a gasping, raspy breath came from Mantis's body. His chest heaved and bloody drool leaked from his mouth.

"See," Jarryd muttered. "Told ya we should've killed him."

Emory leaned toward Brandon. "He's probably right. If I were you...I would get that key before he wakes up. He might not like you if you're here."

Brandon gulped and stepped toward the door; the henchmen blocked his path.

"Jack, follow him. If he raises any alarm or does anything suspicious, radio back." He gripped the bat with white knuckles. "And he'll listen to Jarryd scream."

Sydney put her foot in the stirrup and swung her other leg over the horse's back. Greyson made sure the saddle was secure one last time. *Good to go.*

Greyson grabbed Sydney's arm, slipped his foot in the stirrup, and swung up behind Sydney, awkwardly close on the saddle. *Where do I put my hands?*

"Just put them around my waist. Get over it."

He shrugged and gently set his hands on her waist.

"UGGHH!" SquareJaw pushed a bale of hay from the pile and found fresh air. His upper body crawled from the dark hole and his eyes locked on them.

"Hold on!"

Sydney kicked and the horse jerked around the gate and toward the scrambling giant of a man.

"Go, go!"

SquareJaw lifted his large frame from the hay and lunged for them; Sydney kicked hard and Dancer swung her large haunches into the flailing man. His body thudded sideways and toppled over the hay avalanche as Dancer broke into a gallop in the open aisle.

Greyson nearly fell off the back end, but Dancer slowed just in time to let his momentum carry him back to Sydney. He abandoned all prudence, wrapping his arms around her and hugging her back to his cheek. *She smells like rain and strawberries.*

"Which way?" she shouted through the torrential rain.

Dancer twirled by the SUV, the rain falling on them in long streaks. Greyson glanced around from his position on her back. "Back to the gator! We need the walkie."

Sydney tried to look at him, but could not crane her neck around that far. Smiling to herself, she whipped the reins around to the tree line. "Yah!"

The speed of the horse started like a bumpy roller coaster approaching the top of the first steep incline, but the next moment they had peaked and began the drop. The wind and rain beat down at them and was soon blowing Sydney's hair over his head in a straight horizontal. Mud and water sprayed behind them in chunks and beads, lit now by the fading bright lights of the SUV. His cheek rubbed up and down on her wet shirt as his glittering eyes watched the scenery buzz past with the clopclop, clopclop, clopclop of Dancer's gallop.

Now this was horseback riding!

Lightning flashed again to their left and the thunder shook in their chests, but Dancer's gallop was fearless now because she was free. Nothing seemed like it could faze her out here.

The trip to the tree line was short, and Sydney pulled up on Dancer's speed. She and the horse deftly weaved around the trees toward the dark green vehicle planted against a tree. When they got closer, the light suddenly shifted, spinning away from them and through the forest. The SUV was leaving.

"Get it."

Greyson pushed off her back and spun on his butt to swing his legs off the saddle. He landed with a muddy plop and sprinted to the downed vehicle. The smell of gasoline and hot oil rose from the hissing beast.

Sydney watched the SUV drive from the ranch at maniacal speeds and glanced at Greyson. He held up the black object; the bottom half looked normal, the top half was in sharp, plastic splinters. "It's shot! Literally."

She sighed and pulled him up and over again. "To the pool?"

Greyson hugged her back and glanced at his watch. "Nine o'clock! It's only been an hour – the dance isn't even over yet."

Sydney turned Dancer toward Morris and along the gator's tracks. House lights flickered well beyond the tree line. "Dancer. To the dance. Yah!"

Brandon walked slowly, trying to allow his thoughts to catch up. *What can I do? Run? Turn and fight? Yell? I have no real choice. Whatever I try, the stupid guy behind me's going to call in and have Jarryd killed. And for what? Keys? The boys didn't even know what the keys were for. But then again, whatever they were for, they were worth a lot of money...and pain.*

He turned into the pool hall and three girls in colorful swimsuits passed him on the left, giggling and smiling. They passed Jack, too, oblivious to the firearm he hid under his jacket. *Ignorance is bliss...*

The smell of chlorine filled the hall and splashes of water echoed until they came into view of the swimming pool center. The bright blue pool shimmered with the light that came from beneath and above. The tiled floor was visible to the left in the shallow end, but a rope floated as a barrier where the floor dropped off into the darker deep end.

Brandon stopped and scanned the area – boys belly-flopping off the diving board, girls hitting each other with noodles, a counselor supervising while swimming laps, and a lifeguard sitting on a lawn chair listening to her iPod. Behind the pool, large bleachers filed backward. And in the back left corner, by the exit-door, the boys sat, huddled closely and talking.

He began his walk over and could see the boys' pleasant reaction turn sour when they saw the man behind him. They frantically murmured to each other and Nick spoke helplessly into the walkie.

Brandon slowed, hoping to allow them more time to warn Greyson, but Jack passed him, splashing through the pool's runoff. He dashed around the corner and approached the group of anxious boys with his right hand in his jacket pocket.

"No running!" The lifeguard gave Jack a death stare but quickly plugged his ears with the earphones, passing him off as an ignorant parent.

"Give me the walkie," Jack demanded.

Nick handed it to him, and the man sat next to him, his voice calm and direct.

"Who were you talking to?"

"Uh...no one. He didn't answer."

"Who didn't?"

Nick looked to Chase; Chase shook his head.

"Brandon!"

Brandon sulked over to them, his eyes hanging low. "Don't try anything boys. He's armed."

He looked to each one – Chase, Nick, Ryan, Austin, Sammy, and even Patrick. But no Liam. *Where was Liam?*

Jack nodded. "Give us the key and your friend Jarryd doesn't die."

Nick's eyes shot open. "What?"

Brandon hurriedly pulled Nick up and held him close. "It's okay Nick. He'll be okay."

Jack stood up. "*If* you give me the key, right now."

Each boy's face spoke a thousand words. Chase squinted and his knuckles cracked; he wanted nothing more than to pound the man's face in. Austin's deep, sad eyes grew weary and withdrawn, focusing on Nick. Ryan held close to Patrick, both frightened more than they ever had been before.

But Sammy; Sammy grinned wide, trying to glare at the man with both eyes but failing. "Keeeeey? Whaaaaat keeeeey?" He blinked rapidly and grinned wider.

Jack sneered in disbelief.

"Sammy," Brandon said. "Give it to him."

Sammy turned to him. "But whhhhyyyy?"

"For Jarryd, Sammy."

Nick suddenly shot from Brandon's grasp and flew to Sammy. He pulled at his bag straps with both hands, saliva and tears slurping at the corner of his lips. "Give it to him! Give it to him!"

Sammy squealed and squirmed, attracting the attention of the counselor in the pool. Brandon noticed and, thinking on his feet, jumped to the boys and pulled Nick from Sammy, tickling his sides and laughing.

"Oh! I made you cry even! You are ticklish!"

The counselor pulled her goggles down and blinked her eyes, watching them suspiciously. Brandon released Nick and shot to Sammy, tickling him as well. The boy squealed again and his bag fell loose to the bleacher behind him.

"Sttaaahhhhp – hehe – stttaaahhhp!"

The counselor smiled and shook her head once before putting the goggles back on and diving back under.

Chase scooped up Sammy's bag, unzipped it, and dug inside. His hands wrapped around the peanut jar and he threw it to Jack.

"What is this?"

Chase pumped his chin. "Look inside, genius."

Brandon released Sammy and put his hands on Nick's heaving shoulders as Jack untwisted the top of the peanut jar with both hands. Chase and Brandon exchanged a quick look. The same thought crossed their minds.

This is our chance. Now or never.

They leaned in, but Sammy suddenly leapt between them, lunging for his nuts. "Hey! My nuts!"

Jack merely planted his hand in the boy's face, pushed him aside, and took two steps back, eyeing the group with a fierce suspicion.

Brandon dropped back and cursed at the ceiling as Chase pulled Sammy to the bleachers and held him down with a scowl.

The lid spun off to the bleachers and a moment later Jack's hand dug deep into the peanuts. He quickly grasped what he was looking for. Pulling it out, he blew the salt off of its smooth, golden exterior.

"Thank you, boys." He slipped it in his left jacket pocket and pulled out a cell phone. "Just sit tight. I got to make a call."

Dr. Emory's earphone beeped and he tapped it. "Yes?"

"I've got a key. What now?"

Emory winked at Jarryd and sat down on his comfy office chair. "Tell them they can go. Of course, inform Brandon that if one of them talks, screams, whispers, or somehow manages to mess things up for us, we'll end the eldest Aldeman's life."

"Let them go, sir?"

"Yes. We need the camp to continue to run. Brandon and every one of his kids missing could lead to a lot of confusion and suspicion.

Greyson's absence will be handled shortly. Jarryd's absence...well, tell his brother that he needs to be both of them for tonight. Someone catches on to the act, and his brother will pay."

Jarryd buried his face in his arms as Dr. Emory stood up. *Poor, Nick.* He was sensitive and very protective. They hadn't been apart for more than a day before, and when they had, both had whined for an hour straight until their parents agreed to end the little experiment.

"Give me the gun."

Jarryd's face shot up and his hand snapped to the holster. Emory's hand was already over it. His shorts had fallen down, revealing the hidden strap. Emory slipped the gun out and held it firmly around the handle.

"Boy, you could have done some damage with this thing."

Jarryd bit his lower lip in disgust. Emory smiled at him, walked back to his desk, and dropped the gun into a drawer; he locked it away.

Now, there was nothing left. Their only hope was Greyson...and Deergirl.

Chapter 18

The Runciman family sat together at the dinner table where every piece of silverware had its place. A wet breeze rushed against the large window behind them and their heads turned as the motion light clicked on, sending its blurry rays through the dark backyard. Glittering rainwater overflowed the sides of the kids' pool to the trimmed grass where two toy guns lay as the children had left them. Beyond, two swings swayed gently in the wind, suddenly casting shadows over a horse's muscular haunches as it trotted past with two children on its back. Mrs. Runciman dropped her fork.

Dancer trotted around the guns, its graceful hooves lightly patting the smooth grass and its massive frame casting a long shadow to the tree line.

"Which way?" Sydney asked through the static downpour.

"Let's stay in back. The SUV will stay to the roads."

They peered down the long line of backyards; aside from a few picket fences, only sheds, birdbaths and lawn gnomes seemed an obstacle in their path through Morris.

Sydney pumped the reins and pushed in Dancer's side with her heel. Dancer responded with a soft gallop.

Greyson held his hands together around her waist, finding a rhythm with the horse's gait. "You know? We could just hide the key!" he shouted through the storm. "Or destroy it!"

Clopclop…clopclop…clopclop.

"And then they never would have a chance to launch their missile!" she replied.

Missile. The word snagged in his mind as houses passed through his field of vision one by one. TVs flashed in living rooms. *He could see it striking the town.* Candles flickered in dining rooms. *A flash of light, vaporizing homes.* Complete suburban families taking their peaceful lives for granted.

"Greyson?"

He snapped from his daydream. "But if we destroy it…and we're caught…they'll have no reason to keep us alive!"

Clopclop…clopclop…clopclop.

"Then we hide it! Someplace only we can find!"

Releasing one hand from his firm grip, he reached into the fanny pack and grasped the cold metal. He held it up in his fist with reverence.

A black shape buzzed behind it, out of focus.

He lowered the key, squinted into the wind and waited for the next gap between houses. It passed, but only a road and more houses beyond were in view. And no headlights.

"I think I saw something."

"Huh?"

"I think I saw something!"

"What?"

"I don't know. Maybe the…"

VRROOOM!

The SUV blasted between the houses in front of them and cranked a hard right just feet ahead, sending a stinging wave of water and wind into their sides. Its tires spun like a giant tiller, churning the grass into flying gobs of mud as the side of its frame crashed into a red picket fence, smashing the boards from their place like splintering dominoes.

Dancer jerked away from the chaos and Greyson's fingers slipped from Sydney's wet shirt; before he knew what happened, the ground flew at him and he hit it in a wild flailing roll.

The sky and ground twisted around him, his arms and legs banging into mud and wood. Dirty water splashed his face and soaked his body until he finally jerked to a stop, stomach-down in the middle of the SUV's tracks.

The blood still spun in his body, pushing him in an invisible ocean. He spit out a chunk of sour mud and wiped his eyes. Gasping for breath, his lungs gave him no air.

"Greyson! Are you alright?"

Don't panic. The breath just got knocked out of you. You'll be alright.

He shuddered a long breath and coughed. The mud seeped through his wet and tattered clothes to cold skin. He looked ahead of him where, inches from his face, a jagged shard of fence jutted from the ground toward his eyes.

Vroom! Vrrrroooomm!

The SUV curled to a stop in the yard ahead, taking out an electric grill with a loud crash. Its tires spun out again in wet grass, but caught traction on a cement patio.

"Greyson, get on!"

He pushed himself out of the sticky mud, still not getting the oxygen he needed. His knees ached with fresh bruises and he hobbled through the pain. Sydney stretched out her hand, her gaze fixed on the SUV racing toward them.

He snagged her hand and his foot found the stirrup. In a flash, Dancer snapped behind a thick tree with both children on her back; the SUV barreled past, splattering them with another rush of wet air.

Greyson hugged her close, but his hands wrapped too easily together. Something was missing.

"The key! I lost it!"

He jerked around, searching the littered ground for the shiny gold key – boards, dirt, tire tracks, more boards. Suddenly, red and blue lights reflected off the wet grass from the houses' side panels. A siren followed.

"Police! A good thing?"

"No. There it is!"

Greyson found it, sticking up from a chunk of mud thirty yards behind them. *How far did I roll?*

"Go!"

"Yah!"

The SUV turned toward the back of a house and reversed, blasting its headlights toward the children. It had no need for stealth anymore.

Dancer spun facing the key, the red and blue glittering off her shiny brown coat.

"Hold my hand!"

Sydney kept her left hand on the reins, but offered her right to Greyson; he snagged it tight and leaned over the side of the horse. The key approached quickly, but his arm didn't reach down that far.

The headlights flashed in his eyes and grew brighter; the key silhouetted in front of them, a bold shadow sticking from the mud.

"Lower!"

His left arm trembled with the weight and Sydney grunted, lowering his body down Dancer's side.

Clopclop…clopclop…clopclop!

The ground buzzed past and he reached out, stretching his shoulder to its breaking point.

"Aaaaghhh!"

The key slapped in his palm and he yanked it free with a slurp.

"Ha!"

He held it victoriously, smiling to himself. And then he looked up.

"AAAGH!"

A stone birdbath careened at his face.

Sydney jerked him up and Greyson swung over the stone in the nick of time. He ran his hand over his face. *Did it brush my eyelashes?*

Dancer dug in, its hooves pounding deep for traction, and bolted left as the SUV hit its brakes to make the turn. They flew toward the narrow pass between houses, but a siren pierced the air as the squad car skidded to a stop in front of them, blocking the pass.

Sydney gritted her teeth and kicked hard.

"Hold on!"

Greyson grabbed tight and felt her abdominal muscles contract as she tensed for the jump.

Clopclop…clop clop…and silence, the air brushing over them like in slow motion. Clang clang! The hooves met the hood briefly, and the horse vaulted over, knees bent like it had done this in its dreams over and over.

Clopclop! They hit the ground with a short bump and flew toward the streets glazed with rainwater.

Greyson stole a look over his shoulder. The police officer opened the door and gaped at the horse with two children on its back; shaking his head, he turned the other way and watched the SUV buzz through the backyards seeking another way out.

Sydney patted Dancer's neck and stroked its mane as it continued its flawless gallop to the next row of houses. "Good, Dancer. Thatta girl."

"Geez! I think…I think I just peed myself!" Greyson warned.

Sydney turned to him. "No way. You didn't."

"Well, everything's wet. It's hard to tell."

She shook her head. "You're such a boy."

They managed smiles and relished the fragile moment of peace and relative quiet, Dancer doing all of the work.

Mrs. Jensen hung up the phone in her office and stared at her husband, Bob. "I can't believe it. We have to get him now, before the dance is over."

She glanced at her watch – 9:20. Ten minutes left.

Bob nodded and looked over Greyson's file and the man's documents. "After 26 years, some things still surprise you."

They walked from their office to the balcony railing and looked over. The boy in the red hat still danced in the middle.

"Let's go together."

Dancer's breaths blew saliva and rain in slimy beads that trailed from its mouth to its chest in long strings.

"She's getting tired! Are we almost there?"

Greyson squinted through the rain and a flash of lightning draped the horizon in white. Over a line of trees past the park ahead, the campus buildings rose toward the dark, hovering clouds soaking them with rain.

"Through the park."

Dancer leapt another curb and found grass again in the soccer field. Just past the far soccer goal, a line of trees and a surging creek ran the length of the park, effectively blocking the way to camp – except for one small opening where a pedestrian bridge cut through, just hugging the top of the high water.

The rumbling thunder almost masked the roaring engine of the SUV, but its bobbing headlights revealed its presence as it bounced from a curb.

"He's back!"

Clopclop...clopclop...clopclop.

"Come on girl, just a little farther!"

The SUV smashed over the curb with a metallic groan and a shower of sparks underneath; it came down hard, bouncing on its shocks and quickly making ground on the tired horse.

Greyson glared over his shoulder. SquareJaw glared back through the windshield, his face growing larger and more sinister as the SUV's engine whined higher and higher. SquareJaw's face distorted in anger and his white fingers curled around the steering wheel.

"Turn! He can't turn as fast!"

Sydney tugged on the reins and Dancer took a hard left. SquareJaw flinched and pulled the steering wheel left as well, but the large vehicle's momentum was too much, carrying it through the soft field with waves of splashing water.

Anxious, Dancer stopped and whinnied in the bright headlights, huffing for air as SquareJaw stared through the windshield with rage and desperation, the wheel cranked to the left and the car's wheels digging a muddy perimeter around the horse. The children watched in fearful wonder as the SUV continued to circle around them in a steep donut as if its front bumper were tied to them by rope.

"See the bridge?" Greyson shouted over the hard engine.

The vehicle flashed past her line of vision.

"Yeah!"

"Around the soccer goal! Use it as a block between us!"

Sydney nodded and Greyson held on. She waited; the vehicle flew past once more before SquareJaw finally slammed the brakes.

"Yah!"

Dancer shot through the SUV's tracks toward the soccer goal. SquareJaw cursed to himself and pulled the vehicle around in another whirl of spraying water.

The horse swerved around the goal and galloped at its top speed, but it wasn't enough. The headlights lit them from behind and the SUV shot toward the open goal, accelerating until it slammed into the middle of the goal's net; it stuck with a perfect fit, carrying the goal over its grill and hood. SquareJaw bent low over the wheel, peering through the net as the headlights shined brighter on the horses' haunches.

"Faster! Go!"

Dancer chugged back in line with the bridge as Sydney pressed her feet to its side.

Please, please, please!

Greyson glanced behind – SquareJaw grinned evilly and the SUV's grill flew toward them with the goal hanging over it.

He glanced in front and the bridge-opening suddenly engulfed them, Dancer barreling between the metal rails and its hooves hitting wood.

VrrrrOOOOOMMMMM!

The SUV's front bumper slammed the narrow bridge's metal railings, snapping the bolts and curling the steel on both sides of the horse. Greyson felt the engine's heat on his back and grimaced, bracing for impact.

But then it happened – the goal's net snagged the edge of the bridge rail and pulled the metal frame down like a clamp around the hood; the front wheels dug into the bridge and stopped, but the back of the vehicle carried the momentum and swung over top, the rear wheels spinning loudly as they pointed toward the falling rain. The speed carried the huge metal beast over the net and flung it at the children from behind.

Dancer leapt from the bridge just as the SUV struck it like a colossal pendulum, exploding in a cluster bomb of splinters and a tidal wave of water. The shockwave of wood and water washed over them from behind, hitting them with stinging shrapnel as Dancer galloped with the wave into open field.

Sydney pulled on the reins and Dancer curled to a stop. Breathing heavy with adrenaline, Greyson watched in awe as the upside down vehicle bobbed down the swollen creek, taking on water in large gulps. What was left of the bridge moaned its death cries and followed its killer away.

Both kids shook their heads in disbelief. Greyson rubbed his eyes and slapped his cheeks, the water running over his head like a constant shower as he watched the aftermath. The SUV's metal frame dipped lower and rolled in the rushing water, churning into the distance with the bridge's planks and rails. *Was SquareJaw inside, clawing at the windows, gulping water and cursing their names? Or could he have gotten out?* The SUV ducked under the water, the last of its underside succumbing to the deep.

He was goners.

Greyson blew at the rain running to the corners of his lips and wiped a large splinter from his shoulder. "You okay?" he asked.

"Yeah, I think so…"

"Uh…I was talking to Dancer."

Greyson patted Dancer and smiled at Sydney.

"Jerk. Well, I'm fine, too, in case you were wondering that as well." She shook her head and opened her mouth to the rain for a drink.

Greyson shivered for a restful moment as the night finally grew cooler with the rain. "I can't believe that just happened. If we'd got that on tape, we'd be millionaires."

Sydney smiled and sat straight. "Were you videotaping it?"

"No, I said if we *were*."

She turned and furrowed her brow. "Then, what *were* you doing?"

Greyson recoiled. "What?"

"Dancer was running; I was steering…what were *you* doing?"

"I was…I was watching your back."

She laughed. "Yeah…real closely." She smiled again and lifted her head for another drink.

As Sydney gulped in thin amounts of rain and Dancer recovered her breath, Greyson eyed the dark outline of the Rec Building where Mantis would be waiting – in his dark blue raincoat and sinister hood. His faint smile faded. He turned and scanned the lines of houses behind them.

We could escape…and never go back.

A stab of guilt made him twist in the saddle.

The terrorists might not find us and they wouldn't have the key to launch their missile. We've done our part then, right? Even if the terrorists get away, we'll still be heroes. Someone else will hunt them down. After all, we're just kids. And Mantis wouldn't hurt the other boys when they're at camp, would he? But…Liam wasn't at camp. Had they found him? What would they do to him if –

Dancer jerked forward and began the trot toward campus – toward the terrorists – and Greyson sighed in relief. The tense knot in his neck eased away and the silent pull of conscience tugged him closer to Sydney's back. *Enough questions.* Until there was nothing more he could do, he wasn't done.

Besides, he had to get his hat back.

Mrs. Jensen filed through the group of sweaty and tired dancers toward the boy in the red hat and Bob followed close behind, smiling at his campers.

"Greyson. Greyson!"

Chris swung around. "Uh, oh."

Mrs. Jensen arched her brows. "Oh. I thought you were Greyson Gray."

Chris' lip quivered. "Where's Greyson, *where's* Greyson! That's all people have said to me all night! What about me? Does no one care who *I* am?"

"Sure we do…hun. But you're wearing his hat."

Chris swiped it off his head and pushed it in her hands. "Fine! You take it! I'm going home!"

Bob stopped him. "The dance is over in a few minutes. Stick around here and find your counselor."

Chris huffed and tried to hide his teary eyes.

Mrs. Jensen raised her finger. "Sorry for asking, hun...but...*do* you know where Greyson is?"

Chris scoffed and shook his head. "No. Don't care."

He stormed toward the bathroom.

"Judy. Check with Brandon. I'll wrap things up here."

"Alright. We'll find 'em."

They had waited as long as they could after Jack had left them alone. The pool was closing and Greyson had still not returned. Thinking on his feet and making sure he was not being watched, Brandon opened the back exit-door and dropped a thin goggle strap in the locking mechanism before it shut. *Just in case he makes it back to the rendezvous, he'll be able to get in.*

"Time to clear out! Last time I'll tell you!" the lifeguard shouted to them in the corner. "Go back, get changed, and meet your counselor at your shield."

"I'm their counselor. They're with me!"

"Sorry, but I'm paid 'til 9:30, not 9:35."

Brandon shook his head.

"Do we have to Brandon? What if he comes back?"

"If he comes back, he'll find our note and he'll get out of town, I hope. As for us, we don't say anything, remember? Jarryd will be okay until the FBI comes, but only if we stay quiet."

"But..."

"But nothing. Please. Let's go."

They trailed from the empty pool, Nick holding on to Brandon's waist. The lifeguard waited until they left and then shut off the lights.

Dancer trotted up to the Rec Building the back way, avoiding streetlights and homes. Sirens and police lights spread throughout the neighborhood behind them, searching for the fugitives on the run with a stolen treasure. But in and of itself, this treasure was not worth much; steel crafted into a unique shape and painted over with gold paint was not desirable for much other than a paperweight mostly, but this particular piece of metal served a sole purpose worth millions of dollars and who knows how many lives. And he carried it in his fanny pack.

They rode quietly and whispered as they dismounted behind the last wall before the pool entrance. "It's past 9:30. I bet most of the kids are back in the dorms by now."

"Here. Tie her up here. All we need to do is find a spot to hide the key before the FBI comes."

Sydney tied the reins to a drainpipe. "Do we go back to our rooms?"

"They'll be looking for us there, I'm sure. But we need to contact Brandon and Jarryd and the others somehow. Let them know what's going on."

"Should we hide it here? Just bury it?"

Greyson eyed the muddy edge of the building. "This works. But if anyone asks – we hid it…in the stables. Stall 6, by GreyOne's water.

Sydney nodded. "Got it."

They knelt and dug in; the mud sloshed away with ease and before they knew it, they had a six-inch deep hole. Greyson took it from his pack and threw it in. Covering it up was even easier and they made it look just like any other patch of mud.

"Good. Now to the rendezvous. Maybe they left us a walkie."

Judy Jensen walked with purpose to Brandon and his campers at their shield. She looked over them in a quiet desperation but didn't find what she was looking for.

"These all your boys? Where's Greyson, Brandon?"

Brandon froze. *How did they catch on so fast? How am I supposed to cover for this?*

He looked over his shoulder at his kids, and something caught his eye – their shield with its bright golden letters spelling 'Cowboys Gold', and right below it, the single word that now seemed especially profound, even prophetic.

DARING.

Wow. Nothing fit better than that word. Except for maybe, 'screwed'.

"Uh…," he looked back at Judy, searching for the words, "…Liam and Jarryd are in the bathroom. Greyson…um…I'm not sure. He knew to meet us here after the dance…"

She searched his face and reached toward it. He jerked back reflexively.

"Hold still. Is that blood?"

He put his fingers where she had reached. A dried flake of blood stuck to his cheek. He pulled it off. "Oh…yeah, I cut myself shaving before the dance."

She smiled worriedly. "Hmm…well, we need to find him. Send your kids with CJ. Follow me."

Shocked, Brandon obeyed.

Greyson slid to the door's window and peeked in. Dark and empty – only the pool's lights were on. Listening in the light rain, they heard footsteps and excited voices leaving in front. They were streaming to the dorms for hot showers and soft beds. *Oh, that would feel so good.*

He pulled on the handle and it opened easily as a thin strip of rubber fell to the ground. "They propped it open for us," he whispered to Sydney.

She followed him into the wafting humidity and chlorine, tracking in mud but not really caring. He scanned the room, but there was no walkie; only a piece of paper lay folded on the bleachers next to them. He reached for it.

"Greyson?"

His head snapped across the pool; Judy Jensen stood straight, her small glasses dangling on the tip of her nose. "Is that you?"

Run?

He glanced back at Sydney; she stood without an answer, frozen to the floor.

Brandon came walking in behind the director, staring at them.

"Where have you been?" she asked.

Judy took quick steps forward and Greyson turned to the door.

"No, no, wait!"

He pushed on Sydney. "Go!"

Judy rushed around the corner and stopped. "Greyson, you're not in trouble!"

He froze again, nearly out the door. His face shone with waving hues of blue and white reflected from the pool.

And he saw it. In her small, wrinkled hands, she held his red hat. Her eyes were tearing.

"We're not?"

"No, Greyson…" She gulped, choking on her words.

And what she said next shattered his world.

"…your dad…he's back."

Chapter 19

The words passed through him like an icy sword; it sliced through his fear, cut at his doubt, and pierced the walls he had erected around his heart. The moment passed like an eternity – the kind old lady crying for him before he could manage any response. As the adrenaline pumped ceaselessly through his young body, his light head wobbled with the slow waving blue light.

The world turned to shades of grey. He had to sit down.

"Greyson!"

He had fallen, but someone held his arms and dragged him to the bleachers. There was murmuring all about, but it faded inches from him. He could think of nothing else than the words he had finally heard – words he'd been waiting for every day he would come home after school, every morning he'd woken up, every time the phone had rung, every time they'd received a letter in the mail – and now, of all times, he'd heard them. He had to shout!

"He's alive! I knew it! I knew he would come back! He's alive! My dad's alive!"

Or at least that's what he thought he said. In reality it came out, "Hehsuluh! Ahnuwt! Ahnumhuwudcompat. Hehsuluh. Myduhsuluh."

"Greyson. Look at me, Greyson. Get some water."

Water splashed his face once then twice. Color returned and he recognized the shape of Brandon's face in front of him. "Greyson? You back with us?"

He gulped and blinked deliberately. "Where is he? Where's Dad?"

It felt unnatural, so immature to say it. *Dad.*

Judy knelt in front of him. "He's here, hun! He's waiting for you in our office."

He stood up too fast and almost toppled into the pool. Brandon held his shoulders with both hands. "Careful. You look kind of banged up already."

Judy suddenly seemed to notice. "Oh, my. What have you been up to? Sneaking out for a little mud wrestling, huh?" She elbowed Sydney. "I knew a boy here one of the first years of camp who was known for such things."

Greyson looked up at her, his eyes sparkling with new life.

"That's right. Gregory Gray. Your dad."

"Can we see him now?" Greyson's mind was still swooning.

Judy looked at Sydney and Brandon. "Why don't you say good bye to your friends here first so they can get back to their dorms?" She took some steps back, folding her hands at her neck in a grandmotherly show of affection.

With a quick glance back at her, Brandon knelt to Greyson's eye level. He paused, unable to restrain his smile for the boy's happiness. "I'm really happy for you, Greys. But there's some things to clear up, as you know." He looked back at Judy, then whispered to Greyson. "Do you have the key?"

Greyson breathed heavily, his eyes a mix of confusion and excitement. "We hid it. They'll never find it," he replied in a husky whisper. "And Dad...he will help us. I'll tell him everything and he'll believe me. He always does the good that should be done - and he's not afraid of anything."

Brandon nodded. "And Sydney knows where it's buried?"

Greyson looked at her and flinched. A sudden worry popped back into his world of bliss. "We'll keep her with us. They won't get to her if my dad's with us."

His counselor searched for more words, but nothing came. He hated to see the boy leave, but it was best; the more of his kids he could get away from the bad guys the better. *Should I tell him about Jarryd? About Liam? Does he know, somehow? What could he do about it if he did know?*

He looked at the boy one more time and smiled weakly. He couldn't risk Jarryd's life by telling him. Their hope was running out, but Greyson's was just beginning.

"We'll figure it out here, so don't worry. I'm happy for you."

Greyson squinched his eyebrows. "Wait. I'm not leaving. I'll tell him everything. We're not going to leave you."

Brandon stared blankly, his eyes bouncing around Greyson's face as he searched for the right thing to say. Before he could make up his mind, Greyson thrust forward in a strong embrace and whispered in his ear. "We'll be right back." Then with a quick release, he slipped past him, jogged to Judy, and took his hat from her.

"Come on, Sydney. I'll introduce you to him!" He put his hat on over his wet, muddy hair.

Sydney looked at Judy who shrugged her approval. "That would be fine! Brandon, I'll talk to you later tonight after I get this young one off and running."

He nodded helplessly. "Okay. I'll be back in Bickford."

"Thanks. Let's go kids!"

Brandon watched them walk away, Greyson twitching with anticipation and whispering enthusiastically with a very confused Sydney. He smiled, but a deep sadness shook at his soul. The door closed slowly behind the kids, but Brandon still stood there with the quiet lapping of the pool.

Jarryd. Liam.

Greyson bounced up the stairs at a frantic pace. His aching knees and body seemed numb to the pain and he was too happy to hurt anywhere

He flew around the corner – his thoughts and hopes racing with him. *Where had he been? What had he done? Did he change the world? Will he insist on taking the key for himself and taunting Dr. Emory with it? Or will they go get an army of FBI agents? Would he approve of Sydney? Will he want his hat back?*

He ran down the balcony, past the darkened doors. Only one was open. Only one had light pouring from it into the hall. The one his dad was in.

Tears welled in his eyes as he ran with abandon, the last of the mud falling behind him in spinning chunks.

"DAD!" he screamed, coming to the light.

"Greyson?"

His heart leapt and he flew around the corner. Before he could even see his face, the man took him into his strong arms and pulled him to his chest. They spun around in the embrace he had been missing for ten months and sixteen days.

Greyson laughed and cried at the same time, tears soaking his face and lips. He pressed closer and closer, never wanting to leave. Finally the wait was over. His hat fell from his head, but he didn't need it anymore.

"I knew – you'd come back!" He gasped through tears and sniffs. "I knew it! I missed you – Dad – but I never gave up! I knew it!"

His dad stopped spinning and held him out toward the hall.

Greyson gazed up at him through blurry, teary eyes.

"Look here, boy."

The gruff whisper startled him and he wiped away the tears.

His heart stopped; the air sucked from his lungs.

IT'S NOT HIM.

The man pulled his head to his chest and whispered his hot, stale breath in his ear. "You scream...you say *anything* other than *'yes'* and nod, and I will have your friend Jarryd *killed. Got it?*"

Greyson choked on a sob. *Jarryd? NO! NO! Dad! Where is he? What had they done with him?*

"Judy!"

The man held Greyson close with one strong arm and reached out to Judy with the other. The elderly woman joined them in a teary group hug, Sydney watching from the doorway.

"Oh, what a moment! I'm so glad I got to be a part of it."

The man stared at the boy, smiling. Greyson stared blankly, overwhelmed.

Dad...it can't be...he was still gone.

"Okay, okay. I could hug forever, but you two probably want to get back to Mrs. Gray!"

The man set Greyson down and laughed, taking the boy's hand. "Oh, yes. It's been too long. *Way* too long. Oh, who's this?"

Sydney took an awkward step closer and timidly held out her muddy hand.

"Sydney. I'm Greyson's friend."

The impostor shook her hand and gave her a hearty smile. "Pleasure to meet you, young lady. Looks like you two have had quite a night."

She laughed nervously, glancing at Greyson, who watched the ground as the man continued to squeeze his hand in his own.

"If it's okay, Judy, I'd like to take her back to her place – Binz is it still?"

Judy smiled. "Yes! Great memory! Yeah, if you want, you could just drop her off on your way. It would save us a trip."

"Sure. It would let them say a better good bye."

"That sounds wonderful." She bent over and looked Greyson in his tired, sad eyes. "A bit overwhelming, isn't it?" She pinched his cheek and shook it back and forth. "You okay with leaving camp a little early?"

He stole a look at Sydney but the man wrung his hand. "Yeah…"

"Okay. Your huddle will be sad to see you go and so will I! Come back next year!"

Avoiding her eyes, he noticed the familiar object on the floor. He reached down and pulled his red hat from the floor. Lightly, he set it on his head, and the memory of his mother fitting it on him –

The imposter pressed it flat on his head and laughed.

Hatred rose violently in his chest and almost exploded into a fury, but it fizzled in his clenched fists – one of which grappled three of the man's fingers.

He could hear him fight the pain, and the corner of his eye flinched.

"Good bye, Judy. Thank you so much."

"Thank the Sudanese ambassador! And call anytime! Good bye!"

The man pulled him out the door and into the dim balcony. The gym – where there had been over a hundred dancing, sweating, rowdy kids ten minutes ago – was now lifeless and abandoned. The curtains were

238

up and all the doors were closed; it was only him, Sydney, and the complete stranger carrying him along like his own son.

The man immediately pulled his fingers free and put his large hand around the back of Greyson's neck.

"So, Sydney, what did you two do tonight?"

How long would he play this game?

"Uh…just some mud wrestling…I guess."

The man eyed her suspiciously and she couldn't keep her eyes off Greyson. *He didn't look nearly as happy as he did before. He was bouncing off the walls, and now he's a whipped puppy. Something was wrong.*

"Mud wrestling, huh?" The man laughed – a sickening, rasping laugh that sounded eerily familiar. In fact, the man looked familiar – nothing like his dad – but someone else.

They walked down the stairs and headed to the front entrance where another SUV awaited them. Greyson and Sydney shared a look of disdain in the headlights, recent frightening memories piling on top of the one happening now. *What would he do to them once they got in the car? Would he point out that he had killed two of their men and then simply kill them in retaliation? Or would they torture them…for the key location. That was what this was about – a clever scheme to get the key.* And he'd fallen for it hook, line, and sinker.

The man opened the car door for them and motioned them inside. As they hesitated outside, the pitter-patter of the rain sunk into the fabric of his hat.

Well, he thought, *at least there's one small thing to appreciate before stepping inside the last car I'll ever ride in… I have my hat back.*

Dr. Emory pulled Jarryd up from the seat and pushed him to Jack. "It worked. We'll have both keys soon."

"Do we still need this one?" Jack sneered at Jarryd.

"Bring him back. Just in case this Gray is as stubborn as his father was."

Jack nodded and swung the squirming boy out the door. "Hey! Child abuse, geez!"

Emory shut the door to his office but stayed behind. He immediately looked to Mantis, who winced in pain, holding his forehead with both hands as he rested his back against the wall. He noticed Emory watching him and looked up.

"Need your brother to clean up your messes, do you, Jacob?"

Emory sneered. "I'm very capable."

He pulled his gun.

Peeeuuw! Peeeeuuw!

Mantis's body shook with the bullets' impact. Small puffs of smoke rose from the silencer, and Emory sniffed its scent.

Then, smiling and humming to himself, he walked to a thick safe the size of a microwave and set the gun on top. Spinning the dial, he found the correct combination.

09...11...01. It was a date he'd never forget.

The safe clicked open and he reached inside to grab the lone object in its belly.

He carefully held it in his palms like the tiniest baby and escorted it over Mantis's outstretched legs to his desk. Kneeling to get a better view, he stuck it to the underside of the desk, just beneath the computer that held vital encrypted messages that authorities in several countries would love to get their hands on. Then, with two simultaneous button presses, the red light flickered on. The bomb was armed.

He smiled even wider and locked the door behind him when he left, humming a tune.

A moment later, an electronic buzz interrupted the stillness. The fax churned to life and the paper filed through the feed in small jerks. Coming out the other end, the loose piece of paper fell lightly to the floor. It read simply:

Known alias for highly dangerous man. Wanted internationally for espionage and murder. Do not approach. Units on the way.

Chapter 20

Mmm! Mmm! Mmmpppfff!

The duct tape pulled his cheeks into his lips and muffled his screams. The blindfold digging into the bridge of his nose was also quite effective. The only thing he'd seen since he'd been pushed into the car was…nothing. He could still hear, though, since they didn't think of earplugs. He could hear Sydney's feet being dragged behind him and every once in awhile he'd hear a thud and a man would curse.

"Freaking, girl! Knock it off or I'll tape your ankles to your neck!"

Thud.

"OW! You little--"

Beep. Click!

The third door. They were in deep.

And this room was different. More light filtered in through the dark cloth and the noise was airy and echoing. There was such a loud hum it felt like passing a semi-truck on the Interstate, but without windows or driver. The sound of hissing gas combined with the soft patter of liquid dropping on cement also made it feel like it was a massive mechanic's garage. Or maybe a semi passing through a mechanic's garage.

But either way, he knew where they were. He'd seen it before. And when he was thrown to the cement near the loud hisses and underneath the liquid dripping, he knew *exactly* where they were.

They were under a massive missile – where the fuel met with spark and ignited into a giant flame that burned with enough energy to send thousands of pounds of steel hurtling through the lower atmosphere.

It wasn't comforting.

"Here. We brought you some chairs."

Oh. That's better.

"Now we can have a nice fireside chat. HA! Get it?" The man burst into a fit of nasally laughter. The other man ignored him and pulled

Greyson to the chair by the armpits. For the first time, he wished he had pitted out more.

"Here, girly, have a se--"

Thud.

"OW! Freaking girl! I'm gonna…"

"Calm down."

Slap!

"There. That'll calm her down."

He heard her plop on the chair, then sniffling. *They had hit her!*

"Mmm mm mm-mm mm mmm." *I am gonna kill you. Hear that?*

The man laughed. "What? You want to be tied tighter? Okay!"

In an instant his arms were pulled back and wrapped behind the chair's back; the rope flew around his wrists, his thighs, and around his chest. He inhaled and held it in, sticking out his chest, hoping to get a loose tie, but it was still snug. They were serious about keeping him in his chair. It was like going back to 3rd grade.

The man grunted and yanked.

"MMMMM!"

The rope tore into his wrists and cut the circulation to his arms. He tried to scream more, but the rope around his chest was still tight.

"There we go. Girlie next."

He could only listen to them tie her up. She groaned when they pulled it tight, but she didn't scream. *They must not have tied her as tight.*

"Okay. That oughta do it. The doctor will be with you shortly. Ha!"

"Mmm…mmm."

"Oh, wow. You kiss your mom with that mouth?"

I kiss your mom with this mouth.

"Kyle, let him be. He's got more guts than you and me combined."

The other man scoffed. "What? This kid? Let me feel."

"MMMPPPFFF!"

The fist punched the air from his lungs and nose in a wet mess.

"Mmmmm!"

The pain forced tears from his eyes that merely soaked into the blindfold.

"Kyle, knock it off! He's just a kid."

"A kid who almost took our paychecks! I already bought a house and a freaking awesome home entertainment system I can't afford."

"He was just doing what he thought was right. Give him a break."

Kyle scoffed. "Okay. Then why don't you watch your new little junior-high friend? You can play truth or dare while you wait."

"Fine."

"No wait – I got one. Boy, I dare you to stand up."

What an idiot.

"Ha! Nope. You lose."

The man left, laughing his head off.

Beep. Click.

Greyson breathed in as deep as possible and let it out, shuddering.

"You okay, there?"

He felt the man leaning close. A drop of fuel dripped on his forehead and the man wiped it away.

"Forget him. He's like that to everyone."

"Mmmm."

"But I'm not like that. I feel for ya."

He felt the man pat his thigh. *This is when Mom would tell me to run.*

"And I'm not going to lie to you…you're not going to make it out of here."

The words sunk in. He'd already known it, but somehow he'd fought to ignore it.

He sniffled and tried to tighten his lower lip.

"I know you're tough; we all know it," the man spoke with compassion. "But even you have a limit."

Greyson lowered his head to his chest. *Was Sydney still listening? Was she okay?*

"From someone who wants the best for you…give up. Being tough now will only cause you more pain.…pain beyond anyone's limit."

He had been right. They were going to torture him. Images of every horrible movie he'd snuck to his friends' houses to see flashed in his mind – images of knives, chainsaws, sledgehammers, electrical wires, pliers, needles, drills, and blood.

And then, a worse image came to mind – an image he had never seen, but only imagined. Eye of Eyes – the old oracle with skin barely clinging to his bones, with bloodshot eyes and crooked teeth – reaching toward his thin-skinned neck with the sharp knife, ready to slice his neck and watch his blood flow to the floor in a thick stream, winding to the clearing on which the observatory was built. The legend would be complete. He would be the thirteenth child.

"You can avoid it. And all you have to answer is…where's the key?"

He raised his head and pulled at the ropes tearing at his wrists. They already hurt; his whole body already hurt. He couldn't take a knife to the throat. *I'm too young to die!*

He imagined the key, under the mud…far away from the missile that towered above them. It all came down to the key. *How ironic.* The key gave him the choice – die slowly and horribly while saving the potential victims from the missile's wrath…or die quickly…while giving in to terrorists and being responsible for whoever stood within range of the missile's blast.

When he thought of it that way, the conclusion was clear.

"Mmmmpff!"

The tape came off in one burning swipe. The pain was delayed, but when it came, it came in a swell of fire.

"OOOWW!"

The blindfold slipped off next and light bombarded his sensitive eyes. He squirmed and squinted until his pupils retracted enough to make sense of his surroundings; the man stood over him, legs spread and leaning in, expecting an answer.

"I buried it. In a stable at the ranch. In the sixth stall by GreyOne's – he's my horse – by his water."

The man stared blankly and crossed his arms. "You're lying."

"No, I'm not! Ask Sydney! She buried it, too!"

"I'm telling you. Tell us the truth, or we can get it the hard way. Kyle – he's good at the hard way. Me – I prefer the easy way."

245

Good cop, bad cop, huh? They think my generation doesn't watch TV anymore?
Greyson shrugged and spoke slowly. "The last stall…"

The man leaned in so close Greyson could smell his foul breath. "We know it's not there, boy. Lie to me one more time. I dare you."

Greyson leaned back and swung his right foot up like any good goalie would kick balls out of the box. And he connected with great force.

The man stood up with a shocked yelp, then fell to his knees as his face scrunched in pain and anger. "Uhhhhh….ehhh…you…ehh…"
I think I just lost all my Fairplay points.

And then, just to keep to the man's dare, "The sixth stall. By GreyOne's water."

But then he thought of his 'last words' Nick had recorded to tape. He thought of his mom watching the video on their TV from their couch at home, curled up in a blanket with their dog, GrayHound, playing the scene over and over again. His image lit the dark room and reflected in her watery eyes.

Play. Cry. Rewind. Play. Cry. Rewind. Into the night.
Sorry, Mom.

But it was the good that had to be done.

"He left? He couldn't just leave!"

The stunned group looked to Brandon from Jarryd's empty bed.

"I'm sorry. He did. But the key is safe and the FBI will be coming, I'm sure of it."

He felt so helpless. Five boys were mourning the loss of three of their friends – two of their leaders and Liam. Now, they looked up to him searching for a solution, expecting him to solve an impossible problem. *I'm 21. I barely know how to do my own laundry. How can I handle a hostage situation?*

"Liam's still in there! We can't just leave him!"

"Ryan. If we were to try anything, they'd hurt Jarryd."

"But…but…"

The rain picked up again outside, spattering the windows in dull thuds.

"I wish we could do more, but all we can do is wait." He sighed dreadfully and paced to the door. "I don't know…if you go to sleep now, maybe it will all be over by the time you wake up."

The boys' dark eyes were sullen and without hope. *How could they sleep? How could Nick even breathe?*

He walked to Nick and motioned for him to follow. Shoulders sagging like his brother was literally weighing on him, Nick rose and trailed Brandon to the hall. Brandon took him to the side in privacy, knelt to his level, and put his hands on his shoulders.

He mustered his confidence. "He'll be back. The FBI will come anytime now and they'll know what to do to get him safe."

Nick nodded, his expression not wavering.

"If you need someone to talk to, I'll be around right after the counselor's meeting that you boys obviously know all about."

"Nick?" A boy suddenly called out from down the hall. "Have you seen Jarryd?"

The boy's voice flipped a switch in Nick's demeanor.

"Yeah," he smiled. "Uh…he's inside. Let me get him."

Nick ran around the corner and stopped only to reach deep in his pockets and take out two large tootsie rolls. "Jarryd, a Purple wants to talk to you!" he yelled at the wall.

Opening his mouth wide, he pressed each tootsie roll to the outsides of his top back teeth. When his lips slipped over them, his cheeks puffed out over the large lumps. Brandon smiled. *Genius.*

Nick rustled his own hair into his twin's messy style and leaned out the doorway. "What's up, Purple dude?"

The boy walked up to him in the hall, giving him an odd look. "Uh…here's your Slim Jim. I'm still impressed."

Nick stared then suddenly snapped forward and grabbed the Slim Jim. "Yeah…I knew you'd come through."

The boy glanced at Brandon then back at 'Jarryd'. "How'd you do it? Tell me and I'll give ya another one."

"Uh…" He had no idea what he was talking about. "…It was easy! You just have to be in the right mindset. Think to yourself – I can do it. Focus. Then ACTION! And you're done. You'll be able to do it someday, my young friend."

Brandon cleared his throat, trying not to laugh. He knew his brother so well.

The boy looked confused then content. "Hmm…okay. Thanks."

"Yeah, no prob. Check ya later."

The boy swung around and scampered to his door. As soon as he was out of sight, Nick flipped the switch off again and violently threw the Slim Jim at the wall. Without a word, he pulled the tootsie rolls from underneath his cheeks and turned toward the doorway.

"Nick, wait."

Nick stopped in the doorway as Brandon reached down to pick up the snack. Holding it out to him, Brandon arched his eyebrows. "Put it under his pillow. He might want it when he gets back."

Nick sniffed and paused.

Glancing toward Brandon with a weak smile, he snagged it from him and scooted in the room.

The boys' faces disappeared as the door shut them out. *Geez. What the heck? Why did this have to happen to me? And to them? Of all places, why in the middle of Iowa?*

The fake good cop had been called away and left the room limping and cursing under his breath, vowing revenge on Greyson for the near-fatal kick to the groin. Greyson had wanted to brush off the threats with a witty and confident remark, but had come up short. Instead, his mind began to swarm with the reality of the situation and the possibility of the death threats coming true.

His eyes rolled to the silo around him, wearily surveying his surroundings. The missile was impressive, even from underneath. Three thrusters pointed at Sydney's and his head, dripping with heavy drops of rocket fuel that smelled like powerful gasoline. He'd always loved the smell of gasoline. *Until now.*

Above the thrusters, the shaft was as thick as a redwood and as tall as Bickford Hall. They must have been underground, because two stories up, the once-tinted window to the control room looked out over the silo at about midway up the missile's height. The missile's four tail fins were sharp and red, like a ninja star, and they reached the ground all around them, acting as a balance in addition to the one pillar of crisscrossing steel that jutted straight from the floor all the way alongside the missile to the tip; every three feet or so, metal clamps held the missile tight to its frame.

From the top down, the room was brightly lit steel. The observatory's rounded roof was layered, ready to split open to allow the 'telescope' to see the sky, and all the way to the floor, a winding, metal staircase with retractable metal scaffolding spiraled around the walls of the circular room. There was no one on the stairs or scaffolds now, or at least as far as he could crane his neck to see.

And there they were – two damp, muddy children tied to wooden chairs below the magnificent man-made tool of destruction. He felt a little out of place.

"Sydney?"

"Mmmm?"

Oh, yeah. Tape and blindfold.

"You okay?"

"Mm hmm."

This is stupid. How do I get her tape off?

He shuffled his feet and the chair moved slightly; he tried to throw his momentum up, but that didn't do anything; he could still get some mobility sideways, so he swung his legs to the right. The chair spun with a squeak – a little closer.

He swung his legs the other way, pushing off with his toes at the same time, and the chair shifted inches. It was possible.

"Eh! Uh! Eh!"

"Mmm mm mm mm mm-mm?"

"I'm almost there. Hold on."

He glanced up at the control room; he could see shadows of movement, but no one was watching. The door at ground level had remained shut since the 'good cop' had left.

"Uh! Eh! One more. Ehhh!"

He sided up to her, facing the opposite direction, and squeezed as close as he could. His right hand could just barely move to hers. He grabbed it and she squeezed back.

"I can't reach any knots. It's all tied below."

"Mmm hmm."

"But I think I can reach your blindfold with my teeth. Bend toward me."

She bent her neck over. Licking his dry, parched lips, he bit at the blindfold at her nose. He could feel her breath coming out hot through her nostrils. He pulled at the tight cloth, drawing his head and chin down, but it didn't budge. *Not quite strong enough.* He let go.

"Push up as I pull down."

"Mmm."

He chomped down again and yanked with all the strength in his neck as she pulled up. It came loose with one yank, falling over her face and down to her neck. Her pupils were as wide as dimes but shrunk swiftly. She blinked twice and looked over at him.

"Mmm!"

"Hi."

They stared for a moment.

"Mmm?"

Her eyes bounced down to her lips. She nodded.

"Oh! Uh…"

Geez. How was this going to work?

He looked up at the thrusters. *Had they started heating, or had it just gotten hotter in here?*

He gulped and leaned in a smidgeon. She watched him with a gleam of fear and anticipation both nipping at her brow.

"Close your eyes."

"Mmm?"

"Close 'em. I can't focus."

She rolled her eyes and closed them.

He exhaled audibly and leaned in toward her cheek. Closer. Her cheeks were covered in the thinnest blonde hairs which glowed white in the light. Closer. Her skin looked soft and had no blemishes. *Make up? Don't think so. Natural beauty? Yeah…*

He drew close to her with lips curled, teeth bared. He slid his bottom lip against her skin until he found the edge of the tape with his bottom teeth. He pushed at it, digging into her cheek to pry it loose. She opened her eyes wide, looking down at the boy with his mouth wide open, biting at her cheek repeatedly like some perverted zombie.

The tape curled just enough at the corner for him to get his top teeth over it, and he bit down. He ripped it upwards and the tape pulled from her cheek a few inches. He let go, scooted closer and she leaned further over. He bit down on the inches and curled it further across her mouth. His bottom lip met hers.

He jerked back, pulling the tape with him at a horrible angle.

"Aaagghh!"

The tape still remained stuck to one of her cheeks, but she was free.

"Ooooowwwwah!"

He laughed nervously. "Oops."

"That counts as one, jerk."

"Uh, uh. No way!" *My lips barely touched hers!*

"Yes way. Now get this tape off of me and get your second."

"Huh?" His eyebrows arched and head cocked. *Did I hear right? Well, better not let her change her mind…*

He leaned in…hesitated…then guided his lips to hers. They met briefly in a dry smack before he bit the tape and yanked it away.

He spit it to the floor and smiled wide. "Thanks. We'll call it even."

She shrugged and rubbed her lips together. "Well…that first one really *was* just a half."

Beep. Click!

The heavy door creaked open and both children swung their necks to see who had entered.

"Greyson. Sydney." *Emory.* He held another wooden chair in his hands and set it down back first. He straddled it and put his arms casually over the top. "I see you've managed to escape from your blindfolds and gags – another accomplishment to add to your list of deeds for the night, including killing two of my men and severely humiliating another. So out of deep respect for you, I'll cut straight to the chase. You won't give up the key, right?"

"Right. And we didn't kill your men. A horse and a river killed them."

"Ah, just like this missile will kill people, not me," he smiled mischievously. "Let me sum things up for you so you don't have to do any more of that thinking of yours that has gotten you into so much trouble today."

A henchman held the door open, another stood, looking into the hall.

"What do you value more? The key or your life?"

"The key."

"The key or Sydney's life?"

Greyson swung his gaze to her. She nodded.

"The key."

Emory nodded. "Hmm…commendable." He turned back to the henchmen. One of them nodded, reached into the hall, and pulled a boy around the corner. *Jarryd.*

"Jarryd!"

"Greyson! They got you? And Deer-girl? We're screwed!"

Yup. That about summed it up. Emory laughed and Greyson almost did, too.

Jarryd looked up at the colossal missile. "WHAT THE HECK?"

The henchmen grabbed Jarryd's neck and squeezed it. Jarryd tried to squirm, but his hands were tied behind him.

"The key…" Emory continued with his raspy laugh. "Or Sydney *and* Jarryd's lives?"

Greyson paused.

252

"Ah…not so easy anymore. How many does it take? Shall we add more?"

"Don't…"

"Nick, Austin, Sammy, Ryan, Chase, Brandon…your mother?"

He gasped. *Nooooo…*

"That's right! I'm being blunt with you…one fearless leader to the next. Jarryd said it right. You're screwed."

"Greyson, don't…," Sydney advised, but Emory interrupted.

"You have a simpler choice now. The key and let us do with it as we will…or we kill everyone you have ever loved. I will personally cut their throats in front of you and force you to watch them bleed and die." He stood up and walked to Sydney. "If you want to be the hero, do you want to die saving strangers, or these…," he wrapped his hand over Sydney's neck and slid it across her throat, "…delightful people."

"No!"

The legend – Eye of Eyes cutting the children's throats and making the boy watch – was coming true. *But I'm not like that boy in the story, Josiah Morris. I won't watch them die in front of me!*

"Let them go – all of them – and I'll do it. I'll tell you."

Emory raised his hands in joy. "Deal! Once we have the key, we'll let them go."

Greyson balked. His chin shook and the skin under his eyes crinkled. "W-what will happen?"

Emory cocked his head.

"W-with the missile. Why – what are you doing?"

The doctor stroked his thin, blonde hair sideways. "Heh. Want me to share my 'evil' plan with you before I kill you, huh?"

Greyson shrugged.

"Key's location first."

Doubting and fearful thoughts loomed over him, but Sydney and Jarryd's throats seemed to gape open in front of him. He blurted it out without much thought. "Behind the Rec Building, along the wall and by a drain pipe, six inches down."

Emory looked back. "Go." A henchman bolted. Then he turned back to Greyson. "Ohhh...I hope for all of your sakes that you aren't lying."

Greyson looked down at his shoes to avoid Sydney's gaze.

"Now then...my plan. We came into possession of the material first – nuclear material that is..."

What?

"...and we needed a location. We had options of course, for delivery – suitcase, airplane, et cetera...but a missile – a missile could spread the payload beyond any other option...and imagine the indignity, the shame this country will feel. Bombed in their own heartland from a bomb *built* in their own heartland. A mighty country with a mighty weakness..."

Nuclear. Nuclear. The word rung in his ears. *What have I done?*

"So...we searched for an adequate place to build and launch a missile, and lo and behold, we discovered an old government secret – an observatory that had been fashioned into a secret missile silo during the Cold War. When the Soviet Union collapsed, the silo was dismantled and the observatory abandoned."

Cold War? Soviet Union? Who would have thought history class would have come into handy in this type of situation?

"So we established relationships with the university and camp, hired the crew, 'remodeled' the place, and built our 'telescope'. Years of planning. Years of preparation and hard work. Tens of millions of dollars from several investors. But it was an investment well worth the costs. We'll all be set for life, and the country will never be the same." He laughed. "And to think. A twelve-year old almost ruined it."

He stood up and motioned the henchmen holding Jarryd to tie him to the chair. The henchmen pushed him to it and sat him down. "Hey. Gentle! Oh, and Dr. Emily..."

"Emory."

"Whatever. Where are you shooting it?"

Emory flinched. "Why? Do you have family nearby?"

"Yeah. Chicago," Jarryd replied.

"Well, that's where we'll shoot it then. Goodbye kids."

He strode toward the door but stopped suddenly and turned back. "Wait. I almost forgot." He crossed his arms and held one finger to his lips, tapping in thought. "I knew your name sounded familiar...Gray. I'd heard it somewhere before, but just couldn't place it. Then...of course as it often happens...the answer was right under my nose."

Greyson stared blankly ahead – not caring what he had to say.

"This camp. I went here as a boy. That's how we first included it in our search by the way, but that's beside the point. The point is...I attended this camp alongside a troublesome boy my age named Gregory Gray."

Greyson's eyes shot up.

"Haha! Exactly my reaction. Can you imagine that? The coincidences are just marvelous...." He lost himself in a daydream with a corny smile on his lips.

"But anyway – when you meet him in your afterlife, make sure to ask him about his week at Morris All-Sports Camp with Jacob Emory. He won't look back on me fondly, I'm sure, but we had our share of adventure as well."

The news would be shocking any other day, but on this day...this day would be newsworthy enough for the entire world for a decade.

"Well, I'm afraid I've got to go. I'll wave to you from above before liftoff. Good bye."

Emory walked out with a quick step, humming a tune.

Brandon looked at his watch, pacing the halls. 10:45 – Five minutes until a useless counselor meeting. *How will I be able to sit and gossip and rant about kids when my kids could be dying for all I know?*

He wandered into Liam and Greyson's empty room, shaking his head. Light from the sidewalk lights filtered through the blinds. Slowly building intensity, red and blue hues circled on the curtains. *Could it be? They were here!*

He rushed to the windows and threw open the curtains in a flash. In

255

the far distance, to the right – there! A single squad car parked at the far entrance of the observatory and a lone, portly officer ran toward it.

His heart sank. Somehow he knew the man's name. He threw the curtains shut and cursed. *Sheriff Roberts.*

Sheriff Roberts waddled up to the men at the front entrance.

"I need to see Dr. Emory, right away," he panted, sweating in the rain.

"No one gets in now."

"But …he's not answering my calls!"

"What's your message? We'll relay it to him."

The Sheriff shifted in his dark blue uniform, adjusting the equipment belt around his wide diameter.

"I took a call from the FBI…they now have a high-value target listed here. And I mean the *highest* value."

The guards looked at each other, spooked.

The Sheriff gulped, still trying to catch his breath. "They ordered us to secure the area, but I've managed to keep this from my deputies so far. They've been occupied with the little search Emory put us up to."

A guard pulled out his phone and muttered into it as the Sheriff looked around, paranoid.

"They are on their way! You guys better get out of here right away and let my men move in." *And we'll 'discover' this dirty plot. I'll be a hero. Or should I move my men in on them now? Could my forces take this place?* He eyed the electronic lock. It looked complicated. *We'll wait until they leave.*

The guard whispered into the phone and listened.

"Dr. Emory says he'll double your pay if you keep your men away until the signal in the sky."

"Signal? What signal?"

The guard smiled mischievously. "Oh…you'll know it when you see it. You'll know."

Chapter 21

Chase looked over at his roommate from his dark bed. He could just barely see Austin's profile in the yellow glow of the parking lot's lights. He was sleeping. *What was he dreaming about tonight? What was he seeing?*

Ever since Austin had told him the secret, he'd watched him sleep for several minutes each night, looking for signs of some supernatural occurrence. It was creepy to watch a roommate sleep, he knew, but Austin was even creepier.

The first day they'd met, Austin had asked, "Can I please share something with you that you promise never to tell anyone?"

He remembered thinking *'how the heck did I get this roommate?'* but since he'd met his other huddlemates, he'd realized that he didn't have it so bad.

Austin had then closed the door for privacy – he'd thought this tiny-framed, big-eyed boy was going to kill him – but he merely told him that he dreamt more clearly than others. He'd described it just as dreaming tomorrow's dreams. Like everyone else's dreams, his were sometimes jumbled and didn't make any sense, but unlike others' dreams, his included images, people, and events that hadn't really happened yet.

Austin had made sure to tell him that he was often wrong about what he'd seen, but that he was also often right. He'd even gotten quite good at guessing certain events throughout the day.

The first night, Chase had awakened to Austin's light screams. He sat straight up in the middle of his bed, muttering unintelligible words and staring blankly with his deep, large eyes. It had freaked the crap out of him. And then it happened again the next night. And the next.

Chase watched him closely tonight. He seemed to be mumbling some silent words. His mouth was moving and his feet twitched. *What was he dreaming? And had he already dreamt what had happened today? If he had, why hadn't he stopped it? He could have warned Jarryd, could have warned Greyson and Liam. Did he have some responsibility in all this?*

BeepBeepBeepBeep!

Austin jerked from his sleep, threw off his covers and slammed his alarm clock.

10:51.

Why the heck?

"You know he's not going to let us go, right?" Sydney looked at him through disappointed eyes.

"He might," Greyson responded.

Jarryd pushed himself closer, bound just as tightly as the others. "He won't let us go. We'd go screaming at the top of our lungs and he knows it."

"What does he care? It's not like you could stop him now."

Sydney scoffed. "No. The point is…why should he even risk it? To keep his word? He'll get his key, we'll be useless."

Greyson bit his lip and the tears rose at the corners of his eyes. Jarryd saw them forming.

"Come on. Don't cry. We could spend our last few minutes together in a much better way."

"Oh, like how?" Sydney looked at him, annoyed.

"I don't know…making out or somethin'?"

Sydney and Greyson shared an awkward smile. Jarryd missed it.

"Or not. Maybe uh…what was your biggest regret in life?"

He looked excitedly at both of them. Greyson shook his head and sniffed. *How did he have such energy, even to the end?*

"Hmm…" Sydney thought. "I regret taking basketball as my first minor. When that Anti-Terrorism spot opened up, I knew I should have taken it."

Jarryd clapped his knees with his palms and shook the entire chair with his laughter. Greyson chuckled and sniffed again. *She's great. I regret not being able to introduce her to my mom.*

"Do you even want to hear my list of regrets?" he asked, quickly killing the atmosphere.

"No. I don't. I dare you to give us your biggest."

Sydney watched him closely.

He thought for a long moment, sorting through the list. And then he found it.

"I suppose it was leaving Liam behind."

The henchman ran through the rain and mud, his breath puffing in front of him as the sidewalk lights streaked over him. The rain fell in heavy drops and drenched his black outfit, flowing over the fabric on his arms to the tip of the golden object in his gloved hand.

"Open up!"

He bolted between the guards and through the entrance. The sound of pattering rain disappeared and the cold air chilled him through his damp clothes. His boots smacked the tile as he passed doors on his left and right and ignored the men with automatic rifles guarding them.

The control room opened ahead of him and he stopped on a dime at its edge, arms at his side, golden key sticking out from his fist. Emory walked to him without a word, smiling and whistling. The henchman handed him the key and then, almost dancing, Emory skipped to the control panel where another henchman stood holding the key that smelled of peanuts.

They shoved the keys into their appropriate holes and made eye contact. "One...two..."

They turned them together at the exact same time.

Click! Vrrrrrrooooooooo....

The keys locked in place and lights lit anew across the control panel. A horn began blaring and red lights spun around the ceilings.

Waaaaaaahhhhhh! Waaaaaaahhhhhh! Waaaaaaahhhhhh!

Emory's face beamed and he leaned on the panel to look down at the kids. They looked up and he waved.

Brandon's weary body hit the sofa like a sack of concrete, and its springs groaned as a comfortable crater formed around his backside. Camp counselors filled the lobby of Bickford Hall, some rubbing red, swollen feet while others sprawled out on the floor, their arms shielding tired pupils from heavy fluorescent lights.

CJ sighed wearily, massaging his own neck. "I don't know *what* went wrong during these kids' childhoods, but someone must'a dropped them on their heads or somethin'."

The counselors grunted in agreement.

"Well, at least your group's not as bad as Brandon's," Tristan declared. "His group reminds me of a circus – they look like a freak show and act like animals!"

"Hey!" Brandon pulled himself up to the edge of his seat and glared at Tristan. The laughter melted to silence. "Don't talk about them that way, okay?"

Tristan looked up. "Yeah, okay, sorry dude, I was just joking. I actually do admire some of them, like that kid with the red hat. He's somethin'."

He sure was, Brandon thought to himself.

"You keep good track of him at night? That cop car pulled up outside and I immediately thought it was for him."

Everyone laughed – except for Brandon. He knew the kid was already gone.

"There's a trainer watching our hall. He'll be fine," Brandon lied.

"Unless he tries to go out the window," Tristan joked, "good thing it's three stories to asphalt."

CJ laughed. "From what I've seen, I wouldn't put it behind him…"

Brandon's mind began to wander as he looked past Mac, who was coming in from the rain, to the gleaming observatory in the distance.

Jarryd was still with that man somewhere. Liam hadn't been seen for hours. Nick was curled into a ball, moaning in fear. Greyson had left them. And I sit here.

But what can I do but wait and hope for the FBI to know who 'Ray Yavil' is? For all I know, that's just an ID he'd stolen from the real janitor he'd killed. Maybe he would store Jarryd's body the same place he stashed the janitor's. And maybe after they were done here, he'd clean up all the loose ends. Nick, Austin, Sammy, Chase, Patrick, me...

He sighed and watched the counselors laugh at Mac's story. *They had no idea. Any moment, the observatory would open like a wakening eyelid and send a flaming rocket burning through the clouds and rain. Would they even see it? Or would they just think it was —*

"Whose kid is this?"

Brandon broke from his daydream to see Austin standing in the center of the room like a drugged zombie. "He's mine." He rushed over to him.

"8."

"Austin, are you awake?"

"He's counting down. What is he counting down to?"

"I don't know."

"7."

The room grew tense as the counselors sucked in their breath and slid to the edge of their seats.

"6." The boy's whisper grew louder — his eyes opened and stared blankly out the window.

"Austin. Look at me."

"5."

Brandon knelt and grabbed the boy's arms, looking straight into his eyes. "Austin. Wake up, Austin!"

"4."

"Austin, listen to me, what are you counting down to?"

Is it what I think it is?

"3!"

The counselors in the room stood up, muscles taut, eyes frantically darting from the boy to the observatory, where his gaze led.

"Wake him up! Quick!"

"AUSTIN! Wake up! What happens at zero?"

"2!"

"What happens? WHAT HAPPENS AT ZERO!"

Austin snapped awake and turned toward Brandon with a desperation and fear he had never seen before. The boy's dry lips formed the last word...hesitated...then spoke.

"One."

BEEEEEEP!BEEEEEP!BEEEEEP!BEEEEEP!

Red lights flashed from the ceiling and the alarm blasted shrilly through the entire building. Counselors held their ears and cursed to themselves.

"Fire alarm!" Mac shouted above the noise, "Get your boys and get outside! Go!"

Brandon ignored the blaring alarm, holding Austin's shoulders and peering into his eyes, searching for an answer. Austin's lips curled up and he smiled, the lights flashing all around him. "It was right on time."

Brandon cocked his head and yelled over the siren. "How'd you do that?"

"I didn't do it. Chase did."

"Why?"

"The cops will come. You'll tell them what they need to know."

"What? But Sheriff Roberts..."

"Sheriff Roberts can't stop this."

Sirens and lights from the outside merged with the ones inside. They were coming.

"Go. Tell them."

Brandon stood up.

"Brandon!" Mac yelled. "Get your kids! BRANDON!"

He disappeared into the rain.

Red warning lights spun in circles around the walls, synchronized with the soft wail of a horn.

Waaaaaaahhhhhh! Waaaaaaahhhhhh! Waaaaaaahhhhhh!

Clank! Clank! Clank! Clank!

The metal clamps loosed from the missile, releasing it from the support scaffold rising from the ground.

Jarryd, Greyson, and Sydney craned their necks, watching the clamps release one by one. When the last had undone, the scaffold pulled away through a slot in the floor. The missile now stood on its four fins alone.

"Oh geez," Jarryd moaned. "Oh geez. It's gonna light. It's gonna light!"

Emory tapped his earphone. "Yes, brother?"

"The cops are moving in on a fire alarm. Is the launch sequence started?"

He glanced at his watch.

"It is. Four minutes to launch." He motioned a henchman to his side and whispered in his ear. "Reinforce the front entrance. Rifles ready. Any cops approach, kill them."

"Yes, sir."

He turned and listened to his receiver again, now alone in the room.

"Good, Jacob. I'm proud of you."

"Thank you for your help. I will see you soon."

"Soon."

Brandon began to shiver in the rain, standing near the squad car's headlights. The officer eyed him suspiciously. He turned to his partner.

"David, get a load of this."

Brandon yelled out. "There are men who kidnapped three of my boys in the observatory. I swear. There is no fire; we only had to get your attention because Sheriff Roberts is in on it with them!"

A fire truck pulled into the drive in front of Bickford and firemen jumped out, sprinting through the front entrance.

Officer David stood up, his door still open. He nodded his head. When he had heard Roberts' name something had clicked inside of him. "Let's check it out. It can't hurt."

The other officer shrugged. "Whatever. Better than a wild goose chase for two kids on a horse."

They shut the doors and turned the sirens back on. The car skidded in the wet pavement and flew around the drive toward the observatory.

Emory tapped his earphone again, frustrated. "What?"

"Emory! A squad car is on its way up the hill, and I swear I can hear a heli in the air."

Emory cursed and looked around the room – the two keys still stood erect, a flashing red button blinked in the center, and to the right, the boy's fanny pack rested on a side counter. He looked at his watch. A little over three minutes.

"Alright. Full evacuation. Have a ride ready, I'm coming."

"Yes, sir."

Emory whipped his earphone off and threw it down the hall where it smashed and skidded in several pieces. But after a few deep breaths, he caught one last look at the missile. He grinned. Even if he didn't make it out of here, at least he knew in the back of his mind that he'd succeeded. The missile would launch and as a bonus – a Gray would die.

Officer David pulled the car around, looking out through the swiping windshield wipers to the front entrance.

Swish, swish. Swish, swish.

"You see two men, there, Tommy?"

Swish, swish. Swish, swish.

"Yeah. They're watching us pretty close. Swing around."

David swung around, closer to them, approaching slowly.

Swish, swish. Swish, swish.

He could just begin to make out their faces when they suddenly jerked at their jackets and metal flashed in the streetlights.

"HOLY— "

RATATATATATATATTATA!

"AAAGHHH!"

Sparks cascaded as lead met metal. The side windows and windshield burst into white, and sharp shards sprayed inside the car.

"BACKUP NEEDED! SHOTS FIRED – Uggh…at the….observa…tory!"

The men held their fingers to the trigger, rocking the car with bullets that streaked from the bright muzzle flashes to the side of the car.

The officers felt the thuds pierce their bodies. The last image their dimming eyes saw was three men running to a black SUV. The last noise they heard was the light thumping of an approaching helicopter.

Brandon watched the muzzle flashes burn through the dark. Little pops followed like a string of small fireworks. *Gunshots.*

Heads began to turn and they matched his gaze. A fireman walked up to him in a methodic trance and gave him a sideways glance of uncertainty. Boys began flowing from the building, and soon an audience had gathered under the rain.

"Were those gunshots?"

"Who's setting off fireworks?"

"What's going on?"

"Can you see them?"

"Is that thunder?"

"It sounds like a helicopter. It's coming closer."

Brandon took a step forward from the crowd. He took another step, this time quicker. The next moment he was running at full throttle. From three different angles, police cars were racing him there.

Waaaaaaahhhhhh! Waaaaaaahhhhhh! Waaaaaaahhhhhh!

The alarm sounded like the cries of pioneer mothers, weeping and crying out in hopeless anguish and sorrow, mourning the violent murders of their young children at the hands of savages. Ancient screams still rose from the ground, but after such a long and lonely wait, the old mothers' cries would soon be joined with a new set of voices.

I can't hear myself think!

The alarm and lights together overwhelmed his senses. Even the missile groaned in annoyance and leaked fuel in greater quantities. It churned and beeped and seemed to twist from inside itself. It was preparing for what it was made to do. And there was no telling when it had made its final preparation. *Unless…unless the ceiling starting to open had anything to do with it.*

"Rain. It's raining inside." Jarryd mentioned casually.

Greyson squinted and found the right focus. Spots of moisture pooled quietly on the floor in a wide circle around them. The ceiling had opened to the sky.

He'd failed. They'd all failed, but he'd failed them all. He was really going to die. His life would end any moment from now. There would be a flash and then nothing. Real nothing. He wouldn't get to reflect back on how it ended or what his last thought was – it would just be over. No regrets, no do-overs, no laughing at the charred corpse and waiting for the black screen to fade to credits. *This was it.*

Sydney started to cry and he reached out to grab her hand. She grasped it tight.

"I'm sorry," he choked. "I did this to us. I'm sorry."

Sydney's red eyes pleaded with him – *fix this. Fix this!* But he could do nothing. He shook in his chair, screamed out, and he felt blood trickle down his wrists. "Aagh!"

"Greyson!"

Saliva and tears dripped from the corners of Greyson's mouth, and his face distorted in fear and complete anger.

"Greyson!"

He turned to Jarryd, who hadn't shed a tear.

"What was your biggest regret again?"

He sniffed and confusion fought his anger. "Wh…what?"

"What was your biggest regret?"

"It…it was leaving Liam behind."

"Well I think you might want to change that."

Greyson, still confused, followed his gaze. Two stories up, kneeling on the edge of the control panel and nearly doing jumping jacks trying to get their attention., was a small boy with buzzed blonde hair and freckles.

"*Liam?*"

Chapter 22

"G-g-greyson! J-Jarryd!"

He shouted at the thick pane of glass and their small mouths below opened wide like they were yelling back, but he could hear nothing but the increasingly annoying waaaaaaahhhhhh, waaaaaaahhhhhh, waaaaaaahhhhhh!

His eyes shot around the room and into the silo. What could he do? Break the glass? Push random buttons? His eyes fell on the larger, blinking red button in the center of the panel. There were no words above it, but it begged to be pushed.

His fingers hovered over it, touching its smooth surface.

But no. It couldn't be that easy. He looked to Greyson and Jarryd and Sydney. They all seemed to be shouting the same word. He crawled over the control panel up to the glass. Their mouths moved slowly. Their tongues started between their teeth and shot down. *The!*

Then they started with barely open mouths and bared their teeth, open wide like a vampire going in for the kill. *What was that? A 'k'?* Greyson's eyes motioned toward his own hand and Liam followed it. He seemed to be gripping something invisible with his thumb and pointer finger and turning it over and over like it was starting a car...

The key!

He scooted off the control panel, obliviously hitting a lever with his knee on the way down. A light blinked from green to red.

He jumped to the key on the right and pulled it out.

Ugh!

Wait. It didn't come out.

He twisted it.

It didn't twist either.

It was stuck!

He ran to the one on the left and tried it. Stuck! They didn't even move!

Then standing between them, he desperately stretched his arms out to both sides, straining as he reached for both at the same time. But it was useless. He'd need another person.

A mechanical whir slipped past the alarms and into their ears. The shadows in the silo shifted and the air pressure changed.

"What's that?"

"The rain stopped!"

"Did he just close the roof?"

They craned upward, but none could see. A metal clang confirmed their suspicions.

"Did he do it? He stopped the launch?"

Liam appeared in the window. He shrugged and shook his head. He pulled at an imaginary object, but it didn't budge.

Jarryd turned to Greyson in desperation. "What happens when the missile goes off with the roof over it?!"

"Boom?"

Brandon ran toward the back entrance of the observatory as the helicopter zoomed over, its spotlight beaming down on him.

Whumpwhumpwhumpwhump!

He looked up at its dark shape, but the spotlight blinded him. He covered his eyes and stopped. Two squad cars buzzed around him in the grass and the spotlight swung away and moved on, flashing above the rounded roof. He read the bright white letters on its side.

FBI.

He had to get down to them! Liam ran to the room's only door; the keypad glowed red and the door wouldn't budge.

No!

He turned on his heels in frustration and caught a familiar sight out of the corner of his eye.

Greyson's fanny pack!

He dashed to it and unzipped it; he dug in and found the smooth white card. Gasping and smiling, he ran to the door and swiped it.

Beep, click!

The flashing red hall opened ahead of him, doors on both sides. Left.

Beep, click!

A stairway.

He bounded down through the echoing alarm with an urgency in his legs he had never felt before.

Another door. He passed it going down and nearly tripped.

His shoes slapped the cement on the bottom floor and he rushed to the door. Swipe!

Beep, click!

The silo spread above him, the giant missile rising like a monument from its center.

"Liam!"

Emory ran toward the SUV, where two of his men waited with automatic rifles leveled toward the sky.

WHUMPWHUMPWHUMPWHUMP!

A spotlight cut through the rain and lit their vehicle with its rays.

"This is the FBI!" The loudspeaker blared. "Put your guns down!"

He stopped feet from the SUV and turned to the helicopter. Two men in full black aimed long, scoped rifles from its open side.

RATATATATATATATATA!

His men opened fire with deafening roars, and sparks and metal shrapnel flew from the helicopter into the night sky.

Emory ducked under the fire to the ground.

RATATATATAT— BANG!

One of his men flew into the SUV's side panel with a loud thump, a spray of blood mixing with the rain.

BANG!

His other man spun violently and his rifle fell to the wet grass in a splash of water.

The helicopter swung around and the spotlight fell on the front of the vehicle.

BANG! BANG! The front two tires exploded into shreds of rubber and air.

Panicking, Emory dashed to the side door and opened it.

"Shoot it! Shoot it!"

The driver snarled and pushed himself out. Emory ran for his life, the door of the observatory feeling a mile away.

RATATATATATATATAT!

His feet spattered water and mud behind him as he dashed, panting for breath.

RATATAT – BANG!

He looked over his shoulder, the rain flinging from his limp blonde hair as his last man fell lifelessly to the soft ground. The spotlight lit his dead body without remorse.

He looked forward and slammed into the door; his hand shot into his pocket and fumbled with the card.

WHUMPWHUMPWHUMP!

Sirens blared and squad cars raced around the corner. Doors opened. He swiped the card through.

Beep. Click!

"FREEZE!"

The spotlight burned into his back. He threw himself toward the hall as the rifle shot ripped through the air.

Greyson pulled up and the rope fell loose all around him. Liam smiled and reached under Jarryd's chair next as Greyson threw his chair back and knelt under Sydney's. His fingers pulled at the tight knot, searching for the loosest length.

"Just go!" Sydney shouted. "Stop the launch!"

"No! I'm not leaving anyone behind!"

He yanked at a piece of the knot and it pulled free; tugging again and again, the knots loosened. She pulled up with her legs and arms, taking the rope with her.

"Let's go!"

Waaaaaaahhhhhh! Waaaaaaahhhhhh! Waaaaaaahhhhhh!

Beep. Click!

The kids hobbled up the stairs, the blood returning to their sore thighs.

"Wuh-wuh-one more flight!"

Greyson looked at his watch pointlessly. There was no knowing when the thrusters would ignite, sending the nuclear-tipped missile into steel at high velocity. There would just be a flash, the walls would disintegrate around him, and Morris would burn in a fiery shockwave.

Beep. Click!

They flew around the hall and into the control room.

Emory slid on the floor, the bullet shattering the tile next to him. He rolled to his right and scrambled to his feet. Staggering down the hall, he took a fleeting look at his watch. Thirty seconds. He wanted to watch.

The two keys stood like two golden joysticks, ten feet apart on a giant game console. Liam and Jarryd flew to the left, Greyson and Sydney to the right. Eyes flashing from the missile to each other, Greyson counted.

"One…two…turn!"

The keys turned with a loud click and they tugged them out simultaneously; each pair held them in their hands, staring ahead.

Waaaaaahhhhhh! Waaaaaahhhhhh! Waaaaaahhhhhh!

"It didn't work!"

The missile shook, steam pumping from valves on its side in puffs.

"The button!"

They flew to the button.

"No! You're never supposed to push a big, red, flashing button!" Greyson screamed.

They leaned over it, faces side by side, its red hue fading in and out on their faces. Jarryd's mouth hung open over it, Liam's white eyes reflected its shape, Sydney bit her lower lip, and Greyson gulped. Glowing red sweat dripped down their cheeks and soaked their shirts.

"We should push it," Jarryd stated.

Greyson slapped his hand away. "No. It could have worked, already."

"Y-yeah!" Liam agreed.

Suddenly Jarryd pushed Liam away. "Dude, your breath stinks! Get away."

Liam staggered back and sat on the lone swivel chair, watching dejectedly.

"We need to push it! It's going to launch!" Sydney yelled.

"No it's not! It's defusing!"

"How do you know?"

"I don't!"

"Then shut up!"

"Push it!"

"Maybe we should…"

"We have to!"

"No we don't. We have the choice."

"The choice is obvious."

273

"No, it's not! Obviously."

"Look at it! It's blinking!"

"That's a warning! It's saying, 'stay away'!"

"It's getting attention. 'Push me'!"

"If you touch it, I'll push you over a cliff."

"I'll push *your mom* over a cliff!"

"Shut up! Do we push it?"

"I don't know!"

"Yes!"

Greyson sighed and hushed them. "Shhh! Shh! Alright. Oh, geez. Maybe...maybe we should."

"Yeah. We got to."

"You know, if we're wrong, we'll probably never know it."

"Okay! Then no guilt. Do it!"

"Fine! Let's do it together."

Greyson put his hand over its smooth plastic, Sydney put hers on top of his and Jarryd joined them. They breathed in deeply and –

"N-n-no!" Liam shouted from his chair.

They turned to him, hands still hovering over the red button.

Liam licked his lips. "D-don't push it."

They followed his gaze, hands shaking and hearts racing. His wide eyes peered into the silo. The metal support shaft pulled in toward the missile and hugged its side. The metal clamps snapped shut from top to bottom, locking the missile to its side.

Waaaaaaahhhhhh! Waaaaaaa…..

The red lights spun their last and blinked off. A restful silence gradually replaced the echoing horns, and a sudden stillness revealed the ringing in their ears.

Their hands still hovered over the red button. Sydney laughed nervously and pushed Greyson and Jarryd's hands away. Together, they gawked at the round button, wondering the same thing.

"What would have happened if we pushed it?"

"Boom!"

They swung around. Emory loomed behind them by the closed door, dripping rain from the hands at his side. His head tilted low and his eyes glared through the kids. He stepped slowly in their direction.

"It's an abort button. A small charge inside the missile blows, usually dismantling it once in the air." He took another step closer. His blonde hair fell over his eyes. "But in our case, we needed no abort. Instead, the charge is placed inside the warhead. Press that button...you'd have what we call a 'dirty bomb'. Nuclear material all over the place. Deformed children, sterile adults, skin falling off...all that good stuff."

Emory bared his teeth and tensed his shoulders.

Greyson stepped in front of the button and planted his feet. "No! Don't do it."

Emory chuckled. "I push that button, we all die. Why would I?"

Greyson clutched the key in his right hand. *Try it. I dare you.*

Jarryd, Liam, and Sydney looked to Greyson. He puffed out his chest and turned his hat backward. "He *doesn't* push the button."

"FBI! Open the door!"

Emory turned and looked at the door. Footsteps and radios approached in the hall. They were coming for him.

"RrrrrruuuUUUUUGGHH!"

He turned and burst toward them with his full weight like a charging rhino. The kids' hearts skipped a beat and their muscles tensed for the impact.

Greyson gritted his teeth. *This would be real rugby.*

Greyson dove shoulder-first into his shins; bone met bone hard, and he heard a sickening crack. Emory's torso flew forward, his arm stretched toward the button in mid-air, but Jarryd jerked forward and collided with Emory's ribs just as Sydney snagged his arm, pulling him just to the right of the button; his hand slapped the panel beside it before he smashed to the ground.

Jarryd fell with his momentum and landed on Emory's back at Sydney's feet. Emory tried to push off, but Sydney jumped on him with fingernails bared.

Greyson groaned and held his collarbone. He felt a lump where it should have been smooth. Broken.

"GET OFF!"

Emory raged and slid from underneath Jarryd and Sydney. He grabbed Jarryd's shirt and pulled himself to his feet. Then, with nothing but fury, he yanked on the boy's collar and flung him into the steel wall – his head hitting with a bang and body folding to the floor.

Without hesitation, Sydney grabbed the man's arm and pulled him away from the panel just long enough for Liam and Greyson to join her effort. Liam dove into a gymnast's somersault and came out of it directly behind the man's legs. He latched on for all he was worth, yanking at his legs as they churned toward the panel.

With a fresh adrenaline rush, Greyson went in fists punching. His left fist felt useless so he abandoned it, but his right found soft stomach. He struck it once, twice, then leaned back for a third.

SMACK!

Emory struck Greyson's cheek with the back of his hand. Greyson's hat toppled across the room as he twirled away, clutching his jaw.

When Liam found a good grip and pulled the man's legs together, Emory instantly lost balance and fell hard to the floor again. At once, Sydney kicked him in the side of the head and dove on his back with both hands pulling at his hair.

Growling like a trapped cougar, Emory suddenly jolted and thrust his legs out; his left connected with Liam's chest and sent him sliding toward the center of the room. He then flung around, bleeding from the mouth and nose, and pulled Sydney's hands from his hair. Her hands ripped free with two handfuls of blonde.

"Agghh!"

Emory twisted her hands around her frame and threw her into Liam where they collapsed awkwardly. He turned, his eyes fixed straight on the flashing button.

He took one step forward, but something flew at him from the right; the careening black chair struck his legs out from under him and sent him head over heels; he did a full flip and landed on his back with a breath-taking blow.

Greyson slid to a stop on the swivel chair and ran to him before he had a chance to recover. He grabbed the man's leg with his good right arm and yanked him away from the panel. Greyson pulled and tugged as he felt his gash open with drips of wet. This was his tug of war. Emory groaned and choked for air, but he still had the strength to lash out with his legs.

Greyson suddenly found himself hurtling backwards with Emory's shoe. He landed on his back, banging his broken shoulder to the ground. Instantly, the adrenaline rush faded and his crumpled shoulder felt like someone was pushing a knife into his bone and twisting it around and in. He grew weak and a nauseous lump rose in his throat. While the room spun, he could see Emory trying to stand again.

"Stop him!" Greyson cried desperately.

Liam and Sydney scrambled to their feet, but Emory took an unexpected turn and flung himself straight at them; their bodies bounced off of his shoulders like dolls, flailing to the floor, and just like that the only one left between Emory and the button was Jarryd – who had crawled to a stop in front of the button, holding the back of his head and breathing heavily. With one long, last gasp, Jarryd's eyes swam to the back of his head and he lay down.

No…

Victorious, Emory stood over them and smiled with bloody teeth at their writhing bodies. He glanced over his shoulder at the button, then back at Greyson. He spit a gob of blood and smiled condescendingly as Greyson pushed himself up with his good right side, grimacing with the pain.

"You know…you look just like he did."

A tear streaked down his swollen cheek and met with the trail of blood from his nose.

"He looked at me just that way once. But back then, I was his size. Now, I think I have the advantage."

Emory lunged for him, but Greyson had anticipated it; he sidestepped and cut behind him. He took a long stride toward Jarryd, but something caught his foot and he sprawled to the floor. Emory had tripped him.

His good shoulder took the brunt of the impact and he skidded along the tiled ground all the way to Jarryd, who lay mouth agape, eyes gazing up at the underside of the control panel. Greyson rolled to his back and looked at Emory, who sighed one last time and bent his knees for the last run.

They wouldn't be able to stop him this time. Sydney and Liam watched woozily from the ground to the side, Jarryd was in dream world, and he was a broken one-hundred pounds.

The red button flashed its warning.

After so much, this is it.

"Skeeshooing."

Greyson turned. Jarryd's eyes were fixed above and he was speaking gibberish. *'Skeeshooing'?*

He bent lower and followed his friend's line of sight – clamped to the underside of the panel was a large shotgun with a deep mahogany pump and stock.

Skeet shooting!

Emory burst forward, running like an Olympic sprinter, his eyes set straight ahead, arms pumping and legs churning.

Greyson grabbed at the clamp and the gun fell heavily to his chest.

And suddenly the world broke into pieces. In a flash, an explosion of sharp ringing absorbed every sound into silence as debris flew from the door in horizontal streaks of sparks and smoke. Pieces of door and metal sprayed into the room, pluming in a cloud of silent chaos behind Emory.

The explosion shook their bones, and the bright shockwave hit Emory's back like a crashing wave. He flew forward as if in slow motion, his body stretched in desperate longing, led by his right hand, which seemed guided by some invisible magnet to the center of the flashing red button.

Greyson fought for consciousness and blindly found the trigger. He pulled it up toward the flying man, and out of instinct alone, he pointed it and pulled the trigger.

Emory crumpled into an invisible wrecking-hammer and dropped to the floor at Greyson's feet like a heavy piece of meat. His outstretched arm lay limp as smoke wafted over it.

Something hot and liquid dripped over Greyson's face and arms, but he couldn't move to wipe it away. The pieces of the world dimmed, fading in and out as the ripping sensation in his shoulder numbed like melting ice.

Men in black, crouched and gliding like ghosts, emerged through the smoke toward him. Their visored helmets were shiny and beautiful, like halos. One of them knelt beside him and reached toward his face. Then, something caught his attention as it reflected in the man's visor.

The giant missile stood, still pointing to the sky.

Exhaustion came over him like a warm blanket; he curled in to it and fell asleep.

Chapter 23

The dark was long and silent.

Then he woke with a start and there was nothing but white.

Sydney! Jarryd! Liam!

Someone stroked his cheeks and hovered over him. A woman. Her cheeks were pink, her eyes a vivid green, like his.

"Greys? Honey? You're okay. You're okay," the woman whispered.

Gradually the white dimmed and he began to relax, sucking in large swaths of air. He sat upright in a bed with an IV snaking down his arm to the top his hand where its needle inserted into a vein. His left arm was in a sling that strapped over his shoulder. *A hospital.*

"You're okay," the woman repeated. "You broke your collar bone and you were dehydrated, but you've been getting fluids for almost nine hours now. How do you feel?"

He recognized her. "Mom?"

"Yeah," her voice wavered.

She embraced him gently and they cried together. *I'm safe. I'm alive.*

"Mom!"

She pulled away. "What?"

"How are they? My friends! Are my friends okay?"

She grabbed his hand and squeezed it. He blinked away a tear and watched her for any signs of an answer. *Please let them be okay. Please.*

"Yes, dear. They're all okay."

"All of them? Liam? Jarryd? Sydney?"

She laughed and nodded enthusiastically. "Yes! They're outside in the lobby, waiting for you to wake."

He embraced her again, happier than he had ever been since...well...since he'd thought his dad had returned.

"Can I see them now, Mom?"

A woman in a body-hugging business suit walked in, clicking her high heels on the tile. She had a kind smile. "He's awake."

His mother turned to her. "Yes. Just now."

"I'm sorry, Mrs. Gray, but can I just have a moment with him for now? It'll only be a minute and then we'll debrief with him in more detail later."

His mother turned back to him and rubbed his cheek gently. "She's with the FBI, dear. I'll be right outside and then we'll see your friends."

Greyson flinched but nodded his approval. His mother smiled and walked out, watching and waving at him from the doorway. The woman in the suit closed the door.

"Hello, Greyson. I'm Agent Feldkamp. It is truly an honor to be the first to talk with you, but I'll keep it short."

"We stopped it, right? The missile?"

Agent Feldkamp walked closer to him, nodding and smiling. "Yes you did. There are thousands of people indebted to your service for this country."

His heart jumped and the heart rate monitor beeped at his side. She glanced at it and laughed. "You *should* be proud." She paused and looked at her clipboard. "Now, just quickly. Can you take a look at these pictures and tell us if you recognize them?" She held out a picture of the man he knew as Mantis.

"Yeah. Mantis. He didn't like me very much. Did you catch him?"

She shook her head in disbelief at the boy's bravery. "We believe he died in an explosion in Jacob Emory's office. DNA will confirm or deny it later."

She held out another picture and another. SquareJaw, the bearded man, the man he kicked in the groin, Dr. Emory. He knew them all, and all had died. He felt no anger toward them now, and even a small twinge of regret and guilt coiled in his heart.

"One last one, Greyson."

He looked at it. His pulse quickened and he drew in a deep breath. The regret and guilt sprang loose and hatred took its place.

"Did you kill him? Is he dead?"

The woman drew back and took out a notepad. "How do you know him?"

He searched for the words. "I…he pretended to be my dad. He hugged me, then told me he'd kill Jarryd if I told the truth. The Jensens believed him, too."

She scribbled a note on her pad and nodded her approval.

"Thanks, Greyson. We'll talk to you more after you've recovered fully."

"No, wait! Did you kill him?"

She sighed and clicked toward the door. "No. We didn't. But we'll get him. We promise."

Greyson's lip trembled. "Who is he? What's his name?"

Agent Feldkamp glanced at the ceiling, searching for the answer. When she looked down, she spoke softly. "Everett Oliver Emory. He's Jacob's older brother and among the most wanted men in the world. He's masterminded many of the attacks against this country and our allies. They call him their Eye of Eyes."

Greyson sat, breathless, his memory taking him back to places he didn't want to go. There was no way. The coincidences were just too real.

She turned back toward him. "And one more thing, Greyson. I think it would be best if we clear your name from all of this. It would be for your benefit – for your safety."

He blinked, confused. "What do you mean?"

She set her hand on his. "If we take you out of the story…the part where you killed his brother…it might help prevent an incident in the future."

An incident? She calls the most wanted man in the world killing me an incident?

"Of course, that would mean the public wouldn't know as well. Effectively, you'd be a victim…not a savior."

TapTap. His mother knocked on the door.

Agent Feldkamp gave his hand a pat. "Something to think about Greyson. Once again, you have the deepest thanks from the Bureau for your bravery and heroism. We'll be in touch."

"Thank you, ma'am."

She smiled and opened the door for his mother. She got one look at his face and rushed in for an embrace.

"What'd she say to you? Are you okay?"

What can I say to her? I threw a golf ball at the angriest, most powerful horse in the entire world?

Greyson merely smiled reassuringly. "Yeah, mom. I'm fine! I just miss my friends."

She looked into his eyes suspiciously and ran her hand through his hair. "Okay. If the doctors say it is okay."

"Brandon!"

Brandon stood in the doorway, hands behind his back. He walked forward smiling. "Hey, bud. How're you feeling?"

Greyson shrugged and grimaced. *Ouch. Note to self. Don't shrug.* "I'm okay."

"Well. Maybe this will make you feel better."

He swung his right hand up with a flat wooden paddle the size of his arm. He turned it to its front side and showed him the two dark brands burned into it. "They're the perseverance and dedication brands. I think you more than earned them."

Greyson laughed. "Nice. Thanks."

Brandon noticed his lackluster response and winked at him. "Don't worry. I know what you really want. I saw you being wheeled out hatless so I told some FBI guy you'd die without it."

His left hand rose, holding his red hat.

"Awesome! You're the best!"

Brandon put it over the boy's head and smacked the bill playfully. Greyson reached out and shook his hand. "Mom, this is my counselor, Brandon. He believed me."

His mother smiled at him and tried to hold back her continuous urge to cry. Instead, she hugged him and patted his back.

"Greyson!"

Liam and Jarryd sprinted in and flung themselves on Greyson, hugging him tight. "Ow! I'm broken!"

"So am I!" Jarryd wore a hospital gown as well. He looked back at the doctor waiting for him at the door and bent over to moon him out the back slit of the gown. The doctor laughed and left, shaking his head.

"I-I-I love you!" Liam continued hugging him and almost strangling him.

"Love you, too. Mom?"

His mother pulled Liam up by his shoulders, smiling. "Were you there, too?"

Liam looked at his mother and nodded enthusiastically. A butterfly band-aid covered his split upper lip.

"He saved us, Mom. We'd be toast without him."

Suddenly, Jarryd hit Liam on the shoulder.

"Ow! W-why'd you d-d-do that?"

"You never told us. How'd you get in the control room?"

He shrugged and rubbed his shoulder. "C-c-climbed on a fridge and b-b-boxes to the v-v-vent. And I used – I used – I used the r-r-rope to climb d-d-down. I p-p-put the carib-carib-carib-carib…"

"Carabineer?"

"Yeah. In-in-inside a b-b-bullethole. It was dark."

"Geez. You're amazing, Liam."

"Way to be!"

The doctor came back with two male nurses. "Jarryd. Three concussions in 48 hours might have broken some kind of record. You need food and rest."

Greyson laughed. "I think he needs a bath, too. He stinks."

Jarryd recoiled. "*Your mom* stinks!"

Greyson's jaw dropped and he looked at his mother. Jarryd's eyes lit up and he turned to her. "Uh…it's just an expression. You don't really stink."

She laughed, bewildered.

Jarryd grimaced and turned back to Greyson with a nervous laugh. "Well, bye Greyson. I'll be around."

"Bye."

He walked to the nurses but turned quickly. "Oh, and I think I saw some girl waiting for you outside."

Greyson smiled and the heart monitor beeped again.

"No, wait, it was three girls. They looked like eighth-graders." Jarryd laughed and punched one of the male nurses in the stomach playfully. "Ow. Rock hard. You *must* tell me your secret." He disappeared around the corner.

Greyson's mother eyed him. "He's a character."

Greyson chuckled. "Yeah. He's not the only one. Brandon, how's Sammy and Austin, Chase, Ryan, and Patrick?"

He shrugged and nodded. "They're good. Their parents came and got them pretty fast. Chase is staying with the Jensens' until his folks get back. Sammy's grandmother gave me a hug, Ryan opened the door for his mother on the way out, Austin told me he'd see me again soon so I didn't give him a long goodbye, and Patrick's mom slipped me a hundred."

"Nice! You can buy yourself something nice."

"I might just get a nice toothbrush. I have a lot of thinking to do."

Greyson smiled wide and winked at him.

They paused and sighed, the vibrant atmosphere finally relaxing as the sun filtered in through the white curtains, peeking out from the clouds for the first time in over a day.

"Well…I should let you get some rest, bud. Maybe your mom and I will go find you something to drink."

Brandon pulled at his hat teasingly and nodded good-bye.

"Bye, Brandon."

Brandon left and his mom followed with a smile.

Finally alone, Greyson's finger snapped to his ear. He dug inside, picking at something itching him. Black mud chips sprinkled out as he dug away at the dried clod.

"Need some help?"

He jerked his pinky from his ear and more dirt came out. The girl laughed.

"Hey."

"Hey."

The bright lights and sun lit her golden hair with rings of white, and her heart necklace hung loosely around her neck. She stood in the doorway with her hands behind her back and head tilted low.

My girl.

"I got you something." She walked in casually, watching him try to catch a glance of what she held.

"What? What you get me?"

She bit her lip and smiled coyly. "Guess first."

He scanned her face and body language. "Umm...bacon?"

She rolled her eyes. "You're such a boy. Guess again."

"Umm...a new fanny pack?"

She scoffed. "What? No way."

"Then I don't know. What else could I possibly want?"

She set her hips. "I can think of one thing you want." With a sly smile, she pulled out a white sock tied at the top with a shoelace and threw it at him before turning on her heels and exiting the room.

He jerked up and grabbed the gift from his lap. He hastily untied the shoelace, threw it to the side, and turned the sock over. A small object fell with a plop and rolled to a fold in the blanket.

A half-eaten chocolate kiss. Exactly what she owed him.

End of Book 1

Did you love the book? Want to help the series become the next big adventure movie? You can! Just review the book on Amazon! Each review goes a long way! We dare you!

And good news…

Continue the adventure with
Greyson Gray: Fair Game

Find it at GreysonGray.com

Stopping the terrorists only made them madder.

The twelve-year-old secret savior of thousands, Greyson Gray, is given a new identity and forced into seclusion to hide from the Eye of Eyes – the most wanted man in the world and the leader of a rising terrorist group trying to divide the United States in a new civil war.

But Greyson can only be secluded so long. Drawn toward suspicious activity at the massive Iowa State Fair, Greyson and his faithful friends uncover a plot even more insidious than before – one that threatens the fibers of the nation and possibly the next president of the United States. For Greyson everything is on the line – his father's whereabouts, his relationship with Sydney, and the lives of everyone he loves. With new weapons, a new rival in love, and new enemies, there's no holding back. It's all fair game.

ABOUT THE AUTHOR

B.C. Tweedt lives in North Liberty, Iowa with his beautiful wife, Julie and his son, Maverick. Because he can be a big kid at times, even at the age of 31, he enjoys hanging with other kids. He volunteers at a youth group and mentors boys in his free time. There is nothing he loves more than seeing kids grow in wisdom and character. The characters in the Greyson Gray series are a conglomeration of many of the real personalities and humors he knows and interacts with on a daily basis. Because of this, kids feel the characters are authentic and relatable.

Though *Greyson Gray: Camp Legend* is the first book published from B.C. Tweedt, he has plans for a fairly long series, following Greyson as he grows up in an increasingly divided and threatening world. B.C. has thoroughly enjoyed brainstorming ideas for this series while running, listening to epic movie soundtracks, and researching in exotic places like the Bahamas.

Made in the USA
Lexington, KY
05 August 2019